Regency Love

By TL Clark

Published in the United Kingdom by:

Steamy Kettle Publishing

First published in electronic format and in print in 2019.

www.tlclarkauthor.blogspot.com

www.facebook.com/TLClarkAuthor

ISBN: 978-0-9956117-2-6

Acknowledgements

My humblest yet greatest thanks must go to Jane Austen, Fanny Burney and Charlotte Brontë. These brave women laid the foundations upon which I now stand.

Hubby, as always gets my deep gratitude for his forbearance and support. Living with a writer is certainly challenging, but he is always there, quietly supporting with love.

Thanks also to my beta readers, editor and proof readers. You offer invaluable advice and help spot those naughty little errors.

And thanks to you, dear reader, for selecting this book. Without you, my writing is empty.
I hope you enjoy Lady Anne's story.

Cover design by the wonderful Robin Ludwig Design Inc.
http://www.gobookcoverdesign.com/

The main image on the front cover was featured in Ackerman's Repository (of arts, literature, commerce, manufactures, fashions and politics) – a popular British periodical 1809-1829

A poem for my own amusement and for some clarification:

The Naming of Aristocrats by TL Clark

(inspired by The Naming of Cats by TS Eliot)

The naming of aristocrats is a difficult matter,
For titles are listed in a fashion most militant.
Confusion might arise should one pop by for a natter.
For dukes, one name is insufficient;
A duke's son will borrow the next title in his line,
More than one duke of any one place? No sir.
The son of Lord Benford becomes Lord Dowbry; how
fine.
But what of the fair ladies, which name for them is
demure?
When daughters of dukes, their first names are used.
As for the rest?
To the titles of husbands and papas they do refer,
But for daughters of barons and knights, Miss is best.
For years of tradition and acts of bravery
Have gone into the history behind each title.
It is a matter of pride which if ignored is highly
unsavoury.
Dignity to them is of importance most vital.
Now you know who and how to name with formality,
Cast a bow or curtsey should aristocracy you meet,
As you acknowledge the full respect owed to their
family.
My lord / my lady / Your Grace, you say, whilst
looking firmly at your feet.

1

Introduction

Dear Reader,

I would like to take a moment to clarify my purpose before you begin reading this delightful tale, if you would so kindly permit.

This book has been written with the purpose of giving a voice to women who had none at the time. To show what they may well have really been thinking and feeling beneath the façade of civility. But do bear in mind that it is written some 200 years following 1814 (the time this tale is set in).

The language has been carefully selected to lend an air of authenticity yet allowing it to be easily readable by the modern reader. Great pains have been taken to include words and phrases in use during the Regency period. But I beg your indulgence of artistic license. This should also be applied to the story, for it has a foot in realism yet remains a novel, which insists on some elaboration for the sake of excitement.

And I would remind you of the caution stated in the book's description; that there is an attempted seduction which may be shocking to some readers. As well as some arousing scenes which may not be suitable for gently bred ladies.

Also, the age of consent in Great Britain at the time was twelve years old. It was raised to sixteen in 1885 and has remained at that point ever since. At the time this book was set, girls were still married at fourteen, but this was in decline, and ages of marriage were increasing. Our heroine is seventeen years old, and by no means out of the norm.

Some real life events and settings have been included, but the characters are all fictional (except the brief mentions of the likes of the Queen, the Prince Regent, the Duke of Wellington and Beau Brummell; and even in these cases the conversations are fictitious).

Thus arming you with my intention, please settle yourself into a comfortable seating position, inhale deeply, and enter into Lady Anne's world.

I bid you a most hearty welcome (*opens the door with a curtsey*).

❧ Chapter 1 ❧

Gazing upon my reflection in the looking glass, I am startled by the transformation. My long chestnut hair has been formed into an elaborate work of art by my hairdresser. Pale blush flowers intersperse the cascading ringlets hanging about my pinked cheeks. Yet this is not the transformation which I find startling. It is more that my reflection shows the image of a young woman, no longer a girl. Today I make my 'come out', and my mind is all awhir.

Outwardly, I am everything a lady ought to be as she enters Society, with even plumpness residing in all the correct places and an air of elegance in my deportment. Inside, my heart is fluttering wildly, more from trepidation than excitement. For me, this is no joyous occasion, but a torment which must be borne.

Having been cursed with the terrible fate of being born female, I must be married post haste now I have reached the age of maturity; that being the ripe age of seventeen. My body has shown signs of my readiness for marriage, the vile traitor that it is.

My entire life has been building to this moment. One has been bred for purpose, barely better than one of the estate's prize pigs. Much attention and care has been invested in my upbringing. Papa has spared no expense in obtaining the finest tutors to ensure his daughter attracts the best match; painting, singing and dancing all form my repertoire of allurements.

The pigs in the pens I happened upon during my adventures on horseback had been born unto selected parents, fed the best nourishment and shown at their very best at the county fair. I confess they were endearing creatures. I returned often and spoke with the farmer, without Papa's knowledge of course, and the snuffling animals never failed to relieve my melancholy. And like them on a show day, I am about to be exhibited too, fully brushed and preened. My parents were matched according to breed, and now it is my turn.

Being a daughter to the Duke of Hesford carries a heavy burden. I have little real say in the matter of my marriage partner. Happily, my disposition is not romantic; that is a luxury I can ill afford when the field is so narrow. Admittedly, my elder brother James has eased the situation a little by making a fine match himself. However, a weight still remains about my shoulders. One cannot bring disgrace upon one's family.

My wish is that my husband be not hideous, neither in features nor disposition. I pray God that my husband be not cruel, but rather a cordial fellow. Such hopes serve no purpose, but they will not be entirely silenced. With an inner shrug and a sigh, but a smile to the world, I must admit that he shall be whomever my parents deem worthy.

So you see, outwardly I am the very essence of gentility, yet inwardly I am in turmoil. The most important mystery of my life may be about to be solved. Whether this is for the better is yet to be seen.

Clément, my lady's maid, has run off to locate a vital item, leaving me alone for a short spell. She really is a marvel. I've no idea how she makes my lotions and cosmetics, but my pale skin is flawless thanks to her efforts. My eyelashes and brows are even a little darker by her hand, and my breath is violet-scented having been administered a cachou. A tin containing more lozenges is in my reticule, along with my spare dancing slippers.

There was just enough time three days ago to dispatch a letter to my sister, Margaret, which I recall now with a heavy heart.

Letter to Margaret, 14th April 1814

My dearest Margie,

I hope this letter does not find you still in a miff. Perhaps these few short lines will aid your recovery. Please be assured once more that your turn will soon come, and it is not something you should long for so ardently. I urge you again to find pleasure in your maiden years.

The journey from Hampshire to London was a long one, but we have arrived safely. We made several stops along the way but were met with warm welcomes wherever we went, despite being at inns, which are equally as tiresome as I had supposed them to be; full of noise and confusion.

I fear the length of the journey exhausted even my own enthusiasm for the bright colours and fresh scents of the season. The coach was comfortable, but the roads were not. Mama and I were quite shaken and weary by the time we joined Papa in Piccadilly.

Preparations have begun already with the greatest flurries of activity. And this is only the beginning. I am keenly aware of your excitement over the purchase of dresses, and I shall update you on my wardrobe as it develops. My only wish is that I could share your enthusiasm for such things. My time here would then be a far finer prospect.

Of course, the dressmaker paid a visit here on our first day, but there is nothing out of the ordinary to report there; I have sufficient gowns to wear for the present. Only to say that the court gown promises to be every bit as hideous as predicted. It will take a few days to prepare due to the excess of layers and frills. There is no hope of my appearing before Queen Charlotte as anything but an oversized white apple. Her insistence on this dress really is astonishing. Hooped at the bottom and coming out from under one's bosom. Well, at least a corset is rendered useless; one's waist shall ne'er be seen, if you will forgive my mentioning said garment.

Mama has of course sent to the Chamberlain, requesting to present me at the next Drawing Room, but we still await confirmation of the date. It seems her Highness maintains poor health. But the dress is to be readied so as to avoid any panic once we are granted audience.

I do not have much time at present, but I promised to send word of our safe arrival. I shall write again soon. Please send word of yourself. Do not give Miss Swanson any trouble. It is not her fault you were born after me, and her intentions are all for your betterment. Forgive my plainness, but your lessons are important. You must listen well, for it will be your turn before you know it.

This letter is sent with my love to you and a big hug for Prince.

Your ever affectionate sister,

Anne Frithringham

Prince is a Pomeranian of advancing years and is a most faithful dog. He brings joy to us all, I believe, with his silly antics. I shall miss his judgement on this trip; he has never once bitten a person of good character.

"Anne, Anne, what are you about? Hurry yourself," Mama calls on her approach to my room.

"Coming, Mama." My fingers run over my curls to ensure they are truly in the correct position.

"You look very well, Anne, but we must be ready to receive our guests who will soon be upon us."

Mama looks younger than her years and is wearing a magnificent mauve silk gown with a train, comfortable in the knowledge she may sit out all the dances this evening. She is dressed to impress yet to also blend in and not be on show.

My white gown flies around my ankles as I walk briskly to keep up with mama as she hurries us to the ballroom. This evening's dress is one of the few I brought with me. It is mainly white, with a gossamer net overlay. Pink flower embellishments adorn it and is completed by pink Spanish slash sleeves with white crepe folds and silver trim.

Invitations went out prior to our departure, but the long list of people is too immense for me to recall. This is to be a grand ball full of carefully selected suitors and prominent persons of the Ton.

The room is splendid; flowers fill the air with their scent, the floor is beautifully chalked, and candles are lit all around. The musicians are in place and start softly playing as we enter.

Papa is already there, dressed finely for the occasion. Tall and imposing, with more than a little grey hair, strong jaw and a firm set to his brown eyes, which he shares with me.

He approaches and takes my white silk gloved hands in his.

"I challenge even the Prince Regent himself to produce such a magnificent daughter," he tells me in an uncharacteristic display of sentimentality.

I'm forced to swallow hard to avoid an embarrassing display of emotion.

"Thank you, Papa," I manage to reply with a deep curtsey.

My mouth gapes in a most ungainly fashion as Papa strides over to Mama and begins leading her in a dance, just the two of them. She is forced to hold up her train as they hop around like young fools.

I cast my glance away, aware of my intrusion on this very personal and deeply shocking moment. They look so happy I daren't draw attention to myself by walking away. However, the clattering sound of carriages outside soon comes to my aid and halts their merriment.

Finely attired guests begin to file in and are greeted as expected. I am introduced but know not how to recall all the names scattered towards me.

All too soon it is time to begin the dance. My papa and I take the top position, and call the dance, being careful not to make the figures too complicated.

A look I'd not previously seen on him crosses Papa's face; he smiles with parental pride as we make our way between couples. My nerves soon dissipate as my feet are carried along by the music, already knowing their correct placement after my many hours of practice.

The dance finishes and Papa hands me over to the Duke of Tilbourne, who is far more advanced in years than I but is looking for a wife. I accept him as a dance partner with as much good grace as I can muster. Is this to be my lot in life? United with a relic? A shudder is barely contained.

As the music ends, a great commotion erupts, rippling out from the direction of the doors.

"Heavens, did you begin without me?" Beau Brummell asks the room loudly whilst striking a pose.

Papa hurries over to welcome the distinguished guest who, as we are all well aware is deliberately late in order to make this grand entrance.

"Brummell, how good it is to see you. Might I introduce my daughter, The Lady Anne Frithringham?"

"Delighted," he returns with a quick yet not entirely indecent bow.

My breath and heart halt in anticipation of this man asking me to dance. But a sigh, as silent as I can manage, escapes when, with a few words of flattery, he disappears into the crowd.

Beau Brummell rarely dances, preferring to merely be seen, and that meets with my satisfaction in this case. He may cause many to swoon, and he may be handsome, but his reputation precedes him, and I have no desire to unite myself in matrimony to such a man.

Instead, a rather tall, simply but finely dressed man takes his place.

"If I may have the honour?" he asks my papa, who assents.

My partner is Henry Gildcrest, Marquess of Dellingby, heir to the Duke of Wenston, whose seat is up in the north country. Too far away from my family for my liking. However, he has kind brown eyes under the mop of dark blond hair; not unattractive. Perhaps a little advanced in years. I cannot discount him entirely, for his rank recommends him and Mama has pointed him out already.

Smiling slightly and with downcast eyes, I curtsey to begin the dance. "My lord."

He bows in acknowledgement but remains silent. At least this gives me ample opportunity to settle my thoughts. The spectacle of this evening has rendered me quite giddy; it is nigh on impossible to absorb it all. And I'm still regaining my senses after meeting the famous Beau Brummell. Oh Lor', how fortunate I am he did not raise his quizzing glasses.

"You hail from northern lands, I understand," I try, hoping to bring about some conversation.

"That is correct."

"You do not sound much as if you are."

"Ee by 'eck, should I sound like some common miner, lass?" he asks in a pronounced accent akin to the one I'd expected.

Blushing wildly, I shake my head. "I see my error clearly."

The only example I had heard of the dialect was indeed from a servant. How mortifying I should expect this marquess to sound alike.

"Lady Anne, I own you have me at a disadvantage, for you should call me ungallant if I were to point out you do not much sound like a country bumpkin from the south."

"My lord, I have owned my error."

He raises his brow and I am utterly silenced and attempt no further discourse.

An Earl of somewhere-I'm-not-paying-attention-to takes the place of the marquess and once more I'm led about the room. We exchange a few pleasantries, but he does not draw much of a reaction I'm ashamed to say.

By the time the set finishes, fatigue is setting in so I stand aside before any other gallants can drag me into their power. Holding out my hand, a cup of punch is placed into my grasp by Forbes. He's a good man. Papa brought him up from the country, along with many of our servants. I'd not be surprised to learn that Margaret is home alone with only our governess Miss Swanson, and a cook. Papa does not keep too many staff here in London usually, so he brought some from home, knowing they're trustworthy as well as hiring some new from town.

Sipping the thirst-quenching beverage, I draw breath and look about the room. Many of the eligible nobility and gentry are here, and even some from France. However, due to the recent tragic occurrences over there, it is perhaps advisable not to dwell on them for long. I should forever fret whether my head was safely upon my shoulders should I marry one of them. Perhaps now there is a King back on the French throne he shall restore their former glories, but as it is, I cannot be sure I'd have a home to go to. No, I must not think of them.

Thinking of kings, I can only be thankful I was born no closer to the throne. To be a princess must be unfathomably unpleasant. Then I would have no say whatsoever over my marriage partner. In all likelihood, I'd be sent to an entirely different country to be married to a prince, with no consideration given to his character whatsoever. Dreadful!

I cannot help but smile broadly when I see Miss Compley advancing. Julia has been my friend since early childhood. She's already made her come out. In fact, this is her second Season. As the daughter of a baronet, she's not of the nobility, but I refuse to let that deter me from my dearest friendship.

The rest of my punch is veritably gulped down so I may be rid of the glass to accept my friend into my embrace.

Julia looks splendid in her cream muslin gown which is stamped with daisies and decorated with lace. Her blonde hair is elegantly done. She's looking at me with wide blue eyes, her mouth smiling perhaps a little too broadly.

"Oh my dear, I have never beheld such a sight. What a wonderful ball your papa has thrown for you, and so many distinguished guests. I am quite lost. And you are the fairest belle of them all."

We stand huddled together, holding up our fans so we may have a moment of private discourse.

"You are too kind and present a pretty picture yourself. I am so happy you are come. I have been quite desperate without you. You must come to the house tomorrow. I shall be in grave need of your company after my dance partners have taken up my morning," I implore, my eyes looking heavenwards.

"Of course. My aunt and I would be honoured."

"Lady Anne, might I be so bold as to claim the next dance?" a man enquires, intruding upon our privacy.

"Certainly, my lord," I reply with a slight curtsey.

Really, I have no idea who this man is, but lord seems a safe form of address in a room such as this. I recollect being introduced, but his name quite escapes me. I am in no position to refuse, as much as I would like to continue my conversation. Oh, poor Julia shall be left stranded. I glance about to see if I can spot a suitable companion for her also.

"Rohampton, I believe you are neglecting your duty," my intended partner calls over his shoulder.

Rohampton? I recognise that name. A baronet, if I recall correctly, his papa having recently passed away. Yes, he will do nicely for Julia. And he's rather dashing which goes in his favour.

As we are led to line up for the dance, I'm better able to take in my beau's appearance. He and his friend are both dressed more in the dandy fashion of Beau Brummell, in well-fitting dark blue coats with brass buttons, tight breeches and brown top boots. It becomes them both.

My gentleman's dark hair is fashionably short and brushed forwards, following the Brutus trend, also favoured by Beau Brummell. His sideburns are pleasingly long, and his bright blue eyes are gleaming in my direction.

The music starts, we step together and join hands. I almost pull mine from his grasp as an odd sensation travels up my arm, seeming to affect my heart, but he maintains his firm hold.

"Lord Felsenworth at your service, my lady," he announces, making my heart thunder.

What is this stirring within me? I cannot explain it. It is most unnerving. He leads me round elegantly, paying modest yet seemingly earnest compliments as we meet and then part in the dance.

It takes me a moment to recognise the earl who regrettably takes his place, and he pales in comparison. My world is shaken, and time drags on as I'm forced to perform steps by rote, my mind certainly elsewhere. Blue eyes follow me from a few partners away, I feel them burning into me.

Fortunately, this dance ends the set, and I walk out to the veranda, desperate for some cool air. The ballroom had become over warm and confining and had begun to wobble in front of my eyes. My fan flutters furiously as I gain my exit.

"Are you quite well, Lady Anne?"

Dratted man, I was fairing much better until he burst into my presence again. Lord Felsenworth is precisely who I was running from.

"I thank you, yes," I try to say dismissively.

He does not take my meaning. "Might I get you some wine?"

His eyes are full of concern, but they serve only to increase the pace of my heartbeat again, especially as I realise we are the only two out here.

"Is everything quite alright, your ladyship?" the Marquess of Dellingby asks as he joins us.

"Yes, quite so, thank you, my lord. I was merely gaining some fresh air for a moment."

"What are you about, Lady Anne?" Mama admonishes, seeing me alone with not one, but two members of the opposite sex.

"I fear the room was over warm, Your Grace," Felsenworth ventures on my behalf.

"Is this right?" she asks, looking at me.

"Yes, Mama. I had no idea of causing such a fuss. I thought I may slip out unnoticed for but a moment."

"Thank you, my lords," Mama says, dipping her head, making it plain the men are dismissed.

"Apologies for any intrusion," Lord Felsenworth replies with a quick bow before making his exit, with Lord Dellingby close upon his heels.

"Mama, I am sorry —"

"Do not discomfort yourself, I observed what transpired. The fault does not lie with you. I am only sorry it took me so long to reach you. Here, why do we not sit a minute?" she asks, leading us towards the seating outside.

The darkness of the night is relieved by the glow of the full moon, its silvery fingers touching the tips of nearby branches and balustrades and reflecting in the water of the fountain below us. Night-time creatures echo calls from unseen boughs.

"Thank you. I do not know what came over me," I declare, still wafting my fan.

"It is your first ball. The experience can be overwhelming. And it is rather warm indoors. I have ordered the doors and windows open."

Forbes appears with a glass of wine for each of us on a silver platter and disappears without a word. I sip slowly, allowing the liquid to refresh me a little.

Once our glasses are empty, Mama asks, "Are you fit to return? Our guests are waiting."

I bow my head and allow her to assist me to my feet, taking my time to ensure my footing is secure.

Those same feet, it turns out, are danced raw by several more suitors upon my return. It is with great relief that I am escorted to dine by the Earl of Emsby. At least, that is to say, I am grateful for the respite it offers. My partner is quite a different matter.

I do hope Papa doesn't intend him for me, as can be feared from this escort to supper. He must be at least five-and-thirty; far too old, no matter what his fortune may be. He is not handsome at all. He is too portly, his features are dark and severe, his hair overly greased, and there is a rather pungent odour emanating from him. My lack of romantic tendency may be stretched a little too far if pressed into marriage with the earl.

By the heavens, must I endure this for the rest of my life? The man is slurping his soup so noisily I am sure the guests at the far end of the table must hear. If my teeth clench any more firmly it shall become obvious to any onlookers.

With my eyes fixed on my own bowl of white soup, I attempt to shut out all else around me.

"Lady Anne, do you not enjoy your supper?" he asks between mouthfuls.

The look in his eye rather worryingly suggests he'd gladly eat the contents of my bowl as well.

"Quite the contrary, I assure you. It is quite delicious. I am merely savouring the flavour."

"Jolly good, jolly good."

He sits fidgeting, watching as I finish. When I look up it's to a pair of gleaming blue eyes across the table.

"Lady Anne, how are you enjoying your come out?" the owner of the eyes asks.

"Very well, thank you, Lord Felsenworth," I reply, quickly returning my gaze to my bowl.

Really, the man is terribly disconcerting. I cannot look at him long. The mirth in his countenance is incorrigible.

"Have you any plans the day after next?"

"I think it best if you quiz my mama on the subject, my lord."

"But of course. I merely inquire as I myself am planning an expedition to Hyde Park for a breakfast. Perhaps you'd enjoy such an event, wot?"

"That sounds agreeable. I shall ask Mama if our plans will allow for it."

The returning smile I receive fills my entire being with a warm glow. Excitement ripples through me at the prospect of meeting this person again. I hide my smile behind my cup of hot negus but am sure my eyes give me away.

"What's this? An expedition to Hyde Park. What a splendid idea." Oh, for pity's sake, the Earl of Emsby is inviting himself along; I shall have to have words with Mama.

Supper continues in an odd mixture of forbearance and fervour. I barely taste my coxcomb and chicken. However, it is enough to lend me energy, despite my inner heaviness, and dance with renewed vigour (and my replacement slippers).

Finally, Viscount Ringsham claims me to dance *La Boulanger* and the most extraordinary evening comes to a close.

❧ Chapter 2 ❧

Letter to Margaret, 15th April 1814

My dear Margie,

I hope this letter finds you well. I have not received a response from my last, and I begin to grow concerned.

I shall not sport with your patience by regaling all of the events of my come out ball, for I wish nothing but happiness for you. Suffice it to say I had a merry and exhausting time of it. Beau Brummell is every bit the character we have heard him to be, and I took great amusement in his posturing.

Now, I must urge you to pay particular attention to Mr Townsend's dance instruction, for his teachings served me well last night. I was barely given a moment's rest. This may sound terribly exciting to one with as much spirit as yourself, but do be prepared, my darling sister, for it was a lengthy evening. My bed was most welcome when I was finally able to claim it.

All the morning was taken up with callers whom I'd danced with, and the drawing room now resembles a hothouse there are that many flowers adorning it. Do you wish to know who paid calls? Well, I shall tell you the main contenders. The others I am yet to form an opinion on.

Mercifully, the Duke of Tilbourne sent only his card. I sincerely hope this is a sign of his disinterest, as I have none for him. He appears every one of his years, perhaps more. He must be Papa's age. Surely too great a gap for him to form any serious designs upon me.

The Earl of Emsby arrived in person first. He is not at all what I expected, which is most disappointing for us all. Mama has urged me to give him a chance, as perhaps he had a bad day and may yet reveal himself in a better light.

The Marquess of Dellingby came. I still say he resides too far north to be seriously considered, especially taking his age into consideration, which I believe to be slightly above the desirable. But Mama pleads his case also.

Lord Felsenworth. Now, I fear you shall become over-excited if I confess I felt a fluttering in his presence. I know how you obsess over these having read the likes of Sense and Sensibility. But I do urge you to follow more the example of Elinor, and be rational, for I fear you are infecting me with such trifles. He seems pleasant enough, and I shall not be sorry to see him again tomorrow. There, that is all I shall say upon the matter.

We are all to go to Hyde Park tomorrow. How you would have laughed to see Mama's face as I invited Miss Julia Compley. I do believe she was attempting to strike me down dead with the glare she shot me over her teacup. And she gave me such a dressing down once they had departed, but there is no retracting the invitation now.

"Really, Anne," she scolded, "I do not know what you were thinking. It is one thing to invite Miss Compley here for tea without consultation, but quite another to be seen out with her. I have encouraged your friendship far too liberally."

I had the audacity to argue, "But Mama, she is here with her aunt, who is one of us. I cannot neglect my duty to my friend, please do not ask it. This is her second Season and I could not bear it if she were to return home without a husband again."

"You talk of duty. What of that you owe to your own family?"

"Surely I can perform both. The barouche will look happier when full. Every person about knows my standing, so surely her company cannot degrade my own? But mine may yet elevate hers. I am determined to do her this service."

There was a long pause, during which Mama turned different colours, and I feared she may faint away. Oh, Margaret, it was very wrong of me to speak so and I do not know what came over me. Perhaps it is unwise of me to recount it to you. I would not encourage you to follow my example. But I have nobody else I can confide in and I must have it out. Did I truly do wrong? Julia is my dearest friend and I only intend to do well.

Mama saw my resolve and is unable to retract the invitation as it was gladly accepted by Julia. Her aunt looked a little wary, I must confess. But what is done is done, and I shall be more at ease having a friendly face in the carriage. I have not yet had chance to converse with the other young ladies, but I saw and heard much twitching and whispering, enough to make me ill at ease. Am I forever to inspire jealousy and intolerance?

Please write to me and confirm at least you forgive me.

Your ever loving sister,

Anne Frithringham

As I gaze in the looking glass, having finished my letter, I fear I am already changed by my short experience here, and not for the better. I must strive to control my exuberant manner and behave like the lady I know myself to be.

Perhaps these first few days have over-excited me, and now the first ball is over with I can begin to calm my demeanour once more. Mama shall receive my apologies in the morning before we leave. She must think me a foolish, thankless girl. I feel so ashamed. Blowing the candle out, I retire for the night.

Clément opens my curtains at a reasonable hour in the morning, but it feels anything but as I reluctantly awake. My eyes are as heavy as my limbs as I try to stretch my arms.

I force myself to catch up with other correspondence before venturing into breakfast. Mama and Papa are already seated.

"Good morning, Papa," I greet, risking a kiss on his cheek before repeating this with Mama.

She looks at me warily as I take my seat.

Slicing my honey cake into smaller pieces, I start, "Mama, please accept my apologies for my conduct yesterday."

"What's this? You have not disgraced yourself already? Anne, I expect better of you," Papa admonishes.

"It was nothing, Your Grace. Anne is making a great deal of very little and we shall say no more about it," Mama intercedes.

"Good. Perhaps we may then enjoy breakfast in blessed peace."

Yes, Papa is back to his usual quiet ways already. He will soon retire to his study to carry out his own duties, silent as the grave.

"Lady Retland has sent word Julia has taken to her room with a headache," Mama informs me, making Papa's eyes roll.

"Oh no, that cannot be."

"It is for the best."

"We must call on her to enquire after her health before we go to Hyde Park."

"We must do nothing of the sort."

"I shall not enjoy the day until I know she is alright," I insist.

"It should not be necessary to make my voice heard on the subject, but I will not have bickering at breakfast. My dear, should you wish to have any peace yourself for the rest of the day, I suggest you pay the blasted visit. It will not take much away from your time and will restore harmony at this table." My papa is clearly cross with us both, and we both fall silent after this heated speech.

My cake and hot chocolate are harder to swallow as the atmosphere hangs heavy around me like a dense cloak. Mama's shoulders stiffen and her countenance resembles a stormy sky.

Finishing as swiftly as possible, I retire to my room and ready myself for what should be a pleasant day but is already marred by this latest unpleasantness. I had meant to make it up to Mama but seem to have made a poor job of doing so. There is nothing else to be done but to pace about my room until it is time to leave.

I refuse to let these false sensibilities hinder my friend's progress. I should have thought Julia's aunt would be favourable of my plan. Should she not champion her niece's advancement? They are being most old fashioned, which irks me.

The barouche had been readied, so we arrive at the house in that transport to avoid delaying any further.

"Did you not receive my note?" Julia's aunt asks as we are shown in.

"Yes, Lady Retland, but I fear Lady Anne was greatly concerned for her friend's health, so we are come to enquire after her," Mama says apologetically, with a look which conveys far more than her words.

"Is she abed?" I ask, stepping towards the door.

"Well, yes, but—"

The good aunt's response falls into the space where I had been standing as I dash out of the room.

"Apologies, Lady Retland. As I intimated, my daughter is most concerned," I hear Mama explain.

"Julia, Julia, are you quite alright?" I call, a servant indicating the correct room.

My friend is fully dressed and sitting in a chair in her room.

"Oh, Anne, you are come. I knew you would. Aunt Retland says you had spoken in haste and did not intend for me to accept your invitation, but I knew it could not be so," she says, her words tumbling in their haste.

"And since when could anyone change my mind once it is made up?" I ask, receiving her into my arms as she rushes into them.

Stepping back, I regard her with dismay. "There is no need for tears. Hurry, dry your eyes, and we shall go out as planned and spend a jolly day together. You are not really ill, I trust?"

"No, I am quite well, merely relieved to have such a brave friend." Her lip trembles as she speaks.

"Come, gather your things and let there be no further delay."

We return to the matriarchs, and I gaily announce, "Good news, Mama. Miss Compley is quite recovered after her rest. Isn't it marvellous?"

"I am pleased to see it," Mama replies, her look hinting the reverse.

"My apologies, but I am not dressed for the park this moment," Lady Retland rallies.

It is a brave attempt, I grant you, but she cannot believe this will now halt proceedings.

"There is no great hurry. There is time for you to change, Lady Retland," I return.

"Lady Anne, please do not forget yourself, otherwise nobody shall be going anywhere," Mama reproaches me.

Turning to Julia's aunt, she says, "Please accept my apologies for my daughter's high spirits, Lady Retland. I fear she is rather too excited about the day. The exuberance of youth in a new town is sure to be heightened under such circumstances. However, she is correct. We are happy to wait if you wish to dress. Or, if you prefer, I shall be responsible for both girls and you may remain here."

Pardon me, is this Mama not offering any option for Julia's absence? There is a painting on the wall I suddenly find fascinating. I turn to study it more closely to conceal my countenance, fearing it would give away my feelings of triumph all too readily.

"Your Grace, I could not think to allow you to endure the day alone. Julia, ring for tea. I believe there should be some at the ready. Ladies, please excuse me."

She nearly inspires pity as she bustles out of the room. I did not mean to cause offence. Really, so much fuss over a simple park outing.

"This does not mean I approve of your methods," Mama whispers at my side as Julia goes to ring the bell.

"Of course. Thank you, Mama," I whisper back, risking a small smile in her direction.

I wonder what transpired as I went to fetch Julia. Lady Retland must have said something most shocking for Mama to now be on my side. What a pity I missed it.

We are not halfway through our tea when Lady Retland rejoins us, wearing a most sombre gown.

"We took the liberty of pouring tea for you, Lady Retland. Will you partake before our departure?" Mama asks brightly, handing the delicate teacup across.

"Why, thank you, yes, Your Grace."

I really am missing something. What did occur? Mama is pricking this woman more and more with every movement and gesture.

Everyone's spirits seem a little lifted by the tea, and we make our way to the carriage at last. Mama and I, of course, take the front-facing seats; our charity does not extend so far as to hide me away behind the driver. The four horses carry us towards our destination.

There are a great number of carriages, and we are quite stuck along the causeway as others keep stopping. There are various entertainments, which are quite a sight, but I am anxious to arrive amongst friends. And it is rather bright. Thank heavens for bonnets and parasols; it would not do for a drop of sunshine touch my fair skin. One must sadly live in perpetual shade and wear a blank expression.

I hear hooves clattering up behind me, and for a moment I fear we are to be robbed, the person is so close and in so much haste.

"Good day, ladies," the rider greets, doffing his hat as he pulls up alongside.

"Oh, Lord Dellingby, you gave me quite a fright," I respond, one hand on my chest.

"That was far from my intention. Pray, excuse me."

And with that, he trots up to our driver and has a lengthier conversation with him before continuing on his way. Well I never, the cheek of the man. What does he mean by this?

The carriage soon turns off and we have an easier time of it the rest of the way through.

"Ah, Lady Anne, you are arrived. I had quite given up all hope of your attendance," Lord Felsenworth comments as we approach his party.

"Please accept my apologies, my lord, we were unavoidably detained, but we are here now."

"Your Grace, Lady Retland, Miss Compley, a pleasure to see you all," he greets with a bow.

The rest of my group give head bobs and curtseys accordingly.

"Have you met everyone? I am acutely aware you are new to London. Might I introduce Lady Rathburn, Lady Rosen, Lady Glaston, Lord Alverbury, and of course, you know Lord Emsby and Lord Dellingby?"

Curtseys, head nods and bows are exchanged as we take our place amongst them.

"Lady Anne, you are recently arrived from Hampshire, I understand?" Lady Glaston asks.

"Yes, I am just come out," I am forced to confess.

"What a pleasant change London must be for you."

"Oh, indeed. But I am fond of the country."

"I suspect you will soon be completely won over once you have had the opportunity to experience all the delights London has to offer. Have you attended the opera yet?"

"I fear I have not yet had the chance but shall do soon."

"You simply must. The operas in London are only surpassed by those in Rome."

"Then I shall be sure to attend."

"We go in three nights time," Mama puts in for me.

"I'm glad to hear it, Your Grace. Perhaps I shall see you there," Lady Glaston replies, a snide smile sliding across her visage.

"Our diary is quite full, I assure you." Mama narrows her eyes at the condescending woman.

"Tell me, is Almack's part of your itinerary, Lady Anne?" Lord Felsenworth interrupts, I suspect to prevent any escalation.

"But of course, I go this very week, my lord."

"Jolly good, I must have the first dance," Lord Emsby announces.

"Of course," I reply, inclining my head.

Oh, hang him, I was conversing with Lord Felsenworth, who I am sure was about to stake his claim.

"Ah, but I claim the first waltz," my favoured partner says, victory shimmering in his eyes.

"Certainly, so long as the good ladies there permit," I demur, hoping to accept graciously without causing offence to Lord Emsby.

I have not yet attended the famous Almack's, but the patronesses are renowned for being particular about who they select to dance the waltz.

"A lady of fine standing and obvious good character such as yourself, I am sure, shall win them over."

"I suppose that leaves me a cotillion?" Lord Dellingby asks, and I assent.

Goodness, I'm not even at the venue yet and my evening is already getting filled.

"Lady Anne, do spare us a dance partner, won't you?" Lady Rathburn whines.

"My good lady, never fear, we shall all make a merry evening, and you shall be by no means short of partners," Lord Felsenworth assures her, flashing one of his dashing smiles.

"Most kind," she replies with her own smile.

I am already regretting having come here. As delightful as it is to be with Lord Felsenworth, I cannot say the same for the company he keeps. And the amount of fuss I created over Miss Compley seems hardly worth it now.

As soon as it may be considered polite, I rise. "Miss Compley, won't you join me for a turn?"

"What an inspired idea."

We are fortunately not joined by any others. They are too occupied trying to impress one another.

"I am so happy to have a moment to ourselves. What proud, disagreeable people," Julia confides as soon as we are outside hearing range, grabbing onto my arm.

"Please forgive me for dragging you to this place. If I had any idea —"

"Do not trouble yourself. You could not have known. I too had thought any company Lord Felsenworth was associated with must be a good one."

"What do you think I have done to Lady Glaston to make her so cross?"

"I think she meant only to boast her superior knowledge of the town."

"She most certainly succeeded. I am so glad you are here with me. It is good to know there is one friend upon whom I may rely."

"Always. I suppose this is what comes of mixing in the Ton."

"Oh Lor', you do not think all the rest shall be the same?"

"For your sake, I very much hope not."

We fall to discussing Julia's plans and more pleasant topics, so our mood is much lightened by the time we complete our circuit.

"I trust you found your promenade pleasant?" Lord Felsenworth remarks as we return.

"How could I not? The Park is most pleasant, is it not?"

"Wait until you visit Vauxhall Gardens. The sights there will astound you."

"All in due course, my lord."

"Quite."

He seems a little startled, I hope I wasn't too abrupt.

The conversation is far more amenable the rest of the afternoon, and I begin to warm to the entire company. Perhaps the ladies were merely inquisitive, and I have done them a disservice.

❧ Chapter 3 ❧

At first, the promise of a day in on Sunday has merit. I have been hustled and bustled about from pillar to post. Mama had had the foresight of anticipating my need for solitude. I am not used to this hive of activity. She had initially intended us to go out in the carriage today but graciously altered those plans owing to our expedition yesterday.

Not wishing to be entirely cooped up indoors, I take a book out into the garden so I may read in peace. What a fine prospect.

However, after a full thirty minutes, my page has not been turned. My eyes follow the words on the same page over and over, and yet they do not observe what is before me. My traitorous mind keeps dwelling on Lord Felsenworth. He really is a most charming man and fearful handsome.

Surely Papa could hold no objection should I choose him as a marriage partner? He is not a duke or even a marquess. But he is an earl. Even as the thought occurs, I doubt my reasoning. Well, we shall have to prove his worth, which, in terms of fortune, I believe to be not insubstantial.

It is of no use, the harder I attempt to put him from my mind, the more he insists on taking up residence there. Every glance of those fine blue eyes haunts my memory. And this from a girl who holds not a single romantic notion.

My shoulders shake as I pull myself together. I am an honourable young lady, one who is determined to do her duty. Really, this fancy is surely a passing moment. My head should not so easily be turned by a few looks and words of flattery. Have I not been prepared for this very thing?

If only we were at home, I should take a ride out on my horse, and outrun these wild thoughts. Regrettably, there is no chance of doing so here in town. Papa has been unable to secure a riding horse for me, although I am in some doubt as to how hard he attempted to do so.

Taking my book back up, I renew my attempts at reading. Only to be thwarted by Forbes seeking me out.

"Pardon me, m'lady, but Lord Beauvrais is arrived."

"Very good. Thank you, Forbes," I reply whilst inwardly turning somersaults.

Lord Beauvrais is just the tonic required. He was friends with my brother George. My heart still aches when I think of dear George. As the second son, he was in search of a profession.

Much to our chagrin, he settled on a career in the army, and Papa reluctantly purchased a commission for him in the horse guards. Papa had intended him for the church, a far more honourable profession, in his opinion. But my brother was not swayed, seeking to bring honour to our name in battle.

George fell during the Peninsular War last year, devastating our family. Papa has become even gruffer ever since. It is partly owing to this tragedy that my own match has come under more pressure than otherwise it should.

We have not seen Lord Beauvrais since. I suppose his reason for visiting has been removed. But he is such a fine fellow, we love him dearly. In fact, I am not sure why we cannot be done with this whole sorry charade of a marriage mart and have me married to him without delay. He has title, fortune and amiability enough, and is a man of parts. It would be a good match and I would remain close to home.

"Lady Anne, what an honour to see you again. It has been far too long," he greets, standing as I walk into the room.

Mama is, of course, there also, glaring at me so as to remind me not to run into this man's arms as I wish to.

"Lord Beauvrais, a pleasure indeed." A curtsey and hint of a smile are all that are permitted before I take a seat next to my chaperon.

"I do hope you will pardon my absence from your ball. Believe me, I tried all in my power to attend, but pressing business matters regrettably demanded my presence elsewhere. Can you ever see fit to forgive me?" he implores, his brown eyes full of earnest concern.

"Perhaps I can forgive you, if you dance with me at the Grainger's ball this evening," I reply, looking at him from lowered lashes and smirking a little, ignoring Mama's cough.

"An easy promise to uphold, for I shall indeed be there."

"Splendid. I will be pleased to have another friend present."

"You do not find Society here welcoming?"

"Oh, they smile enough, and allow me access, but I am as yet uncertain of much here. London life differs so much from the one I am used to."

We both ignore Mama's persistent cough.

"Then allow me to be your guide."

My heart melts at his smile and offer. No wonder I have been at odds without his reassuring presence here. He was always a balm to my nerves in days gone by.

Of course, Mama rebukes me severely for my wanton behaviour once Lord Beauvrais has departed. It matters not how much I point out that I consider him one of the family, and he was as much at fault as myself. I was clearly the one in error for encouraging him.

But I have secured a dance this evening, and so pay no heed to Mama's reprimand. She really makes too much of nothing at times. Besides, should I not be encouraging Lord Beauvrais? Her stern words are really quite puzzling.

Knowing the rigours of another evening of dancing lies ahead, I do try to rest, truly. But my nerves are on edge. Or is it excitement? The promise of a dance with Lord Beauvrais fills me with hope. And perhaps Lord Felsenworth shall be there. However, fear is also flooding my body. I am all atremble. The more I am in society the less I am fond of it, and the nearer I come to matrimonial vows. Perhaps this is too soon.

"Clément, Clément, come quick," I call.

My maid scurries in and curtseys.

"Clément, regard my face. What do you see there?"

Peering at me, the honest girl replies in her French tone, "Oh, my lady, a spot. *Ooh là là*. Never fear, we shall soon remedy this."

"How did this happen? We have been applying pastes."

"Apologies, my lady, but I do not know. I am sure I have been following the recipes in the articles you gave me."

Retrieving pots and jars, she sets to work. The first application makes me wince and suck in air through my teeth. The stench of sulphur makes my nose wrinkle.

"My apologies, my lady, but this is the best way."

"I understand, Clément. Please do what must be done. I am out at the Grainger's this evening and must be presentable."

"Ow!" I cannot help this exclamation as she squeezes the offending blemish.

"How am I ever to go out into Society looking this way?" I cry, catching my reflection after her ministrations.

"My lady, if you please, I am not yet done."

A stinking paste is then applied. My fingers run over the pots and brushes on the dressing table in front of me as I wait until the revolting concoction can be removed. And when it is, my skin looks red and angry.

"Pray tell me it will get better than this."

Clément nods and applies powders. "There, you would never know a blemish had occurred, my lady. Regard."

Peering closely into the looking glass, I must agree. She's done a fine job of avoiding this disaster. I am even a little paler than usual as more pearl powder had to be applied. And the clever girl's darkened my brows a shade deeper to attract attention there, and not the cleverly concealed offender on my chin. This is precisely why she remains in my employ.

"Very good, Clément."

I am cinched, laced and adorned until I veritably glisten. My gown this evening is white with gold embroidered net and puff sleeves. My hair is simply curled, a small gold comb and ribbon are the only decoration. Elegant purity is the overall effect.

Gliding into the ballroom at the Grainger's like a swan, my eyes dart about, seeking my prey more like a fox. My heart sinks as Lord Emsby inserts himself into my presence. One must not grimace; it is not becoming of a lady of gentle breeding.

"Lady Anne, a delight to see you here. Come, I must claim the first dance."

"As you request, Lord Emsby," I reply with my politest curtsey.

I am made warm by my ire. Where are any of my other suitors? Why did they not step forwards at once? They had the power within them to rescue me from this ill fate.

It takes a great deal of effort not to roll my eyes and sigh at the man's plodding as we travel about the room in the country dance. He clearly still believes himself in with a chance. I feel sick at the notion.

Surely my family cannot consider this man to be my equal? But if they do, can I argue a strong case against him? I am fully aware many before me have made a similar alliance. Why should I be any different? I am not so very extraordinary.

But there it is. That small voice of hope, whispering promises of a better husband in my ear. Something I have no right to desire. Have I not already likened myself to a prize pig? The only difference is the pretence of civility in my case. The pig is far more honest a beast.

They dress me in fine clothes and parade their grand offering. I smile, curtsey and dance. But is my fate truly a life of servitude? To become a good wife and mother, forever holding my tongue. I should welcome it so long as it is not to such a man as is before me now.

Sombre thoughts continue to whir around my head as my feet skip around the room with my next partner.

But then, as if in answer to my question, Lord Felsenworth takes me through the paces of a dance. Our hands touch, his blue eyes shining brightly into my brown gaze as we step agonisingly close to one another, only to be parted as we weave between the other couples. His presence sparks life into my veins, our separation leaves me cold.

"How do you enjoy London so far, Lady Anne?" he asks in one of our joyous unions.

"Very well, I thank you, my lord."

"Ah, the polite, rehearsed response."

We are infuriatingly forced apart by the dance before I can justify myself.

"It is perhaps better at certain times than others," I manage to tell him in a pass.

I observe his grin from my position down the line.

"Might I inquire as to when these times might be?" he asks as we pass again.

"You may, but it would be indiscreet of me to respond," I tell him with a wry smile as we join hands.

We join others in a circle and spin around. This may be the happiest I have been in a long while.

As we meet one-on-one once more, Lord Felsenworth asks, "Wednesday is too distant. Where might I meet you before?"

A small gasp escapes me. "My lord!"

"Not alone, you understand. But perhaps we may meet as if by accident in the company of others?"

"You may call tomorrow."

"Lady Anne, you tease me."

"Very well, if that is not enough to satisfy you..."

"Indeed, it is not."

"Then Mama and I shall be at the theatre tomorrow evening. Or the opera the night following."

"Perfect," he says, smiling as he kisses my gloved hand at the end of the dance.

Yes, he has beauty and wealth enough, but Lord Felsenworth begins to lose manners and forget propriety. I truly believe if I had been so imprudent as to offer a clandestine meeting he would have accepted. A strange wariness falls upon me, which to my shame, only adds to the fascination of this entertaining earl.

Ah, here is Lord Beauvrais at last.

"As promised, Lady Anne," he says, taking my hand and leading me into the next set, a smile trying to tease his rosy lips.

I wonder why he has waited so long. The evening is waning fast. It is surely not due to lack of confidence, for he is still the finest dancer I have ever cast eyes upon. He is so light of foot that he glides about the floor with full elegance and grandeur and is really quite dashing.

He stands almost a foot above me in height, and I cannot help but observe how his tight-fitting breeches and blue coat become him even more than it does Lord Felsenworth. Lord Beauvrais seems designed for the dandy fashions.

Yet, he is unusually quiet. A crease seems to have taken up permanent residence above his forlorn brown eyes, beneath his Titan styled brown hair. I am at a loss to smooth out that look at all during our dance, despite my best efforts.

"Please excuse me," he whispers hoarsely before bowing himself out of my presence.

Not waiting for another partner, I walk swiftly across to the punch bowl, puzzlement addling my mind. In my path to refreshment, I come across two familiar faces.

"Really? Have you ever seen such a neckline? She is positively prudish," Lady Rosen says, looking down her nose in my direction.

Had I been left in any doubt as to whom they were referring, Lady Rathburn's scornful glance would have allayed it. "Quite. Too wholesome by far. There being such a thing as false modesty."

It is true that my gown this evening covers a good deal of my bosom, but it is by no means prudish. Pretending not to have heard, I stride past them and on to my original destination. Helping myself to a glass of punch, I try to quell my burning fury. These ladies were my friends but yesterday. What have I done to earn such contempt?

"Do not pay any heed to them. Lady Rathburn is only sour as you are now the belle of the Ton," a pretty young lady whispers at my side, helping herself to the same beverage.

"You assign me too great a credit…" I am at a loss; we've not yet been introduced.

"I do beg your pardon. My own manners were quite forgot in my haste. Miss Plimpton," she tells me with a curtsey, her brown curls bouncing.

"It is a pleasure to make your acquaintance. Lady Anne," I inform with a returning curtsey.

"Oh, I know who you are, Lady Anne," my new friend tells me with a small smile, her brown eyes alight with mirth.

"I would beg you do not believe all that you hear."

"Only good things, I assure you. That is why you have inspired their jealousy," she says with the slightest point of her head in the direction of my so-called friends.

"But I have been nothing but pleasant to them."

"My dear, that will only serve to add to their resentment."

"But why?" My brow furrows a little.

"It is the way they are made. In Hertford, they are used to having command of every room. But here there are rivals. And you are currently top of the list."

"You are from Hertford yourself?" I ask, taking another sip of punch.

"Yes, not that I am good enough for them to keep regular company with."

"You too have enflamed their jealousy?"

"Sadly, I must confess I am beneath their notice. They are both daughters of earls. I, on the other hand, can only claim a baron as my papa."

"That may be the most ridiculous snobbery I have ever heard."

"I thank you for saying so. You are too kind. I do hope we can be friends."

"I think I should like that very much."

Relief washes over me upon finding an amiable companion of *Le Bon Ton*. Julia wanders across and joins us.

"Miss Plimpton, might I introduce you to my good friend Miss Compley, daughter of Sir Cecil?"

"Miss Plimpton," Julia says with a curtsey.

"Miss Compley."

"Miss Plimpton and I were just discussing the snobbery of others."

"I fear that may be a conversation of some duration."

All three of us giggle at Julia's comment and heartily agree.

"I notice you were dancing with the esteemed Sir Reginald," I point out.

"You are funning me. You know he only dances with me at the request of your Lord Felsenworth."

"He is fearful handsome, is he not?" Miss Plimpton remarks, bringing more giggles from us all.

Before I am able to comment further, we are all approached and taken back into the dance.

❧ Chapter 4 ❧

Letter from Margaret, received 18th April 1814

My dear sister,

Thank you for your letters. I had not time to respond when your second reached me. I believe you grew anxious before time, and this in itself is troubling for it is so unlike you. I do hope you succeed in finding amusement during your stay, even though I am not with you.

I am in full health but feel your loss keenly. Life continues dull without you. We are too quiet, and Miss Swanson persists in my lessons, even although nobody is here to witness them. We have had a spell of sunshine and I longed to spend some time out of doors, but alas I was not permitted even this small joy.

However, I have observed some glances between her and Mr Rawlinson when he arrives to teach me more arpeggios. Incidentally, I am learning a new Beethoven piece, which I confess is rather exciting. But back to the important matter at hand, I feel it prudent to encourage the friendship of these two tutors, and by that method perhaps gain a little more freedom. Only a little is all I ask. I thank you for your reminders and am sensible that one must not neglect one's education. But surely a little leisure would not be amiss? I shall await your scolding for my flighty thoughts.

I trust you will forgive me for laughing at the image you painted of your court dress. It really does sound ghastly. Have you a date yet?

Lord Felsenworth sounds intriguing. I should very much like to meet the man who stirs such flutterings in my sister. Tell me, how was your expedition to Hyde Park? Did he take you for a promenade down a leafy lane and ravish you? Pray tell me of every flutter and smile he extracts. News of this nature enlivens my day most pleasingly.

And I must beg you tell me every detail of your dress fittings. Is your London wardrobe so vastly different from that here?

That you quarrelled with Mama is most alarming. You dared stand up to her? I am not quite sure what to make of this. Please do not return home too much changed. Must I caution you, in turn, to pay heed to your own conduct? Surely not in so steadfast a sister as yourself.

It seems I must live vicariously through you, so send as many letters as your time permits.

Prince wagged his tail at your hug; a most grateful recipient.

There is nothing further worthy of note, so I shall sign off with great sisterly affection,

Margaret Frithringham

Letter in reply to Margaret – sent 18th April 1814

My dear Margie,

Firstly, pray do not meddle in matters of the heart for your own amusement. I beg you would leave poor Miss Swanson alone, lest you should lose her as a governess entirely. Consider yourself reprimanded indeed for such thoughts. It must not be attempted.

My time here seems a bit of a blur, so forgive me for hurrying your reply. I am caught in a whirl of activity, which is both exciting and terrifying, yet I long for the peace of home.

Mentions of flutterings shall desist entirely if you are going to create them into a far greater fancy than they are in reality. Lord Felsenworth is pleasing on the eye and does stir some emotion, but I am as yet not head-over-heels in love with him. Please do calm yourself and attempt a little more solemnity to your manner of letter writing.

Besides, Lord Beauvrais is arrived, greatly relieving my discomfort.

In an attempt to appear less of a harridan in your eyes, I shall divulge details of my day, as there is much to tell you of my dressing adventure.

Clément had told me of a funny shop she had seen an advertisement for in the Belle Assemblée and filled us both with such curiosity we simply had to pay a visit. Well, what do you think? In Clark & Debenham, which is situated in Mayfair, there were dresses for sale which were already made.

"How do they know they shall fit?" I asked Clément in a fit of giggles.

But the dear girl was as much in the dark as I. Surely a seamstress would still have to be employed for fitting, so we were bewildered as to their reasoning. However, we did purchase some silk and sarsnet there so as not to appear impolite.

One was not confident in that establishment's soundness, so on we travelled to an entirely different curiosity, but one which was far more amenable. We were armed with plates from Lady's Magazine. And how pleased I was that I was permitted a copy of The Gallery of Fashion, favoured by good Queen Charlotte.

Oh, how you will love the fashion designer. Everything you could wish for under one roof; I ordered gowns, hats and gloves without so much as a visit to a milliner. What a fine thing!

I do believe we were quite carried away with the excitement of it all. I now have a full complement of walking dresses, day dresses, evening gowns, shoes, some wonderful half-boots, gloves, stockings, bonnets, shawls, parasols, a new spencer and the finest of all, a pelisse. It is of the best brown sarsnet, decorated with golden oak leaves.

I make no mention of undergarments, naturally, but rest assured there are some. As well as cloaks, reticules and headdresses all to match my apparel. I do hope Papa shall not grumble too much when the bill arrives. But really, it is all his fault for making me attend a Season.

Perhaps the visit to Ackermann's repository after was a little excessive, but I was not yet ready to stop.

What a fine time we had! I begin to see why you enjoy this so much. There were so many pretty things. The Ladies Rosen and Rathburn were most disparaging over my gown last evening, so I have ensured a greater amount of flesh shall now be on display. I had thought a little modesty may be advisable, but I was made to feel like a country bumpkin. I was sure I could have died of shame had Miss Plimpton not come to my aid. She seems most pleasant, and I hope we shall be good friends.

We saw such a sight as we passed by Piccadilly, we could scarce believe our eyes. Several young men were racing down the street on something called a Dandy Horse. It is a sort of metal frame with a wheel fixed at each end. The men were propelled along by the strength of their legs alone.

I do so wish you could be here. We would have such larks together. But alas, you are there, and I must make ready for the theatre this evening.

I must sign off, your amused sister,

Anne Frithringham

Clément has dutifully lain out my white and blue silk gauze gown for this evening. Prettily finished with silk net and blue satin, it is, I am assured, suitably virtuous for a Lady of delicate upbringing, whilst displaying my figure to full advantage. For, I am told, the aim of theatre visits is not to see, but to be seen. As seems the general standard to which I am held accountable for all ventures outside this house. How wearisome it is to always be on show in this manner. Eyes are forever upon me, scrutinising.

My hair is once more draped and ringleted, with a few flowers and a blue ribbon its only adornment. There is quite a nip in the air as Mama and I step into our awaiting carriage, making me quite glad of my new shawl.

We make our arrival and greet others with all pleasantry befitting the evening. Mama and I are duly seated in our box, which is well lit. The chandeliers above the auditorium are every bit as dazzling as I have heard them to be.

Lord and Lady Grainger, along with their daughter, Lady Charlotte are sitting with us. It is her first visit here too, and we both happily observe the spectacle before us. But try as we might, we can barely hear a word uttered by the actors. There is such a hubbub from our fellow audience that whichever play we are supposed to be watching is rendered useless.

We are therefore left to talking to one another. But alas, the silly girl witters on about her gowns endlessly. I care not a jot which trimmings her dressmaker has employed. Regrettably, she seems unable to be turned to any other discourse.

By the end of the first act, I am quite ill-tempered with boredom. The heat of the room is stifling, which does not help matters. It is a combination uncomfortable enough to vex a saint, and I am certainly not worthy of such a title.

My fan is busy, but I begin to grow concerned that another person may misconstrue its fluttering, so confine it once more to my lap. The voices about me grow louder and the heat increases until there is such a drumming in my ears I fear I shall soon swoon in a faint.

"Pray, excuse me, Mama," I plead, turning to the good lady.

"Dear, Anne, are you quite well?"

"I shall be in due course. I must beg a few moments to gather myself in the box-lobby, however."

"Of course, we shall go immediately."

"Please do not trouble yourself. Your friends will think me most ill-mannered. I shall be but a door away. No harm can befall me, I am sure."

"Very well but be quick about it. I shall soon be out if you are too long absent."

"Thank you, Mama."

With a curtsey, I make my departure and draw air in deeply as I gain my momentary freedom. Oh, but it feels good to be away from there. My very future seemed to encroach my soul in that moment, stealing the breath from my body. It leaves me pondering how long I may endure such evenings and outings. How I long for the vast open lands of home, away from so many crowds, and where I may breathe easily.

Fanning my face freely now there are no eyes to misinterpret its actions, my senses begin to return. But no sooner do I regain them when I am alarmed by the presence of a man striding along the corridor.

"Lord Beauvrais, I was not aware of your being here this evening," I greet the so-named man, along with a curtsey

"Indeed, Lady Anne. I had not planned it so but found myself brought here quite against my own will by my friends. I beg you would allow me to make my retreat."

"You leave so soon?"

"I fear I must."

"Lord Beauvrais, we were always friends, were we not?"

"Of course, but what a question," he replies, taking hold of my hand.

I catch his gaze with my own. "Then answer me truthfully, if you please. Might I inquire as to why you have not called on me? You ought to have done so this very morning, but I did not receive so much as your card. Have I done something which offends you?"

"Lady Anne, why ever would you think such a thing? Pray, make yourself not uneasy on my account. It is I who am unworthy of your good self. I did intend on calling on you in person, of course, but I was unavoidably detained and had not the opportunity of sending word. I dare not tell you more. Please accept my sincerest apologies."

"At once. I am sorry to have doubted you. I do not know what I am about anymore. I seem to live in constant confusion. And then you were arrived and helped bring order to the chaos. So, when you were again absent, I felt it perhaps more keenly than I should."

Both my hands are now within his grasp as he tells me, "Dearest Anne, you poor little dove. You must be suffering greatly to make such a speech. How keenly you make me feel my neglect. If you but knew how your words strike my very soul. You make me determined to make amends and prove myself your worthy friend in these lands you find so strange. I am at your service."

My hands are kissed as he bows down to them upon finishing this fine speech. The battle between my will and my tears is bitterly strong at this moment, and I fear my will may the be losing party as droplets pool in my eyes. My heart is brimming with gladness at his promise. I had scarce admitted to myself what I have confessed to him. Indeed, I do not know what force dragged the words from my lips. But what a happy outcome they have brought about.

"Alas, I really must beg my leave this moment though, for my friends shall soon notice my absence. But I leave with the promise of calling on you in the morning."

"Go, go, Beauvrais. I would not have you dragged back in there for the world. I only wish I could accompany you."

"You are too good for such an act. Adieu, my friend."

And with that, he's on his way. Rapid footsteps behind me have me spinning on my heel.

"I say, was that Beauvrais?"

"Lord Felsenworth, what a surprise to see you here."

"Lady Anne, forgive me. I am in haste. I did not recognise you. Might I add you look very well this evening?"

"Why thank you, my lord. But I must return to Mama. She shall be wondering where I am."

With a curtsey, I hurry away from his flattery, as I do not trust the look in his eye whilst alone with him.

"Your colour is quite returned. I trust you are recovered?" Mama asks as I retake my seat.

"Quite, Mama, I thank you."

In truth, my heart seems to be racing faster than ever before.

❧ Chapter 5 ❦

The next morning, after breakfast, Clément is helping me into one of my new walking dresses just as the butler alerts Mama to Lord Beauvrais' presence. I hurry down before she may discourage his attentions, as I fear she may do based on our earlier discourse.

"Lord Beauvrais, you are true to your word," I tell him with a smile and stretch out my hands towards his.

Poor Mama is coughing again.

"Lady Anne, have I ever given you cause to doubt me?" he replies with a bow before taking my gloved hands in his.

"I am sure you have not."

"I am arrived on an errand, if your gracious mama permits?"

She raises her brows at him quizzically.

Turning to her, he asks, "Your Grace, would you permit your daughter an excursion this morning? Only so far as Hyde Park."

"That seems amenable," she grants.

He smiles and turns back to me. "Splendid. Did you pack your saddle and riding habit, my lady?"

"Why yes, but Papa has not yet procured a horse for me here."

"Then it is well for you that I have brought one for you to ride."

"Really?" I fail to contain the joy bursting from me.

"Lord Beauvrais, I granted permission on the assumption we were to travel in a carriage," Mama interjects.

"Your Grace, if you please, regard the joy your daughter so clearly has at this prospect. Would you deny her this simple pleasure? And with such an old and trusted friend? You may choose her companion to accompany us. Do you have a footman to spare?"

Mama ruffles in her seat at his impertinence. "Of course."

"That's happily settled then. I shall ensure all is prepared by the time you make your exit," he tells me before bowing and bouncing out of the room.

Now, there is the Lord Beauvrais I know. Full of mischief and surprises. What a darling man he is, to have gone to the exceptional trouble and expense of bringing a horse to me. Taking my leave of my rather stunned mama, I away to make ready for my pleasure ride. How I have missed riding my horse.

Two fine mares are pawing the ground with their hooves as I leave the house.

"She's beautiful," I tell Lord Beauvrais, slowly approaching to stroke my horse's grey nose, who softly whickers at my touch.

"Lady Anne, this is, rather suitably, Lady, here at your service as am I."

He is standing close to me, holding the reins of both our horses. If it were not for my watchful footman chaperon, I would risk planting a kiss on his cheek, for this is the greatest gift anyone has ever bestowed upon me. Surely this shows an inclination of more than friendship, on both parts. Perhaps soon I shall receive the one truly welcome proposal?

"I have not words enough to thank you, Lord Beauvrais," I tell him, fighting back tears.

"Your happiness is reward enough. I know how much you ride when at home. And am also aware of the difficulties in finding riding horses in London at present. You looked so forlorn last evening I was determined to restore your smile."

"If only I could return the favour."

"You think me unhappy? Come now, we dally. A marvellous day awaits."

Calling the footman to hold his horse, Lord Beauvrais gives me a leg up and waits for me to settle comfortably into my saddle before swiftly mounting his own horse.

"Are we ready, my lady?" he asks, his eyes twinkling.

"Onwards," I call, kicking Lady into action.

Riding along London roads is really quite a different skill to the one demanded by my country jaunts. There are many horses, donkeys, carts and carriages to contend with. It makes for slow going until we reach the park.

Glancing at Lord Beauvrais as we gain entrance, I spur Lady into a trot. Her gait is a little shorter to that of my own Rosalind, and it takes me a minute or two to grow accustomed to her bouncy movement. She has been an absolute angel thus far, and not at all deterred by our journey here.

"How do you find your steed?" Lord Beauvrais asks, riding at my side.

"She is fine indeed," I manage to say somewhat smoothly.

Hyde Park is quieter today, and our progress is unhindered, but I slow us back down to a walk nonetheless.

"Everything alright, Lady Anne?" Lord Beauvrais asks at my unusual slow pace.

"Oh, quite," I say with an unladylike wink.

"Oh, what is this beast about?" I announce for the benefit of the footman whilst subtly kicking underneath my riding habit.

Slowing to a walk had been a mere ploy to discover how fast Lady gathers pace once allowed her head. I'm delighted that the answer is that she is rather rapid indeed, as we canter off. Lord Beauvrais is, of course, close upon her hooves in pretence of catching up to this damsel in distress. Only once we are out of earshot do I allow my laugh to ring out.

"You really are still a sly fox, Anne," Beauvrais observes with a chuckle as he draws beside.

Lady and I cannot allow that, and she launches into a full gallop, making me squeal with joy. This is the freedom and the pace my heart had been missing this past week. The wind rushes past my cheeks, wrenching water from my eyes. My skirts are flowing freely as we fly onwards.

All too soon we must slow, however. I am supposed to be on a runaway yet mustn't cause too much of a scene. Allowing Lord Beauvrais the chance to pull up in a charade of taking charge, we slow to a walk.

"Your Mama will not allow me to accompany you anywhere again if we do not return to your poor footman. The poor man. You are too cruel. See how he runs to come to your aid? You shall exhaust him."

There is no mistaking the comical form in my family's livery, even from afar.

"You have the right of it. Let us close the distance for him. I would not give anyone else discomfort for the sake of my own enjoyment."

"Yet, nor should we hurry too greatly, for Lady may bolt should you risk anything above a walk."

How my heart dances at the sound of his chortle. It is my belief that this brief escapade has restored us both to our former selves.

Leaning towards me he cautions, "Do try to not look quite so merry. Recall you were carried off by this brute."

I giggle at his faux-serious disposition. "You are quite right. One must be affronted by such events," but a laugh escapes us both as I speak.

"Oh, but it is good to laugh again, Lord Beauvrais."

"I would always have you so well pleased."

"Why must we grow old? Why can we not always stay as we were when we were children?"

"Some of us will not have the privilege. You should not speak so. It betrays your selfishness," he says, the joy immediately vanishing from his visage.

"But what wrong did I infer on you?"

"I was not speaking of myself," he retorts gruffly, urging his horse to a trot.

I am at a loss. What did I say? We were having such fun, the radiance was back in his eyes, and now it has vanished. Am I never to keep it alight?

Trotting Lady on in an attempt to keep up with the sullen lord, we do not take long to reach my footman, who fusses greatly.

"Oh, my lady, are you alright? I was so worried for you. Are you quite safe? Should I send for the carriage?"

"Do settle yourself, Barnes. I am quite well as you see. I was not even thrown. The daft beast got spooked and ran away with me, but she is calm again now. There is no reason not to continue as we were."

"Perhaps we should return you home?" Lord Beauvrais contradicts.

"What? Return already? Lord Beauvrais, I had thought you would be sensible of my meaning, but I see I am quite alone. Very well, as you wish it."

Why does he speak against me so? I must have upset him terribly, and after he had been so kind. Is his friendship lost to me by means of a few careless words? Too upset to stay near, I urge Lady into a trot and make my way out of the park as elegantly as possible.

His face looks like a storm, at least each time I catch sight of it.

"You need not accompany me home. I shall have Lady returned to you," I tell the foolish man haughtily as we reach the park gate.

"I would prefer to see you safe."

"Lord Beauvrais, I claim old acquaintance, so shall not mince words. What you prefer is clearly to bring an end to this outing. Having so earnestly promised to be my friend, I see your struggle to uphold that pledge. Therefore, I release you from any obligation. Good day."

Turning Lady away, I ride towards home, with only Barnes behind me. Lord Beauvrais did not even try to insist himself into my presence to see me safely home. I must conclude our friendship is indeed at an end.

Confound these busy streets. Delay is as inexcusable as it is unavoidable. My resolve is slipping further with each slow step. But I must not show my feelings, not yet. How far from home we seem. How long can this anguish be contained within my bosom? My lip begins to tremble, forcing me to bite down to halt its treachery.

Will this torment not end? Move, you interminable coaches and carriages. Clear the way and let me pass, for I seek refuge from you all. None must see the agony of these tears which at this very moment threaten to rain down.

I do not know how, but I manage to swallow hard enough, to bite hard enough, and breathe deep enough to keep my emotions in check. Sliding off Lady, I whip off my gloves and sling them in the direction of a waiting servant, along with my hat.

"Please, not a word, Mama," I beg, sailing past that good lady, who looks askance.

Heading straight to my chamber, I launch myself upon my bed and allow the dam to burst at last. And oh, how the torrent threatens to overwhelm me.

How ridiculous of Lord Beauvrais to call me selfish. The impudence of the man! I had merely wished for the simpler pleasures of our childhood for us both. For then there were no social barriers between us, no awkwardness as there now is.

There was hardly ever a cross word between himself, George and I. James thought himself too mature for our games, and Margie too young at first. But we three would run into the woods of Papa's grounds and conjure up all manner of adventures. I am sure our elders would have censured our frivolity had they ever witnessed it, for I behaved almost as one of the boys at times. With them, I was not Lady Anne; I was but myself. And now I am quite lost.

Tears rain unchecked as once more the loss of George fires its flaming daggers through my heart and stomach. As I mourn the loss of my dearest brother as well as our innocent childhood.

How much a stranger this Lord Beauvrais is to me. No longer the Bamber of times past, who is lost to the annals of history, it seems.

How cruel of fate to snatch all this away from me. My anger truly has turned to sadness and back again.

"Aaaaargh!" I yell to the canopy of my bed until any witness would think me deranged.

Attracted by the unearthly sound, Clément enters. "My lady, what is the matter? May I be of assistance?"

Sobering at once, I reply, "Only if you can rewrite history."

"If it were but in my power I surely would, my lady."

The dear girl is so earnest in her pledge that a weak smile is brought to my lips. "I believe you would. How sweet you are."

The compliment forces a curtsey from my maid.

"I suppose it helps me not to rally against what cannot be changed," I tell her glumly.

"It has often been said it is best not to dwell on things past, my lady."

"How wise those words are. We must reflect on what is before us now."

"Which reminds me, your mama sent me to request your company once you have regained a more dignified demeanour."

"Oh, you wretch," I scream, raising a pillow in my hands.

She holds up her hands, and squeals, "*S'il vous plaît*, please. Them was her words and not my own. I would never dare speak so. You know this."

Lowering the pillow back to its place on the bed, my head also lowers. "My apologies. I should not have believed it of you, Clément."

"You must have had a great shock today, my lady."

Smoothing my skirts as I rise, I tell her, "Just so. But one must make the most of the situation."

"If you please, my lady, if you would allow me to re-arrange your hair before you go to her grace?"

❧

"Well, what have you to say for yourself?" Mama asks down her nose as I enter her presence with neat hair and a change of gown.

Kneeling at her feet I respond, "Please forgive me, Mama. Lord Beauvrais and I had a quarrel and I do not wish to do so with you. I was too cross to find words upon coming home."

"Did I not caution you against encouraging him? But the pair of you insisted on going out on those confounded horses. Barnes tells me you were carried clean off."

"Oh, indeed I was. But it was but a moment of fright for the horse more than I. No harm befell me, except from Lord Beauvrais' words."

"He spoke harshly?"

Getting up to sit on a couch, I continue my explanation and recount the details of the outing.

"I shan't pretend you have not been foolish, for I believe you raised your hopes too high, despite my caution. However, you are paying dearly for that, so I shall say no more about it. Nor should he have spoken so and was most neglectful in not accompanying you home. You see what happens when you go out without your Mama?"

"Please, Mama, no more chastisement. I see my error and am most heartily sorry for it."

"Very well. You may spend the rest of the day in quiet contemplation. I shall cancel our evening engagement, excusing you with a headache."

"Thank you, Mama," I tell her, grasping her hands and kissing her cheek before rustling out of the room and seeking the tranquillity of the library.

Chapter 6

Be still, oh beating heart. How rapidly it beats in my breast, thundering in hope that this evening I may yet regain Lord Beauvrais' hand. Clément busies herself about my toilet as I gaze on in the looking glass. We have changed my gown twice already, for it must be perfect if I am to lure him into a dance at Almack's this evening. Then perhaps he will remember our friendship and his mind will be reconciled to me. We are a near perfect match, as close as any can be upon entering the marriage state.

It is with trembling limbs I climb into the carriage which transports Mama and me to the thrills tonight holds. My dearest wish seems to be to find my dance partner and make love, with the music heralding our union.

Have I not repeatedly stated I am not romantic? For shame, my heart does protest and rail against me. For in Lord Beauvrais I place my trust. Surely, he cannot betray me so entirely? He would not abandon our friendship so easily. Not for the sake of a few poorly chosen words.

But what has he thus promised? Has every look, every word not denied me the closeness we once shared? How am I to regain what has been lost? He seems so far away. His eyes betray thoughts which stray elsewhere. If only we could but share a few moments alone, discuss what we were, and may yet be.

Perhaps I should not favour him so, but how can I not? He has been the life companion of my childhood. Is it wrong to hope he shall continue that through to my adult life? And yet I dare not hope and know I must not outwardly single him out. There are other beaux I am expected to court.

Where is he? As I gain entrance to the hallowed ballroom, Lord Beauvrais is noticeable in his absence.

Lord Emsby and Lord Dellingby both happen upon me at once.

"Lady Anne, I believe I was promised the first dance," Lord Emsby greets with a bow.

Dash it, but I did, at the breakfast on the park. But as I am about to accept his proffered hand we are interrupted.

"But I was promised the cotillion, which has been declared the first this evening," Lord Dellingby states.

What is the proper response? I am so afraid of causing offence to either that my gaze turns alternately between them in astonished silence.

"I would not wish to make you break a promise, my lady," Emsby supplies, bowing out gracefully but with a dark glower at his competitor.

It was indeed gallant of him to stand down. But now I am left with Lord Dellingby.

"Thank you, Lord Emsby. Should the first dance have been a minuet, as I believe you had anticipated, I should relinquish my claim," Lord Dellingby says, bowing to the now retreating man.

Claim? Neither one has a claim upon me, not yet. Never have I felt so much the prize pig as I do at this moment. I am led to the floor as if to my slaughter.

"How glum you are this evening, Lady Anne. Is there nothing I can do for your relief?" my dance partner asks.

"Please excuse any appearance of such. I am still recovering from the headache of yesterday. It shall pass."

"Perhaps you should sit the next one out? I would be willing to sit with you until you are recovered."

"I thank you, but that shall not be necessary," I reply, bowing my head a little, and trying to place a small smile on my lips.

How is one supposed to display civility when one's heart is breaking? Lord Beauvrais has still not arrived, and I am losing all hope that he ever shall.

Really, the man does not know how to accept defeat, for here is Lord Emsby to claim the very next dance. With my stomach turning, I curtsey my acceptance.

"Lady Anne, you are a magnificent dancer," he tells me, supposedly in the hopes of raising my spirits.

"Why, thank you, Lord Emsby," I politely respond.

My attention is caught by a movement amongst the onlookers. Was that? But no, alas, I cannot see Lord Beauvrais now. It must be my mind playing its wicked tricks.

The dance seems eternal as my feet are forced to perform the steps that tap out my doom. Each smile, each dance takes me nearer my fate. I must give myself over to it as I was brought up to do. Why do I resist it so?

Coming to London, I knew full well what my duty was. Lord Emsby seems not unkind. His aroma is perhaps a little unpleasant to the nose and his manners are lacking, but I do not think him vicious. Papa must consider him a fitting match, therefore so must I.

"Enchanting, as ever," he tells me as he hands me to the next.

Passed from one man to another, my evening is whirled away in a dreary circle of dances. But wait, what is this?

"The fine patronesses have granted us the waltz," Lord Felsenworth tells me, his blue eyes twinkling with a mirth which matches that of his lips.

"Surely..?" I quiz, but as I glance over to one of the fine dames, she nods her assent, which I curtsey back to.

"Well, what a fine thing," I say, my own smile playing at the corners of my mouth.

Warmth begins to thaw my veins, and is that a flutter in my breast again? I had thought it could only beat so rapidly for Lord Beauvrais. Have I so much neglected Lord Felsenworth as to forget the pleasing effect he has upon me?

Oh my, but he draws me close as the orchestra strikes up. I have only danced this with my tutor and oh, dear George when he could be coaxed into practice with his sister, which was uncomfortable for us all.

"What cloud is this which dims the sun?" my charming beau inquires.

"Beg pardon?"

"Ah, but you are back here with me now. The sun begins to shine again from those brown pools of chocolate."

My smile widens at the compliment, but how can it not when it is delivered in tones which would make the hardest winter frost melt?

A deep blue gaze holds mine as we begin to step into the waltz. Our eyes never look elsewhere; thrills ripple through me. Oh Lor', how scandalous this dance is when it is danced with one such as Lord Felsenworth. The touch of his hand upon my shoulder makes my knees tremble as we turn together, our bodies facing.

We reunite with the other couple in our circle and sway back and forth in a manner which heightens my desire to reunite alone with my dance partner. Relief floods through me as he once more takes me into his embrace, and we turn and travel alone. My breath hitches as we glide.

"You are quite lovely, you know," he whispers low, bringing a blush to my cheeks.

To and fro at the hand of another whilst struggling to maintain my placid countenance. It takes a great deal of effort to remind myself this is no more than a mere dance. And my resolve almost gets washed away entirely as Lord Felsenworth grasps my shoulders and turns me about. Words escape me entirely.

All sense of propriety abandons me as the next attitude swirls us ever closer into an embrace. Lord Felsenworth has one hand firmly on my waist. I cannot begin to describe the warm sensations spreading throughout my person, emanating from that point of contact. The fingers of his other hand touch mine above our heads before our arms arc down as we turn in circles. My breath catches. Without such a tight grip on my waist, I am unsure whether my legs would support me at this moment.

Our arms interlink in front as we promenade, leaving me cold without his hand upon me. How I yearn to feel his hand again, how at home it seems when present, and how lost I am to this man.

By the time the dance reaches its conclusion I am quite enthralled. Life, I am convinced, could be quite merry indeed should it be spent with Lord Felsenworth. There is always such mirth in his countenance, a mischief bubbling below the surface, yet with a tenderness of affection. Yes, if Lord Beauvrais is not prepared to make me an offer, Lord Felsenworth is an admirable match.

Chapter 7

A few callers attend upon me this morning, Lord Felsenworth being amongst their number. He may have bewitched my mama, as she has agreed he may escort me to Vauxhall Pleasure Gardens in two evening's time, with no more than Miss Compley and Sir Reginald Rohampton as companions. It does not seem quite decent, even to myself but it is a public enough place. If Mama holds no objection I cannot.

Having sought refuge in my room in order to carry out some correspondence, my solitude is interrupted by none other than the arrival of Lord Beauvrais. How my heart pounds upon the announcement of his name. My feet skip on the stairs as they carry me towards the man I hope is now to be my friend again.

"He is in the garden, m'lady," Forbes says from behind me as I am about to enter the morning room.

How curious. He must have something of the utmost importance to share with me to dare such impropriety. But he is a trusted friend, so is perhaps allowed the liberty. Taking the offered parasol from Forbes, I check my pace upon gaining entrance to the grounds. One cannot be seen to be hastening too rapidly. But the effort not to run is an enormous trial.

Lord Beauvrais is immaculately dressed as ever, but his tawny hair is slightly dishevelled, which is a great endeavour for him. My progress is paused as he looks at me with sorrow-filled mahogany eyes as he stands up from his bow. His looks do not convey a message of reconciliation, but quite the reverse. I fear my heart shall break.

"Dear Anne, please do not look so concerned. My purpose is not to injure you. Come, shall we not sit?" he asks, indicating the stone bench beneath the tree.

So considerate, even now. A fine spot of shade for our discussion, whatever his intention may be. With my nerves jangling, I gratefully take my seat. It is both a pleasure and a pain to be so near him once more.

"First, I wish to apologise for my recent behaviour—" he starts.

"Please, it should be me who apologises. I am sure I caused offence with my carelessness."

He takes my hands in his own and gazes directly into my eyes. "Dear, dear, Anne, do not attempt such a thing. The fault was all mine, and I must own it."

"I cannot—"

"Please, I must insist. Hear me out. And yet I barely know how to begin now we are here."

He stands and begins to pace most alarmingly. I have never seen him so out of sorts. His hands rake through his hair, I suspect not for the first time as that would explain its unruly appearance.

Turning to me, he starts, "You see…well…the fact is…"

"Lord Beauvrais, please say what you must. You cause me great alarm, but I shall endure what you have to say to the best of my capacity."

He strokes my cheek, but I cannot mind at present.

"Oh, you are so like him. So brave, so encouraging," he mutters.

"I beg your pardon, but of whom are you talking?"

"Why, of George."

"Whatever brought him to your mind? Do you miss him so keenly? I confess I do, and there are days I am not sure how to bear it. But I had not thought any other shared the sentiment so deeply. Nobody seems to dare even speak his name."

Coughing, he turns so his back is to me. As he takes a minute to collect himself, I attempt to do the same. Sharing my grief with another is a tempting comfort, but I should not like to unman Lord Beauvrais for my own purpose.

Clenching his fist, he continues, "Dash it all, I shall have this out."

His back is still towards me. Getting up, I take his hand, rotating him in my direction. "Lord Beauvrais, we have shared much across the years as friends. I would not have you pained this way if it is too distressing to attempt."

But instead of bringing the comfort I intended, my words send droplets trickling down his cheeks. His hands wash over his face as he takes his seat again.

"Anne, oh Anne, if only you knew."

He is so overcome I am forced to remain silent for several minutes and wonder if I should depart and give him privacy, but he stays me with his hand when I make the attempt.

"I have not long. I would tell you, my only friend. You, who have been nothing but constant. For the truth must be shared less I should be driven to madness by it."

He again takes up his dreadful pacing. My heart thunders in my breast and there is a pounding in my ears. Something terrible must have occurred, but what could cause someone so steadfast such distress?

Getting down on his knee at my feet, he takes my hands back in his. "I may tell you a dark secret, might I not?"

I nod frantically. "You need not even ask. Surely you know you may."

"And you shall conceal it in your bosom forever, even though it may scorch the innocence hitherto unblemished?"

"But of course. Although what you have to say must be frightful indeed, I shall hold your secret if that is your wish."

"I thank you. I do not wish to burden you at all."

"Bamber, I shall call you such, it is evident you must share whatever terrible news burdens you. And I am a willing friend. It pains me to see you crumbling under this apparent weight you carry."

His tears have been halted, but I cannot be certain how long for.

"You are all goodness. Too good. My little dove, did you truly never notice? You are so innocent, so lovely. Oh, I tried to be brave for us but I have failed you. And for that, I shall be eternally remorseful."

"Failed me? I begin to doubt your senses. What nonsense is this?"

"I had thought that I should allay the fears of my father and honour my love's memory by making you my wife."

The gasp is dragged from my bosom before I can stop it. But surely he would not be so distressed by a marriage proposal? I hold my tongue and await further explanation.

"But you are too like him in every way."

"Him? You still mean George?"

"Pray, still your sweet words. Yes, I speak of George. Anne, you I love as a sister, but he...he I loved far deeper than a man has any right to feel for another of the same sex." His eyes turn earnestly upon me.

I am all astonishment. "You...loved...my brother? As a man should love a wife?"

"At last, she sees it plain. Yes." He stares at me with such openness there can be no room for doubt as to his meaning.

"And he loved you in return?"

He grasps my hands. "Please, I would not have you think less of him."

My shoulders stiffen as I hold my head high. "No indeed. Nothing in the world would make me think less of such a beloved brother. Nor of you either."

Tears spring forth from both of us at my declaration.

"It is a relief to hear you speak so. No other could be more forbearing. If I thus openly declared to any other person, I would be escorted to the gallows without delay."

"Bamber, I could never, would never doom you to such a terrible fate."

"But I am so unnatural."

"I shall grow angry if you continue in that reasoning, for there is no reason there at all. You shared a love, and is not love a grand thing? And would you be so spiteful to George?"

"Of course not. Oh, but if the world could share your generosity."

"I am sure we must not be the only ones to feel this way."

"I pray you are right. But by the laws of the land, I would be tried and executed. Should I marry I could perhaps stave off my demise by diverting suspicion."

"Yes."

"I beg pardon?"

"I freely accept your hand."

"Dear, sweet Anne, I do not offer it."

"Oh?" My mouth is left agape.

"When I heard of your come out, I had pledged myself to that endeavour. But the longer I was in your presence the more plainly was the futility of such an idea laid bare. Instead of being comforted by such a likeness, it pained me. I am sorry to speak thus and mean no offence."

"Am I so very much like him?"

"He is in your eyes and every move. You share his mannerisms."

"I am sorry for it."

"No. The fault is not yours. It is all mine. You cannot be sorry for such a wonderful gift. I had thought that to give you a comfortable home would bring some recompense, to honour George's memory. And I should like to do so. If it were not so entirely against the sentiments of my heart. The harder I try the more I rebel against it. If only you but knew the struggles I have suffered."

"Are you quite certain it cannot be achieved?"

"What I would give for your goodness. I cannot commit you to such a life, Little Dove. You deserve so much more. You are too full of life for me to ensnare it only to extinguish the flame. Doves should not be trapped in such a dreadful cage. I cannot pretend it would be otherwise. Did I not witness your gaiety in the arms of Lord Felsenworth in a waltz? It was apparent then that another should have the honour of calling themselves your husband. To give you the life you deserve. I would not make you miserable for the world, yet I could not make you happy."

"You were there?"

"I confess it. I had hoped to try once more to steel myself, to become the man others expect."

"I should be content indeed to be married to such a fine, brave man. No, I would be honoured."

"There is no bravery. If I were then I could execute my plan. But like a coward, I admit defeat."

Taking his face in my hands, I tell him, "You are wrong. To tell me all this has taken more courage than I ever witnessed before or could even conceive."

"But it is to no purpose. I am able to tell you as I know I shall never see you again."

My cry of alarm echoes about us. "You do not mean that."

"Without wishing to cause distress, it must be so. I am soon to sail to Canada."

"No. It is too dangerous. Do not think me ignorant of the terrible fighting there. I would marry you tomorrow if it shall save your life. Do not make me mourn a dear friend as well as a brother."

"You worry too much. I do not intend to fight. I never did long for it. The only reason I even entered the army was to follow your brother. I would have followed him anywhere." He sighs heavily, his shoulders slumping.

"That is all well and good. But what do you mean to do if not to fight?" I ask.

"My father has investments, and I go to protect his interests, as an investor only. The Yanks are putting up a good fight, but Canada must remain under British rule."

"It is settled then," I remark, folding my hands in my lap.

"If there was any other way I would choose it. But you must see the impossibility of any alternative."

"Even if I declare again my willingness to be your wife, in full awareness of the consequences?"

He touches my cheek with the back of his fingers with a featherlike touch. "Even then. You do not know what you are saying. I shall leave you to think upon the abject misery of a life spent with one such as me."

"Can we at least part as friends?"

He holds me to his chest as he declares, "Always. You are as dear to me as any sister ever could be."

As we part, I have to ask, "So this is truly goodbye?"

"A ship departs in a week. It is probably best for us not to meet in the interim."

"But you shall write?"

"Expect many letters from one Jane Fairley."

That makes me laugh. "Jane Fairley?"

"Well, I should not like to bring your reputation under any doubt by writing as myself."

"Most kind," I say with a curtsey.

"I shall miss you."

"You shall make me sad again. And I do so wish to remember you laughing."

"Then, I take my leave whilst reminding you of the best pirate captain who ever sailed the Sea of Sludge," he says, bowing with a grin.

I laugh at his retreating back. It is true, I did make a fine captain, and lorded it over the two scurvy boys with great aplomb. Drying the traces of my terrible display of emotion, I head back towards the house, much bereft but a little humoured.

❧ *Chapter 8* ❧

Mama is lingering in the morning room as I re-enter the house, unavoidable on my way to my room.

"Do you care to tell me what Lord Beauvrais had to say?" she enquires.

Surely, he spoke with her beforehand?

"Lord Beauvrais is to leave the country and merely wished to say his goodbyes."

My stoicism surprises even myself. I do not launch into the hysterics, but merely impart the vague details of what passed. There is no need for Mama to know the poor man's secret, it is mine to keep, which I mean to do until I meet my grave.

"I do not care for your tone, Anne. You really are become headstrong. I have a good mind to take you home, husband or no."

Good, I wish she would.

Instead of the curt response on my tongue, I say, "Sorry, Mama. Please allow that news of his departure has saddened me greatly." I add a curtsey, so there is further no question of my humility.

"I do not know how many times I told you not to encourage the man. But at last he shall be out of your path entirely, and you may think no more about him."

My eyes must be like saucers at her reply, but that involuntary reaction is all the outward appearance I allow. And even then I cast those tell-tale orbs towards the floor.

"As you say, Mama." With another curtsey, I continue on my way, every bit the calm lady of breeding I am supposed to be.

Upon reaching my room, the façade starts to fall, however.

"Clément, a sherry, if you will, quick as you like. I have had a shock."

"Right away, my lady," she says with a dip before disappearing.

I sit in my chair near the window and fan my face. It is too much. Lord Beauvrais denies my hand, declaring he cannot think of ever taking it, and that because he was in love with my own brother. However did this happen? And why did I not see?

Sunny memories of carefree days spring to my mind. The boys would often play-fight, but surely this is the same for all of their sex? But as I think upon the later years, there were perhaps secret looks, and, oh, there were more touches. They seemed so innocent at the time. But now I see the love that was there if I had but opened my eyes.

And now I have no George to speak with, to ask if he truly felt the same. But Bamber told me so himself, and he would not say so falsely as he knows how it could sully my memory of a much-loved brother. No, it must be true.

They were with each other a great deal in the army. This much I know from George's letters. How he must have secretly told me. I go to my letter box and pull out the items I'm thinking of.

"Thank you, Clément. That will be all," I tell her as she places the small glass on my desk.

Ever obedient, she leaves me alone to paw through the letters.

Letter from George, dated 19th June 1813

My dearest Anne,

Things continue heavy here, but I have seen so much on my adventures. Most are too horrendous to describe to my darling sister. I shall not be held accountable for corrupting your soul. And Wellington is doing a fine job, so we shall soon taste victory, I am sure.

Nor am I able to tell you my location, but we are soon to enter battle. It is a daunting prospect, to be sure. I shall not pretend otherwise to you, who I am able to be frank with. And how grateful I am to you for that. You are so sensible that I can tell you almost all. There is no pretence of excitement at the prospect of fighting for the honour of my country. Although I am proud to do so, it is more terrifying than exciting, for now I know the horrors of battle.

Lord Beauvrais remains at my side, and together we shall chase off these rascals. He says to tell you how fine we look in our blue coats still. He talks nonsense, I am sure, for you are not so easily swayed by mere clothing. And it is starting to become a little worse for wear, despite our best efforts. But he insists we shall soon return to parade them for your inspection, Captain Nobeard.

I maintain you should be more impressed by the number of hours we have been in the saddle and the gloriousness of our steeds. It is almost as if we were on our Grand Tour after all, so far have we travelled.

How proud you will be of your heroic brother as he returns quite the figure of a man. James shall be turned quite green by my glory. Perhaps even our father shall see me as more than merely a second son. But perhaps I hope too much. I shall be satisfied if I manage to do the family name credit.

Time is short, so I must bid you adieu for now. Papa should receive his own, different version of this letter, so allow him to tell all of my loving wishes. This one is intended only for your good self, so you may know your silly brother is still thinking of you and misses our pretend adventures, which were far grander than any here, and always ended with a fine tea in the nursery.

Yours faithfully,

George of the Horse Guards, a real soldier

Oh, dear George. Yes, you earned the accolade of hero, and indeed, your family are proud, and you were a credit to our name, but at what cost? It is too high a price to pay, and not one of us would have asked this of you.

Tears rain from my eyes, unchecked as my fingers curl around this precious letter, the last one I am ever to receive from him. How blind I was. He speaks of Lord Beauvrais being at his side. I had viewed it as two friends, almost brothers bravely marching forth. I now know they were marching to the Battle of Vittoria where Wellington claims victory, where I feel only defeat. Bonaparte may have been defeated, but not without claiming lives of too many, my own brother one of the fallen. No, I cannot view victory in this.

Knowing what I do now, he speaks of a lover, not a friend. But, taking a deep breath, I must find comfort in this even so. Beauvrais was clearly a source of support, and they surely helped one another face that fateful fight. I can only be glad they fortified each other.

There are still questions I would have answered, but they must remain forever silent within my bosom. The sherry warms its path down my insides. If only I had such a companion to help me through these dark times.

My loss is all the greater, for now both boys from my childhood are lost to me. Lord Beauvrais is bound for Canada and to be a stranger to me now. It is almost like losing George all over again. I have never felt more alone.

A knock on my door shakes me from my stupor.

"Beg pardon, my lady, but should I dress you for supper?"

I had not even noticed the passing of time, I had become engrossed in letters written as if beyond the grave, reading them with new eyes when they were clear of tears enough for me to make out the words.

"Yes, of course," I reply.

Saying nothing, Clément prepares a soothing eyewash and cold compress. By the time she is through, none should ever know I had been anything but calm. I do not betray her efforts as I make my way to join my parents, head held high, shoulders back and taking dainty steps. My serene mask is carefully sitting in place.

"Good evening, Mama. Good evening, Papa," I greet them with a curtsey before taking my seat.

"You are for the opera this evening?"

"Yes, Papa."

"See to it that you obey your mother, and do us credit," he warms gruffly.

"Of course, Papa."

That is all the conversation permitted. I may as well dine in my own room, where it would be cheerier. But some sort of duty obligates us to join in this charade. Breakfast and evening meals are a torture to be endured. Which is precisely why I eagerly accept any evening invitations to dine with friends. But there are few of those in this vicinity so far. I shall seek out Miss Plimpton; she should prove welcoming, I believe, and perhaps help introduce me to others.

It is with this aim that I venture out with Mama to the opera house. And I do not have to wait long for she is in the saloon where we converge before finding our box. She kindly accepts my invitation to join us, which spares me a little of Lady Charlotte's conversation.

"You are recovered fully, I trust? You were sorely missed the other evening," Miss Plimpton quizzes quietly as we take our seats.

"I am sorry for that. But yes, I am now well, I thank you. It was a passing headache, that is all."

"Brought on by all this constant liveliness, I daresay. One is pushed from pillar to post with little regard to our vitality."

"Indeed. It has been quite a shock to my system, but I believe I shall better endure it now I am becoming accustomed to London life."

"Oh, I think it a marvellous thing to be forever entertained. There are so many delights. But this very day my aunt took me for a promenade down Bond Street," Lady Charlotte puts in.

My eyes only look towards the heavens for the briefest of moments. Yes, she would see it all as larks and games. I daresay it has never occurred to her the seriousness of her situation. Her education seems sadly lacking in so many respects. She seems oblivious to the fact we are not here to have fun but to entice some poor unwitting man into marriage. But I doubt a sensible thought has ever entered her red head and remained there.

"How pleasant for you," I reply with barely a trace of a sneer in my tone.

"Oh yes, it was exceedingly diverting."

My mind wanders as she drones on, I'm afraid. My attention cannot be kept by such idle fancies as hers.

"And you will never guess who we happened to see next. I shall tell you. Lord Beauvrais. And he was even so good as to recognise me."

My attention is piqued. Lord Beauvrais?

"Oh really? How kind of him," I say with as much nonchalance as can be mustered.

"He had been to his outfitters, readying for a trip. I know not where, for he could not be drawn to say. But I am sure it shall be somewhere exciting, for I fancy him for an adventurer."

"Whatever put that notion into your head?"

"Is he not a man of the world? He has fought the French, don't you know? What a hero he is."

I must have visibly baulked, as Miss Plimpton intervenes. "Well, I wish him well wherever he ends up. But tell me, what did you do next? Was it to visit the milliner to purchase that fine hat?"

I could kiss her. She has successfully diverted the topic back onto one the stupid girl can prattle on about without any input from either of us, allowing me space to recompose myself. The little upstart. Of course I know he fought the French. Does she forget my brother entirely? Does she not know they fought side-by-side? Unfeeling, thoughtless girl.

A delicate hand is placed on mine, ever so lightly. "I am sure you will tell me of the offence when you are quite ready but know there is no obligation or rush to do so. But I should like not to be the one to cause such a reaction," Miss Plimpton whispers.

My returning smile is almost too wide for public display. Yes, I am confident we shall be firm friends. What a keen observation and ready wit this lady has. I flatter myself, we could be sisters.

"Perhaps you would like to dine with us tomorrow, if you are not otherwise engaged? We are to have a small party of close acquaintances, but I should be happy to count you amongst them."

"I speak for Mama, we have no prior engagements."

"Good. Shall you come a little before, so we may make a merry afternoon of it?"

"How very gracious. I thank you. I should like that a great deal."

"Then it shall be so."

We fall back into silence and feign interest in Lady Charlotte's tales of feathers and lace. Why Mama thinks this girl a good companion for her daughter is beyond me. I believe Mama is old friends with Lady Grainger, but must this involve me? I don't mean to be ungracious, but we share precisely nothing in common. I am sure I am as much a bore to Lady Charlotte as she is to me.

My attention strays away from her talk of fashions. Glancing about, I try to make out who else is present this evening. Who amongst these spectators is to share my future life?

Practically speaking, with Lord Beauvrais now off my list of husbands, perhaps I had better turn my attention fully back towards Lord Felsenworth? He dances almost as finely and must be viewed favourably in financial terms. A smile rests on my cheeks as I reminisce about our waltz.

No others seem to take my notice. It is solely the shimmering blue eyes, shining like sapphires which draw me in. Lord Felsenworth nods his head in acknowledgement. I return the gesture before forcing my gaze away, lest any observer should witness our flirtation. But I am left wondering when we will next meet. Two days seems an awfully long time.

It pains me to see other ladies in his party here. If I must own it, jealousy grips my heart in its clutches. I should not deny them their right to try for him. But what is there for me to do to ensure my place as the winner of his heart?

❧ Chapter 9 ❦

The next afternoon, Mama and I arrive at Miss Plimpton's house. It is almost as fine as my dear papa's London dwelling. Fine artworks adorn the walls and plinths as we are led through to the drawing room.

Sadly, I did not encounter Lord Felsenworth on our outing to the park this morning. Many others were observed and observing as we took our promenade. How dull it seemed without his cheerful presence. And I have no hopes of him being here this evening, as he does not seem to be in Miss Plimpton's circle of close acquaintance. But I am determined to make the most of it. And I am looking forward to making new friends via my new companion who has promised as much.

Miss Plimpton hastens to greet us as soon as we are announced, her brown curls bouncing with each step. Her delicate white hands hold mine as she tells me, "Lady Anne, I am so pleased you are come. You do us a great honour."

A small cough sounds from behind her.

"I beg your pardon. I am quite carried away. Your Grace, this is my mother, The Lady Plimpton," she says, turning and curtseying to my mama. "Mama, this is Her Grace, the Duchess of Hesford."

She is met with one of mama's indulgent smiles as the senior ladies become acquainted. Mama's tall, elegant frame is dipped in reverence as her blue eyes take in the other Lady's appearance. Miss Plimpton's mama is shorter and shares the same brown hair and eyes as her. I have often wished I had the same eyes as my mama; hers are so beautiful. Mine are positively commonplace in comparison.

"Come, let us take a turn about the garden," Miss Plimpton says, taking my hand and gently pulling me.

I go most willingly, glad to be out of the shadow of the matriarchs who are already engrossed in their own conversation which turns to us as we pass on our way out of doors, and they believe us to be out of earshot.

"What a pity we do not live closer, they have become so close already," my own mama remarks.

"Quite the reverse could be true. I am sure my daughter is too independent, and I fear they would set the entire county aflame should they both reside in the same vicinity."

We leave the room as giggles ripple around it.

The grounds here are not extensive, but there are some pretty shrubs, and we succeed in gaining a seat beneath a tree.

"So, tell me all," Miss Plimpton urges, eyes wide.

"I do not take your meaning."

"Lady Anne, there is much going on with you, I am convinced of it. Unless I am greatly mistaken it relates to Lord Beauvrais."

A frown darkens my features, I feel my brows furrow as I form my response. "Sorry to disappoint, but there is not much to tell there. He is an old family friend and is now to defend his family interests in Canada. It was merely Lady Charlotte's carelessness which caused me distress last evening. She knows my brother George fought alongside him in France and did not return."

"Oh my dear, I beg your forgiveness. I meant only to sport with an idea of an attachment."

I lay a hand over hers. "You were not to know. I am happy to share the memory, for we rarely speak of poor George now. It's as though he never existed."

"It must have been a great loss to your family."

"Certainly. But my older brother, The Marquess of Ellingsmoor is continuing our name."

"I am glad of that. But let us talk of happier things. Such as Lord Felsenworth, perhaps?"

We both giggle at the rapid change of topic and take some time to list his finer attributes. She seems as smitten as I at the dashing gallant.

Growing serious, she cautions, "But, let us not forget there are other contenders."

"But I do wish to forget it. I fear Papa means me for Lord Emsby."

I laugh as Miss Plimpton pulls a face of disgust. "Surely not."

"I am hoping to steer him in a happier direction."

"Well, let us supply him with a selection."

My mouth drops open.

"Do not look at me so. Would you limit yourself so narrowly?"

She leaves me pondering this in silence. Then a thought occurs to me. "But who is leading your list?"

She waves a hand as if swatting a fly. "Oh, I am quite intent on marrying Lord Meltcham."

This is surprising as I have not seen them together.

"Really? And you are happy to limit yourself thus?" I tease in return.

"He has won my heart."

"Please excuse my asking, but how are you here if this is the case?"

"Papa is trying to make up my mind to the contrary," she says with a roll of her eyes.

"He does not view the match favourably?"

"He believes I should set my sights higher than a viscount."

"Oh, I see. How funny life is. Here I am trying to broaden my horizons, whilst you are attempting to narrow yours. How simple it would all be should our papas simply agree with us at once."

We both laugh at the notion.

Leaning her head towards mine, deepening her voice in imitation, Miss Plimpton reminds me, "We are to trust they have our best interests in mind."

"You must be a credit to your family," I reply, mimicking my own papa.

"Do not play the flirt."

"But entice a good man using your feminine charms."

We both fall into laughter as we put words into our papa's mouths.

"Have you ever known such absurd contradictions?"

"We must make what we can of it though, must we not? I believe our true duty as daughters is to play the politician and demonstrate our case strongly in favour of our chosen partner."

This makes me laugh again. "We must take care then that we know with all certainty which our partner should be."

Miss Plimpton may be the most peculiar young lady I have ever encountered. She ventures her opinions so decidedly that she encourages me to do the same. And the topics she introduces are verging on the outrageous.

Whilst fun, I must take care not to alter my true behaviour. For Papa really has been quite indulgent, and it would be very wrong to go against his wishes, however sorely I am tempted. But perhaps there is a power of persuasion I may yet bring to my purpose.

Then again, I was so entirely mistaken by Lord Beauvrais that I cannot be sure of anyone any longer. Perhaps my papa does know best. Is his opinion or mine to be trusted the most?

It is soon time for the other guests to arrive, so we re-enter the house. Mama and I are delivered to the reception room, so nobody is made uncomfortable by our preferential treatment. And even Mama seems lighter in spirits following her own discussion. How pleasant this evening promises to be.

Introductions are made as new people arrive. Some of Miss Plimpton's friends are elegant, some not quite so splendid, but one shall not judge on appearance alone. But it is rather disappointing that the Ladies Rathburn and Rosen should be present. Understandable, as they hail from the same county, and Miss Plimpton must have been obligated to extend the invitation to them. But I would not have thought they should accept.

In my quest to expand my choice of a husband, I make an effort to be my most charming to the men present. Most suit my ideal of age, but whether their family and fortune are up to standard is in question. Although they must be in close approximation, as several of the young ladies are preening wildly.

Mama has impressed upon me previously how much simpler it was during her come out. Changing times have muddied the waters of breeding, as others climbed up the ranks on fortune alone. And there is a deplorable lack of labels about these persons' clothing indicating which is which.

It should be wonderful to judge on character alone, but this is a foolish notion. With so little power over my life, a comfortable home must be ensured, else I shall end a seamstress or governess when all comes crashing down about my ears. A most revolting prospect. Indeed, I shudder at the thought. And one can hardly be expected to sway Papa with arguments of, 'but he is ever so amiable.'

Bearing all of this in mind, I turn to be introduced to a man of average looks and blond locks.

"Lady Anne, at last, I have the pleasure of being in your presence," he says with a bow, and it must be noted, a smirk.

"Lord Trunton, a pleasure," I reply with a curtsey.

Already his manners appear flirtatious and over-familiar. However, I attempt to quell these thoughts as one must allow not all conduct themselves equally.

"Your reputation precedes you most truly."

"Does it indeed? And which is that, might I ask?"

"Of being the grandest beauty of the Ton."

Well, really, is this to be borne?

"Trunton, do spare Lady Anne her blushes," a known voice interjects.

"Lord Felsenworth. I had not expected you here."

His smile is broader and his eyes brighter than ever as he bows his greeting and replies, "You would be amazed by the venues at which I make my appearance. I trust the surprise is not an unwelcome one?"

I find my hand in his as he brings his lips to brush it, leaving me in astonishment.

"I shall take your silence to mean you are pleased."

My mouth moves, but no words will fall from my lips.

"Come, Lady Anne. This is not like yourself. I believe we should have some conversation."

"I...thank you, my lord. Of course. Forgive my lapse."

For shame, why do I struggle so? My sensibility dictates I move away, but my heart commands my feet to remain. I had thought Lord Trunton familiar, but Lord Felsenworth's actions would have others believe we are intimate friends. But we are to attend Vauxhall Gardens together tomorrow, so maybe he can claim such? The progression is happening so rapidly I am not sure of the proper conduct. Have I erred?

"Shall you join us for a game of cards?"

"Thank you, yes."

Too late, I discover our fourth in a game of whist is to be Lady Rathburn, who smiles too broadly as she meets us. There is no escaping now. I must remain to face my challenger.

I lose the first draw, as Lord Trunton and I hold the lowest cards. Well, it shall be a good opportunity to discover more about him. And Lord Felsenworth may be observed all the better.

Lady Rathburn shuffles the French deck for Lord Felsenworth with great skill. Perhaps a little too much for she seems over practiced in the art, leaving me to cut the deck. He deals the thirteen cards with great aplomb too.

The first card is laid by Lady Rathburn with a tilt of her head and an air of superiority. Lord Trunton lays a card in the leading suit, but I lay a trump. Only to be outdone by Lord Felsenworth with a glance of apology as he collects all four cards and lays the next.

Lady Rathburn's card is strong, but Lord Trunton trumps her, as do I, and so collect the trick with no apology whatsoever. In fact, there may be a gleam in my eye, a firmer set to my jaw and a slight rise in my brow.

Lord Trunton disappoints with his next, but he beats Lord Felsenworth. Sadly, Lady Rathburn takes the trick with great mirth and even a laugh.

"Lady Anne, I declare you are better than I expected," she declares as I win the next.

"When you know me a little better perhaps you shall discover more admirable accomplishments," I reply with a wide-eyed look which hopefully feigns innocence.

"Oh, a fine hand," Lord Felsenworth declares, meeting my gaze.

His look fires flames through me and I have to blink before I can reply, "It is all luck, I assure you."

Lord Trunton wins a trick, closely followed by Lord Felsenworth, and then me. By the end of the game, my team is declared the winner.

"I praise your skill," I tell Lady Rathburn with good grace, rising to my feet.

"What, will you not allow us to regain our honour?" Lord Felsenworth requests.

"My lord, I do believe one should know when to best enjoy victory," I tell him with a smile before walking away.

"Oh, well played," Miss Plimpton praises as we meet.

"Pah, a little attention is all which is called for."

"You do not give yourself enough credit."

"Perhaps. But come, what can you tell me of Lord Trunton?"

"I will not pretend you would not do me a favour by removing him from my sphere. But, as your friend, I must declare you could do better. He is fine, but his family is raised too high too quick," she whispers as we walk arm in arm.

"It is as I feared," I say with a sigh.

"But be of good cheer. There are others I would have you meet," she says, leading me towards such a man.

I am met with a thin smile beneath kind blue eyes and fashionable brown hair. He is perhaps a little portly, but his clothes are of a fine cut, and he is not too much my senior. Papa should be satisfied with the son of an earl.

"A pleasure to make your acquaintance," he says with a bow.

"The pleasure is mine, I am sure, Lord Nordfield," I reply with a curtsey.

"Might I tempt you into a dance, Lady Anne?"

"You may indeed."

There is a small gathering of dancers, which we join as the next piece begins. It is a simple country dance, but Lord Nordfield dances it beautifully. He has a bearing of authority without conceit. His grip on my hand is supportive but not over tight. So why do I look into his eyes and think of another?

Before Lord Felsenworth, this suitor would be the best in the room. But how he pales in comparison. My pulse remains steady at his touch and my cheeks do not burn under his scrutiny.

We continue to supper together and enjoy the most pleasant conversation. He proves himself to have intelligence. But no matter how I try, there is not a single flutter in my breast. Why must I compare? This is unworthy of me. I must fulfil my duty first. Thoughts of romance must be quashed, else I set myself up for a life of torment.

My conviction falters as Lord Felsenworth takes me through a dance after supper, however. Oh Lor', please save me. I have lost all power of rational thought as he guides me through the movements. How alive I am in his hands, how much lighter my feet, how rapidly my heart beats. And how he knows it, for every look both acknowledges what is and encourages more.

"I trust you are not as put out by Lady Rathburn as she is by you. She is most unsporting, and I had to spend the entire supper calming the poor girl," he tells me as we unite in the dance.

"I had no intention of putting her out of sorts."

"Well I know it. You are quite unaware of your influence, my lady. It is part of your charm."

We part and weave between other partners as we progress down the line. An uneasy feeling weighs heavy on my shoulders. It is true I had desired to win, but I had not meant to annihilate her chances. Merely to make her aware of my intention, which seems to insist in the direction of Lord Felsenworth.

"She shall recover. Pray do not make yourself uneasy," he tells me as we meet again.

"I hope you are correct."

"Your tenderness and charity are most becoming," he says before other couples join either side of us.

His words bring some comfort but do not settle my misgivings entirely.

"I hope this unfortunate occurrence has not changed your mind as regards our plans for tomorrow?" he asks when we are alone, worry creasing his brow.

"Certainly not. I look forward to it."

As the dance finishes, I make my way towards Lady Rathburn to apologise for any offence I unwittingly caused. However, on my approach, I overhear her bitter conversation with Lady Rosen.

"How many husbands can she want? Must she stake her claim on every eligible bachelor in town?"

Her friend placates her, and I judge it best not to make any attempt of apology. The timing is most unfortunate. Swallowing my disappointment, I move in another direction and find Lord Trunton in my path.

"Lady Anne. You dance so gracefully. Might I ask you to join me in the next?"

Reluctantly, I agree. Fear makes me rigid as I worry my way through the entire dance, that this too may be mistaken as another conquest. Everything I do seems to cause upset in some quarter. It is enough to make one quite discouraged.

The rest of the evening passes by without any further drama, but without excitement either.

"Well, I think we need not visit that house too often," Mama comments as we drive away.

"Mama, I thought you got on well with the lady of the house."

She bobs her head a little. "Her, I like. And I approve of the daughter. But her friends leave much to be desired."

I reflect on some of the conversations during the course of the evening.

"I was surprised to see Lady Rathburn and Lady Rosen there."

"Quite. But they were not the ones to whom I was referring."

My mind recalls the other people present. "There were some young ladies present who seemed of the bluestocking persuasion."

"Precisely. It cheers me to know you have not lost all sense after all. I know you shall not let us down."

"Of course not. I am fully sensible of my place in the world."

"Are you quite certain of that?"

"Mama, how can you bring me into question so?"

"Miss Compley's friendship is understandable. She was a close neighbour, and you grew up together. Having a baronet as a father is unfortunate, but we allowed it as you were so happy together."

"Indeed. You had no qualms over our friendship that I recall."

"However, this Miss Plimpton."

"Her papa is a baron, Mama. That is not so bad."

"But hardly highly bred."

"But gently all the same. Please allow me to make a case in her favour. For truly, who else should I befriend? There is none, bar Miss Compley, who is of such a similar disposition as myself. She is a little forthright, perhaps and has modern tendencies. But she is good, Mama. Her heart is full for her friends, and she is of the nobility."

"Barely."

"Mama, you are too severe, if you pardon my opinion. Of course, I should defer to yours alone, and I do. Please, I do not believe her to be a bluestocking herself. Please do not deny me a friendship I have already begun to cherish."

"Anne, how warm you are become on the subject. Of course, I should not deny you a beneficial friendship. But mind it does remain beneficial. I would not have your reputation tarnished, especially at this delicate point of proceedings."

"I hope never to have my reputation brought into question, Mama. I am sensible of all you and Papa impressed upon me. I endeavour always to conduct myself in the way you would approve."

"Very well. Let us speak no more about it for now. Keep your friend, but caution is all I urge. I am sure you will act accordingly," she says, patting my hand as the horses pull us through the darkness of the night.

❧ Chapter 10 ❧

I awake the next day with happy visions in my head, having dreamed of home. Ah, can there be anything more joyous than a stroll around one's gardens on a warm summer's day?

The sweet scent of roses and lavender permeating the air as one drifts past. Birds singing their melody whilst bees buzz between dancing butterflies. It is most intoxicating and fills my heart with joy.

Yet how cruel shall it be to be torn asunder and thrown into a barren wilderness of a destination as yet unknown. But it looms on the horizon like a horrifying dark cavern, ready to swallow me whole. And yet I must persist. My parents' bidding is mine to obey.

As much as Lord Felsenworth lures me towards him, I grow evermore troubled that my parents shall not approve. Or even whether I should be able to secure him. He was so attentive to Lady Rathburn last evening.

And if not him, who should I expect to make an offer? Lord Trunton is not to be encouraged, which is a pity. Lord Nordfield could be a possibility, but we have only just met. The gathering last night has not been as beneficial as I'd hoped. Thus remains Lords Emsby and Dellingby.

If only this was not a marriage mart, I think my time here would be joyful. There is much amusement to be had. But always the question of who I am to wed plays on my mind. It is enough to drive me quite into madness.

Here is Clément, ready with a smile to start my day. How simple her life is. I do wonder if hers is not the better. How gloomy I am this morning, and after such a pleasant dream. But that is perhaps the source of this melancholy, for it reminded me of bright, happy, summer days whereas I have awoken in this busy place with its parading beaux.

Hoping to raise my spirits, I venture into the garden once Clément has dressed me and tied my bonnet. But my outlook is a pale comparison to the vast grounds of home, and only serves to make my heart ache all the more at first.

However, continuing my stroll and bending down, I breathe in the heady scent of an early rose and immediately relax my shoulders a little. A cheerful rainbow of tulips adorns the next bed. The small box shrubs are kept in their neat ball shapes. A peace descends, and I pick one of the last daffodils, almost without thought, and twiddle it between my fingers.

One can almost pretend the world has ceased to exist amongst such tranquillity. Still restless, I let my feet carry me around the garden again, breathing in the aromas with every step, a smile upon my visage.

"Anne, what are you about? Breakfast is called," Mama shouts across, disturbing my reverie.

"Coming, Mama," I chime, rapidly walking towards her.

I had not heard anyone announce breakfast, and I wonder at her presence as opposed to that of the likes of Forbes. It is of no consequence, for I have landed myself in trouble either way. Papa detests lateness.

Fortunately, Papa seems preoccupied this morning, and there is no conversation whatsoever, not even a word of remonstrance. But this is a far more suffocating silence than the serene one I just left in the garden. My moment of contentment has been snatched away.

More primping and preening follows breakfast, as today I am to have my first sitting for my portrait. Apparently, one's come out is occasion enough to warrant this extravagance. Papa insisted, and Mama made the appointment before our arrival, as the flattering services of Sir Thomas Lawrence are much in demand.

As one must endure this back-aching procedure, I requested Prince be painted at my feet. Convincing Papa that it would reflect my obedience and duty, he agreed. But secretly, I am amused by the idea of a prince being brought to heel, especially as the royal is so exuberant and beyond such a feat. What a fine joke!

My purest white cotton dress goes on with lace undersleeves, with a pale pink sash tied at my high waistline. White flowers are pinned into my hair, and a simple topaz cross is at my throat. The very picture of sweet innocence which any man must want in a wife.

Reaching the studios, I am positioned carefully on a chair and am told not to move. My shawl is strategically placed about my arms, and I am become a statue, silent and still. Not long into the sitting, my fingers flinch as they long to scratch my itching nose.

"Hold," the august painter warns, having caught the slight movement.

I am left wrinkling my nose in an attempt to quell the urge to scratch. It does not help, and it becomes distressing. As Sir Thomas' head is behind the canvas, I quickly lower my head to my hand to relieve the discomfort and quickly sit erect again before the man can chastise me. It is a relief when he doesn't notice.

My aching body is forced into rigid lifelessness for above an hour, but finally, I am set free. I stretch my arms, and lean my head from side-to-side, trying to bring life back to my limbs. Slowly, I rise to my feet and am escorted to my carriage, which I mount with more effort than is customary. The coachman takes me straight home where I change into a walking dress.

"You must re-animate your limbs," Mama tells me as we promenade.

"Must it be done so publicly?"

"But of course. Anne, I do not know what has got into your head. But surely you are sensible of the dual purpose of our excursion."

"Sorry, Mama." My head hangs a little until she coughs, at which I consciously right it again.

We bow our heads and dip curtseys to our counterparts, all undertaking the same task. Will the Lord not have mercy upon my soul?

"Well, you have not been so very bad. We shall find a good match for you yet. Perhaps some reward is in order."

Looking in the direction she is now taking, I observe we are heading towards Hookham's circulating library in Bond Street.

"Oh, Mama, thank you," I say almost too loudly. Of course, I refrain from offering the embrace which my arms wish to offer.

A vast room lined with books is before me as we enter, the heavy scent of literature permeating the air. What a fine place. Many other people are busy at their selection, and my heart sings as I join their number.

After much deliberation, I select *The Wanderer by Frances Burney*. Its predecessor, *Evelina* was most enjoyable, and of some service, even although I am of a different class to that worthy heroine. Indeed, I have endeavoured not to be as wholly reserved as that poor creature, and to educate myself into the ways of the opposite sex as much as the information at my disposal would allow. For too much modesty may be just as faulty as too little if the lessons in that tome are to be fully understood and adhered to.

I understand the author has been in the employ of Queen Charlotte herself. How scandalous she is at liberty to write as she does then. She must have considerable insight into matters of the heart amongst the aristocracy. Perhaps there will be more wisdom in store to help my own foray into matrimony.

But as I begin reading this afternoon, disappointment reigns as it bears no resemblance to the former great works. It is dark and most dreary. Although I pity the poor émigrée, forced to flee France without a single penny. I have observed such personages here in London, now turned to work, such as my own dear Clément. It is quite uncomfortable to read so intimately of their plight.

Never matter, at least no great expense has been paid out, and the book shall be returned to the library once I am finished, which I am determined to do. Perhaps the book shall improve further along.

Time moves on, and thrills run through me as I am dressed for the evening's amusements. The prospect of seeing the famous Vauxhall Gardens on the arm of Lord Felsenworth is great indeed. I can scarce sit still whilst Clément applies her powders and the hairdresser decorates my locks. My company are all to convene here so we may take the carriage together.

"I am all excitement," Julia exclaims upon her arrival.

"What fun we shall have," I reply, no less gleefully.

"Ready ladies?" Lord Felsenworth enquires as he joins us with Sir Reginald.

They each offer their arm and help us to the vehicle, and we are off, a merrier party you ne'er did see.

There is a moment of consternation as we reach the north bank of the Thames.

"No, no, we cannot all travel in the boat if your footman comes along. Really, whoever heard such a thing? He may wait for you here with the carriage to see you home safely. Pray, what harm can befall you with no other means of escape?"

"But —," I start to form an objection.

"Come, you are not going to be missish now, are you, Lady Anne? Faith, how skittish you are. Let us not raise a breeze over such inconsequential matters. I had not thought you so straight-laced. Perhaps we had best not continue our outing after all, eh wot?"

Mortified at my apparent prudish sentiment, my cheeks burn as I am helped into a boat, along with my trusted friend, Miss Compley. What must she think of me? I almost ruined her evening before it is begun.

Any ill humour is soon forgot as we ascend the stairs, pass through the gates and behold the magnificence that is Vauxhall Gardens. So much vaster than I could have imagined. At this hour of twilight, I had expected the lanterns to be lit, but not a single one is illuminated.

We are led through the impending darkness, with not a little trepidation, following the vast throng of fellow revellers who seem not at all perturbed. Excitement buzzes through the crowd, and I begin to be swept along.

I am almost frighted out of my wits by a sudden noise, when all of the lights are illuminated at once, wrenching gasps of amazement from all about.

"There there, I am here by your side," Lord Felsenworth says with a chuckle whilst patting my hand.

"I would thank you not to be so free, my lord. Who could wonder at my astonishment at such a sudden action?"

"You are in the right, Lady Anne. Please accept my apologies for my impudence. So often have I witnessed this spectacle I quite forget what the first time was like."

Inclining my head, I force a smile. It is all the acceptance of his apology he should expect. Mocking me for such a trifle. I merely jumped. It is not as though I screamed.

As the band plays and we continue our promenade, I begin to be diverted once more. There are so many sights to be seen. Musicians, tightrope walkers, acrobats, Indian jugglers, circus horses, all lit by the wondrous coloured lamps.

As the weather is fine, we do not require the ornate colonnade's protection. Stately elms line the Grand Walk as we make our way up, marvelling all the way. Our beaux lead us through to a magnificent canal, and over one of the two Chinese cast-iron bridges. Should I be so inclined, I would say this was the most romantic place ever beheld.

Once we have promenaded sufficiently to tire us greatly, Lord Felsenworth finds us a table within one of the beautifully painted boxes. I believe Hayman is the artist responsible for the rather bawdy scene here.

A man soon brings us refreshments in the form of small chickens, perhaps the smallest I have yet seen, and some ham which is sliced thinner than some of my muslin gowns. However, after such a lengthy walk, I am grateful for any nourishment.

Music drifts through the air most melodiously. Dancers are scattered about, making full use of the lively tunes. I am quite overcome by such gaiety.

We are all ease and geniality through our meagre supper. My suitor is most convivial under these circumstances, and he is revealed as my clear favourite. In fact, I begin to wonder at my ever favouring Lord Beauvrais. What carelessness on my part made me neglect such a fine fellow?

"Alright, be off with you," Lord Felsenworth tells the servant once he has placed a bowl of rack-punch on our table.

"One cannot spend time in Vauxhall and forego the pleasures of this fine beverage," he announces, pouring each of us a glass.

"Oh, it is perhaps not quite as sweet as I was expecting," I tell him, hoping not to sound ungrateful.

"Well, it is made from lemons among other things. Try some more now you are prepared what to expect."

Not wishing to appear ill-mannered, I drink the rest but decline any further offerings from the bowl.

"Zooks, the hour is getting late. Hurry, or we shall miss the best spectacle here," my partner announces, standing and offering me his hand.

The pace he sets is a little alarming, and my breath is quite taken as he pulls me along the walks. Sir Reginald and Miss Compley are forced to run to keep up. Most unseemly.

A bell rings out and the dark curtain before us is drawn back, revealing the most beautiful scene of a bridge, water-mill and cascade. A sound of rushing water echoes around as figures and wagons cross the bridge. Gasps and applause surround us as we are all amazed by this dazzling spectacle which lasts a full ten minutes.

Lord Felsenworth is wearing a boyish grin and is as lively as a spring lamb after.

"Let us enter the Dark Walk so we may better see the fireworks," he suggests.

"Oh yes, lets. I do so love fireworks," Miss Compley eagerly agrees, her blue eyes widening.

But as we approach The Grove, my steps slow.

"Go on, we shall catch up. I need to catch my breath one moment," I say to my friend.

Before she can argue, Sir Reginald guides her away.

"Lady Anne, are you well?" Lord Felsenworth asks, concern furrowing his brow.

"I shall soon be after a moment of rest."

"Here, let us find a more peaceful location," he says, taking me away from the path and in amongst the trees and shrubs.

"Oh, I fear I must find a bench," I tell him, my hand going to my forehead.

"There is not a single one present, but no-one shall observe should you sit here on the grass, hidden from view."

I allow him to seat me down on the ground, fearing a swoon if I remain on my feet.

"Take some deep breaths. You shall be all right again in a few moments. The evening is quite overwhelming is it not?"

"Yes, quite. Such splendours," I say, my voice becoming weak to my own ears.

"Whilst I have you alone, there is something I must ask. I had hoped it would be better timed, but it cannot be helped, and it must be said."

A sense of a question of great import pumps my heart faster, reviving me to some extent.

"Lady Anne, you must allow me to declare my great regard, nay, my affection for you. It cannot have gone unnoticed, I am sure. And your very acceptance of this evening's invitation leads me to hope your response shall be favourable if I should ask for your hand."

The dizziness returns in an instant, my free hand stops me from falling full on my back.

"Lord Felsenworth, this is hardly the time. Should you not ask when you may go to my papa?"

"Ah, I would, all too readily if I could be sure of his acceptance of me as a son, but I fear he will not."

Trying hard to remain alert, clutching my head, I lean forwards, but the motion brings forth a bout of nausea.

"Why ever not?" I manage to ask, my hand holding my mouth closed as I swallow the subsequent bile.

"Zooks, you really are unwell. The curst chicken here is at fault, for certain."

His arm wraps around my waist in support, and I am so grateful that my sense of propriety offers no resistance whatsoever. My head rests upon his shoulder.

"If I ask it, would you come away with me? We could marry from my aunt's estate, and then there would be no chance of your papa to refusing us. I have given the matter a great deal of consideration and conclude this must be the best course of action."

"Without asking Papa? You cannot think that I..." but another fit of nausea halts my tongue.

"I had thought you would say that but needed to hear it from your lips before taking more drastic action," he tells me.

My eyes want to close most fervently, but his words frighten me so that I force them to remain open. I make the attempt to get to my feet, wishing to find my friend and flee, but the trees spin in the darkness.

Lord Felsenworth's hands are upon me, and I am forced back to the ground with a thud, fully flat, making me scream. All shining light has vanished from his eyes, only darkness remains as I look up into their depths. My addled brain fancies it perceives a snarling wolf as it pounces upon me with snarling jaws.

"My lord, what are you about? Please unhand me," I demand, all too quietly, my words slurring, my limbs refusing to answer my call to action.

"What the devil?" someone shouts.

"It cannot be…" I murmur, quite sure I have abandoned all sense.

"Lady Anne, are you harmed?"

A pair of brown top boots blur within my vision.

"Lord Beauvrais?" I ask.

I find myself enveloped in his arms in a sitting position, and I am saved.

"Stay back, fiend, else I shall not be held responsible for my actions," he yells above my head.

"What has come over you, man? You seem to believe me about some great wrong-doing. Will you not see sense? Lady Anne has been taken unwell. I was trying to look after her, damn you."

"He was—" I try.

"Hush, I know full well what he was about," he soothes.

I am jostled slightly. "Damn me, would you? I damn you to the devil himself. Lady Anne is like a sister to me. No finer lady has ever breathed God's clean air, yet you seek to defile her honour."

"You are quite mistaken, Beauvrais. You are not yourself. We are friends, remember?"

"Has any before suffered a falser friend than you? No. You go too far, Felsenworth."

Lord Beauvrais stands, taking me with him. His arm is the only means of support available to me. I grow ever more tired.

"Unhand her this instant," another voice calls.

I only make out a few fuzzy words, as the world comes and goes in my ears. They drift as if from afar, unclear and echoing. My eyes see only darkness behind my lids.

"Don't…ninny…She…fall if …"

"…vile scheme."

"… glad to hear…trust you to…boat…I must…a lesson…"

On the outer edges of my awareness, my body is passed into another set of hands, the motion is almost my undoing. A hand roughly pats my cheek.

"…salts…"

"Not…reticule…"

My nose wrinkles and an, "eww," is forced from my lips as a familiar foul stench meets me. I clutch my head in a vain attempt to quieten the ringing therein.

"Lady Anne, who were you here with?" someone asks with hollow words.

"Miss Compley," I manage to say with a groan.

There is some discussion of locating her, but then I am directed towards what I believe is the exit. My shawl is pulled up about my face.

"No, don't adjust it. Trust me on this please, Lady Anne," a somewhat familiar voice tells me softly.

I cannot make out to whom I am indebted. I am secured under his arm and am unable to look up from my position. But he is kind and is walking slowly with me, taking care I do not fall. Something inside tells me to trust my new companion. The boots are not those of Lord Beauvrais, that much is clear, and that is all which seems important to me now. There are elaborate tassels upon these ones.

My head hurts, and the music assaults my ears as we pass by, causing me to groan. My footsteps are hastened a little by the arm about my waist pulling me along.

"Lady Anne, oh my dear, I should never have left your side. I did not realise how unwell you were. Can you ever forgive me?" Miss Compley asks as she catches up to me near the water.

"Good man, I am forever grateful to you, but we can manage from here," Lord Beauvrais says.

"You are sure?" the voice rumbles in the chest against my ear.

"You still doubt me?"

"I am sorry I ever did."

"No apology is necessary. It must have looked bad for me. But come, I am anxious to get Lady Anne home."

"But of course."

Lord Beauvrais carefully accepts me under his wing, and my chaperon bows himself away into the night. I catch the merest glimpse of his coat as he does so but cannot look behind me to verify the identity of its owner.

My friend's arms are all the strength I require as he helps me very slowly into the boat at the foot of the stairs, before helping Miss Compley also.

"Perhaps a further application of your smelling salts shall aid your recovery?" she suggests.

"Yes, won't you try?" Lord Beauvrais encourages.

I fumble in my reticule before my fingers clutch onto the small vial.

"Meurgh," I exclaim rather inelegantly as I sniff the contents.

"Better?" Miss Compley asks.

"I thank you. A little."

I look from her to Lord Beauvrais to our other companion.

"I do not believe I know your friend, Lord Beauvrais," I hint.

He chuckles. "Lady Anne, might I introduce you to my valet, Mr Gibbs?"

"Oh. How do you do?"

"Let us forget formality this once, my lady, for fear you should swoon with any movement," Lord Beauvrais suggests.

"Hm, quite," I say, laying my hand on his arm to ensure my steadiness.

Oh, how my head seems to swim in the waters, how much my stomach lurches with each pull of oars. Fortunately, the boat journey is of short duration and we reach the other side without injury or incident.

Lord Beauvrais sends his man to find our carriage. A shiver runs through me, to which he answers with a discreet rub of my back.

"Not to worry, Little Dove. We shall soon have you back safe and warm in your nest."

I see Miss Compley raise her eyebrows.

"Lord Beauvrais, I believe you embarrass my friend."

"Oh, dear lady, my humble apologies. A mere habit of childhood. Please do forgive me. Concern renders me neglectful of respectability."

She bows her head in assent, but her eyes never leave him from that moment, clearly unaware he is the hero of the hour.

My tongue is dried to the roof of my mouth, so can make no argument for him.

The carriage arrives, with Mr Gibbs mounted at the rear. An odd look passes between the men as we are lodged into its confines.

"Remind me, if you please, my lord, why you have taken the place of Lord Felsenworth and Sir Reginald?" Miss Compley quite rightly enquires.

"Pardon my lack of explanation, Miss Compley. My primary concern was for the welfare of our mutual friend. Lady Anne was taken unwell, and I happened upon her in her moment of distress. Being an old family friend, I thought it best to play her protector in her vulnerable condition, and Lord Felsenworth wished to stay on to enjoy the fireworks with his friend. It is of little consequence."

Finally, able to move my mouth, I add in a slur, "Indeed. Lord Beauvrais is like a brother to me, Miss Compley. I am most grateful to him for his assistance."

My eyes glance across to him as I speak, and hold his gaze, conveying my deep gratitude.

"Pah, I am happy to be of what little service I may perform," he dismisses with a wave of his hand.

He has no intention of warning my friend of the perils of our earlier companions, and I wonder at it, but hold my tongue. I trust his judgement above my own, which has been poor in the extreme.

We take Miss Compley to her house.

"I am not sure I should leave you again. You do not know how deeply I regret my earlier failing," she says.

"I am in no danger. Please do not trouble yourself. This is my carriage, with my footman and driver. You cannot think, even if Lord Beauvrais wished me ill which he does not, that he could ever succeed under such a watch."

She gasps. "Lord Beauvrais, I meant no offence. Please —"

"Not at all. Your consideration does you credit as one of Lady Anne's greatest friends," he tells her with a nod of his head.

"Well, so long as you are recovered and are able to reach home." She squeezes my hand before alighting from the carriage.

Once we are back on the road, I am given cause for doubt as to my defence of my friend as he takes me firmly into his embrace as he sits beside me.

"Oh, Little Dove, I have never been so scared in all my days," he declares, squeezing tight and kissing the top of my head.

"Nor I."

The shock of the ferocity of his actions having worn off, I squeeze back. Reaching down, he sweeps my legs up and over his lap so he may hold me all the closer.

"If anything ever happened to you I would never forgive myself," he says, his voice cracking.

"Oh, when I think of what may have occurred had you not happened upon us."

"Do not dwell on it. I cannot bear to think of the consequences. Had I not thought to take Gibbs to see the fireworks before we depart London…"

"Gibbs? You were alone with him?"

"This is the point your mind dwells on, Anne?"

"I beg pardon."

"Do not ask for forgiveness where none is due. Yes, I was there alone with Gibbs. He is my valet and is to accompany me to Canada."

"And you took your valet to the fireworks?" I ask, peering into his eyes.

"Ahem, he may be a little more, but let us not speak of such things," he whispers.

"Oh. Um…" A blush explodes across my cheeks.

"Well, at least red is better than the deathly pallor you had earlier," he tells me, chuckling, holding me closer once more.

Accompanying me to my door, Lord Beauvrais explains to Forbes about my ill health, and leaves me to his care, disappearing into the night with his valet.

❧ *Chapter 11* ❧

My dream turns towards a woodpecker making busy about my forehead. Bees begin to sting my cheeks. I open my mouth to scream, but no sound comes forth.

"Eurgh, heurgh," I cough, spitting water and sitting up, finding my bed and not a forest floor under my hands.

"There, she is awake," Mama states with a scowl from beside me, before turning and exiting my room.

"Oh, my lady, although I am glad you are awake, I am greatly sorry for the method. You would not stir, and I was so worried that I fetched your mama. I never thought she would throw water at you in such a manner."

It takes me a while to absorb Clément's words, I fancy part of me is still in the dreaming state. My hands run through my wet hair.

"Come, allow me to right your appearance, my lady," she encourages, coaxing me out of my bed.

Every movement is woefully slow and lumbering as I make my way to the dressing table. My face scrunches at its reflection. How dishevelled my appearance is, how small my eyes.

Even Clément's expert ministrations are not enough to conceal the darkness beneath my eyes this morning. But it is an improvement all the same.

"Sorry, my lady, it is as well as I can manage."

"Do not trouble yourself. I fear this is a challenge too great for all but the greatest conjurers."

My bed beckons me to return to its warmth, but Papa's rules force me to the breakfast room. I am able to rise from my bed, so must partake in the family meal. A groan escapes as I open the door and cautiously step onto the landing.

Forbes places a cup of chocolate before me as I take my place at the table.

"I think tea this morning," I tell him, pushing the cup away, clutching my stomach.

"She shall not put you to the trouble. Coffee shall suffice if chocolate is unpalatable," Papa contradicts.

My eyes are kept low as I butter my toast with slow, deliberate movements. My knife seems unwilling to cooperate and it clatters to my plate. Papa glowers in my direction.

"I would speak with you after breakfast," he tells me in an authoritative tone.

My nerves jangle all the more at his demand. Truly, I am not able to withstand lectures this morning. But mine is to obey, so I knock at his study door after forcing a few morsels of food and lots of coffee into my unwilling body.

"Enter," he shouts.

With my head hanging down, I slowly approach.

"What do you mean by entering the house last night in such a state? I am ashamed of you. I had not thought to ever witness a drunkard for a daughter."

My head shoots up. "You believe me to have over-indulged? Papa!"

"Do not Papa me. I shall hear no toadying or Canterbury tales."

"But Papa —"

A thwack thunders through the room as he bangs his hand on his desk and stands glaring. "I said I shall not hear it. Do not think to contradict what is abundantly clear. I say you were foxed. Your insolence is not to be tolerated. Is this the gratitude you show for my over-indulgence of your whims?"

Tears roll down my cheeks and I make no attempt to halt them. Papa should know how much I am injured by his treatment. He makes me afeared to be in his presence. My wobbling knees would carry me away should I allow them.

"I told your Mama what would happen. Spare the rod and ruin the child. But she would have you raised in the modern way. I have a good mind to have you carried off home this instant where you cannot disgrace us further. But far better to marry you off all the sooner and remove you entirely."

My mouth is gaping at this severity. Lord Felsenworth has utterly ruined me without even fulfilling his evil scheme. Why will my papa not see I am the injured party? If he would but listen.

A rapping at the door interrupts my next attempt to explain.

"Not now," Papa bellows, but the knock is repeated.

"In heaven's name, it had best be of the utmost importance."

Poor Forbes hunches as he steps into the room. "Beg pardon, Your Grace, but news of the most alarming nature has reached our ears, which it is perhaps best you hear at once."

"Well, out with it," he snarls.

"Pardon, Your Grace, but perhaps Lady Anne should not bear witness."

"Balderdash. I am not finished with her yet. Say what you must and be away."

"Well, it's Lord Felsenworth, Your Grace."

"That fop of a boy? What are we to do with him?"

"Pardon, Your Grace, but he has been shot dead."

"And what—"

My cry of alarm interrupts them as I lose myself to the darkness.

The next I know, Clément is by my side and I am laid on the chaise.

"No, do not move yet, if you please, my lady," she says softly.

Papa looks more a bear than ever, so I ignore her advice and attempt to sit. The room spins a little, but a bottle of smelling salts soon has me upright.

"Let us get you to your room, my lady. You are not well."

My answering nod sets the room in motion again. I hold her arm as I get to my feet. Leaning on her heavily, she escorts me from this room of horrors.

Felsenworth dead? Forbes is at the door and catches me as I swoon. He props me up and helps Clément get me to my room. My fingers fold around a piece of paper as it's placed in my hand.

Forbes quickly removes himself from my presence, so Clément may remove my corset, allowing me to recline in my chemise.

Sobs burst forth as the news hits me with full force. But even as I cry out my grief I question it. For was he not a demon who would have befouled my honour? My heart does not seem to fully appreciate his treachery as it bleeds for the loss of a former favourite. One who deserved a swift end. My mind sallies back and forth between grief and gratitude as my tears hit my pillow. Head versus heart in full conflict.

"Oh, what calamity," I wail to my bed canopy, turning to my back, only to roll over again to my front.

Clément hurries to my aid, but rescue is impossible. My friend or foe is lost to me forever.

"Lord Felsenworth…" I start but cannot finish.

"Please try to calm yourself. For you are in such a state I do not know what to do. May I fetch some wine, perhaps?"

"Aye, do," I agree, if only so I may be left alone to my sorrow for a while.

Trying to collect myself, I breathe deeply. What hope did I have any right to own? That the events of last night were a momentary lapse of propriety? Now I shall never know.

Reaching under the covers, I retrieve the letter I had concealed there. I am sure Forbes meant for only me to see it from his surreptitious placement. Wiping the tears from my eyes and inhaling deeply I read the contents.

Letter from Lord Beauvrais, 24th April 1814

My dear Lady Anne,

I would prepare you for a great shock, for I risk causing alarm with the news contained herein. I have had this letter delivered direct to the hands of your trusted Forbes, but with a sum of monies to ensure his utmost secrecy. I pray he has followed instruction and only delivered this unto you, for it is of the most serious nature that it should commit me doubly to the gallows should it reach the wrong hands. With this in mind, please destroy it as soon as you have read the contents without delay. Only the flames of the nearest fire will serve this duty I must beg of you.

How my heart retreats at these terrible words. The next breath is trapped within my breast and my marrow is quite frozen. But I must read on.

However, the cursed maid's hand is upon my door. The pages rustle as they are rapidly placed beneath my covers once more. I can only hope the noise did not reach her ears.

"Your tears have stopped. I am pleased," she observes, laying the glass on my nightstand.

"I shall be well. Perhaps it is best for me to rest quietly for a while longer."

"Of course, my lady," she replies with a curtsey before leaving me to my solitude.

I have no doubt she shall inform Mama who will be forced to cancel any plans she had for the day, which will vex her greatly.

My attention is drawn back to the letter, however.

The terrible intentions of Lord Felsenworth were all too clear. I do not for a moment believe you to have been naturally unwell. Your state of lethargy was most unnatural, and I suspect from the administration of laudanum. For what else would cause you to fall so drowsy?

And if this be the case, which I am sure it was, who else would have supplied it you but Lord Felsenworth himself? And there must be only one aim in mind of such a man. I cannot bring myself to write the words and do not think you a simpleton requiring further explanation. You must be aware to what I refer.

My dearest Anne, keeper of all my secrets, and sister of my heart, such an insult could not be left unanswered. I have challenged the blaggard to a duel. There, that very word condemns me should I yet live.

Do not blame me for this, I implore you, for how else could I respond? The scoundrel must answer for his actions. Any doubt I had was dismissed in his acceptance of the contest.

You should not receive this letter until after you have breakfasted. So, I am now either on a coach away from London or lying in a ditch in Hyde Park at this moment. I pray God I am permitted the former. Victory must be mine. Such a despicable fiend must not be permitted to draw breath.

I am sorry he was ever in your presence. I had suspected him of being a rake and had even begun to distance myself from his friendship. I had previously dismissed his tall tales as a bag of moonshine but had of late witnessed such base behaviour to corroborate his stories. If I had suspected for a moment him capable of attempting to take any woman's virtue, I should have ensured he never came within a mile of yourself. To think what almost befell you. It boils my blood.

How I despise myself for not perceiving his true nature and warning you off such an undeserving creature. Even if you are capable of forgiving my utter lack of foresight and counsel, I never shall. The torment I now suffer is as deserved as it is wretched.

Whilst I am here with my pen, I would also inform you of the fine qualities of my valet, but he shall never replace who was there before. He does me a service only. I hope you grasp my meaning, for I dare not be more explicit. Perhaps even this is too much for your delicate ears. But some explanation was necessary.

Canada beckons still, I trust, and will endeavour to gain passage on an earlier ship, although it should not be too difficult to lay low until my intended one sets sail. I cannot wait to leave this cursed country; excepting you and one other, it has brought me nothing but misery. And even then, well, you know my feelings.

All being well, I shall write as promised once I am safely abroad. Pray for my safe passage, my dear friend. And pray for my soul.

With brotherly affection from one who dares not sign his name.

X

My hand covers my mouth. Such a letter to have written!

Daring any repetition of dizziness, I dash to the fire which is happily lit, and throw the damning letter into the flames, prodding it with a poker to ensure its total destruction.

Poor Beauvrais. What agonies he has suffered. What risks he has undertaken in my name. He is victorious to be sure. For have I not heard of Felsenworth's demise? And I am no longer sorry for it at all.

I had been willing to suppose he merely attempted to take advantage of my weakness, but no, he was far more calculating. He planned it just so. And thank the Lord for Beauvrais who answered my scream. Had it been any other who…no, I shall not dwell on that line of thought. It makes me shudder to think.

But is Lord Beauvrais now safe? Is it known Felsenworth was killed in a duel? Or has it been hushed up? And my name was associated with his. Have I not been seen dancing with him and courting the attentions of Lord Felsenworth? Oh, Papa, your daughter may have brought more shame on your family name than you could ever possibly imagine.

❧ Chapter 12 ❧

Inertia holds me within its grips all day. I seem unable to stir myself out of my bedroom, not even to take some air. My mind insists on thinking of the recent terrible events. There was surely some way of avoiding it. I appreciate what has been done cannot be undone, but still I puzzle over it. Did I err?

And now Lord Felsenworth, for whom I had such high hopes, is no more. I can scarce believe it. How a healthy person can meet such a sudden demise is shocking. My own brother met an early end, but that was in battle, and not on the streets of London. And if Lord Beauvrais is caught, he shall also find his life snuffed out like a candle. Is death to forever plague me?

And more selfishly, what is now to become of me?

"Oh, Beauvrais. By coming to my rescue you know not that you have doomed me also. For who am I to marry now?" my heart cries.

The looming figure of Lord Emsby dances in my mind, badly even in imaginary form. I cringe at the thought. But if Papa truly means to marry me in haste, is he not the most likely partner? Lord Felsenworth, how I despise you now. The repercussions of your vile actions may yet be far-reaching and of lengthy duration.

In the early afternoon, Julia bursts into my room without warning, in too much haste even for anyone to announce her arrival.

"My dear friend, you are still about your room. But I am glad to see you in your chair. No, do not get up on my account. I could not rest until I had seen you were recovering and insisted on my aunt bringing me to you to offer what little comfort I could."

"You are very good."

"I shall never again dine in Vauxhall Gardens. I am most fortunate my chicken did not poison me on this occasion, as it did you. You still look quite ill. Do you feel any better at all?"

"A little—"

"I daresay being confined here that you have not heard, so I shall tell you the dreadful news, for surely it is better to come from a friend than any other. But, my dear, you must prepare yourself for a shock. For it is too terrible."

I adjust my position, ready to feign surprise at what I am sure will be a repetition of what I already know.

"But I do not know what could have possessed him. For surely Lord Felsenworth and Sir Reginald over-indulged after we left them. There was a great deal too much liquor flowing in that place for them to resist. And it must have made his hand unsteady. What could have entered his head to rise early and attempt shooting practice? But he did. And, oh, Anne, I am sorry to say, a great tragedy has occurred from his carelessness, for Lord Felsenworth is now dead by his own hand."

My eyes widen as I gasp. Julia places a comforting hand upon my arm.

"I tried to prepare you, did I not? But I have not done wrong by informing you?"

"No, you were quite right to be such a good friend. But are you sure this is the truth of it?"

"Oh yes, all of London is talking of it. What sad news. I can only guess at how it must affect you. Yes, I see it does. Shall I call for your maid?"

"No, do not trouble her. There is nothing but time that can heal this wound. Poor Lord Felsenworth." I manage to sound sincere in my sympathy.

"Such a fine young man. How cruel to have such a vibrant life taken away in such a manner."

"It was foolhardy of him, to be sure. What a notion. But I suppose young men will insist upon their sport."

"It makes one thankful to be of the gentler sex. We shall not meet such a grizzly end."

"Quite," I reply, my shock real. What a graphic picture she paints.

"I shall leave you to your recuperation. I fear you shall not be amongst society this evening?"

"It is unlikely."

"Well, you shall be sorely missed. You must recover soon, for I shall be desolate without you."

"I shall do my best, to please you," I tell her with a smile.

Laying a kiss on my cheek, the sweet-intentioned girl leaves and I sigh deeply. At least there is no talk of a duel. Whether all believe this version of events remains to be seen, but at the very least it casts gazes away from my direction. Perhaps I shall not bring us into disgrace after all.

Left to myself once more, my mind returns to what occurred in Hyde Park. Was I in any way to blame? I have prided myself on not being too green, of making men's behaviour my study. Admittedly, most of this was from book learning, so perhaps I erred.

Recalling my every interaction with Lord Felsenworth, there was surely nothing in my conduct which encouraged such an outrageous attempt on my virtue? I received his attentions with perhaps too many smiles, a trifle too much eagerness. He is, was, an extremely charming person, who made it impossible for me to do otherwise but like him.

Did I ever utter any words of anything more than would be expected of a girl of delicate breeding? My teeth worry my lip as I mull over our conversations. But I can think of nothing untoward. Not until I accepted his invitation to that fateful evening's entertainments. Was that my error?

Mama herself approved the excursion. If it had been in any way inappropriate she would not have permitted it, and certainly not without her presence. And there were a great many couples about without a chaperon; this was no extraordinary occurrence.

Perhaps I should have insisted my footman follow in a boat behind us. It had been my intention to allow him to follow at a distance, so as not to intrude, but to protect me from this very thing. However, I allowed Lord Felsenworth to convince me of the excessiveness of this plan. He was at the point of returning us home, and Julia had looked so desperately saddened by that notion that I complied with his wishes. There. There was my most grievous decision.

Whilst trying to further determine my own guilt, I judge myself to have shown nothing but propriety in my other actions. And surely, if Lord Felsenworth had thought for one moment I was loose enough to accept his offer of elopement he would not have taken the drastic measure of adding laudanum to my punch. And there it was surely concealed, for I recall mentioning it was not as sweet as I had thought it should be. What a fool I was not to have given that more consideration. So entirely did I trust him.

Whatever possessed a man of breeding himself of forming this scheme? Had Lady Rathburn herself not called me out as a prude for my earlier form of dress? Was this what misled him? The lowering of my neckline? Was it a temptation too far?

Round and round my thoughts travel, picking apart every move, every whisper and every interaction.

I am none the wiser when Clément returns to dress me for dinner. More hours have passed than I realised. To her credit, she succeeds in brightening my countenance this time.

Following a dinner I barely touched, Mama calls me to a private audience.

Patting the seat next to her, she commands, "Come sit with me."

There is naught to do but comply.

"You may have noticed your papa's grave mien."

I nod, not wishing to disclose I had not. He looked just as stern as is usual.

"He is much angered at what has transpired. I myself am quite out of favour with him, but it is perhaps as well not to dwell on that. We must speak of you."

"But Mama, what have we done which upsets him so?" I ask, my eyes widening.

"Why, encourage the attentions of Lord Felsenworth."

"But why should we not? He is of the Ton, or was."

"Well, my dear, it seems he was of dubious character. I will say that your papa should have shared the information with me sooner. Had I but been made aware of the talk in his club, I should have kept you far away from the man."

"Pardon me, but what talk, Mama?"

"There were rumours of his excesses, of gambling himself to ruin, and, well, perhaps it is best not to go further than that."

I put a hand on hers as I tell her, "Please, I would hear it. Perhaps it shall relieve my mind."

"Quite the reverse, I assure you. They say he was a rake. But I cannot lend this any credit. He was perhaps a little over flattering and too handsome for his own good, but a rake? How could one be so deceived in his character?"

I remain silent.

"You appear quite as perplexed as I upon hearing this news. But if The Duke withholds such details, how can you be blamed for not being aware of his true character? Forgive me, I rant over your papa's faults. But he gave me such a scolding as I never thought to receive. And now he makes a demand I know you shall not receive well, but really, there is nothing to do but obey."

"Do not hold me in suspense, I implore you," I beseech as she pauses and fidgets.

"My dear, he insists you court the attentions of Lord Emsby."

My hand flies to my open mouth. "No, he cannot be in earnest."

"As he quite rightly pointed out, what else is there for it? The Duke of Tilbourne declared himself out at your come out, you know. 'Who in all good sense would seek to cage such a vibrant bird with an old buzzard?' were his words, I understand. Your papa tried to persuade him otherwise but had to concede."

"I had no notion this had transpired. Although I had thought it odd not to have seen him again."

"The Duke of Tilbourne is an excellent man and has spared any embarrassment you may feel by ensuring not to appear in your presence. He truly is a considerate man. Such a pity he is so far your senior. Although, I may be tempted to change his mind if Emsby is to be the alternative."

"I beg you would."

"No, it is too late for such things."

"How can Papa intend me for Lord Emsby? I have never met a more ill-mannered, odious man."

"Now, I shall not hear such disparaging remarks. He is an earl and manages his affairs sensibly. He will provide you with a comfortable home."

"No. He shall not. I cannot do it." The words have leapt off my tongue as if of their own accord, without my knowledge of their existence beforehand.

"Anne! This really is too much. It shall not be borne. I never thought to hear such impertinence from you. Of course you can and you shall."

"I tell you it cannot be done."

"No offer has yet been made, but you will bring one about. You will receive and encourage that good man's attentions."

"Mama, you cannot condone this. I never thought to disobey or make myself disagreeable to my excellent parents, but I must repeat, I cannot do this." Tears have welled in my eyes, and my hands plead as if in prayer.

Staring me down, Mama, through gritted teeth, tells me, "If you do not, Papa says all the birchings you have been spared thus far shall be visited upon you all at once, rendering you unable to sit down for a week."

I sink from the chair to the floor at Mama's feet, grabbing a hold of her skirts. "Mama, please, please spare me. Oh, won't you save your daughter this hideous fate?"

Mama stands, brushes her skirts, and therefore me, down. "I suggest you take time to consider. This outburst is not becoming of you. Remember who you are. This is what is expected of you, and indeed, you shall obey as is your duty. Or would you live your life alone and penniless?"

"I shall have my annuity, such a life is not ever to be my fate," I rally.

"Go against your papa's wishes and see how much income you receive from him. His mind is made up, and you should not receive as much as a shilling."

With that, she walks away, leaving me in a heap, crying in earnest. What despair plummets my heart into hell? Before my arrival in London, no, I had not been romantic. But then my heart was awoken by none other than a rake. And now it is verily crushed, by his betrayal as much as the prospect before me.

Have I not before said I would be satisfied with a husband who be not hideous, either in action or features? That, so long as he be not cruel, I would perform my duty?

But Lord Emsby *is* hideous. His appearance is corpulent, his manners revolting, and there is a cruel gleam in his eye. Why, when he was out-manoeuvred by Lord Dellingby he looked quite murderous. He is everything I had most feared upon entering the marriage mart. And now I am to make love to him? To encourage an offer from the most odious man of my acquaintance?

My fist hammers the floor as resentment fires my arm into action, and a cry more befitting a wounded animal than a lady of distinction bursts from my throat.

"God in Heaven, why hast thou forsaken me? Have I not been a dutiful daughter? Followed every instruction? What mortal sin have I committed to warrant such a marriage partner?"

"If you please, m'lady, I thought some refreshment may be in order?" Forbes quietly suggests, offering his silver platter with a glass of Madeira upon it.

Taking a deep breath, mortified he should see me in such a dishevelled state, I take a sip. My back leans against the chair, my eyes turned towards the ceiling as I hiss out more deep breaths.

A small cough alerts me to the presence of the butler I had thought to have gone as soon as his duty was carried out.

"Well, what is it?" I snap.

In lowered tones, he informs me at a fair rate of knots, "Beg pardon, m'lady. I wished to inform you I did my utmost to reason with The Duke. I was sure you would not have allowed yourself to be top-heavy, for you have never been so before. I surmised, as much as I dared, you were unnaturally tired. But your papa would not hear of it. And I most sincerely offer my apology for not having been more successful."

"It is of no consequence now," I tell him with a wave of my hand.

"Very good, m'lady," he says, bowing and finally leaving me.

His interruption verged on impertinence, but I am sensible of the honour of his intentions. Papa has clearly made the entire household uneasy with his wrath. It is enough to make me almost pleased he would not listen, for how much greater would his rage have been if he were made aware of the close ruination of his prize pig...daughter?

Even those porkers are spared by a quick death, so I am informed. My own torment, I fear, shall be most prolonged and arduous. Is it possible to live one's life entirely shut off in one's room? That is surely the only possible glimmer of hope there is to be had.

❧ Chapter 13 ❧

"Come, I will not have you lay about in such blue devils," Mama commands me the next morning.

Thus far, I have refused to stir from my bed, in part owing to the supreme lethargy which renders me immobile, but also from an unwillingness to meet with my papa at breakfast. A scene we would both be ashamed of can be the only possible outcome. Mama fails to see this.

"Mama, not this morning, I beg you."

"Such obstinate petulance. Stir yourself immediately and face the day with the grace becoming of your station."

"You ask the impossible," I mumble from beneath my pillow.

Said pillow gets snatched away and thrown across the room. The yelp informs me it either hit or narrowly missed poor Clément.

"I shall not ask again, Anne. You *will* rise and partake in breakfast. Or shall you force Papa to prepare his birch?"

Bringing my knees up, curling into a ball, a moan escapes me. It is far from dignified. Mama knows only too well it signifies my reluctant compliance, so swishes from the room.

"Dear Clément, you see what your mistress is brought to? Did you ever think to see the like?"

"Indeed I did not," she replies, a blush spreading across her cheeks, her gaze held to the floor.

Dragging them around, my legs hang over the side of my bed. My fingers dig into the mattress, arms rigid. My own gaze finds the floor, as hair falls into my face.

"There there, my lady, all will come right, *n'est ce pas*?"

"That is kind of you, but woefully inaccurate on this occasion. Imagine, if you will, the most onerous and odorous man your mind can conjure. Now, try if you can make him worse. Loud, obnoxious, in short, the most tedious person to ever draw breath. Now, envision yourself a bride marrying such a man."

"Oh *non non non*," the good maid gasps.

"Quite."

"But surely this cannot be? You are so beautiful and graceful. The best Society could ever hope to behold."

"Dear Clément, do not get carried away with your description. But I must own I had thought a better fate may await me, but alas, this is indeed the man I am to set my cap to."

"He must be a great deal better than you imagine, I think."

"Oh, I am sure on paper he is a fine match," I tell her, smirking. "But enough, I must face my fearsome papa first."

I said too much. My sense of propriety really has gone awry. But who else am I to pour my lament out to? Mama is clearly not in sympathy with my plight.

For once, the rule of silence is a welcome one over our repast. My occasional pointed glares at Papa are sufficient to convey my displeasure, as are his in return. Every scrape of the knife and chink of glass seems amplified this morning. It makes for the most uncomfortable meal of my life. Oppression fills the air like a velvet cloak, closing my throat until it takes considerable effort to swallow each and every mouthful.

Another sitting for my portrait is not precisely appealing but is a more attractive proposition than remaining in this house of gloom a moment longer. Something bordering excitement fills me as I am made ready in the same attire as before. Clément excels herself in the preparations, and I appear exactly as before in the artist's studio.

This time, I have remembered to bring the small likeness of Prince for Sir Thomas to incorporate into my portrait. I receive only grumbles when I request a glimpse of the work so far. Apparently, it is not permitted. Really, artists and their temperaments are enough to try one's patience.

"Hold here. Yes, your arm just so. Your head slightly more to the left," I am ordered.

Drapes are opened and closed until Sir Thomas Lawrence is satisfied that the light is as it should be. My thoughts drift to this evening's ball, making my heart sink and my shoulders slouch.

"Ah ah ah, hold still, if you please, Lady Anne," he admonishes.

Rolling my eyes, I hold myself erect again. What a bore! Fighting the urge to rest my head upon my hand, I sit as still as one possibly can whilst lamenting one's future. Lord Emsby is to be at the ball this evening. How am I to make love to him when I feel only revulsion? How can Papa truly intend me for him? It defies belief.

Certainly, family names are to be considered, and fortune. I am sensible of these going in Emsby's favour. Had I not noted as much myself, and feared this very outcome? But Papa must have witnessed his obscene conduct at my come out?

"Soft face," Sir Thomas moans.

"I beg pardon," I apologise, doing my best to smooth my brow.

It is most grievous to have Papa in such a rage that he would marry me to the first man he thinks of. How can he doubt my sense of propriety so? He must know I would never over-indulge, and most certainly not in public. How can he lay the blame at my door? And punish me thus?

"Lady Anne, remember if you will, a serene scene before you. I must not paint such frowns. You are an elegant young lady of *le beau monde*."

Again, I school my features.

My mind wanders back to woes. Besides, even if I had erred, is an entire lifetime of torment just punishment for one moment's lapse of judgement?

With many sighs from both Sir Thomas and myself, we get through the sitting in bearable fashion.

On the way home, I request the coachman to tour the park before heading home. Fresh air is a welcome relief after the stuffy studio, and I would delay my return as long as possible. Nobody can think ill of this small detour. Perhaps Mama would even welcome it. The weather is dry, so the top of the barouche is down. I am being seen, which is surely commendable. I confess, there is a slight hope that an alternative may present himself.

But no beau dares approach as I am alone inside the carriage. And no women of my close acquaintance are about. I must be satisfied with distant head nods and my solitude.

Trying to escape these persistent thoughts, I spend the rest of my day hiding in the library. But my eyes are not reading as they should. The same pages are read and re-read with alarming regularity.

This evening looms like a murderer in the dark. And worries of Lord Beauvrais plague me too, for I have received no further word from him. Yet, nor have I heard anything of the demise of Lord Felsenworth other than his 'shooting incident'. I suppose all have accepted this version of the truth, and there is no search party after my friend. Or, at least I hope this to be the case. And then he has a long sea voyage, which is also troubling, for I fear for his safety on the waves also.

It would seem that my childhood, having been so blessed, all these concerns have been saved to arrive all at once. Never have I been visited by such dismal difficulties. I grow more homesick with each passing day.

Getting up, I cross to the writing desk. Perhaps updating Margie on my progress, or lack thereof, may help rid me of these troubling thoughts. They shall be away from me, and down on paper.

But the feather of my pen teases my lips as I stare blankly out of the window. A fine drizzle on the panes blurs my view. Or is it my tears which do so?

My task complete and reviewing my situation set down clearly and simply on the page does help me see things in a clearer light, but no avenue of hope has emerged from my scribblings.

Returning to the comfortable, stuffed chair, I continue my efforts to escape into the novel I have been reading.

I am more successful in this attempt, as the next thing I know it is time for me to make ready for the ball.

"Please be generous when scenting my handkerchief with violets, Clément."

"Very good, my lady. Would you like a few drops on your fan also?"

"What a capital idea. Then it may be wafted directly to my face in a gesture of feminine grace."

Smiling, she proudly dowses my accessories accordingly. That should offer some defence to part of Lord Emsby's offence.

My gown this evening is a white silk gauze and has a pattern of blue leaves, is trimmed with blue satin, and has simple puffed sleeves. It does feel rather lovely against my skin, and the hint of colour does something to soothe my nerves a little.

I have to control my smile as Miss Compley hastens towards me, her blonde locks framing her elegant face. Her gait is as close to a run as is possible without being so as she crosses the room. It is on the far side of dignity even so, but my heart overflows.

"Lady Anne, you are come, you are come. What a pleasure to see you," she almost yells.

Her exuberance is as contagious as ever, and my smile spreads wide as my shoulders are encased in her hands and my cheeks receive her kiss.

"Miss Compley, you cannot conceive how glad I am to be in your company. Come, for I have news to impart," I tell her, leading her to a quieter corner.

She grimaces and is taken aback when I divulge the plan to marry me off to Lord Emsby. Such a dear, sweet girl – she is quite mortified on my behalf. Having known me most of my life, she knows my sensibilities intimately.

Unfortunately, the man himself weasels his way into my presence before I can greet my newer friend, Miss Plimpton who may be observed heading in our direction. I leave Julia to update her on this gossip as I line up in the first dance.

My eyelashes flutter, my smile is sweet and my blush creeps along my cheeks in the most appropriate way as we dance. I take a few opportunities to rest my fan on my left cheek, indicating a 'yes' to his advances whilst inhaling the sweet scent to help carry me through.

A cold sinking sensation runs through me as I look about for the blue eyes I realise too late shall ne'er be seen again. He is not worthy of so much sadness, I am sure, but it cannot be helped. However, it sits but a moment on my countenance, as one must outwardly display charm, grace and poise.

"What a pity to spoil such fine chalk work with one's feet, wot?"

"Indeed, a most intricate pattern," I reply, not truly caring what may lie beneath my feet.

A loud chortle erupts from his thin lips before he says, "Regard, Lady Anne, I do believe we dance among the stars, wot?"

Noting the chalked stars, I manage a delightful giggle before telling him, "Oh, how droll. So we are, Lord Emsby, so we are."

May the heavens themselves lend me the fortitude to endure this.

Taking even greater care, I smile as Lord Emsby and I join hands. But how my hand wishes to recoil from his touch. Schooling my thoughts, I focus on trying to discover his better points, for every man must have them.

Such distinctions are not to be found about his small mouth. There is a tooth amiss towards the back, revealed by the stupid grin widening his round, red cheeks. The other teeth are so yellow as to make me wonder whether they have ever seen a brush and powder.

His eyes are beady and dark; his smile does not bring light into them. His greased hair seems to be racing towards the back of his head.

There, his nose is straight and inoffensive. And his legs are shapely, but for ought I know, this may be the result of clever padding; I have heard men use such deceptions.

It is of no use. His appearance has not improved under my scrutiny. And his conversation is as dull as ever.

"You are a delight, as always, Lady Anne," he says through his nose as we walk away from the dance area.

"I thank you, but the pleasure is surely mine," I declare with a smile and curtsey, quelling an attack of bile.

He seems intent on carrying on our discourse, much to my chagrin, but it must be encouraged, although not without some remedial action. Reaching into my reticule, I take out my container of cachous and delicately place one on my tongue.

"Won't you partake of a pastille, Lord Emsby?"

"If only to be obliging, I shall. Although, I confess I do not like them much."

I silently add 'apparently' whilst offering the container. The clever sweet goes some way to combatting the breath being blown my way as Lord Emsby vents his hot air. He offers misplaced condolences on the surprising demise of our mutual friend.

"But you should not concern yourself that no offer may be made. I may go so far as to say it increases your chances," he says before taking a pinch of snuff.

"*Merci beaucoup*. Your kindness is of great comfort and I thank you for such thoughtful observations."

"There is no need for gratitude. There is much I would do to enhance your comfort, Lady Anne," he says, but in a manner which makes my skin crawl; his smile is more a sneer and his tone frankly lecherous.

"You are too good," I reply, my mask of civility firmly in situ.

"Lady Anne, it is good to see you here. Might I beg the next?" I am asked.

"Lord Dellingby. You may, should Lord Emsby be good enough to release me?" I look pointedly in his direction as I speak.

"I would by no means deny you any pleasure," he says in his most nasal tone whilst bowing.

"You are very good," I remind him with a light touch on his arm before allowing myself to be led away.

Glancing at the floor, the model of modesty, my breath catches. "Your boots!"

"You needn't look quite so horrified. I should not have you think I am a coxcomb. But I do confess a fondness for fine footwear and took the opportunity of being in town to commission these. They do not meet with your approval?" His brow rises as he asks the last.

"They are fine, of course, but unusual. The colours are richer, the shape, the elaborate tassels placed..."

"They are perhaps a little foppish."

"Oh no, I do not mean...they are handsome. But I have seen them before."

"I should think you have," he says with a smirk.

He seems bewildered and my own anxiety only increases.

"It was you!"

"Pardon me, Lady Anne. But to what are you referring?"

"That night. In Vauxhall Gardens. You were the one who helped me away." My heart is beating so wildly I fear it shall break free of my person.

"And this surprises you?"

A blush fills my cheeks with warmth, unbidden, and I am forced to look away. "I confess it does. Please do not make me admit I was ignorant as to your identity until this moment."

"Oh my dear, shall we perhaps sit this one out? Let us find you a chair. You fly so many colours as to astonish me greatly. Come rest a while."

In silence, I let his arm lead me towards some seating by an open door. Yes, this was my protector, so considerate and gentle. That arm which was so strong and welcome around my waist that fateful night now supports only my hand.

Landing a little heavily in my seat, I look up at Lord Dellingby with new eyes. His dark blond hair is fashionably styled without being overly done and hangs above kind brown eyes which are looking into my own.

"Might I fetch you some refreshment?" he asks.

"Yes. Oh, but I would not put you to any more trouble."

"No trouble at all. Please, it is my pleasure."

My heart quickens further still as I watch his tall frame walk away, his coat hugging his figure closely without squeezing the air from his lungs. The hint of a swagger is in his stride taken upon fine calves. My hand flies to my breast as I attempt to draw in more air.

Be still my beating heart, recover from this revelation. For what you feel is gratitude alone. Gratitude for the saviour who walked me away from danger. One's head cannot be turned with every act of kindness, no matter how great.

Upon reflection, Lord Dellingby's appearance does seem a little improved of late. O fie! Such foolish notions are of no consequence, for I have my orders.

Oh, but those orders condemn me to one who can never measure up to the one now returning with two glasses of what turns out to be ratafia. As he approaches, he takes a sip from one, and with his back towards the room, he switches glasses, so I take the one he sipped from, winking as he does so.

"You know all!" I say, gasping.

"Do not look so astonished. It was my mission to run to your rescue. But Beauvrais was mercifully there before me."

He glances about before continuing in lowered tones, "But perhaps it is best not to discuss such matters here. Might I call on you tomorrow?"

"But of course."

"Do sip your drink. You begin to turn all manner of colours again."

I do as bid and swallow in a large gulp. The noise makes the man at my side smile.

"I do beg pardon," I say, looking up at those amused eyes.

"Not a word of it. Pray continue," he says, patting my arm.

His action induces me to take another large mouthful. The intimacy is quite overcoming.

"But you may wish to slow a little," he cautions with a cough.

"Do you find amusement in my distress, Lord Dellingby?" I ask, a smile of my own dancing about the corners of my mouth.

"I would not dare," he says, his voice deep and low and filled with his concealed mirth.

The corner of his mouth twists and it is my undoing. I laugh despite myself.

"There, that is a better sound. I'd wager it would grace the orchestra of Vauxhall Gardens itself."

"Pray, do not mention that place."

"Oh fie, do not blame the location. I would remind you of the wonders it beholds."

"Perhaps, but nothing shall induce me to return."

"Not yet, but perhaps in time," he says, inclining his head.

He allows me to slowly finish my beverage, standing guard by my side.

"Now, I do believe you are recovered sufficiently to attempt that dance I was promised?"

"Indeed, I believe I am," I agree, taking his hand, getting to my feet.

The first sensations of happiness return as we skip and hop our way about the room, dancing between the other couples, caught in our own world for the briefest of moments. The moon and stars underfoot almost becoming real as we swirl amongst them.

But the illusion is broken once the dance finishes, the musicians fall silent, and the real world re-emerges. I followed this path before, and it led me towards near ruin. Duty beckons and I must obey. To do otherwise would be folly.

Other partners dance with me, and I am sure I partook in supper, but all is numb to me. I fear my heart should break beneath this façade of amiability, though none would know it. A sadness far greater than that of the previous days grips my heart as the carriage takes us home.

Only once safely alone in my room does the mask crack, and the tears flow. Had I not been so blind, so foolhardy, I could have yet chosen to be married to one whom I hold in higher esteem. What ridiculous churlish notion rid me of that opportunity?

Oh, how I willingly gave my heart to one so wholly unworthy instead. One with fine blue eyes and merriment concealing the devil incarnate. Or even to one who could never return my love. Oh, a fine pair of men to fling my heart away on. A fine mess I have contrived. And all to no avail, for I am to court Lord Emsby.

How cruel to reveal what might have been, now when it is too late.

Chapter 14

My dreams were filled with scenes of dread all night. Amongst which was a vision of me walking up the aisle on my wedding day, Lord Emsby ahead of me. But as I reached him, he turned into a snarling, vicious dog. As he lurched forwards to attack, I awoke safe in my bed. But the terror remains.

I really do make too much of this and must strive to fulfil my duty with good grace. Perhaps he shall make a kinder husband than I give him credit for. He seems to admire me. Surely there is nothing much to fear.

Heading outside, the earthy scent of a fresh rainfall greets me, which I inhale deeply. The clouds are clearing and promises a finer day ahead. Not wishing to ruin my shoes, I carefully keep to the paths as I make my way about.

Forbes finds me and announces, "M'lady, a...errr...gift has arrived for you."

"A gift? For me?"

"Yes. It awaits you by the main entrance, m'lady."

Curious as to why he did not bring it to me rather than leaving it where it was, I follow him back inside. He doesn't stop in the entrance, but opens the door, and what a sight there is to behold. For there stands in all her glory, the fine mare that is Lady.

"Oh, is she really for me?" I ask of Forbes but receive an answer from another.

"If you will accept her, your ladyship," replies the groom holding her reins.

"If I...? Well, of course I accept," I inform him, walking up to the horse and patting her neck.

Walking around, I stand head on and stroke her nose, which makes her whicker. I cannot resist placing a kiss on her velvety soft muzzle.

"Is there no note?" I ask.

"Oh, beg pardon, I almost forgot. Here y'ar."

"Thank you," I tell him in a tone which dismisses him.

"Come, Lady, you must meet your new friends, and then you must make ready for we must ride out after breakfast."

Her hooves clip clop alongside me as I lead her to the stables. Giving her one last stroke before handing her to our groom and making my way to breakfast with footsteps far lighter than they have been of late.

"Mama, would you be very angry if I asked you to cancel any plans we had this morning?"

"There was nothing of any great consequence, but you should wait until after any callers have paid their visit. What is it you wish to do that is so important and has placed a smile back on your visage?"

"Oh Mama, it is the finest thing. Do you recall the mare Lord Beauvrais brought for me to ride?"

"I am sure I do not."

"He has made a present of her to me."

"A present? But he is not here, surely?"

She appears so startled that I almost laugh. But managing to control myself, I merely tell her, "No. You know he is making his way to Canada. I suppose he could not take her with him."

"But why should he make such an extravagant gift to you, pray tell?"

"We were always friends. I rather think he thought of me as a sister. And he knows how happy I would be to receive such a fine horse."

"It is quite improper," she grumbles.

"If it stops her hysterics, the infernal beast may stay," Papa intercedes and thereby silencing us as befitting our meal.

Following breakfast, I retire to my room but do not call for Clément immediately. Instead, I read the letter which arrived with Lady.

Note from Lord Beauvrais, undated.

Dear Lady Anne,

Please accept Lady into your household. I know there is room for her in your stables, and there is no place on Earth where she could be better looked after. She cannot accompany me to Canada. Her stable companion is on her way to my cousin Harriet, but alas, only one may go thither. It grieves me to separate them but needs must. And I am sure they could not be bestowed on two more grateful recipients.

You looked so charming together in the park and there is such a scarcity of fine horses in London, I am convinced there must be no objection to this gift. I pray she may bring you joy, for I would have you happy always.

Adieu,

Your brotherly friend, Bamber Beauvrais

Dratted man, why did he not date his missive? However short a note it may be, surely even he should be sensible of this standard? And now I am left with no idea as to when he formed this plan. Is he still in London? Has he not yet set out on his journey?

His writing has always been so very bad, that there is nothing to be supposed from his scrawl. It could have been written at any time.

Holding the note to my bosom, I offer a prayer up to Heaven, asking again to keep him safe. Indeed, he is more like a brother than ever, for who else could bestow such a gift? One which offers me a modicum of freedom.

Having secreted the note in my letter box, I call for Clément and prepare for my callers. There is one I am excited to see, and one I must endeavour to feel the same for. But I know not who else to expect with any certainty.

Never missing an opportunity, Lord Emsby arrives first with a lovely bouquet of flowers. I must allow for his thoughtfulness. With the promise of a more appealing caller, I must confess I get through this visit with renewed vigour. I am all smiles and compliments, and even earn a compliment from Mama once the man departs.

Lord Dellingby soon arrives, but Mama remains in the room, as one would expect, but it does make conversation rather difficult, at least the one we would choose to have.

Having exchanged pleasantries and exhausting civil discourse, he ventures, "Your Grace, there is something I would disclose to your daughter, but I regret it is for her ears alone. Be not alarmed it is of an improper nature. But pray, might we be permitted a few minutes privacy?"

Mama's eyebrows try to jump off her forehead. "Certainly not. If it is of honourable intent, you may tell her what you must in front of any company."

Unperturbed, he continues, "Of course, I do not mean out of your sight, Your Grace. I would not make you so uneasy. But perhaps, in the garden here where you may yet see us? Truly, if it were my own secret I should not hesitate to declare it."

"I detest secrets," she sneers, looking down her nose at him.

"I confess I am not fond of them myself. But perhaps we could allow this one on this singular occasion? Truly, I mean no disrespect or harm."

Something in his look must soften her resolve. "For a few minutes only," she grants, scowling.

We both leap up and hurry outside, bringing forth the most alarming noise from Mama. But paying her no heed, we make our escape.

"Lady Anne, I fear your mama shall be true to her word. But I must tell you Lord Felsenworth had bragged of his fiendish plan to Lord Alverbury whom you may recall from Hyde Park. He was much alarmed and, hoping for his friend to have been telling 'Banbury stories' but fearing otherwise, he sought me out. It took him some time, for I was not at my usual club."

"Why did he seek you especially?"

"He knows me to be a man of honour, and we are old friends. I blush to admit it, but time is of the essence, so I shall confess he was also aware of my feelings and designs for you."

"Feelings?"

"Please, allow me to finish. So it was that I was sent on my errand of valour. Vauxhall Gardens are vast, but even I am aware of the darker corners where dishonourable people may go. And thus I found and escorted you."

"And I am much obliged to you, my lord. But this much was apparent last night. What is the explanation for this urgency?"

"Our fine friend Lord Beauvrais was incensed by what he discovered, seemingly by accident."

"And who would not be?"

"Indeed. He remained as I accompanied you to safety. What came to pass I cannot be sure. But if it had been me in his place, I should have challenged that dog to a duel."

"I should think anyone of worth would do so."

"Yes, but Lord Alverbury sees this too. He took me aside and asked if I had been the one at the other end of the barking irons. He is no fool, and would not believe it a shooting accident, being aware of the facts preceding."

"But you can tell him in all good conscience that you were not."

"And so I did. But that led him to ask whose hand he may shake. I tried to avoid supplying him a direct answer, I truly did. But he insisted, and in the end I had to give up Beauvrais' name." He hangs his head in shame as he tells me this.

Putting a hand on his shoulder, I calmly tell him, "But this is not so very bad. Lord Alverbury is on our side, else he should not have taken the trouble of finding you, for which I am most grateful. And did he not wish to shake his hand?"

"And if it were just him, I should not have a moment's unease. But that confounded worm Lord Emsby happened upon us as I confirmed the name."

"No! He cannot know. He has said nothing of it. But…oh dear, he did seem rather pleased with himself. He would not think Lord Beauvrais a threat to his ambitions, surely?"

"There, you see it as I do. Lord Beauvrais is not safe. I have known him a long time, and am aware of the impossibility, but Lord Emsby is not."

"Impossibility?"

"Of him being in Lord Emsby's path to you."

"Lord Dellingby!" I shriek.

"You do not know? Are you not aware…?"

"Yes, of course. But your forthrightness astonishes me."

"I beg your pardon, but if the man's life were not at stake I should not find it necessary to be so blunt."

"But have you not heard he is making his way to Canada?"

"I heard some stories to that effect, but are they quite true? Do you know if he has yet boarded a vessel?"

"All too true, but not because of what has happened. It was his plan prior to…to…well, that event. I have this very morning received a present of one of his horses."

He sighs at this. "Then it is true, at least. He would never part with them if he were not in earnest or had the least intention of ever returning."

"Alas no. He is gone for good."

"But is he safely out of the country? He must make haste if not."

"I do not know. I have no way of contacting him and no news has yet reached me. Oh, what are we to do?"

❧ Chapter 15 ❧

Lord Dellingby and I part ways before Mama can protest. He has already sent agents to the likely ports to discreetly make enquiries as to Lord Beauvrais' whereabouts, and to assist a hasty departure should he not yet have done so.

He instructed me to continue my day as planned. But as I mount Lady, it feels highly improper to be enjoying my friend's gift when he is himself in so much jeopardy. My footman is of course with me, and we're making our way to the park. My gaze does insist on wandering over the crowds, on the lookout in case Lord Beauvrais is addlebrained enough not to have fled the city.

When I do not see him, it is an odd mixture of relief yet heightened apprehension which grips my heart and throat. However, the mask of civility is in place as Lady clip-clops along. Her gait really is lovely, long and smooth when at walk. It is no wonder Lord Beauvrais would be loath to part with her.

She seems not to have been exercised since I last rode her, for she is fighting her bit and fidgeting to be let loose. Shortening the reins, I allow her to progress at a trot along the park's paths. Such a swift, bouncy trot.

And yet she is not satisfied. I sympathise wholeheartedly at the restlessness caused by confinement. I look behind at my footman and nod a warning we shall speed away. The poor man is still much frighted I shall be carried off by her. The fault is all mine, of course, for having fabricated such a deceit. And now Lady has her card marked. Hence my warning to him, so he knows the ensuing canter is intentional.

Gathering the reins further, I click my tongue as soon as there is a suitable space, and leg Lady on. She requires little encouragement and lengthens to a canter most merrily. I do have to check her, keeping us away from a gallop. But as we speed along, she snorts her pleasure at having gained this freedom. My laugh echoes her snort as we fly, the wind whipping past us, nothing in our way.

We complete a circuit of the grass and slow to a walk so she may stretch her neck out on a long rein on the way back. Her head and neck shake as she grunts, sending ripples along the length of her body. Leaning towards her head a little, I pat and rub her neck.

As we near the path I collect the reins so we are at a smart walk, presenting our most refined selves. A carriage slows on its approach.

"What a fine specimen," is shrieked at me, causing Lady to tense.

The volume and pitch of the statement were aimed at causing alarm, I am certain, and the content of her exclamation was more barbed than it would appear.

Keeping a firm grip, I nod and smile as I respond, "Why, thank you Lady Rathburn."

"Are you quite alone?" she asks, her eyebrows rising.

"As you see."

"Oh, but here is your man," she comments, looking across at the approaching servant.

"Lady Rathburn, you did not presume I would be without a chaperon entirely? Oh goodness me. But of course, I am only alone in the sense that I am not here in a party," I tell her with a slight giggle.

Of all the nerve! I am most thankful for my footman's timely approach, for she would have her party think me some sort of lady-bird. How dare she insinuate I do not conduct myself with all propriety? She is become quite ridiculous in her envy.

"I say, what a beautiful stepper," a male on horseback hails.

"Quite, just as we were saying, Lord Alverbury," Lady Rathburn replies, all sweetness.

"Say, do I not recognise this mare?"

"Perhaps you do. Lord Beauvrais has made a gift of her to me."

"Zooks! That's generosity, by Jove. I considered his choice highly irregular at first but needs must. And once seen, all doubt was removed, for she rivals any stallion, I wager."

"Certainly, she does. But I'm sure I do not know that I deserve it, but he was always too kind to me, even in our childhood."

"I am certain you must be worthy, else he would not have entrusted her unto your care."

"Lord Alverbury, you are all politeness."

"Haha, perhaps I am. Come, shall we give these beasts a good stretch, eh?"

Giving the ladies in the carriage a courtesy nod, I reel Lady around and take her into a trot. I am surprised when Lord Alverbury slows us back to a walk before long. My footman is not far behind.

"Lady Anne, I confess to being glad of this opportunity to speak with you. Have you seen much of Lord Dellingby of late?"

"I saw him but this morning and must thank you most sincerely for the kind service you rendered me."

"Pray, do not mention it. The least I could do. Nasty business, that. Wouldn't stand for it. But here you are safe and well, so let us mention it no more."

"I am, and again, must venture my gratitude for that."

"So, is the former owner of your beautiful steed also safe?"

My smile fades quite away. "Alas, of that, I cannot be certain. Lord Dellingby has quite unsettled me but is now making enquiries. It is my dearest hope that Lord Beauvrais has left the country as hoped. It would grieve me greatly should he not have."

"Pray, do not concern yourself. He has friends who shall see him protected."

"At risk of becoming a bore, I must thank you again, my lord."

"One must rally in the name of honour. But you are a most divine creature to be so concerned. Yes, I believe I discover why Lord Beauvrais was so sweet on you."

I blush wildly. "Oh no—"

"Pray forgive me. I meant no offence. Do not be so alarmed."

"He was not...I would not..."

"Come, come, do not make yourself uneasy. There was no harmful insinuation intended. It was a clumsy compliment, for which I apologise."

Still at a loss for words, I merely smile and nod.

"I must away before I myself tarnish your stainless reputation, eh?" he says with a chuckle.

"Oh dear, that would never do after your labours."

"Haha, there's that wit. I bid you good day, Lady Anne."

The merry chap is soon off at a trot. I am not entirely convinced he possesses full sense, but he is rather amiable, so one can forgive him a great deal. There is an honesty about his green eyes underneath his dark, slightly foppish hair. An air of wisdom underlies his joviality. He does seem rather my senior in years. Yet one could be forgiven for being disappointed at his ineligibility, being only a second son; he is not on Mama's list for me.

Lady and I complete our tour of the park without further event. We pass a few of my acquaintance, but without any lengthy conversation. And Lady is soon returned to a large helping of grain and a carrot.

Feeling famished myself, I head inside in search of a little nuncheon.

"You seem a good deal cheerier," Mama comments down her nose as we meet in the hall.

"Indeed. I found my ride out to be quite invigorating."

"Well, I am pleased you are out of your sulks," she says before continuing on her way.

"Is there any nuncheon left?" I ask Forbes.

"I believe you are spared a little," he says with a smirk.

I have the room to myself, as Papa does not observe nuncheon as an official meal, I'm spared any unpleasantness of company. My bread, cheese, apple and wine are enjoyed in perfect solitude

However, I cannot but help worrying over the fate of Lord Beauvrais. Lord Alverbury would have me trust to power and influence. My mind is a little eased by his assertion his friends will succeed, but what if they should not?

Would Lord Emsby truly go so far as to send men after him? I cannot think it so very likely. But the Lords Dellingby and Alverbury seem to think it a possibility, or why else should they issue assistance? But what should be his reason to be so brash? There must be more to the matter than my hand alone.

One piffling duel is hardly worthy of anyone's attention. Lord Felsenworth's demise is regrettable, but he was not much liked as I now understand. My fingers break cheese into crumbs on my plate as I ponder the curiosities of this situation.

There must be a detail which alludes me. My reason has not been what it ought. Am I now too trusting of Lord Dellingby? Is this pursuit a fabrication of his making? But his concern seemed so sincere, and to involve Lord Alverbury? No, I shall not believe that.

What other quarrel could Lord Emsby have with Lord Beauvrais? My head falls onto my palms as I admit defeat; the mysteries of men are far beyond my comprehension. Attempting to dissemble the truth is giving me a headache. Perhaps a lie-down before this evening's frivolity would be beneficial.

❧

My headache has subsided, and Mama and I are on our way to the opera to see Artaxerxes. Miss Plimpton, who is becoming more a close friend with each passing day, is to sit with us, much to my relief.

"Lady Anne, a delight to see you again, and looking so well," she greets.

"Likewise. Miss Plimpton, your gown is exquisite."

We take ourselves to one side whilst everyone assembles.

"So, how fare you in your list making?"

"Miss Plimpton, you are quite scandalous, you know. However, Papa seems insistent upon it now containing the name of Lord Emsby alone."

"Oh my dear, you shall not accept such a dismal defeat so easily."

"Shall I not?"

"Pray do not tell me you now have more hair than wit, for I admired your good sense before."

My laugh joins hers like two bells chiming.

"We of sound intellect must design our own futures successfully. A little creativity is all which is lacking," she adds, our heads drawing closer together, "Tomorrow we shall add to your number."

"If it were but that simple."

"Lady Anne, I begin to think I do not know you."

"Forgive me. But I doubt my reason and judgement."

"You do not mean that the demise of one Lord Felsenworth has brought about such a change?"

"But do you not see? I was so misled by him —"

"As were we all, I assure you. If I were not so determined on Lord Meltcham, I am sure I would have given chase."

I gasp at her vulgar term.

"Do not look at me so. They are the foxes and we the hounds in this hunt," she says, her eyes glistening and creasing in the corners.

I giggle. "What a bloodthirsty analogy. Besides, I feel more akin to a vixen of late," I tell her, my merriment diminishing and my nose scrunching.

"Well, perhaps that is for the best, for they are more cunning, are they not?" Her eyes narrow as she speaks, but we both laugh.

"How you make light of serious things."

Buoyed by Miss Plimpton's good humour and exuberance, I am most amused by this evening's performance; the singing is sublime, and the audience is a good deal quieter than usual, surely also enthralled. Although, I wish I had seen it before. How then might I have been more wary of cups and their contents.

❧❧

The day is a fine, bright and sunny one, so Mama and I went out in the barouche. This, along with Miss Plimpton's discourse last evening has lightened my heart, and I am become quite cheerful.

Miss Plimpton has promised singing and dancing at her ball this evening. Mama, upon learning Lord Emsby is to be present, was in favour of our attendance. But she has cautioned me against conversing with any bluestockings who may present themselves, for no man will want a lady whose intellect is brought too high.

So, ensuring to cover my knowledge with my curls, I am dressed in my white satin gown, with a silver embroidered crepe petticoat and spring green bodice; pure yet playful. Tonight, I am on a mission, one I must not fail.

Mama keeps pulling my silk scarf in place about my arms during our carriage ride as my fidgeting is causing it to fall repeatedly.

"Do sit still," she admonishes again.

"Sorry, Mama," I reply once more, my feet still tapping on the floor.

Who awaits inside that house? Can they or I form an attraction?

Miss Compley is already in the room and smiling amongst friends. But my heart halts when I notice Sir Reginald in her party. I must warn her away from him. So far, I have not been able to accomplish this, and I cannot tell her all that happened. But the urgency to find a way has increased and it must not be put off any longer.

"Lady Anne, how good of you to join us," Miss Plimpton welcomes, "And just in time, for Lady Rathburn is about to entertain us with a song."

"Oh, I can barely breathe for anticipation."

She giggles. "You are too cruel. But we must prepare for battle. I see you have outdone yourself with your armour this evening."

"Why thank you," I tell her, curtseying and smiling.

We all gather around the pianoforte where a peacock sits upon her roost. How Lady Rathburn preens is quite astonishing. She even has feathers in her hair to complete her mimicry, and they are now bouncing along with her playing.

Her voice is fine, I cannot take that away from her. And we must all flaunt whatever talents we possess. Every eye is turned towards her, including that of Lord Emsby, which is pleasing and gives me an idea.

Rapturous applause bursts out at her song's conclusion.

Stepping forwards, Miss Plimpton congratulates her before asking, "Who shall we have next? Lady Anne, would you do us the honour?"

My embarrassment must be all too evident, but at the encouragement of others, I take my place upon the stool and sing "When Love is Kind" which I am well acquainted with.

My fingers skip over the keys as my voice carries the notes to the ears of the audience.

"Has ever any songbird sounded so sweet?" Lord Emsby asks at my side once the song is over.

Has ever a man been so woolly-headed? Here I sing about denying unfaithful love, and he takes my meaning of encouraging him as a constant lover. He tries my patience.

I regain my seat, having declared Miss Compley should take her turn, for I know her singing to be angelic. Lord Emsby accompanies me, and as I cannot escape with any good grace, there he must remain.

"How wonderfully you sing, your ladyship," he tells me.

"Your lordship is too kind."

"No indeed. I have never been so captivated."

"Shall we not hear you sing?"

"I could perhaps be tempted into a duet." His accompanying grin makes the skin want to crawl from my bones.

"Very well," I whisper back.

His conversation continues in hissing whispers at my ear until we get the opportunity to sing. Not once does he mention Lord Beauvrais. He is too full of praise for me.

I begin the song of his choosing and do my best to harmonise with his barking. It pains me to discover that singing is not one of his talents either. I very much wonder if he is good at anything.

Muted applause is our reward. And a knife goes through my stomach as Lady Rathburn sings with Lord Dellingby. How finely he sings; deep and resonant. Their voices blend beautifully. My chair is become uncomfortable, forcing me to adjust my position.

Miss Plimpton is next, and a man of not unpleasant appearance accompanies her. Moderate height, brown hair and eyes which match her own, a confident poise. Neither of them are the best performers of the evening, but they carry themselves off with aplomb. I suppose this must be her Lord Meltcham; there seems to be an attachment there, and they suit each other well. If this is indeed her choice I do not wonder at it.

Lady Rosen sings alone, but beautifully. As do many other ladies and couples. But I am stuck by Emsby's side. My scented fan is put to full use as his odour wafts along with the hot air of his conversation. Papa cannot be serious in this scheme of his.

It is a relief when the carpets are rolled up and we are all to begin dancing. Of course, the first must be endured at the hands of my shadow.

"How curious, Lord Emsby. Have you noticed how Lady Rathburn glowers at me but smiles when she sees you? Whatever can she mean by it?"

"Does she?" he asks, looking about for her as we part and weave.

Reuniting, he acknowledges, "I do believe you are correct. And how charming you are not to dissemble her reason."

"Charming? Surely you do me too much credit. I am but curious."

"Of that, I have no doubt. But I would not upset your sensitivities with explanation."

He keeps looking in her direction for the rest of the dance. Even the appearance of flattery can apparently go far with the dimmer sex.

As soon as the music ends he bows away, and seeks her out, leaving me alone with my hidden smile.

"Lady Anne Frithringham, might I request the honour of the next dance?"

"Sir Reginald...I..." cannot think of an excuse, and so I must accept, "Thank you, yes."

To deny him would be improper and lead to questions I do not wish to be asked. But now I must meet with a man I hoped never to see again. His audacity in venturing here is shameful. If I were him I should have fled Society altogether. But perhaps this is how they had been successful? No girl of good breeding would ever make it publicly known what the true character is to this wolf.

"I mean you no harm," he starts.

I look at him through narrowed eyes.

"Your incredulity does you credit. I know how I must appear," he adds.

We are forced into silence as we join in a circle.

"You must believe I thought a proposal only was intended," he says when we are close enough for only each other to hear.

"You are indeed correct in your assumption. I am incredulous," I reply, fire burning from my eyes.

"I do not blame you for it. Please know I am truly sorry."

Dancing is not conducive to such discussion and we are parted again. Miss Compley is looking at me fiercely as if we were not the oldest friends and cannot know I am not encroaching on her territory. To betray her so cruelly would be the last thing I could ever wish.

"I do not know what I can do to prove my innocence."

"I do not care what you are, sir, but I would ask you leave my friend unharmed."

"Dear lady, I would harm no one."

"Your actions speak for you, sir."

We join up in a line of dancers, and scolding must be paused. My smile has not left my face this entire time, but the effort is a strain.

"I did not learn of the truth until the duel," he spits as he whispers, too close to me.

"And yet I remain unmoved."

"I was as shocked as yourself, I assure you."

"I find that difficult to comprehend. I was frighted out of my wits."

Again we part, my anger seething. Shocked as me? How can he utter such nonsense? And what does he mean by even attempting this discourse? He is highly improper and disgusting and vile and abominable and loathsome. I'd sooner dance with Lord Emsby again than remain here with him.

"Lady Anne, I am a good man. I will not have my name sullied by the actions of another."

"Then perhaps you should choose your friends with greater care."

"I was greatly deceived, to my humiliation. But if Lord Beauvrais had not succeeded in his aim, I would have," he says with much force yet still on a whisper, and with a gaze so intense that I am stunned into missing my step.

It is with no little embarrassment that I regain my place in the dance.

"You truly mean that?" I ask when opportunity permits.

"I do," he says quietly, inclining his head.

"Good God above."

The dance comes to a merciful end and he leads me to a chair.

"Lady Anne, are you quite well?" The ever-observant hostess, Miss Plimpton is upon us in an instant.

"It is perhaps a little warm."

"Come, let us step outside," she instructs, linking arms as I rise.

"You look as white as a court gown," she says once we are alone on her veranda.

"Miss Plimpton, I am continually astonished by the opposite sex."

"Sir Reginald astonishing? Lady Anne, he is the dullest bore I ever beheld."

"Really? But his friendship with Lord Felsenworth?"

"Was a recently formed one. I rather fancy it was only encouraged lately so he may be more in the presence of our fair friend Miss Compley. It is most unlike him to be so lively. But truly we can find better for you, do not look in his direction long. Let us leave him to Miss Compley."

"I see." Flabbergasting!

My vivacious friend introduces me to other men of her circle. And I am led into a dance by Lord Sudville. He appears to be of moderate height and temperament. He is the son of an earl, so merits closer inspection. His blond hair and blue eyes lend him some charm.

"Lady Anne Frithringham, charmed. I am recently arrived in London. How do you find it? Are there any entertainments your particularly recommend?" he asks as we pair up.

He does seem perhaps a little young.

"I find it varied. Artaxerxes is amusing and worthy of its fine reputation. I saw it but last evening and already find myself desiring a repeat performance."

"Then it shall go to the top of my list." His accompanying smile is warm and welcoming.

As we dance, an air of uncertainty may be detected about him. But being new to Society is daunting, as well I know, so must make allowance for him.

His conversation is hesitant but hints at a not ill-educated mind when he can find his words. I should not think him the cleverest of my acquaintance but would welcome him. Sweet is the overriding impression. Hardly a bold man, to be sure. No, I would not be sorry to know him better.

I am reunited with Lord Trunton in the next. Another blond beau. Without Lord Felsenworth's comparison, I daresay he improves. But the very recollection of that man unnerves me. And Trunton's boldness does nothing to soothe my nerves. He has a way of holding my hand too firm and of looking too long.

Lord Nordfield engages me after. I had quite forgot how handsome he is. His blue eyes make me regret the traitorous ones of Lord Felsenworth, and how I had preferred them above the kind ones now looking at me. I find myself comfortable in the presence of Lord Nordfield now, as if we had been friends for a long time.

And who should arrive but Lord Alverbury. I rather think him a little old, but he is highly diverting. His easy manners bring trickles of laughter from my lips as we make our way around the dance. He nods in the direction of another and pulls a face, indicating the sourness of the other. Spying Lady Rathburn, he holds his head high and sneers down at me in perfect imitation.

"Lord Alverbury, you are too much," I tell him, giggling despite myself.

"It is good to see you happy."

"Even at the expense of others?"

"My dear, we all live to make sport for the Ton, do we not? Watch and be watched, eh," he tells me faux conspiratorially, tapping the side of his nose.

"It is quite wicked of you to speak so." I cannot help but smile though.

"Oh, have a care," he warns before I turn to take the hand of Lord Emsby.

Just as I was finding pleasure in the evening, he arrives to mar any merriment.

"Dear Lady Anne, your smile lends you more radiance than the sun. You should do so often," he drones.

I attempt to maintain my cheer, which is boosted in timely fashion with Lord Alverbury taking my other hand. He gives is the faintest reassuring squeeze, and I know I am protected. Indeed, it is difficult not to think of him as a fond uncle when he looks at me thus. But he is not so very far from Lord Emsby's age, so that should not matter. I shall not count him entirely out of my consideration, for he is far preferable to him.

My evening flows with agreeable dancing and affable partners. And, as Miss Plimpton predicted, my options have been added to in number. Curious then that the absence of Lord Dellingby still strikes a pang in my heart.

❧ Chapter 16 ❦

My hideous court dress has been checked for fit. How that may be ascertained is quite beyond my comprehension, but it has been deemed such. To my eyes, it may have increased in distaste, but it is what must be worn; Queen Charlotte demands it.

The already heavy mantua gown is, of course, white, and fitted tightly about my bosom, from whence it cascades outwards like a spouting water fountain thanks to the large hooped skirt. Indeed, that must be the overall impression when taken in with the tall ostrich feather in my hair. The vast expanse of white is only relieved by a few pale pink roses strewn about the many ruffles. About my arms lies three entire rows of frills.

With my arms held over the gown at an awkward angle, I am expected to carry my fan and reticule whilst remaining upright. I foresee a most tiresome day yawning ahead of me.

Clément is finally done arranging my, face, jewels and dress to the specifications warranted by Queen Charlotte. And the hairdresser has secured the last feathers and pin. Glancing in the looking glass, I cannot say I am pleased with the result, but that is no fault of theirs.

Taking small steps, that being all I can manage, Mama and I make our way to the carriage. The rain has mercifully held off, so there is no roof for me to contend with. Getting in requires careful coordination however, as this dress is so wide it is a miracle it can be got in. One cannot be entirely sure Mama shall be able to fit as well, being similarly attired, of course. But she manages, much to my astonishment.

I am paraded through the streets as the carriage continues its journey towards St James's Palace. We join a long line of conveyances on Piccadilly Street as we approach amidst gunfire and trumpets. Watching a young lady clamber out of a Sedan Chair I stifle a giggle, for she is required to fold down the sides of her hoop which were sticking up, presumably so she could squeeze into the tiny space. She makes quite a comical sight.

Once my turn arrives, I make my way out of the barouche as elegantly as one can. I wonder how Mama makes it appear so easy, and hope I showed myself in a similar light.

Never before have I envied a man, but today they appear far more comfortable in their velvet suits of blue, purple or green. We are gathered closely in a ring inside the drawing room, and the air is pungent already. This many people on a warm day in such drapery is not conducive to a happy nose. Mix in the scents used to cover the foulness, such as orange water, clary sage, violet, vanilla and cinnamon, and one ends with an overpowering aroma.

Amongst the throng are some faces I recognise, including Lords Dellingby in a fine blue ensemble which becomes him, a dress sword hanging at his side. Lords Sudville and Trunton are also present and looking fine. But I cannot make my way to any of them.

Aching all over, I am forced to loiter, unable to hear a word around me. Girls are forced to squeeze between others upon being called. At least the width of my skirts keeps others at a safe distance; perhaps the only good thing to be said for it, but one I am grateful for.

The sight of others using a bourdaloue is understandable with such a long wait, but I refuse to relieve my bladder in company as I should not like to seek the queen's permission to do so. Although, if I have to wait much longer there may be no avoiding it.

At long last, my name is called. Pushing past people, I approach the queen. Kneeling on trembling knees, my forehead is kissed by Her.

"Hide your brains a little more and you shall yet find a splendid match, Lady Anne," she tells me quietly.

"Thank you, Your Majesty," I humbly reply, getting to my feet, my eyes lowered.

Slowly, I back out of the room, wondering how much the queen knows about me, and how. And then, just like that, it is all over. I consider myself presented, and Mama and I are able to return home. Once we find our carriage, of course, which is no easy task. But eventually, we do succeed in locating it and are carried home so I may sleep before the ball.

�⋙

It is a great relief to be more suitably attired this evening. My white ballgown with gold embellishments is positively feather-light and dreamy. I take a moment to savour its swishing movements as I sway side-to-side, looking at my reflection.

"Much better, is it not?" I ask.

"Far more pleasant, my lady," Clément responds with a smile, "Much more becoming, if I may say."

"You may."

"Oh, Anne, you look very well, my darling," Mama coos as she joins me.

"Thank you, Mama."

"Are you ready to come down?"

"Yes, Mama."

Taking her arm, I am led down to seek Papa's approval.

"Yes, you shall do. The prince should be appeased," he tells me, pointing at the feather laying across my hair.

Quite why one needs to appease the buffoon is beyond me. I congratulate myself on having avoided his acquaintance until now. We are very honoured by his presence, I am sure, but I am hardly courting his good opinion. But for Papa's sake, I shall be civil. Not that he ever has a good word to say about Prinny either.

Our guests arrive, and we are all quite merry as we congregate. Some of the young ladies present were also at the Drawing Room today and are in high spirits.

"Oh, you must tell me all about your day," Miss Compley squeals, holding onto my arm.

She is keen to hear every detail I pour into her ear. Her excitement is obvious, and I wonder at my lack of it. Today should have been jubilant, but it was nothing but tedium. Perhaps I see what she does not, that it is one step closer to being married off.

Pushing such thoughts aside, I smile back at my friend as she comments on the other guests.

"Felicitations, Lady Anne," Miss Plimpton offers with a curtsey upon her approach.

"Why thank you," I reply with a curtsey of my own.

"So, who are we keen to dance with this evening?"

Blushing, Miss Compley confesses, "Sir Reginald is to be my first partner."

A smile plays across my lips. Their attachment seems to grow, and having cleared his name in my estimation, I am inclined to think it a good match. At least one of us should be happy with their marriage partner.

"I am pleased for you. The Prince Regent is to be my first dance partner," I tell them, unable to keep myself from sighing.

"Lady Anne, only you could look so out of sorts at the prospect of dancing with royalty," Miss Plimpton says, laughing.

"Do I? Please forgive me. It is indeed an honour, of course."

"I am funning you, do not take me so serious. I should not take any pleasure in it either."

My hand covers my heart, and a nervous laugh escapes me. "You do confuse me so. Do tell me, is Lord Meltcham present?"

"Oh, you sly thing, you know he is, and it would be greatly amiss of him to dance with any other but myself," she says, her giggle tinkling sweetly.

A great hush descends as the Prince Regent's arrival is announced, and we all curtsey and bow as he enters. My heart sinks as I notice Beau Brummell is here also.

Papa unites me with the prince, and we lead the first dance. He is a most lively and enthusiastic partner and dressed in the most colourful dandy fashion.

Lady Rathburn looks across at me, all smiles, as she dances with Lord Emsby. It is galling how she seems to relish snatching him away from me. However, it serves my purpose, so I cannot be truly upset.

As soon as our dance is over, however, His Royal Portliness disappears into the gaming room. His propensity for drinking and gambling is the main cause of my family's wariness of him. Papa detests both, having lost a friend to the evils of gambling. This, of course, does not assist in my quest for a husband, as what modern man does not take part in both these pursuits?

Standing to one side, I breathe deeply, preparing myself for the arrival of Lord Emsby who will surely claim me for the next. It is a surprise, not a disappointment to discover he is asking another. The man really does lack manners, though. This is my ball, and he is supposed to be an admirer. Really!

"Ho ho, has a fox got into the hen house?" a voice whispers by my side.

"Lord Dellingby, I would thank you not to be so informal. And I am quite sure I do not take your meaning." I admonish, glaring out the corner of my eye briefly.

"Humble apologies, I meant no disrespect," he offers with a ridiculously elaborate bow.

My cheeks burn at his flourishes.

Lord Alverbury is now arrived, sparing me from further discomfort by drawing me into a dance. Perhaps I should not have been so snippy, but I did not appreciate Lord Dellingby's intense scrutiny of my actions, which are questionable. I was taken aback by his close observation.

"Lady Anne, might I say you look even more dazzling this evening?" Lord Alverbury asks as we begin to dance.

"Why, thank you, my lord."

"I mean it. Were I but a better man, I should not be able to resist making an offer."

"You are too kind," I say, hiding my shock at his audacity behind a soft smile.

"Come, come, there is no need for blushes. You will excuse a foolish man his admiration."

"But of course."

"And I have reason to believe it shall not be long before a proposal of marriage is made to you."

"My lord, you astonish me."

He chuckles. "Yes, yes, perhaps I do."

We are parted by the dance, but he refuses to elaborate further even once we are reunited. I rather think he enjoys being mysterious a little too much. But as I am clearly not high on Lord Emsby's list, I cannot suppose he must mean him. So, who else could it be?

It isn't for another two dances that Lord Emsby graces me with his company for a dance. He happily reminds me what a revolting creature he is, and how thankful I am that Lady Rathburn seems to be succeeding in my plan. He even makes observations about her to me. To me! Does he have no breeding whatsoever?

Dear, sweet Lord Sudville brings a smile to my face again in the very next dance. His blue eyes show nothing but merriment as we take our turn.

"I must thank you for the recommendation of Artaxerxes, Lady Anne. I was highly amused."

"I am glad to hear it. "The Soldier Tir'd" is wondrous, is it not?"

"Quite as beautiful as it is poignant. Tell me, are there any others you would tell me to attend?"

Yes, there may yet be hope for him yet.

"I regret to say I cannot. Although, I believe Mama is to take me to Drury Lane tomorrow to see a play."

He smiles his acceptance of my hint.

I am a little saddened when the music comes to an end, and we part ways. But Lord Dellingby takes his place.

"Lady Anne, my compliments on a most hideous gown today—"

"Well, I never!" My mouth gapes in a most displeasing fashion.

"Which you still looked magnificent in, I was about to say. Those court gowns do make ladies look so swollen," he adds, amusement dancing about his brown eyes.

"Oh, the presentation."

"Dear lady, you did not think I meant this beautiful gown here before me now? I am mortified." His own mouth is left agape.

Blushing, I tell him, "I am rather afraid I did."

"A thousand apologies. But perhaps if you had let me speak..?"

"I am too forthright. It is one of my many faults."

"Now, I shall not hear of that. Your faults are few and far between."

"Now now, enough nonsense. Have you news of our friend?"

"Alas, not yet. But bad news always travels faster, so we must remain hopeful."

He glances behind him, towards me, with smiling eyes as he steps away with the flow of the dance. I shoot him a gentle smile before his attention is then taken up by the next lady in line. Further down, I see Lord Emsby dancing with Lady Rathburn again. He *is* keen.

There is little to feel beyond amiability for Lord Dellingby. He seems kind enough, but he is still a little old and distant. I am much indebted to him for his heroics and discretion, but one must not be carried away by gratitude alone.

My opinion is not much improved as he seats me at the supper table. With no news of Beauvrais to acquaint me with, our conversation falls into inconsequence.

"How warm it has been of late," he states.

"Yes, it has rather. Unseasonably so," I reply with a flutter of my fan, "But it is welcome after such a severe winter."

"Indeed. It was most shockingly cold."

"Quite." I shift awkwardly in my seat, my eyes fixed on my plate.

Clearing his throat after a pause, he says, "I am sorry to have missed the Frost Fair in February.

My gaze lifts to his, my eyes widening. "Oh yes, I hear it was wondrous. How beautiful The Thames must have appeared. Swings, skittles, bookstalls, food stalls, all nestled in sparkling winter delights."

His smile must match my own. "I even heard tell of an elephant crossing below Blackfriars Bridge."

"No, surely not."

"I could scarce believe it myself, but I have heard from several sources it was indeed the case."

"How astonishing. How I wish I could have seen such a thing."

"I am sure it was the greatest spectacle ever beheld."

Well, he has stumbled across a point of interest. How enlivened he is by the vision he conjures. His eyes glisten in the light of the candles.

"How say you to me keeping an elephant in the stables of Wenston Hall, wot?" he asks, laughing.

"Lord Dellingby, you are funning me," I respond, giggling.

"Perhaps, but tell me the idea does not excite your fondness of animals. Yes, an elephant you could visit when we…" He coughs as his sentence dies on his lips, and his smiles disappear from view. "Yes, well, nonsense, as you say."

"I think I shall be content with horses."

A flash of a smile crosses his visage. "Indeed. Far more fitting, after all."

Immediately following supper, I discover Miss Plimpton on her own beside a column and hurry to her side. I have consumed too much delicious food, unconscious of what I was doing as I was absorbed in conversation. A delay must be brought about before I engage in further dancing.

"Lord Dellingby seems most attentive," she tells me, raising her brow.

I giggle a little. "Now, Miss Plimpton, do not scheme. He is pleasant, to be sure. But surely you should not unite me with an older man?"

Her brows fly higher. "Older? He is but seven years your senior. You are not so fastidious as to discount him on such grounds?"

"My dear, you do not mean to tell me he is but four and twenty?"

She laughs in earnest. "Oh you silly goose, how many years did you think he had?"

My cheeks warm. "More than that, I confess."

She looks me up and down. "Well, I suppose I can understand the reasoning. He is so subdued and stands around with a quiet air of authority."

"Indeed. I must have remembered my facts with error." I bite my lip as I try to recall all I should know about the man.

"There now. Does he not make a finer prospect now you are in possession of his age? The Marquess of Dellingby, heir to the Duke of Wenston is not beyond your consideration, I hope," she adds with a smirk.

"Very well. You, my friend, shall guide me. I shall allow you to add him to my number as is your wont."

We laugh together and regard the dancers.

"You are not without your wiles," she notes.

I gasp.

"Lady Anne, we know each other well enough not to pretend, I think. Pray, do not profess otherwise. I do not censure you for avoiding what would be a most wearisome match. See, he is dancing with Lady Rathburn even now."

"Again? Oh yes, so he is."

She pats my hand. "It is well done. She is seeking to heighten her family's name. He is looking for a handsome wife. And they are both sour enough for one another."

"You are too cynical," I say with a laugh.

"Merely observant," she replies, a knowing smile and look in her eye.

"Miss Compley seems well pleased. Really, if only you would pay such attentions to yourself as you do others you could be the happiest of us all."

"No, I cannot own that. For you shall have your Lord Meltcham. I could never match such pleasure."

"Well, in that, let us hope you are correct."

"Your papa's resolve is not waning?"

"Not enough. But I am determined."

"I should not like to ever go against you. You shall win out, I am sure of it."

"We can but pray," she says, holding my hand.

❧ Chapter 17 ❧

Amongst my callers this morning is Lord Dellingby who bounds into the room.

"Lady Anne, how good it is to see you," he says with a bow.

Crossing the room as I curtsey, he pays his compliments to Mama but turns his back to her to take my hand in his. "What a beautiful morning it is."

My fingers curl around a small piece of paper, which I conceal amongst my skirts as I pretend to smooth them out.

"It remains warm."

Mama coughs, and he takes a seat across from me.

"I bring glad tidings," he says, grinning from ear-to-ear.

My heart skips. "You do?"

He looks pointedly at my hands. "I do. Along with my sister, The Lady Isabella. She is soon to set sail into the world of matrimony and has come to town especially to tell me her news."

"Oh, felicitations."

"She is eager to make your acquaintance whilst she is here."

"Oh, I see."

Turning towards Mama, he asks, "Would it be agreeable with your plans to come to dine with us this evening? Her visit was most unexpected. I beg your forgiveness at not being able to give you more notice. But I can deny her nothing."

"Well, we would not like to disappoint a young lady before her nuptials. But nor can we disappoint our friends whom we are promised to attend the theatre with this evening," Mama tells him.

My eyes close momentarily as I try to maintain my composure. Lord and Lady Grainger can surely spare us.

"I would not have you neglect your prior engagement. Your friends are most welcome at my table also, of course."

"It really is all very sudden. I shall ask if they are agreeable and send word if we are able to attend."

Getting up, he bows. "I shall await your reply with eager anticipation, Your Grace."

Bowing to me, he bids farewell with a clipped, "Lady Anne."

As soon as he is out of the room, Mama starts, "Really, what a presumption. That we shall be available at his beck and call. Plans have been made."

"Mama, I do think he was sensible of our inconvenience. He must be exceedingly fond of his sister to even venture such a request."

"And what does she mean by running to town to inform her brother of her engagement? A letter would have served the purpose just as well. She must be a peculiar girl."

"Perhaps she is. I must confess my curiosity has been piqued by her impetuosity."

Rolling her eyes, Mama sighs. "Very well, I shall inquire as to whether the Graingers are willing to forego our outing to the theatre."

Rising from my seat, I rush to kiss her cheek. "Thank you, Mama."

"They have not agreed as yet."

"Oh, but they shall. Nobody says no to you," I tell her with a smile before leaving the room.

Glancing over my shoulder as I go, I witness a small shake of her head and a curious smile about her lips. But I am in too much of a hurry to stop in contemplation. I run up the stairs to my room and shut the door, ensuring my privacy.

Note to Lady Anne Frithringham, 29th April 1814

He is gone in safety.

That is all which is written on the scrap of paper I pull from my skirts, but it is all that is required. Tears drip from my eyes as relief washes through me. Lord Beauvrais is safe. Praise be to God in His Glory. I sink to my knees and thank His Mercy. Oh, my dear friend. May God speed you safely as you continue across the seas.

Clément surely notices me swiping away my tears as she enters to prepare me for my final portrait sitting. How am I ever to sit still today? Happiness and excitement beat within my breast with every breath.

But endure it I must. I am whisked away with no idea whether we are bound for the theatre or to Lord Dellingby's later this evening. I simply must thank him without delay. My eagerness for details consumes me as I enter the studio.

Sir Thomas tsks and murmurs the entire duration of my visit. Try as I might to obey his commands, my limbs refuse to be held still. My knee, at least, insists on bouncing. My fingers dig deep into the chair in my attempts but to no avail. That very act has Sir Thomas crying out to reposition my hands.

195

I believe it is a relief to us both when I am finally dismissed. He pushes my small likeness of Prince into my hands, as he is done with it, and almost pushes me from his presence. I do offer multiple apologies, but I am not sure he accepts them with all sincerity. I shall consider myself most fortunate if he does not add blemishes to my painting, or some subtle object of ridicule.

"Oh, Lady Anne. I had not expected you here," Lady Rathburn says with a sneer as we pass each other at the entrance.

"My business here is complete."

"I wish you pleased with the outcome."

"And I you," I tell her with a curtsey, hastening from her presence.

I am in no mood to give consequence to the vexing girl. How someone as undeserving as her succeeded in gaining an appointment is beyond me. But it is of no matter. I leap into the carriage so it may carry me home to discover my plans for the evening.

Immediately upon my return, I seek out Mama and find her in the drawing room.

She holds up her hand. "Yes, Lord and Lady Grainger assented to your contrary ways."

"I am much obliged to them," I say with a curtsey, departing her presence.

"Wait!" she calls.

But I pay no heed.

"Whatever am I to do with that girl?" I hear her plead to the empty room as I creep away.

Deciding it best to rest before this evening, I lie myself down upon my bed but remain restless. A broad smile takes up permanent residence as I think of Lord Beauvrais' escape. I cannot wait to learn the details how he accomplished it. But part of me shall remain anxious until he can get word to me that he has reached his destination. Such a long sea voyage is troubling.

But I must have fallen asleep, as Clément is waking me to dress me for dinner. In the mood for celebration, my gold silk gown has been selected. I hasten the preparations and am readied in good time.

"Mama, make haste," I whine, having gone to her side.

Her maid shoos me out of the way, causing me to scowl.

"We have time, my dear. Why, might I inquire, are you in so much haste?" Mama asks, looking at me from her looking glass.

My hand covers my middle. "I'm famished."

Mama's reflection smiles kindly. "My dear, take yourself off and eat a little something now. I'll not share a carriage with you in this state."

I obey, as truthfully I am ravenous. Not a morsel has touched my lips since breakfast.

Mama joins me at the foot of the stairs as I'm about to go in search of her again.

"Need I remind you to how to behave this evening?" she asks, her eyes narrowing.

"No, Mama. As excited as I am to meet Isabella, I shall contain myself."

"Good girl. Make us proud," she says, kissing my forehead.

It is not a long carriage ride, and we reach Lord Dellingby's London residence, or rather his father's, more quickly than I had anticipated.

"Oh, Mama, is it not a fine house?" I ask, staring at the opulent façade.

"It is pleasant enough."

I had thought Lord Dellingby would be renting a town house, but he must be using his father's abode. It is every bit as grand as Papa's. We receive a warm welcome from our host, and then a tall, blonde, elegant lady emerges. Her hair is a lot lighter than that of her brother and her eyes are blue, in contrast to his brown, but there is a similarity in the shape of their faces and mannerisms.

"Henry, you did not inform me of our guests' arrival," she admonishes with a smile.

"They are only just arrived," he says, rolling his eyes before turning to us. "Your Grace, Lady Anne, allow me to introduce my sister, The Lady Isabella Gildcrest."

"It is a pleasure to meet you," I tell her, performing a deep curtsey as Mama does likewise.

"I am most pleased to meet you too, Lady Anne. Your Grace," she returns with a similar dip.

"We are going to be the best of friends, are we not?"

"I do hope so."

"You have not visited before, I believe?"

"No, I have not had the honour."

"Come, let me show you then. Henry, do make sure the Duchess of Hesford is made comfortable."

"But of course," he replies with a bow, offering Mama his arm.

Lady Isabella leads me through the hall and down to the morning room.

"We haven't long, but my brother wished me to convey a message to you. He says that your friend is aboard a ship as intended. I must say I haven't a clue what he means. It's all quite mysterious. But he assures me you will understand."

"Oh yes, I do, and please tell him how grateful I am. I received his note."

"Secret notes too? Need I be concerned?"

"Not at all, I assure you. A mutual friend is bound for foreign lands, but there was some question over his safe passage. Your brother was good enough to make enquiries."

"Is that all? I must say that is rather disappointing. I had begun to wonder if you were communicating in code. However, I am glad your friend is well."

She shows me a few other rooms before leading me back to join Mama as we wait for the other guests.

"We are not too early, I hope?" I apologise to the brother and sister alike.

"Not at all," Lord Dellingby dismisses with a wave of his hand.

It seems I was not the only eager member of the party, as the other guests soon start to arrive. Lord and Lady Grainger, along with Lady Charlotte, are of course amongst them. As are Lord Alverbury, and surprisingly, Lord Sudville. I was not aware he was well acquainted with Lord Dellingby.

Despite being an impromptu dinner, there are a good number of guests present, and we are soon seated for our meal. My place is to the left of Lord Dellingby, who sits at the head of the table. His sister is to the right of him, opposite me.

Lord Alverbury is to my immediate left, whilst Mama and the Graingers are farther down, with Lord Sudville as companion. There is a mildly bitter taste in my mouth as I notice this seating arrangement. It is a pity to be so far away from him and to lose the opportunity of knowing him better. And surely Mama is worthy of a seat nearer our host?

However, I must be satisfied with Lady Isabella, who turns out to be a delightful wit. She is but twenty years of age but has much wisdom as well as vivacity. It is perhaps to the detriment of my own vanity, but I am glad she is betrothed, for she would command the attention of all about her in the rooms of the Ton.

Over soup, I learn that Lady Isabella is to marry a lord who is situated but two hours distance from her family home. It dawns on me, that were I to marry her brother, we would be neighbours, and that this is a happy thought indeed.

Even Lord Alverbury is captivated and makes no improper remarks. He behaves in a most gentleman-like manner. Lord Dellingby smiles as he allows his sister to entertain us, seemingly content to observe, only supplying rare comments where absolutely required.

Perhaps if I had a sister like Lady Isabella, I should be stunned into silence too. My brow furrows as thoughts of my own sister hasten to my mind, and I feel our separation greatly. She is a little exuberant at times, but I do love her so, and it has been weeks since we were last together. It feels even longer still, for so much has happened in such a short span of time.

"Lady Anne, is everything to your taste?" Lord Dellingby inquires.

With a delicate 'ahem' I school my features. "Yes, I thank you. In fact, I was wondering how you managed to produce such a feast within a day."

His returning chuckle is deep and rolls like thunder. "You'd be surprised what resources a fine chef has up their sleeve when pressed," he tells me with a wink.

"Well, they have certainly outdone themselves. This fowl and the fruit tart are delicious."

"Thank you. Seeing you so content gives me great pleasure." The light catches his hazel eyes as he smiles, causing a fluttering within my breast.

Sipping my wine, I inwardly chastise myself. He is being a good host, entertaining his sister and updating me on the good news. Talk of fluttering only led me to near ruin before. My fingers grip the glass stem a little tighter in my effort to control my emotions. Of course, this is not love. That, as has been proven, is a foolish notion.

Glancing down the table, Lord Dellingby leans towards me, and in hushed tones asks, "Should you like to hear more of our travelling friend?"

I cast my eyes towards Lord Alverbury and Lady Isabella who are in conversation, before replying, "Well, I should like to be made aware of the facts appertaining to that adventure. However —"

He smiles and indicates with his hand as he assures me, "I see what you are thinking. But know that we are amongst friends here. And there is nothing which may harm him now. Have no fear."

"In which case, please do tell."

Lord Dellingby grins. "Well, what do you think my agents should find? But our most amiable friend in an ale house, laughing and making merry with the very men sent to find him out?"

I cannot help but gasp. This leads to another of Lord Dellingby's rumbling chuckles.

"'Tis true. Upon my honour. That fiend had indeed sent his men after our friend. Such a scandalous act on his part. But upon discovery, he turned them to his favour with not a fist thrown. Their master is such a poor payer that Beau…" He stops himself and lowers his voice. "Beauvrais bought them a meal and ale and they were so taken with his tale they were seen boarding the ship along with him, all seeking a better life in new lands."

"How like him," I declare with a small chuckle of my own.

Lord Alverbury's accompanying laugh is raucous and draws attention to us.

Lady Isabella and I are giggling despite our attempts to stifle them.

"Like who?" Lord Grainger asks.

"Oh, I was recounting a tale of the courageous Marquess of Wellington," Lord Dellingby says in a happy act of deceit.

He is drawn to elaborate on the tale, which he manages to convey without hesitation. The whole table is laughing by the time he is done with the telling, and I am left wondering at the extraordinary ease with which he accomplished it.

Following our sumptuous meal, Lady Isabella rises and leads we ladies to the drawing room. She begins to brew the tea before settling down to a game of cards.

"What a fine room you have here," Lady Charlotte comments.

"Why, thank you. Our Mama had it decorated as you see, before…Well, she had a fine eye."

"The cream walls and gilding are so elegant."

"You should see the drawing room at home. It has a fine aspect."

"I do wish I could see it. Regrettably, it is unlikely I shall ever travel so far."

"It is quite a distance, to be sure."

"If it is not an impertinence, I could not help but wonder at your long journey here," I venture.

She places her hand over mine as she leans in. "To own the truth, Papa has the house in uproar preparing for the wedding, and I simply had to remove myself from there."

"You are to be married from home then?"

"Yes, Papa has obtained a special license. But I begin to regret it. If only Mama were…But it cannot be helped. Papa is doing his best but refuses my assistance. It is not as if it is any great effort. But he is having a room decorated, and a new wardrobe has been ordered for me. So, here I am, on a visit with my brother who has been gone too long from us."

"Has he not recently arrived?"

"Oh my dear, were you in ignorance? He has been in town these two years past."

"Oh?"

"He simply couldn't bear…But perhaps on this, it is best to be silent."

"I would not wish to pry."

"But now I have worried you. It is no sinister reason. Mama passed suddenly, you see, and he felt the loss keenly. We all did. But he found he could not remain in the house with so many reminders, so removed here. I had hoped to persuade him to return with me, but..."

"Surely he will wish to see you married?"

"Perhaps, if he can be torn from the amusements of town," she says, smiling.

"And town has so many delights. I have never been so entertained," Lady Charlotte interjects.

My eyes roll, but I carry the conversation regardless. Speaking about their mother was seemingly difficult for Lady Isabella, so a change of topic must surely be a welcome distraction. My own heart is heavy at the thought of Lord Dellingby leaving London, however. My discourse is therefore not so eloquent as I would prefer.

Mercifully, the men enter the room just as Lady Charlotte begins talking of gowns and lace. From Lady Isabella's deep exhalation of breath, I suspect I am not alone in this relief.

"Come, I shall accompany you in a song," she tells me, stretching out her hand as she rises.

"Please do not make me sing first."

"Would you disappoint my anticipation? I have heard you have a fine voice and insist upon hearing it."

"If you insist, Lady Isabella."

Once all are gathered, I sing, as requested "Tho' You Think By This To Vex me". The applause I receive brings blushes to my cheeks as I meekly seek out a seat so as to watch Lord Dellingby. With Lady Isabella at the pianoforte, he sings "The Joys of the Country". Lady Isabella plays superbly, and her brother sings beautifully.

Before giving up command of the instrument, Lady Isabella plays and sings "The Sapling Oak Lost", and I am sure we are all thrown into silent veneration by her angelic tones. Truly so beautiful that moisture gathers in my eyes.

Lady Charlotte insists on being next, and sings "Black Eyed Susan". A lesser contrast could scarce withstand the comparison, and she carries the song well.

After several more players, I am encouraged to take my turn at the pianoforte with Lord Dellingby in accompaniment for a duet. How my heart quickens as his deep timbre travels through me as my fingers strike the chords. My voice flies from me, clearer than ever, joining with his in blessed harmony.

I am all atremble as we end the piece, and it is necessary for me to draw a deep breath before I take his hand to escort me back to my chair. My knees seem made of jelly all of a sudden, and it is a great relief to reach my destination without incident.

It is with great difficulty that I push away any hopes I may harbour for Lord Dellingby. For Lord Emsby is not yet fully promised elsewhere, so remains a very real danger to my happiness. The thought drowns all and any flutterings as surely as a jug of cold water.

Lord Alverbury sings a wonderful rendition of "Did You Not Hear My Lady", which captures the attention of all. He too has a fine voice, singing with such depth of feeling as to puzzle me. Surely, he has experienced and lost love. So melancholy he seems at its completion. I signal him with my fan to come join us.

"Lord Alverbury, I must compliment you on your superior singing."

"Why, I thank you, but pray, there is no need for flattery."

"Would you have me declare a falsehood? For indeed, I am in earnest and would not say such things if I did not mean them."

"Forgive my gruff response, Lady Anne. It was not of your making. Pray excuse me, I seem to have worked up a thirst," he declares, bowing before walking to the far side of the room to pour himself a drink.

My pity is only increased upon witnessing this sight. Poor Lord Alverbury. What has befallen him to affect him so? He has been nothing but all kindness to me. To think of any person injuring so good a man pains me deeply.

"Do not concern yourself, Lady Anne. He will be well. Lord Alverbury occasionally has a touch of the melancholies, but they always clear," Lord Dellingby whispers at my side.

"But do you know the cause? Forgive me. I do not seek a reply. My concern makes me forget myself."

"I own I do, but it is not within my power to relieve your curiosity, as much as it pains me to admit it. I must ask you to trust this will pass, and you shall soon recognise Lord Alverbury for himself again. The fault is mine. I should not have invited him this evening."

Lord Sudville strikes up a merry ditty, demanding my amused attention. The rest of the evening passes in a blur of gaiety.

❧ Chapter 18 ❧

The appearance of Lord Dellingby this morning comes as no surprise, but his manner is somewhat agitated. Mama is called away from us, and we are left alone in a rare moment of solitude.

Lord Dellingby fidgets in his seat, apparently nervous of being put in this predicament. He rises as if to leave. But no, he stops in front of me, having taken a turn about the room.

"Lady Anne, I declare I know not where to begin. You are sensible, I think, of the regard I have for you. Last evening only increased my admiration. I cannot rest…must not remain silent any longer on the subject. I expect sanction from your good father, and once met with his recommendation, I hope you will see the merits of my case. You are too good to give me false hope. Lady Anne, will you consent to be my wife?"

Stunned! My breath is stuck fast in my breast. Did I hear correctly? Is Lord Dellingby indeed making a proposal of marriage? Ice fills my body. I am able to make neither sound nor movement. What shall Papa say? Would he deny him? Does he not intend me for Lord Emsby? He has declared it to be so. But is this man acceptable?

I must admit to myself that he has caught my interest. He is moderately handsome, is of a good family, and has proven himself noble. Is this not in accordance with the hopes I had upon my arrival?

What stays my reply? The yes forms on my lips but makes no sound.

"Lady Anne, I had not supposed you to be cruel. I must demand an answer. If it is to be a rejection, for heaven's sake speak it now, and I shall say no more on the subject. I had not thought to cause offence with my proposition."

Indeed, I must tell him something. But what? Will Papa admit this man when he has urged me upon another? He is clearly the better of the two in my own estimation, but what of his? I cannot go wholly against his will.

"I thank you, Lord Dellingby, for your proposal," I stammer.

"My good Lady, I beseech you for a favourable reply. You must see what a good match we should make."

"I do."

"So why do you not accept at once?"

"Pray forgive me. I was surprised. This is so unexpected."

"Unexpected? Surely you were not in ignorance of my intentions?"

"Perhaps not entirely. But it is so sudden."

"If convention permitted, I should have asked upon first meeting with you."

It is a good thing I remained sitting, as I fear I should swoon this very moment. Can people fall in love in such a manner? Is that what this is? Or perhaps a passing infatuation? If I accept now, I take this man's hand for eternity. What if he comes to regret his rash behaviour? What if I do?

But I am become foolish, carried away with romantic notions. Surely, we all take the same chance upon entering the marriage state? Who is to know our partner's failings in advance? Lord Dellingby stands before me as a fine prospect. His rank alone should speak highly in his favour.

"Yes."

"I beg pardon, do you truly accept me as your husband, Lady Anne?"

"I do, I do accept," I tell him around a lump in my throat.

"You do? Oh, Lady Anne, you make me the happiest of men. Will you not embrace me?"

I fly into his outstretched arms which prove reassuringly firm. A warm, safe feeling envelops me, and I know deep in my heart that this is the right decision. I have made my choice. Let Papa now see sense. A tear trickles down my cheek as I look up into fine brown eyes.

"But what is this? You do not regret accepting me already, surely?" he asks, wiping away the salty droplet with his thumb.

"No, no. But Papa is yet to give his blessing."

Holding me close, he kisses the top of my head. "Is that all? He can hold no objection. Who would deny the first son of a duke? Come, do not give way to such thoughts. I will go to him directly."

Clasping my hands in his, he brings them to his lips. "I shall not be long from you, my dear."

As soon as he has left my presence I sink back into the chair. Fumbling, I locate my fan and work it about my face. I can scarce believe it. A proposal of marriage? From Lord Dellingby?

He has shown me kindness, but did not that very act of chivalry not deter him? He was absent afterwards. But he has since danced with me. I did not observe any great affection. In fact, he has often teased me. And at other times has seemed so quiet as to be barely perceptible. He did extend the sudden invitation to dinner, which showed some regard. But to this extent?

Now he declares he is in love with me? Can it be true? And do I return those feelings? I had convinced myself merely grateful at his discretion and valour.

Yet had I not suffered disappointment at the possibility of his possible departure? Did I not feel the loss of his presence when he did not attend Miss Plimpton's ball? Surely this does not constitute love, however. I should feel similar loss at the absence of any friend, such as Miss Compley.

And why do I think of love at all? It never formed any part of my plans. Whether he or I feel it is neither here nor there. I am merely doing my duty. Perhaps he is too, and merely believes I need to hear such professions and sought merely to soothe my sensibilities.

"He has gone to your papa," Mama announces quietly as she enters.

"Yes, he said as much," I murmur, in a stupor.

"You look as if you have had a fright. Did he displease you?"

"No, I am not displeased, Mama. I think I am very much pleased."

"But you are not sure?"

"Oh Mama, I am all confusion."

"Forbes, Lady Anne requires refreshment," she calls out.

"Very good, Your Grace," he acknowledges from the door.

He must have entered along with her. I am not sensible of anything. Perhaps I should struggle to supply my own name if questioned now. Oh, what a to-do.

Forbes holds out a glass of Madeira for me, which I sip with fervour. Its warmth trickles down my throat and swells my breast. Taking a deep breath, I let the ruby liquid revive my senses.

"Mama, will…will Papa agree…do you think?"

"I have no doubt of it. Is that what has brought this state about?"

"I do not rightly know."

"Come now, finish your wine. There is no need for all this. Was not the purpose of your coming to London to bring about a proposal or marriage?"

"Why, yes."

"And therefore, have you not succeeded as the good girl we know you to be?"

"Yes, Mama."

"Well then, there is no cause to be gooseish."

"But what of Lord Emsby?" I cry.

"You do not mean to tell me you prefer his company?" she asks, leaning back with widened eyes.

"No no, of course I do not. Only Papa —"

"Papa will accept Lord Dellingby. He is a superior match in every sense. You need not concern yourself with such matters. You will marry Lord Dellingby, mark my words. Let me seek your Papa now to see how they fare."

Once more I am left alone as Mama departs my presence. However, curiosity overcomes me, and I creep out to the hallway after her to see if I can make out what is keeping everyone.

Hearing Mama's voice coming from Papa's study I tiptoe over, and to my shame, listen at the door which is not fully closed.

"My dear, you must allow it has all worked out for the best," Papa is saying in an exasperated tone.

"I will concede it has, but I state again my displeasure at my part in it. You should not have ill-used me so."

"Ill-used? Have a care, madam. You infer wrong-doing. Did I not tell you she would be thrown into accepting Lord Dellingby?"

"Indeed you did, but—"

"And has our daughter, or has she not, just accepted him?"

I stifle a gasp with my hand over my mouth.

"In a most under-handed fashion. Duke, you did not see her distress. All she could think of was that she may be going against your wishes. Her sense of duty has been too heavy a burden. And I am inclined to think it was unnecessary. Had you told her to marry Lord Dellingby outright she would have obeyed."

"Would she, by Jove? Tell me, madam, is she betrothed to Lord Emsby at this moment? I tell you she is not."

"Do not remind me."

"Would you risk Lord Dellingby's name being exchanged with his? No, this was the best way to bring it about with all certainty. I would not risk such a great alliance on her whims…"

I wish to hear no more. My own papa has duped me into accepting the man he intended from the start. How could he?

212

Turning on my heel I notice Forbes approaching, tray in hand. He raises his brow at me and forms a silent 'oh' of astonishment, before shaking his head. His intention, I am sure is to be jovial, but I am in no humour to receive such boldness. Glaring, I hold my finger to my lips, cautioning him to remain silent, and stomp off.

Without thought, I march out of doors and through the garden, beyond sight or earshot of the house. Concealing myself behind a tree, I let out a terrible scream of anguish.

"How could he? How could he?" I yell.

Still, my anger is not assuaged. Spying a stick on the ground I pick it up and start hitting the tree with it.

"Odious, deceitful man. Argh! Unfit to call himself father. Vile deception. Abhorrent behaviour. Utter baseness. Detestable. Deplorable. Argh!" With each exclamation, the tree receives another blow from the weapon in my hand.

"Oh, I say, in what way has this tree offended you?" Lord Dellingby asks, all grins.

"And you. You! I suppose you were in on this."

"I am at quite a loss as to your meaning. But whatever offence has been caused have no fear, I shall defend your honour," he declares dramatically, seeking a stick of his own.

"Take that, and that, you cad. Down with you, bounder," he declares with each flourish of his 'sword'.

I cannot help but laugh at him. "Lord Dellingby, you really are quite ludicrous, you know."

Stopping the tree beating immediately, he turns to me. "Ah, but you are laughing. That is better. Although, you are really quite charming when angry. I could not find you in the house once I'd taken a moment alone following my conversation with your father. Forbes suggested I seek you out here. Little did I expect to discover you thus detained."

"Lord Dellingby, I warn you my temper may yet fly. Did you know of Papa's scheme?"

"And which scheme might that be?" he asks, his brow furrowing.

"The...well...oh, I cannot explain it if you are indeed in ignorance. It is too shameful. Please, I beg your honesty. Pray forgive my bluntness, but were you in earnest when you declared your love for me?"

He scratches his head, smirking. "I do not recall an open declaration of love having been made."

With an unladylike grunt, I begin to walk away from him, throwing my hands up in the air. However, he catches hold of one hand on its downfall and forces me to a stop.

"I could not resist. Do forgive me."

He pulls, drawing me close. Grinning like a fool, and looking me direct in the eyes, he tells me, "Yes, I love you, if you insist upon hearing it openly declared."

"Oh!"

"But to respond to your earlier question, I suppose you must be referring to your having been promised to me. But surely you were not held in ignorance of the fact?"

"I assure you I was entirely oblivious until moments ago."

"How frightful. I had not conceived of this even being a possibility. You put me quite ill at ease."

"And just how long ago was this promise made?"

"I believe there were some vague allusions to it several years ago, but I myself was only recently made aware."

My stomach tightens, as does my jaw. Such long formed plans, and to not have informed me. This is worse than I had imagined. This entire come out has been a charade. Really, to make me go to all this effort; what can be the reasoning?

"Lady Anne, you are shocked, I see. But I would have you know that my offer was made in earnest. As much as I respect and honour my father, I could not enter into marriage so lightly. I insisted upon drawing my own conclusions as to your character before venturing any such endeavour."

"You made quite a study of it, I'm sure."

"I confess I did. It is no longer surprising your attention was so diverted. But I cannot regret even that, for I was better able to observe your disposition from afar."

"And how did you find me?"

"Lady Anne, if you will have me speak plainly, I find you the most admirable woman of my acquaintance. From the first, you impressed me with your rectitude, grace and wit."

I blush to hear such praise, although I remain irked at such under-handed treatment.

He continues, "With this news being so recent, perhaps you need time to consider your own feelings. But it is my hope that you will be happy with your choice. Indeed, I am flattered that you entered into this agreement with no apparent need of encouragement. Perhaps, in time, you could grow to love me with such a promising start as this?"

My eyes turn towards the ground. I had held this man in high esteem and had accepted his offer in all good faith. His charm had won me over. But knowing he was pressed into this arrangement is a heavy blow.

Looking up through lowered lashes, I ask, "You truly acted under your own guidance and not merely from family obligation?"

Before I know what he is about his lips are upon mine, claiming my mouth with an alarming force. Recovering from the initial shock, I discover the pleasant sensations coursing through me at his brazen ministrations. A different kind of fire lights up in my belly. My mouth copies his, and I am lost to his kiss. His hand travels to my waist and I fear I may combust entirely.

But he pulls away from me with an abruptness which leaves me lonely and cold. The back of his fist is at his mouth, making me concerned he is angered. Did I err? Closing his eyes, he hisses out a long breath.

"Forgive me, Lady Anne. I do not know what came over me. I acted without propriety, and humbly beg your pardon."

A smile creeps across my cheeks. "Lord Dellingby, we shall soon be man and wife, if you will still have me. There is nothing to forgive."

"If I will still have you? What nonsense do you speak of now? Do my actions not speak for themselves?"

I giggle. "Well, perhaps they do. But having seen me a moment before…do you not worry for my state of mind?"

"Should I?"

"Well, no. But it is not dignified. Indeed, one could be forgiven for thinking my mind was quite lost. There is no excuse for my behaviour."

His grin is broad, and his eyes are alight with mirth. "My dear, if you may forgive me for what must seem like duplicity to you, I am quite certain I may forgive a little outburst of vexation. I was in earnest when I told you that you are charming when angry. Although I am heartily sorry you should have cause to be so, of course. And greater still is my sorrow for having formed any part of your distress."

My teeth worry my bottom lip. Looking up at him, I say, "I am grateful to you for your present candour. I suppose it is of no consequence how it was brought about, so long as we are both content with the outcome."

His response is to quickly meet our lips together. I would seek a kiss like the former, but he is reticent and pulls his head away immediately.

"Shall we return to the house before we are missed and cause a scandal?" he asks, returning a stray curl to its rightful place upon my temple.

We walk together, hand-in-hand, up the lawn, and into the morning room.

"Ah, there you both are. Felicitations, Lord Dellingby. You are fortunate in your choice of bride. I trust we shall see you in the coming days as the articles are drawn up," Mama tells him.

"Indeed. Your Grace, Lady Anne, I bid you both adieu," he says with a bow, taking his cue to leave.

Once he is out of the room, Mama turns to me. "Now, Anne, you are not yet married. There are rules and behaviours still to adhere to. Go right your attire before your father sees you."

My hand goes to my hair, and I hastily exit the room and seek Clément. Glancing in the looking glass, I see my exertions with the stick have dislodged my coiffure and cap. What must Mama think of me? I gasp at what she may have construed. But then blush as I realise her fears may be grounded.

Clément works swiftly and pins my locks back in place within minutes. As I descend the stairs, I see Forbes making his way up.

"Ah, there you are, m'lady. Your father wishes to speak with you in his study."

"Thank you, Forbes."

Not entirely sure of my readiness to forgive the deception despite the happy outcome, I breathe deeply before knocking on the large mahogany door.

"Enter," Papa enters in his deep, commanding voice.

Shoulders back, head held high, I enter my papa's domain, dipping a curtsey from in front of his desk.

"You sent for me, Papa?"

"Indeed I did. I shall not sport with your intelligence. Nor shall I waste my breath. Let us understand one another. Lord Dellingby has made an offer of marriage which you have accepted."

I bow my head in confirmation, holding my tongue.

"And to this union I have offered my blessing."

"Thank you, Papa," I tell him, hiding my resentment.

He states all this matter-of-factly as if it were a surprise and he had not orchestrated the entire affair. Inwardly, my blood boils. Outwardly, I must maintain my display of respect, else risk the birch. If only I could say all that is within me that wishes to be heard, bursting to find freedom, then he should be surprised.

"We have agreed on an August wedding so you may be married from home upon completion of The Season. Lord Dellingby has graciously suggested you enjoy your remaining time in London before your union. But I caution you there are conditions upon this. You may stand up with other men, but only in his presence. You are not to attend parties where he is absent."

"Lord Dellingby said that?" The question is out before I can stop it.

"As a matter of fact, it is my stipulation, but whomsoever commands it, you shall obey. Are we understood?"

"Of course, Papa," I agree, blushing and staring at the floor.

"Your behaviour of late alarms me, Anne. It is astonishing so good a man is prepared to take you on. I had expected better of you. I do expect better of you. Should you so much as step one foot out of line over the coming months you shall be sent home without delay to await your nuptials in solitude. You shall not disgrace us or your intended partner."

Such language! Have I not tried my utmost to maintain my dignity, to be all that is expected of me? Is it my fault if others made attempts to the contrary? I am sorry for questioning him just now, but it was unintentionally done.

It is not the first time he has brought such scrutiny to my conduct either. It is most unfair. My anger at his own behaviour mixes with my indignation at thus being falsely accused. My lip trembles and tears threaten to spill.

Keeping my gaze directed to the floor in the hopes of avoiding him observing all the displays working about my countenance, I reply with a tremor, "I humbly beg your pardon, Papa."

"Very well, be off with you."

Anxious to depart, I hurriedly curtsey and scurry away. The moment my foot falls beyond the threshold, my tears break their boundaries and trickle down my cheeks. Forbes is in the hall but is so good as to deflect his gaze as I march past, once more seeking refuge in the garden. I am in need of air and a place to cry out, away from the attentions of the household.

Why am I forever at fault? Papa is not aware of all which transpired that night in Vauxhall Gardens. So, what does he accuse me of? Is he angry I avoided matrimony with Lord Emsby? No, he cannot be, for I heard him state otherwise himself. He knew all along I would do so. He intended Lord Dellingby for me. So, I have acted according to his wishes.

He, on the other hand, has duped me and chastises me when he himself should seek forgiveness. It is he who has acted most underhandedly. He who has deceived me, issued unreasonable commands knowing I would be not only upset but would find it impossible to obey.

All the while, I have held my head high, danced with the partners I should, smiled neither too much nor too little, performed and posed and paraded and... I have done it all with decorum and not one word of complaint to any other person.

Tears are rolling big and fat now, blurring my vision. Blinking, I see the discarded stick on the ground and pick it up with the intention of beating out my frustration. But as I hold it aloft, visions of Lord Dellingby spring to my mind and a smile tickles my lips. Sighing a large outward breath, my shoulders slump, all anger leaving my frame in an instant.

What should I care? In a matter of months, I shall no longer reside under my papa's roof. I pray that my marriage partner remains in good humour once we are committed under the eyes of God. There is no real cause for doubt. He has shown kindness, defended my honour and has sought my happiness when it was lost to me. Oh Lor', he has even seen me at my most ridiculous and joined in. It is more than most can boast upon entering the marriage state.

But he may have defects as yet unseen. For had I not thought Lord Felsenworth beyond reproach, and was I not deceived there? What if having seen me in such a sorry state he sees fit to rein me in, and chastise me like my papa? There is nothing for it, but to let things play out as they will. For better or for worse, the choice is now made.

❧ Chapter 19 ❧

Today is May Day, and as I wander the garden before breakfast, a heaviness weighs upon my heart. I picture the happy scenes which are surely happening in the village at home today; the Jack-in-the-Green leading the parade, along with the king and queen of May, chimney sweeps, jesters and musicians, all proceeding towards the maypole. Such gaiety and dancing to enliven even the meanest of spirits.

But alas, here I am alone. We expect the arrival of Lord Dellingby to continue negotiations. One cannot help but wonder at what price I am won. Such matters, I am told, are beyond my concern. Hopefully, Lord Dellingby shall be suitably recompensed for obtaining such a troublesome burden as me.

All that is left is for me to wait patiently, to discover whether he shall wish to meet with me after he has visited with Papa. He may well choose not to do so, as is his right. For what am I to proceedings? I am but a mere prize to be awarded at the end of it all; a shiny rosette bedecked with ribbons.

Silence is, of course, observed as we consume our morning repast. All eyes are upon the table and food. In my head, I attempt to calculate how many such meals are left to be endured. It must number about one hundred. At first, this is a daunting number, but upon reflection, it is bearable. With an end in sight, I think I shall be able to withstand a great deal.

But what then shall be my fate? Shall I ever again be as happy as I was in my childhood years? A sigh escapes as I recollect my brother George along with Lord Beauvrais. I do hope his voyage is progressing well. It shall be an eternity before I may receive word from his own pen.

Lor', how dull I am this morning. I must seek some distraction by means of employment. Once free of the confines of the breakfast room, I find my workbox in the morning room and take up the pocket handkerchief I have been embroidering. I had intended it for Papa, but I am now convinced he is undeserving, so perhaps I shall make a gift of it to Lord Dellingby. Yes, that is the thing. It may show I am honour bound to be a good, dutiful wife.

Carried away in stitching the gold thread of the oak leaves, time passes unchecked. My full attention is poured into every movement of my needle.

"Lord Dellingby awaits you in the drawing room along with Her Grace," Forbes informs me.

"Thank you. I shall come directly," I reply with a start.

Surely he cannot have spoken with Papa yet? How long have I been at my work? Burning with curiosity, I hasten to the drawing room.

Lord Dellingby is standing, and bows. "Lady Anne, forgive the intrusion. Lady Isabella insisted upon accompanying me. She is yet in the carriage, where she shall be comfortable if her visit should be inconvenient. I cautioned her not to expect admittance when she was so unexpected. I blush to make the request, but would her company be favourable?"

"My lord, she shall be shown in at once. Of course I am delighted to receive your sister. There is no cause for concern," I tell him.

"Your ladyship is too kind. Now, with your permission, I shall fetch her before going to your esteemed father."

I curtsey my assent, and off he goes. Mama is looking at me from her chair, with a look I take to be of approval.

"Lady Isabella," Forbes announces.

"Oh, my dear, Lady Anne. I thank you for allowing me to visit in person. I simply had to offer my congratulations as soon as may be. Of course, I knew how it would be as soon as I saw the two of you together. Perhaps I had not expected the news quite so soon. But I am so delighted. Come, let me embrace my sister."

I find myself wrapped up in the excited lady's arms, who then kisses my cheek. A look of horror passes her features as soon as we part.

Turning to Mama, she curtseys. "Oh, Your Grace. Do pardon me. I meant no slight upon your own excellent person. Please allow for my youthful exuberance in gaining a sister in your good daughter. How do you do?"

Mama bows her head, and I see a momentary smirk pass across her countenance. "You are forgiven on this occasion, Lady Isabella, for the occasion is most joyous."

"It is, it is. Tell me, Lady Anne, has it been yet settled where you shall reside? Do please tell me Wenston Hall shall be your marital home. My own nuptials shall be all the merrier knowing I shall have such neighbours as you and my brother. I do miss him so."

"It grieves me to admit I do not yet know where we shall settle."

"Shall you take tea, Lady Isabella?" Mama asks, sparing me from further embarrassment.

"I thank you, Your Grace, that would be most pleasant."

I draw her towards the chairs, so we may sit. And Mama rings the bell for tea.

"How long do you remain in London?" I ask my visitor.

"To my regret, not long at all. My brother fears I may have given the impression I intend to cry off, so is to accompany me back home by next week end."

"Oh, that is a pity."

"Bordering on cruelty, if you ask me. I have never been to London and am not likely to return soon. But there it is."

"You must simply make the most of the time you do have. Lady Anne and I are for the theatre tomorrow evening. If your brother permits, should you like to accompany us in our box?" Mama asks.

"Oh, how gracious of you. I would be overjoyed to be in your company, thank you. Henry can hold no objection, I am sure."

I suppress a giggle. She has referred to her brother by his first name within my presence several times now, and it is both alarming and wondrous to my ears. Henry is a fine name and suits him well. It is suggestive of a strong, heroic ruler. May he also be a kind one.

Mama thankfully distracts and calms Lady Isabella in equal measure by asking after her own upcoming nuptials and home arrangements. I note that our guest soon changes the topic of discussion, however, and brings us back about to the amusements in London.

Lord Dellingby re-joins us as we are finishing our tea.

"Lord Dellingby, will you take a cup?" Mama offers.

"I thank you, no. But, with your permission, if we are quick, we may yet make the May Day celebrations outside Bandaville House, if you are all so inclined?"

"What generosity. Mama, please may we go?" I ask, all anticipation.

"I see no objection."

"Thank you, Mama. Oh, but I must go and dress."

"Time is pressing, I fear, Lady Anne. And you look most charming as you are. My landau is outside, so we need not wait for your horses to be readied."

Caught up in his urgency, we four depart immediately. And just as well, for once out in the streets, we are slowed by a great number of carriages and carts. A great many ribbons adorn the horses of the decorated stagecoaches we pass.

Lord Dellingby's knee will not remain still the entire journey, and there is much wringing of his gloves. I begin to wonder at the excitable nature displayed at both brother and sister.

We arrive in time to see the greatest spectacle. Many couples of chimney-sweeps and their ladies are dancing on the lawn, whilst others are partaking of the feast laid out by the lady of the house. Pyramids of tankards are arranged about, and much laughter rings out along with song. More than one Jack-in-the-Green is bustling amidst the happy throng of spectators. It exceeds even my longed-for celebrations of home.

Other members of the nobility are present, as well as the poorer people of the area. My feet itch to join the exuberant dances, although it would not be proper, so they must be content with tapping on the carriage floor to the beat of the drums.

Lady Isabella is equally as enthralled as I. Catching each other's eye, we laugh and clap our hands, quite forgetting ourselves. Mama fails to cough and even seems to be smiling herself.

"Oh, isn't it the very picture of joy?" Lady Isabella asks.

"I do not think I have ever seen such a merry party."

"Their frivolity is infectious, is it not?" Lord Dellingby enquires.

"Indeed it is. It must surely be impossible for anyone not to be put in good humour upon seeing such a sight."

We linger a while, spectators of the charming revelry. The musicians are enchanting and seem to invade my person with their string, drum and woodwind tones. I begin to fidget as my body becomes increasingly dissatisfied with being denied the dance.

"We are not far from Berkeley Square here, what say you to some ices at Gunter's?"

"Oh yes, let's," his sister pleads.

Unwilling to deny us such pleasures, Mama nods her agreement, another hint of a smile lurking at the corners of her mouth.

My heart leaps into my mouth as a waiter crosses the busy road, careless in his eagerness to serve. However, he manages to bring us our ices without harm. Lord Dellingby leans against the railings, the sunlight is dappled as it shines onto him through the branches of the overhanging trees.

We ladies remain seated, enjoying the refreshments immensely. Mama selected a jasmine flavour, Lady Isabella elderflower, whilst I opted for violet. I'm unsure of Lord Dellingby's choice, but his closed eyes and deep sigh suggest he likes it very much.

The weather is perhaps a little cool for such treats, but it seemed appropriate for such a wonderful day. I am well aware that Lord Dellingby is delighting in being seen out with me, but I cannot criticise for I am of much the same opinion.

Upon re-entering the carriage once we are all done with our delicious ices, Lord Dellingby suggests, "Well, ladies, what say you to a tour of Hyde Park before returning home?"

"Oh yes, let's. That sounds just the thing to complete this wonderful day," I reply, leaning forwards a little.

Mama glowers momentarily but nods her agreement nonetheless. Having spoken out of turn, I am sure reprimands shall be issued later on. But for now, I am intent upon enjoying the rest of my time in delightful company.

My eyes close as we reach The Park proper, enraptured by the surrounding trees and open space, allowing the tranquillity to soak through me. The rest of the world seems to disappear as we make our way along the paths.

"Might we venture towards the north-west enclosure, do you think?" Lord Dellingby asks Mama.

"We may partake in a promenade."

Kensington Gardens lines one side, whilst the Serpentine River is on another. With all due gentility, we walk towards the keeper's lodge. Lady Isabella is by her brother's side; a necessary but vexing formality, leaving me to walk with Mama.

The verdure is a most welcome respite. A longing for home creeps into my heart, which in turn, sinks as my days there are numbered. Shall such a park be present in my marital abode?

The long, low moo of a nearby cow startles me out of my sullen reverie, and I laugh at my skittishness.

"Oh Lor' what a lark. You are also from the country, I understand, Lady Anne?" Lady Isabella chides.

"Aye, yes. Pardon my reaction to so mundane a noise. I was quite lost in my own thoughts, you see."

Gazing around, I observe more cows making their lumbering approach, and a few deer in the distance. One of which interrupts its grazing, raises its head, ears twitching and gazes at me with an air of curiosity. One cannot help but feel more scrutinised by this creature than by even the most fastidious amongst the Ton. What a joke, I do hope it does not find me wanting.

Lady Isabella separates herself from her brother and leads me slightly away, and whispers, "We are both at the edge of a vast precipice, are we not? I find marriage a daunting prospect, if I may confess such. Having successfully deferred as long as possible, I can do so no more. However, I truly believe no greater providence is to be found than your pairing. You will think I speak only as a sister, but my brother is a good man, Lady Anne. You must accept my apologies for diverting his presence, as he is obliged to return me for my nuptials. But he shall soon return and be more attentive than ever. Truly, you must not concern yourself."

"Lady Isabella, not so fast, if you please," her brother calls.

We halt and await the rest of our party. Lord Dellingby is supporting Mama's arm in a most respectable display of good manners.

I am exceedingly grateful for Lady Isabella's forward words. My mind is put at ease by her reassurances, and vow to endeavour to bear our separation as best I can. For I find his absence shall be keenly felt if one is allowed to wallow.

Lady Isabella leads Mama towards an area of particular beauty, leaving Lord Dellingby a brief moment in my company. My heart thunders.

"You seemed to enjoy your ice, Lord Dellingby."

His smile is broad, his hazel eyes intense as they seek mine. "I did, very much. I have found a partiality for violets."

Words fall useless. My breath is fought for. My lips part. His meaning cannot be mistaken. My violet cachous must have left their mark as he kissed me that time, and now a longing grips me, begging he would repeat the experience.

He coughs. "Ah, here is your Mama, brought safely back to the path."

Exchanging walking partners, we complete our circuit, regain our carriage and are carried along beneath a row of trees towards the spring. Lord Dellingby alights and escorts us to the lady who has glasses so we may each partake in the mineral waters therein. There is a sharp tang to its flavour, but we are assured it contains health affirming benefits.

The sun is making rapid progress across the sky, casting its long shadows, so we board the carriage and regrettably make our return journey. It has been such a fine day, and I wish it could last longer. But all good things must end.

By the time we arrive back at the house, there is barely enough time for Mama and I to partake in our light, early supper and have a brief nap before preparing for the ball this evening. It is quite exhausting, but I would not change it for the world.

Lord Dellingby continues to be elevated in my good opinion. Much assisted by the presence of his sister, I am sure. For she seems to bring him out of himself. His cloak of fastidiousness seems dropped, revealing a gaiety with sense and charm which is far more appealing.

This evening's ball is a fitting event for my new pale gold silk gown, with ruffles, frills and dark gold flowers along its hem. Small pale leaves flow down its length. My vanity is swollen as I gaze into my looking glass and notice how well it becomes me.

My long white gloves and white cashmere shawl adorned with gold leaves are most welcome as I step into the chill night air. It is most certainly not as warm as it has been of late. Clément's suggestion of the cashmere shows her good presence of mind. I would not have thought it so cold as to warrant it.

Thankfully, ours is not a long journey this evening, and we arrive at a well-lit house with candles glowing in all the windows. There is quite a throng of carriages and bodies this evening.

Upon entering the ballroom, my eyes dart about in search of Julia and Miss Plimpton, for I simply must share my news with them, having not had the opportunity until now. But I see Julia has beaten me to it, for she is hastening towards me even now.

"Lady Anne, good evening. How well you look. Your gown is exquisite."

"Thank you, my dear friend. You look splendid yourself."

"Lady Anne, you are come. Oh, I have such news for you as will cheer you no end, I am sure," Miss Plimpton greets.

"I have news of my own I would share with you first, if I may. For it is most surprising and you cannot fail but to be pleased for me."

"Then you must tell yours first."

"Well, my friends, what do you think? I have received an offer from none other than Lord Dellingby."

Miss Plimpton emits a ladylike gasp, but Julia squeals. "Oh, what marvellous news indeed. And tell us, did you accept?"

"My dear, I would scarce dare deny such a man."

"And your papa has blessed the union?" Miss Plimpton asks, always the most sensible.

"Indeed he has. I am sure you must be as much shocked as I upon hearing such. It was with some consternation that I received such attentions, I confess."

"Oh my dear, that is far pleasanter than marrying you off to that Emsby creature. Oh, I knew how it would be. He could never have been serious in such a scheme. No, indeed. I declare my approval of your match," she ends, grinning.

I dip a curtsey. "Why, I thank you for your blessing ma'am," I tease, a broad smile dancing on my lips.

We all three have an attack of the giggles and surely create a spectacle. I am immediately reminded of Papa's words, and sober up in an instant, fearing he will be true to his word and send me home.

"Oh, this could be fun," Miss Plimpton declares.

But before I can urge her to expand on her statement, my beau approaches with more confident strides than I have hitherto witnessed from him. There is quite a swagger about his gait.

"Good evening, ladies," he says with a bow, "I do most humbly apologise, but must beg to steal Lady Anne away for the first dance."

Smaller giggles are drawn from each of us, but not loud enough to draw attention this time. My outheld gloved hand is taken gently yet firmly in his as he leads me away from my friends. How far shall I be removed from Julia once I am married? Panic grips my heart at the thought. My hand is gently squeezed, and my eyes are drawn to his hazel gaze, his brow furrowing further and further until I smile.

"Ah, that is better, my lady. Come, let us enjoy ourselves without such alarming looks of disquiet. You are not unhappy, I trust?"

"Pray forgive me, Lord Dellingby. It was a foolish fleeting notion, unworthy of any attention. All is well."

The musicians strike their first notes and the dance begins. We begin sedately enough, and I am swept away with the music and steps. A frisson of excitement rushes through me, setting my pulse racing as our hands meet and our bodies draw near. My tongue runs over my top lip before I know what it is about. Lord Dellingby's eyes darken and his breath is drawn in in haste. Our gazes hold fast until we are forced to part.

Standing in line, I flutter my fan and announce to the lady next me, "It is rather warm in here this evening already, is it not?"

"Really? I had not thought it so," she replies haughtily.

"Oh, I do hope I am not becoming unwell."

We fall into awkward silence, so it is a relief to once more be drawn to my partner to take our turn. Lord Dellingby keeps looking at me all the while.

As we are united in a promenade I venture, "Pardon my asking, but has it yet been settled where we shall reside? Your sister was most anxious on the subject."

"Haha, I am not at all surprised to hear it. But I mean to quiz you on the matter when we have more time as there are options for you to consider."

We are separated and stand facing one another. He smiles with light illuminating his eyes. I attempt to respond in kind but am much taken aback by his response. I have options? Am I to make such a decision? Surely this is one of his jests, for how am I to know where is best when I know nothing of any of them? Choosing one's home? No woman has done as much before. No, he must be funning me.

All perturbed thoughts are swept aside as we swirl together. When we are near my mind seems more peaceable somehow. It is as if his presence calms my tempers whilst stirring up other emotions. It is a heady concoction and makes my head spin if I think upon it too intensely. So, I give myself entirely to the dance.

All disappears in a blur as I am wrapped entirely in a warm sensation. My hand longs for his touch when it is not upon me. To this curious man, I am betrothed. This lord who showers me with such looks of kindness and consideration as to stagger me.

We pay our respects at the end of the set, but he holds my hand to stay my planned departure.

Leaning in close, he whispers, "Let us cause a stir, Lady Anne." He even adds a wink.

Too astonished to do all else but comply, I remain with him as other couples shuffle about us. Lady Rathburn, however, is busy flouncing her deep red skirts. Her every move seems designed to draw attention. What is this? She remains on the floor with Lord Emsby? My mouth gapes, which causes a chuckle from my own partner. Alerted to my expression, I immediately snap my mouth shut, but my eyes remain wide.

Noticing me, she slants her eyes in my direction, bristling her shoulders, enlarging her appearance just like the peacock I know her to be. The sneer of triumph across her countenance is quite outrageous.

"Come, come. Surely this is of no great surprise," Lord Dellingby utters in hushed tones.

"You mistake me, my lord. It is not surprise so much as revulsion. Simply look at her preening behaviour."

"Be charitable, my dear. Allow her her moment. It shall be short-lived," he urges.

I smooth my face back into one of calm serenity and focus on him alone.

"There, see? At last, it has dawned on her rather slow wits that you have made no move either," he says, smiling.

I turn my gaze towards the stupid girl and witness the fall of her victory. Her smirk turns to a vicious sneer before she takes Lord Emsby to the farthest end of the floor, her feet kicking her skirts as she retreats as rapidly as is possible.

"They are well suited, I think. I must be sure to offer my congratulations later," Lord Dellingby tells me.

"My lord, you are too cruel."

"Am I? Well, perhaps I should not wish such a wife upon he who threatened our friend. Perhaps that is taking retribution too far."

My shoulders rise and fall with my sigh. "No, it is just after all, on closer inspection. He deserves no less punishment. And she? Well, she shall receive what she has sought."

"There, we see, a sour back biter and a cunning baggage uniting in unhappy matrimony. They are each as beetle-headed as one another and are falling prey to the parson's mousetrap."

"I confess I had such thoughts myself previously. They shall rub along together with equal dissatisfaction shall they not? However, you do not believe yourself to be leg-trapped, surely?"

"Such bawdy expressions are not to be applied to ourselves, of course, my dear. I should never think to apply such distasteful comments. I follow the rosy path with full awareness and joy. For are we not the very picture of amiability? I flatter myself that we are quite their opposite."

"Such honeyed words, my lord. Take care I do not suspect you of toadyism."

"Abominable reply, Lady Anne. I speak only as I find." He gasps in mock horror.

"Very well, enough said," I tell him, trying my best not to smile too broadly.

Any further such absurdities are denied us as the other couples are finally readied, and the music begins to play us into our second set, our intentions being made clear to the entire assembly.

The couples nearest us offer quiet congratulations as we dance. Many seem happy for us. It is unclear why their sentiments should be surprising, but I find them to be so. Perhaps my dealings with Lady Rathburn have jaded my expectation of others. But there are no jealous remarks made, at least, not within my hearing.

Lord Dellingby leads me back to my station once the second set is complete. I am there for less than one minute when Lady Grainger beckons me to her. Being mindful to respect my elders, I make my way over.

"Lady Anne, I must congratulate you. Felicitations, my dear girl. What a fine match. Two such charming young people," she tells me before kissing both my cheeks.

Her exclamations have drawn other mamas to us, who offer similar salutations. As much as I am grateful to them, I do also wish that more of them would throw off the old fashion of bright lips.

"You are quite delightful, Lady Anne. Pray forgive me if I beg the favour of her company, your ladyships," Miss Plimpton interrupts.

"Are you quite well?" I enquire, taken aback by her rapid intervention.

"Very. But you are in need of some adjustment, my sweet friend," she says, still leading me out of the room without slowing.

"You there! Yes, we require a quiet room with good lighting," she calls to a footman in the hall.

"Ah, I see. Very good, my lady," he replies with a slight bow before leading us to a room with no occupants.

Once alone, Miss Plimpton asks, "Have you any powders and a handkerchief in your reticule?"

"But of course," I respond, pulling the requested items out.

"Those ninnyhammers were overly enthusiastic in their congratulation," she says, taking my handkerchief and wiping at my cheeks.

"Such foolishness in ones supposedly our superiors in sense," she bemoans, moistening the tip of the handkerchief with her tongue, and wiping harder.

"Is my appearance so terrible?"

"Your cheeks look red enough for the stage, my dear, so covered are they in red kisses."

"Really?" I push past her attentions and find a looking glass on the wall.

"Oh Lor'. Pray, continue your ministrations. This shall never do."

By the time she is done with her rubbing, I am sure my cheeks are equally as red from her ministrations as they were from the ladies' lips. But she applies some powder, and I am returned to respectability once more, as is witnessed by my reflection.

"I cannot thank you enough, Miss Plimpton."

"It is of no great import. You would do the same for me. Now, let us return before we are too much missed."

Upon re-entering the room, our path is set to pass by Lord Dellingby who is speaking with Lord Emsby. I lay my hand on Miss Plimpton's arm, slowing our pace.

"Why, what a fine pair you shall make," he's telling the buffoon.

"Quite, quite. She's a fine filly, and one that I shall rein in in next to no time."

Patting Lord Emsby on the shoulder as he begins to walk away, he tells him, "My my, Emsby, if you had full as much brains as guts, what a clever fellow you would be."

He walks off whilst chuckling. Miss Plimpton and I continue past without glancing, and successfully contain our own mirth until we are out of earshot.

"Oh my dear, did you regard his face? He mistook it for a compliment at first," Miss Plimpton tells me amidst sniggers.

"Oh, the juddering jowls as it dawned on him the full force of Lord Dellingby's meaning."

"You have caught yourself a fine and clever husband indeed, Lady Anne."

"So long as he does not turn that sharp ready wit upon me."

"I do not think he would."

"I hope you have the right of it."

❧ Chapter 20 ❦

Alone the next day, I seek some employment before I may drive myself entirely to distraction. Discovering the warmth of the fire in the drawing room, I settle myself beside it, taking up the handkerchief to continue my work.

The design is progressing with minimal mutterings from myself, having only had to unpick one or two small sections thus far. One such area is being neatly resewn as Mama enters, waving a newspaper in her hand.

"My dear, have you *seen* this today?"

I look at her blankly. Mama is in full possession of the knowledge that I have not, for the opportunity has not yet presented itself.

"Your little display with Lord Dellingby has made us subject to idle gossip," she says, thrusting the pages at me, prodding the precise location of the offending article.

I read:

The Marquess of Dellingby, son to the Duke of Wenston was seen last evening at the ball held at Tattinger Hall, dancing two sets together with none other than the daughter of the Duke of Hesford. A great marriage must surely soon ensue.

"Poor Lady Rathburn," I comment, looking up at Mama with a wry smile.

"Is that all you have to say for yourself?"

"She took such pains to be noticed, and there's not so much as a mention of her here."

"This is no laughing matter, Anne." Mama does her best to scowl as she speaks, but the corners of her mouth twitch and her eyes give her away, yet I am far too well-mannered as to draw attention by form of comment.

"No indeed, for she shall be most put out. Imagine how much she must be storming."

Mama's resolve is broken and a full smile bursts forth. "You are wicked to say so."

"But we are worthy of a mention. Must we not view it as an honour to be so singled out? Besides, I was merely following the orders of Lord Dellingby. You would not have me disobey him before he is even my husband, surely? I would not have him think me difficult."

"Very well, when you put it like that, I shall not be angry with you. And you know full well you make it impossible for me to do so. Once I explain it in such words to your father he will calm down, I am sure."

"Oh, is Papa displeased? Mama, I did not mean anything by it. Please don't let him send me away."

"Send you away? The very notion. He was displeased, yes. You know how our name being bandied about upsets him so. He regards it all as causing scandal."

"But the report itself says it will be a great marriage. There is no scandal implied."

"The method of announcing it to the world was perhaps a little faulty, but as you were influenced by Lord Dellingby, this can be no cause of any great alarm."

"Mama, we can hardly be seen in an unfavourable light for not inserting the announcement in the newspaper ourselves, the very periodical which Papa finds so disgusting. And what other method is at our disposal?"

Mama sighs. "You know, sometimes I wonder if you would have better been born a boy, Anne. What a great orator you would have made. A great career in politics could have been before you."

I lift my hands as I shrug. "Well, it cannot be helped. There is nothing to be done. Why dwell on such things?"

"You see, there you go again," she says, reaching to wrap me in a motherly hug.

As she backs away, I catch her wiping at her eye. "How I shall miss you, my darling girl. You do know that, do you not?"

I nod, unable to speak around the lump in my throat which has formed all of a sudden.

"I do hope our husbands will allow visits," she murmurs.

Nodding, I manage to tell her, "I shall insist upon it, and that you bring Margie with you. I could not bear to be parted from either of you for long." It appears necessary for my own eyes to be rid of their excess moisture now.

In fact, as Mama and I hold on to one another longer and firmer, both our shoulders are shaking as our sobs are given free rein.

Letter to Margaret, 7th May 1814

Dear Margie,

I was very sorry to hear in your last that things continue very dull there with you. You really must try to find some employment for your idle mind, my dear, and not pine away the entire summer. These may be the most tranquil times you experience, and they should be spent in pursuit of pleasures around your lessons.

I have scarce had one minute to myself of late. Lord Dellingby has made me an offer, which I accepted and Papa has granted. Mama has surely informed you by now, we shall be married from there, so I may say hello and goodbye to you, my dearest sister, in August. How strange it will be not to be always near you. I implore you to write to me often, and have persuaded Mama to promise to visit along with you as much as may be permitted.

Lady Rathburn has ensnared Lord Emsby. I confess to you alone that I employed the tactic you had threatened towards our good governess. Papa had ordered me entertain him myself, but I could not bring myself to obey this single instruction. And now they are to be married. I would point out, however, that this was done with their good in mind as much as my own. They are both intolerable people so are a far more fitting pair. Had I not felt it absolutely necessary I should not have made the attempt. The rest of my life was in peril, and not a mere few lessons I did not wish to partake in. Therein lies the difference.

Lady Isabella, sister to Lord Dellingby, has been much in our company. She is a lively, engaging sort, and I have been much entertained. However, now they are returned home so she may be married herself. I find myself quite desolate.

Denied the pleasures of attending any balls without Lord Dellingby, most of my time is to be spent at home. And today it remains quite chill. The rain is pouring down, forcing me to remain indoors. But at least it is not quite so cold as it was two days ago when I began to fear winter may be returning. And it lends me opportunity to write, so I am thankful for that.

Lady Isabella was much entertained at the theatre when we were there together five nights since. She has not been allowed to make her come out in London and has been directly promised to someone from their acquaintance. She seemed much miffed by this, which put me in mind of you. You, however, will not have this restriction, so you must be grateful to Papa for his indulgence when your time does come, and be sure not to pout in the interim.

Perhaps you shall be relieved to hear of how I am now confined, at least until Lord Dellingby returns. He assured me repeatedly that he expects to be back by my side within two weeks. I had not thought Lady Isabella was to be married so soon. I confess to having been surprised by her arrival. There must be more I do not know about the case. It is no wonder her intended began to fear she would cry off, fleeing as she did. There must have been some over-indulgence for her to act so rashly with such freedom. I would not have you think ill of her. I repeat, I like her a great deal. It is merely her actions on this one matter which inspire my curiosity.

What do you make of it? Is it possible Lady Isabella really meant to fly into the protective custody of her brother to save her from a bad marriage? But he seems to think it a fine match. Do I trust his judgement? I must, as soon I shall promise to obey him. And surely she would not behave so? But then she was loath to speak of her own upcoming nuptials and would soon change the subject if it came up in discussion. Please do share your thoughts, as it puzzles me greatly. Should I worry about the family I am marrying into?

My mind begins to wander across this page. I shall stop now and find some useful occupation.

For now, I bid you adieu.

Your loving sister,

Anne Frithringham

Well, that outpouring has done little to lift my spirits. In fact, quite the reverse may be true. The pitter patter of rain against the window thrums against my nerves. How frustrating it is to be so entirely confined.

What am I to do? The following weeks promise to be dull indeed. As much as attending balls and parties was weary making, it seems not attending them is worse. How contrary I am!

Perhaps it is best to keep my practice up, for Lord Dellingby has promised me entertainments upon his return. Thus, I sit at the pianoforte and play something suitably sombre for the weather.

Chastising myself for deepening my melancholy, the music quickly turns into sea shanties. Suitable for the water hammering at the windows, yet far more lively than the former pieces. And Papa is not at home, so there is no one to reprimand me for playing them. I cannot help but enjoy playing the skipping tunes.

It is not long before I find myself singing as my fingers hit out ditties. A smiling Mama creeps into the room and saunters to my side. At the song's end, she takes a place on the stool beside me, and we play a duet as we did of old. I am transported back to my youth as we play and sing together.

How I have wished she were able to take her turn amongst company, for she has quite the sweetest voice of anyone. But of course, she is not trying to lure a man, so society dictates she must remain silent, alas.

Such moments are treasures indeed. A private time for us alone. Two women playing and singing simply for the sheer fun of it.

Overcome with joy when Mama begins to play a tune on her own, I stand and dance about the room as if I were a stage performer. No gentility is displayed as my legs kick out through my skirts and I hop around, laughing all the while. Free from her own constraints, Mama laughs along without a single word of chastisement. This is our home, and we are quite alone.

I cannot be certain quite how long we spend in this fashion, but it is as long as possible. Only the quiet, "Duke Hesford's carriage has this moment pulled up," from one of the footmen halts our merriment. Mama and I exchange glances as we right our apparel and go to meet Papa as he returns from whence he came, the very picture of ladylike deportment in our every step.

Papa alarms us both by addressing us over dinner. "You have learned, I suppose, that Wellesley is now Duke of Wellington, Marquess of Douro. Have you ever heard the like? A common soldier being made duke, I ask you."

"Well, err, he is considered a great military hero, Papa," I venture.

"A hero, pah. He has wagered some successful campaigns, to be sure. But to make the fellow a duke? This is the reward of butchers is it?"

I hold my tongue, well aware that Papa's resentment lies in the loss of my brother, George. It was under his command, after all, that his life was forfeit. It must surely leave a sour taste to see him so decorated in the face of such a loss.

Most of London does not seem to hold the same opinion. I have overheard many young ladies veritably swooning over the mention of the now duke. He is not so very common either. He attended Eton and has always been of the aristocracy, albeit in Ireland. His older brother inherited the family title, of course. However, it is of little use to argue any of this with Papa, who clearly wishes only to grumble, which he continues to do during the entire meal. It hinders my digestion dreadfully.

❧ Chapter 21 ❧

My life seems now as if it were one long wait. We are yet to receive news of Lord Dellingby's safe arrival at his home, if indeed such news should be forthcoming. I have no reason to suspect it will. It is not entirely proper to correspond in such a fashion, after all, but I long to hear it all the same.

And of course, correspondence from Canada is yet to arrive. It has not been quite a fortnight since his departure, and Lord Beauvrais' crossing shall probably last that time again. And then he will need to find a residence before sending news, which shall take equally as long to travel back to me. This knowledge does nothing to settle my nerves. I grow ever more restless to learn of his safe arrival. Why must he go all the way to Canada? It is too great a distance for my forbearance.

Here I remain, suspended in time, almost motionless in my languor. The past few days have been spent indoors, trapped by the confounded weather. However, Lord Dellingby's handkerchief has been completed, so it is time well spent.

And another good thing to be said for staying at home is that it has coincided with my monthly curse, so there was little concern over showing stockings displaying red droplets. It really is a most inconvenient occurrence, especially when one seems to be perpetually wearing white. However, it is over and done with for now.

As I'm contemplating painting a watercolour of the water on the windows, I am saved. The skies have cleared, and the sun has made a mildly warming appearance. Having persuaded Mama that Lady is as much in need of exercise as myself, I am reunited with my freedom-seeking friend. Her hooves clatter against the ground as she marks her displeasure at being kept waiting.

She remains impatient, and her hindquarters shift as I attempt to mount the dratted beast. How am I supposed to take her for the long-awaited ride is she refuses to stand still? The groom braces himself, and the footman finally succeeds in helping me into the saddle.

As we make our way through the busy streets, I find myself being jostled as Lady skips and lurches, impatient to stretch her legs. Foreboding fills me with dread as it becomes clear that she means to run, whether at my bidding or not. Perhaps I should have permitted the groom to ride her first, but she is precious to me. The very idea of anyone else riding her makes me recoil. A shudder runs through me even now.

Does the Bible itself not warn that pride comes before a fall? I pray now that I survive what I fear is yet to come.

Leaning forwards, I whisper in Lady's ear, "I am sorry it has been so long, but please do not bolt, my friend, and we may yet both get what we desire."

The ensuing shake of her main and whinny are almost confirmation of her compliance, as ridiculous as that notion is. I fancy it must be wishful thinking on my part. If horses could understand us for a start, her actions could just as easily be interpreted as a shake of the head 'no'.

As we approach the park, I turn to my footman, and apologise, "She seems rather skittish, I'm afraid. Do your best to keep up in case something untoward occurs. I fear Lady is not to be trusted this morning."

"Take care, my lady," he cautions with a nod.

As soon as we enter the grounds, I feel Lady coiling her muscles like a spring under me. I force my weight down through the saddle and take a firmer grip on the reins, which of course she fights against, throwing her head.

"Really, this is most unladylike," I reprimand her.

Every step is an argument between us. I deny her anything above a walk, knowing full well what she is about. My patience is being truly tested as I hold her back, the exertion beading on my brow. Her steps are small and jerky, which is most uncomfortable.

"Pack it in," I tell her through clenched teeth, wrestling the reins as she continues to throw her head.

"Here, take hold at the front," I command the footman.

As much as it pains me, I find myself in need of his assistance. He holds her bridle at her chin and we're walked around as if I were a child learning to ride. My cheeks heat all the more under the shame of it. Others are beginning to stare.

"OK, you can let go now," I tell the servant as she finally seems to settle.

Guilt crushes me as Lady walks on, her head hanging as low as possible. She is utterly dejected, resigned to misery. I collect the reins and urge her to a brisk walk. She complies most begrudgingly and only for a short time before slowing.

"You are determined to make this difficult," I mutter. "If you promise to behave, we can try a trot."

The footman looks at me with worry creasing his brow. I pretend not to notice and kick my steed on. But she lurches forwards, almost knocking me off balance. With some difficulty, I remain seated and try to rein her back from the gallop she's launched into. But it is to no avail, we barrel down the path, narrowly missing passersby.

A fleeting thought strikes me that this may be my just reward for having feigned this precise thing in the past. But little things such as not falling off soon take precedence. If Lady continues at this pace she will hurt herself, and possibly me in the process. I pull harder and harder on the reins, even sawing them, but with little effect.

Panic sets in, as I puzzle what else can be done. If I point her at the fence, she will in all likelihood, jump clear over it. Reluctantly, I steer us in the direction of the pond. It is a risky strategy as she may slip, and I am almost certain I shall end up in the water and return home a bedraggled mess. But rather a bedraggled mess in one piece than with my neck broken.

The thunder of hooves approaches from the right.

"Woah! Woah, there!" Lord Alverbury calls as he intercepts our course, heading Lady off.

She swerves to avoid the new horse and rider, but I brace myself and cling on. Our progress is at least slowed, and my reins are at last having some effect now. Lord Alverbury once more gets in our way, and we are brought to a halt. My breath escapes me in a whoosh as my gaze turns heavenwards.

"Well sat, Lady Anne," my rescuer says with a chuckle.

"Oh my, that was an adventure," I reply through gasps, one hand flying to my heart in an attempt to still it.

Lord Alverbury catches my gaze. "You are alright, are you not?"

"Yes, I thank you. It seems I am once more indebted to your intervention."

"Nonsense. Could've happened to anyone. Glad to have been here."

"You seem to be making somewhat of a habit of it."

"Well, I am to be found hereabouts at this hour most days." His accompanying smirk tells me he did not mistake my meaning.

"I am most grateful."

"Very well, very well, enough of that. Shall we make our way back to your man?"

Lord Alverbury rides close at my side until we reach the puffing footman. "Oh, merciful heavens. Thank goodness you are not harmed, my lady."

"Harmed? She has as good a seat as anyone I know," Lord Alverbury reprimands, all gruffness.

My footman is hushed into silence as he checks Lady over. She is puffing and snorting, having clearly over-exerted her foolish self.

"Would you like me to escort you home, Lady Anne?" Lord Alverbury asks.

"Oh no, I see no need for that. Lady seems to have got that tantrum out of her system. I doubt she has the energy to even attempt to run off again. But I thank you for your consideration."

He bows his head.

Lowering my voice, I add, "I would be grateful if news of this did not reach the ears of my parents, however."

"Say no more. You have my assurance they shall not hear it from me. Although, I cannot guarantee others shall hold their tongue," he says, glancing about the park.

"I shall hold to the hope they thought I had intended to be so reckless. It is not unheard of for me to go galloping about like a gipsy, after all."

"Ha ha, just so."

"Lord Alverbury, you needn't agree so readily."

"I know better than to disagree with a lady," he replies with a tilt of his head.

"I declare you a lost cause, Lord Alverbury."

"You are not the first to say so. Now I see you are fully yourself and are in no danger, I will take my leave. Good day, Lady Anne."

"Good day, my lord."

The footman holds Lady's bridle all the way home, but I allow it. I suspect it is more for his own reassurance than him trying to exert any control over the sweaty steed.

As I make my way into the house, I silently vow to never again leave Lady without exercise for so long. Even if it is solely by means of a groom walking her about by the rein, she should not be so confined. Neither one of us is at her best under such circumstances.

Fortune smiles upon me, and no mention has been made of Lady's escapade. However, riding is still denied as Mama insists upon us taking the carriage instead; a far more dignified mode of transport in her opinion. It being far more agreeable than remaining indoors, I accept with a grateful heart.

We have been permitted our promenades, of course. Regrettably, the recent drop in temperatures has led to an increase in coal fires, which I am told, is the cause of the even thicker smoke enveloping the city. We do not take long walks about the city.

Shops are forced to put on their lights at midday, and one can barely see the dome of St Paul's Cathedral until quite on top of it. The acrid smell seems to have permeated all of my clothes. And I miss the stars, the shining sentinels of the night sky; they are never visible here.

As the carriage takes us through the streets, a sense of foreboding shrouds us as surely as the fog. One hears of horrendous accidents, where carriages are overturned having not seen one another. And who is to say what other horrors hide in the gloom?

Perhaps I had shut my eyes to it before, the nervous excitement creating a veil to this hidden world. My attention was elsewhere. I noticed, of course, but this sense of foreboding was rather reserved for my potential husband. But now that matter is settled, I suppose I am free to worry over other matters. Whatever the reason, my journeys are become most uncomfortable.

This evening, we are on our way to the theatre. Miss Compley is to accompany us, after much pleading with Mama. I should so like to see her betrothed before the Season is out, for she is far more eager to enter the marriage state than I. For me, it is a duty, but for Julia, it is a promise of joy. I cannot, in all honesty, say I understand her enthusiasm, but neither can I censure it. And if it is within my power to forward her hopes in that direction then so be it. She is my dearest friend, and her happiness is of paramount importance.

Offering a silent prayer of thanks for our safe arrival, we enter the theatre and file into the saloon to meet with Miss Compley and her aunt.

"Lady Retland, what a pleasure it is to see you this evening," Mama says.

I know this to be a falsehood. They have not managed to regain any true form of equanimity since that day I insisted on Miss Compley accompanying us in the carriage. However, one must keep up appearances. There is no need for outward hostility.

"Your Grace, we are grateful for your condescension in inviting us," is the rather stiff response.

Remorse sinks my head and shoulders low as I appreciate how much Mama is enduring at my insistence. I thought only of my friend's prospects. How stupid of me not to have thought who would be invited by extension. Poor Mama.

"Lady Anne, thank you for extending the invitation. How lovely it is to be here, and with you. You do look splendid," a rather excited Miss Compley tells me as we walk a short distance aside.

"Why, it is my pleasure to have you with us. And you, likewise, are dressed exquisitely."

"Thank you. Is it not a fine gown? My aunt had it made for me, having declared some of my other gowns too provincial for town."

A small grunt of displeasure springs from me. "Does she, indeed?"

"I am reminded she means to do me a kindness."

"But of course." I bite back any disparaging remarks which were forming on my tongue.

Poor Julia, as if she did not already feel inferior enough to her richer relation. Surely, she could have been kinder in her comments.

"Lady Anne, Miss Compley, you are both as delightful as ever."

"Lord Alverbury, how good to see you. Although I do begin to suspect you of keeping watch in your friend's absence."

His eyebrows rise. "As if I should ever stoop to such underhand dealings."

"Forgive me. I merely meant to tease."

With a wink, he adds, "But, if a certain lord was concerned over your safety, and not at all suspicious of your own excellent conduct, perhaps, if the venue were appealing, I should not be disinclined to be in the same location as her ladyship."

I blush wildly as he confirms my suspicions. It was wrong of me to blurt them out so, but I did not truly believe what was suggested.

"Well, well, you are far too astute. I hope you are not offended at my compliance. I am in earnest when I say it is merely to ensure your safety," Lord Alverbury adds, some warmth apparent in his cheeks also.

"But I am with my Mama and friends."

"And Lord Emsby could say he is likewise here only with friends," he says, his voice lowered.

"Oh, I see. Well, in that case, gratitude must be in order."

"Have no fear. He shall not so much as approach your box."

"You are too good, my lord."

Lowering his voice further, he tells me, "Between you and I alone, I am rather hoping he gives me cause to challenge him. He always has been something of an irritant."

"You do not mean that."

"Well, I suppose I don't. I bid you good evening, dear ladies," he says to us both before bowing away.

How extraordinary. I cannot help but feel somewhat affronted at such an invasion, but it is also comforting to have a strong man such as Lord Alverbury about. He did help stop Lady, after all, saving me from a dunking in the pond. It does seem a little extreme though. Surely Lord Emsby poses no great threat now?

Pushing all such horrid thoughts aside, our party heads to our box, where I attempt to enjoy the entertainment. But my nerves are on edge. The unsettling feeling which began before our arrival has only increased, and try as I might, it refuses to subside.

Miss Compley is merry enough however, and I listen to her comments with pleasure. But then I see him; Lord Emsby is glaring at me from his position. I nod in acknowledgement. He makes the slightest nod in return and quickly looks away, supposedly embarrassed to be caught out.

I am sure I do not know what I have done to earn such murderous looks. Perhaps he is already regretting his choice of wife, and lays the blame at my door? True, they had a nudge from me, but the decision was entirely in his hands. Nobody forced him to it.

Doing my best to ignore any further insolent glances, I concentrate on enjoying the remainder of the evening. The players on stage are fortunately talented and make this a far easier task.

Down in the foyer, there seems to have been a mix-up and we're kept waiting a terribly long time for our carriage. Lord Alverbury is once more on hand and goes in search and to hurry it along.

"No Lord Dellingby this evening, Lady Anne?" a gruff voice asks.

"Lord Emsby, good evening. Lord Dellingby is as yet at home for his sister's wedding. We expect his return shortly."

"Ooh, all that distance and the roads being so treacherous. I hope he returns safely soon." His narrowed eyes would suggest he feels otherwise.

"He assures me that his carriage is well armed against brigands, my lord."

"What's this? Who talks of armed carriages? Surely any man travelling is sensible of such precautions. Why on ever should Lady Anne have any concern? What a notion." Lord Alverbury interjects.

"I was merely stating my concern over Lord Dellingby travelling such a large distance," Lord Emsby replies, his smile as false as it is obsequious.

"Your Grace," Lord Alverbury calls, as Mama is busily talking with one of her friends, "Your carriage is arriving now, Your Grace."

With his arm for support, Mama and I are led to the comparative safety of our carriage at last. A small sigh flies from me as I flump into the seat, which causes Mama to look sternly upon me.

"Thank you, Lord Alverbury," I say out the window.

He doffs his hat as we pull away.

Chapter 22

Lord Emsby's remark is still ringing in my ears this morning. Vexing man! I do so hope Lord Dellingby remains safe on his travels. It is most troubling to be so distant from him without being certain of his whereabouts. He has only grown in my estimation and already it would be deeply distressing to lose him. I take a deep breath to halt any unseemly displays of lament.

The dressmaker shall soon be here, so one must be on top form with no signs of displeasure. All my disquiet is carefully contained within my bosom.

Mama insists a wife must dress differently, and so my wedding wardrobe is being ordered. Surely a few mobcaps and a fichu or two would suffice. But Mama has spoken, so once more I am to be used as some sort of doll to be clothed.

Having had my fill of warehouses, the dressmaker is to attend upon me in the comfort of my own home. I'm even less inclined to venture out of doors following my encounter last evening, so it is fortunate we made that decision.

Mama declares which patterns and fabrics whilst Clément makes notes and murmurs agreements. I have no particular interest or objections to the decisions being made, so remain silent, reminding myself this is the last time I need endure such attentions.

The thought hits me as surely as any hand upon my face. No more will I be able to rely on Mama's fine taste and opinion. These decisions and many more shall lie firmly at my door. My stomach lurches as the magnitude of responsibility lands upon me.

"Mama, how am I to manage an entire house?" I ask her once the other ladies have left us alone.

"Anne, what a question. Have you not been instructed in such matters? Do you think your education lacking, pray tell?"

"In the basics, of course, there is nothing amiss. But you make so many decisions each and every day. How am I ever to do so?"

She strokes my hair aside my head. "You will because it is what must be done. Your life thus far has been uninterrupted by such concerns. But it is no great thing once you become used to it. In the main, a routine develops."

"But what if I should fail?"

"You must not fear errors. We all have made them at some time. The thing is to remain calm and confident in your appearance at all times."

"You have never erred, Mama."

Her eyes wrinkle at the edges as she smiles. "You see how it is. You do not believe me to have ever made an error in my life as I act in such a way as to make it appear so."

She lowers her voice. "But I assure you, there have been several."

"I do not believe it."

Shaking her shoulders, and holding her head high once more, she declares, "Not that there are any I would ever admit to."

She leans forward and kisses my forehead as she stands. "You will do very well, my child."

Then she is gone and I am alone, pondering the shocking confidence. I hope beyond hope that I may live up to her example. Mama has often been stern, but she is also kind. And never ever have I noticed any fault in her. She leaves a lot to live up to.

Lor', I shall be expected not only to be a wife but a mother also. I lie down under the weight of this burden. Can I be a mama? How does one even set about such a thing? This is one mystery I cannot help but think should have been answered during my education.

Hoping to find answers, I seek the refuge of the library. My hands run along the leather-bound spines sitting upon the dark wooden shelves as the delightful musty smell reaches my nose; one of life's finer comforts. Book after book gets pulled down and leafed through, but the mystery remains, answers eluding me in the most vexing way.

I am summonsed to make ready for a promenade, as the day is dry and one should still make an appearance.

"One is not invisible simply for being betrothed," Mama has lectured, "Nothing is for certain until the event has taken place, and it will not do to be entirely forgotten by Society should some tragedy befall us in the interim to bring an end to proceedings."

Seeing the wisdom of her caution, yet fearing for the safety of Lord Dellingby, I follow her advice and walk about the vicinity, stopping to talk with ladies among my acquaintance as is proper, exchanging pleasantries and gossip.

Curious how none ever declare anything but joy at being in London. One is supposed to be constantly entertained. Yes, there are many amusements, but this fog is enough to lower even the brightest spirits. Rain and fog seem to alternate on the most dreary schedule. Yet nobody ever seems to mind it. How does anyone live in such constant darkness? I think I should be happy never to return. Glad as I am to be allowed the honour of saying I have visited, there is no desire to repeat this experience.

As my feet continue to tread the path, my mind turns to that dreadful night in Vauxhall, and a shudder runs through me. No, I do not wish to repeat this experience. Mama tugs on my arm, and I am reminded of where I am and remove the frown from my face.

Inwardly, I wonder how much longer I must wait for Lord Dellingby's return. Surely it cannot be too much longer. Meeting with these other ladies is reminding me of the liveliness I am missing in his absence. It is contrary of me but being so alone is playing havoc with my mood.

A letter is waiting for me as we reach home.

Letter from Margaret, sent 17th May 1814

Dear Anne,

How can I be happy at your tedium? I do not rejoice in your misery, of course I do not. I wish you every happiness whilst also desiring to share in it.

I am supposed to offer felicitations upon your betrothal, which I do. But I cannot pretend to be happy that you shall be so far removed, as it seems likely you shall live up in the north country. But I shall seek every opportunity to visit and look forward to meeting Lady Isabella who sounds as intriguing as she is delightful.

You are far cleverer than I, and if you cannot make out her odd behaviour, be certain I am at quite a loss also. I believe there must be more to this than we are aware of and await further news with great interest. It is as if we are missing a continent in a dissected puzzle as things stand.

How distressing to not have you at home longer before your wedding is to take place, but we shall make the most of it. I miss our bedtime talks greatly, and what details you must have to share with me now which cannot be expressed in writing. I long to hear all without omission.

It is really quite shocking you should adopt my scheme which you disallowed me. I am in good mind to take you to task on the topic. However, from your explanation, and a period of contemplation which is the cause of the delay in my response, I see you must have been driven to such desperate measures by great distress. How monstrously you must have been treated. And this fills me with more sorrow than you can know. How I long to hold you and offer comfort, my dear sister.

And Lady Rathburn does sound far better suited to Lord Emsby than you, my gentle sister could ever be. For should such an angel ever marry a beast? Surely not. And the image you paint of them does bring a smile.

Despite his plan to steal my sister far away, which I must allow is not entirely of his own doing, Lord Dellingby sounds far more amiable. I do hope he shall be everything we expect. Am I to meet him before you marry? Does he come home with you? If only Papa would allow me to come to London, I could meet him now. My mind cannot be at rest until he proves his worthiness of you. It is bad of me not to trust the judgement of you and Papa perhaps, and I do, but yet I must witness it myself before fully believing this to be the case. Please do not censure me for being a sceptic, as it is born of my love for you, and you should think my sisterly affection greatly lacking if I thought otherwise.

Nothing at all is happening here. I am paying attention in my lessons, which need no encouragement from you, but I know it is only your way. And you are right to try to prepare me for what seems to be quite a horrific time in store. I must hope London is cleared of the likes of Lord Emsby and Lord Felsenworth before my arrival. Whoever thought men could behave so? At least now I am aware and shall be on my guard all the more when my time comes.

Yours faithfully,

Margaret Frithringham

It is lovely to hear from my sister; I had wondered why she had not written sooner. My letter must have caused some consternation, but she seems to have forgiven my subterfuge with regards to Lord Emsby. It is indeed a pity she cannot be here with me for I am sure my time here would be so much easier with her at my side.

My afternoon is spent in quiet contemplation and a little sketching. I pencil a likeness of Margaret from memory so I may feel she is here. She may deem me cleverer than her, but I still value her counsel.

       ✦✦

The next day a great hullabaloo erupts as Lord Dellingby calls. I am ushered into the morning room with Mama, and it is all I can do not to run up to him and throw my arms about his neck.

"Lord Dellingby, how pleased I am to see your safe return," I tell him, approaching to take his hands.

My reach is halted however by his countenance which is so stern as to frighten me.

"Is everything well, Lord Dellingby?"

"Quite well. Forgive me, I merely wished to make you aware of my return. I have this moment arrived."

"You must be tired after your journey. Would you like some refreshment?" Mama offers.

"No. No, I thank you, Your Grace. It is perhaps best if I continue my journey directly."

"Continue your journey? Do you head elsewhere?"

"Only my house here," he clarifies.

"But of course. We would not delay you. Thank you for stopping," I tell him with a curtsey, allowing him to bow out directly.

"Well, what do you make of that?" I ask Mama, quite astonished at the change in him.

"My dear, however much they may declare the fairer sex the one who suffers from sulks and miffs, men are just as likely to experience such things. We must learn how best to comfort and mollify them in turn."

"As you speak with Papa when he is enraged?"

"Letting them talk themselves out and offering a quiet word or two does far more good than interrogation at such times. And we must allow that Lord Dellingby must indeed be tired after his long journey. He pays you a great compliment in visiting so soon."

"Perhaps, but it does not feel much of an honour at this moment."

Placing her hand on mine, she confides, "It seems he realised his error as soon as he saw you. He was in too much haste. A good rest and he will be restored to himself once more."

I lean my head against Mama's shoulder. "I do hope so."

Mama reaches her arm around and holds me to her, where I pause, relishing the comforting embrace. Lord Dellingby's gruff appearance has unsettled me more than admitted. I had been so looking forward to his return, but now my hopes seem dashed. Perhaps his father does not look favourably upon our match?

❧ Chapter 23 ❧

It is not with some little trepidation that I await Lord Dellingby's arrival. He is to escort Mama and I to Astley's Circus this evening. I hope that Mama was correct in her assumption that his sour mood yesterday was merely the product of a long, tedious journey.

The clattering of wheels and hooves announces his landau's arrival. I hasten to the drawing room in order to receive him.

"Good evening Your Grace, Lady Anne. I trust you are readied for our excursion?" he asks with a stiff bow.

"Indeed we are. Lady Anne is all eagerness," Mama responds.

"Then let us not keep her waiting a moment longer than needs be." He reaches his arm to me and escorts us to his carriage.

It must be observed that he is not quite surly, but nor does Lord Dellingby seem happy to be in our company. But he extended the invitation. I did nothing to impress upon him any urgency to the continuation of our amusements, or indeed any meetings. His bland civility is as perplexing as it is irksome. Is the vivacious Lord Dellingby a façade and the dull, quiet one the reality, or is the reverse true? He is a mystery.

However, he performs his role of protector with dignity as we make our way through the throng of people and locate our seats. The interior of the amphitheatre is richly decorated with reds and golds. A large circle sets the stage. I can scarce sit still as we wait for the acts to enter.

The crowds of people all around seem to be similarly astir. A great din fills the air along with the thrum of excitement and, one has to add, a rather foul stench. But this deters me not, for I am promised an equestrian extravaganza.

"Oh, are they not marvellous?" I ask of Lord Dellingby, clapping my hands before I can check myself as the performance starts.

The corners of his mouth twitch upwards. "I am pleased to find you so enraptured."

"Oh, quite so, my lord. Such acrobatics upon such fine horses. How clever of you to have brought me here."

"There is more yet to be seen."

And surely enough, acrobats and rope dancers come out to perform their tricks for our amazement. Horse sweat and sawdust mingle their sweet scents with that coming from the people, which renders the odour slightly less putrid. I can even hear the happy snorts of the horses as they gallop in circles.

A gasp is wrenched from me as a rider bends to the floor to pick up a handkerchief whilst cantering. My breath is completely stolen as he then performs a headstand in the saddle.

"Remarkable," I whisper breathily.

My companion allows his smile to lengthen a little, I notice from the side of my eye.

Oh my, a rider is astride two horses as he pipes in an army of horses, riders and cannon are wheeled into place.

"Astonishing," I murmur, wondering how he manages to keep balance and play on top.

The firing of cannon startles me, and I am moved in my seat, my hand flying to my breast as I yelp. Yet the horses continue their rounds as if nothing had occurred. Lady, in all certainty, would have reared then run clean out of the ring upon witnessing such a commotion. Such calmness under such conditions is truly astonishing.

A smirk seems to cross Lord Dellingby's visage. However, despite it being at my expense, my reprimand shall remain unspoken, for I would do anything to lift his spirits.

The air quickly fills with smoke from the military activity below, and one can hardly make out the players for a time. The horses are quite ghostly as they emerge from the grey clouds.

The acts end to rapturous applause from all, and the audience below stamp their feet too, and cheer in a most vulgar fashion, but I should join them if permitted. So much joy and fascination fills me that I do not know how to contain it all. Ne'er before have I witnessed such acrobatic prowess. I fancy a part of me wishes to be a part of the show, to be able to ride horses like those clever people.

Lord Dellingby grins at me. "You are entertained, my lady?"

"Who would not be?"

"I wish you had been with me the past fortnight."

"Me? Surely your time with your family was not so bad?"

The light in his eyes dies in an instant, and I kick myself for my stupidity. It clearly was.

"Oh, I did not mean…of course, you need not tell me…but I should so like to be of use…"

"My dear Lady Anne, you, if I may be so bold, are balm enough simply by being near."

Mama coughs.

"Ahem, well, it grows late. Let us return you to your…home," he adds, and I'm sure I spy a blush on his cheeks.

We are too quiet on the return journey. Whereas Lord Dellingby seems lost in a world of sorrow, I am holding onto the happy memories of my truly wonderful evening. He blinks and attempts a weak smile upon seeing my grin.

Mama steps from the carriage.

"Thank you for such a tremendous evening, Lord Dellingby," I tell him as she descends.

"You are most welcome, Lady Anne."

He risks a quick kiss on my lips as Mama's back is turned. Thrills run through me, and I look behind me with dewy eyes as I alight.

"I am most glad you met with no trouble on the roads."

A frown crosses his brow which is soon smoothed.

"You would tell me if I could be of service, would you not?" I ask quietly.

"You already are."

How my heart flutters at his words as I hasten after Mama and go indoors.

"Was it not a splendid evening, Mama?"

"Most entertaining, I must admit."

"All those riders, how spectacular they were. Have you ever seen the like?"

"Anne, do cool yourself, my dear girl. You are quite over-excited. Off to bed now."

"How can I sleep when so many amazing visions are still fresh?"

"You must try."

"Goodnight, Mama," I bid with a kiss on her fair cheek.

I find myself far too enlivened for sleep, so write all the details of the evening in a letter to Margaret before anything can be forgotten. How fascinated she shall be, for we both have a fondness for horses. Presuming she will be able to decipher my scrawl having written in the light from a single candle.

Lying my pen down, I wonder what is troubling Lord Dellingby. Although, it is a relief to notice it does not seem to be anything connected with me.

"My dear Lady Anne, you, if I may be so bold, are balm enough simply by being near." His words echo in my mind, filling my body with warmth as I climb back into bed.

A few days pass before Lord Dellingby makes himself known again. He is so distant, and nothing like a promised suitor, who should surely call every day. Is this sullen silence and neglect to be what my married life is to behold?

No sooner had I begun to think he was warming to my company when he vanishes as if he were a phantom. What else am I supposed to imagine other than he truly is reconsidering his offer?

It is not entirely unknown for men to cry off. But Papa gave his blessing. There is no family conflict I am aware of. What possible cause could his father have for condemning the match to such an extent to draw such drastic, reprehensible action? And would he not have said at once and not taken us out for a splendid evening?

"Lord Dellingby, m'lady," Forbes announces.

"Thank you, Forbes. Show him to the morning room," I confirm.

"Very good, m'lady."

"Oh, Forbes."

My call halts his retreat. "Yes, m'lady?"

"How does he seem?"

"Seem?"

"Yes. Does he appear in good spirits?"

"I cannot rightly say, Lady Anne. He appears…as ever."

An exasperated sigh emanates from my mouth. "Well, go and direct him."

Bowing, Forbes does as instructed. Really, such a vexing man. Should one ever wish to know anything why ask a servant? How can he be so obtuse? I am certain he knew full well as to what my line of enquiry was pertaining yet pretends not to. Nor does he give any clear response. Servants! False modesty. They surely know more than they admit. It is quite disconcerting. Forbes is one of our own, should he not be on my side?

Well, there is nothing to be discovered in here. Off to the morning room I go to ascertain the mood of the day for myself.

"Good morning, Lady Anne. Please forgive my absence. I had work to attend to which could not be put off. My absence had already delayed it beyond reason."

"But of course. These things cannot be helped."

"I am come to make amends. I offer you the choice of entertainment. Anything at all. Name it and it shall be done."

"In which case, I think it high time you hold a ball."

"Me, hold a ball?"

"Yes. It can be a sort of betrothal ball," I tell him, as the thought crosses my mind that it'll force him to confess it if he is having doubts or hold the ball and confirm his intentions remain steadfast.

"A betrothal ball? I suppose that could be arranged, but you must allow me a little time to prepare."

"Take all the time you need. In the interim, I would beg a further indulgence."

"You grow bold, my lady, but let us hear it," he says with an amused smile.

"Miss Compley is holding a ball, and now you are returned I would dearly love to be in attendance."

"Ah, your good friend, is she not?"

"She is."

"Then, of course, you must be there."

"You do not mind that she…is of lower descent?" I add on a whisper.

"If it is no barrier to you then it cannot be so to me."

"You are very good," I tell him, grasping his hands and kissing his cheek.

Of course, this is precise moment Mama chooses to enter the room.

"Lord Dellingby, so good of you to visit," she says, the trace of a sneer lacing her words.

"Your Grace," he acknowledges with a bow, "I have made my apologies to Lady Anne. Please allow me to extend the same courtesy to you. Business kept me shamefully away. By means of apology I have offered Lady Anne the choice, and she has nominated a betrothal ball to be held at my home."

"Has she indeed?" she asks, raising an eyebrow in my direction.

"She has. However, I have requested she allow me time to make the preparations. I cannot recall the last time a ball was held at Riverton House and fear it may require some attention before it is fit for such an occasion."

"I would not like you to be put to any trouble."

"It is no trouble, I assure you, Your Grace. But it may prove too long a wait, so, with your approval, I would take Lady Anne to the upcoming Compley's ball."

Clever man, he has clearly deduced there was an objection to my attendance other than his absence and is manoeuvring Mama into removing the obstacle. His intellect is admirable.

"Lord Dellingby, if you are of a mind to take my daughter to such a venue, who am I to stand in your way?" The clipped tone alerts me to trouble in store.

"Very well then, it is agreed. Until the ball, I beg to take my leave."

"But it is still two days away," I exclaim.

"With regret, my business is not yet concluded."

"I trust it is not too great a burden, this business of yours?" Mama asks under her quizzing brow.

"No, indeed. It is a mere inconvenience, I assure you."

"Then we shall see you at the Compley's home on the evening of the twenty-fourth."

"Thank you for your forbearance, Your Grace. Until then, I bid you adieu." With a bow, he departs.

"Does his behaviour not seem strange, Mama?" I enquire once he has left us.

"No more than any other man. Anne, they are strange creatures. I shall not remind you again. You must stop this needless worry. And as for your asking to attend the Compley's ball when you know full well I was against such a scheme pushes the boundaries of decency."

"But Mama, he asked. And I made it plain she is not of high standing. He was given ample opportunity to refuse. Besides, I am to start making decisions, am I not?"

A smile tries to emerge on my Mama's beautiful face, it is witnessed in the corners of her lips and in the depths of her blue eyes.

"You are. But need I remind you this is not your house, but that of your Papa. You would do well to remember that distinction whilst you remain here."

"I shall be mindful of that point, Mama," I tell her with downcast eyes lest she should observe my own mirth shining forth.

It cannot be helped, I am growing into a woman who is soon to be mistress of her own household, and my chosen husband seems to be sensible of my comfort, despite his taciturn manner of late. And now, here is Mama forbidding yet allowing all in the same breath. Oh Lor', perhaps I am losing my wits, but it all seems highly amusing.

Dismissing myself from the room, I seek the refuge of the garden. Reaching the tree which received a beating from Lord Dellingby, my smile widens into a grin. Visions of his ridiculous pantomime bring laughter from the depths of my belly and rolling across the flower beds.

The question is more how one can bring him back to such good humour. It pains me to see him so disquieted. Something is surely amiss, but he remains silent on the matter. At least today he seemed a little brighter. Perhaps he is correct, and all I need do is to be at his side. I determine to make him dance away his troubles at the ball. And at the same time, it is hoped that Miss Compley shall be viewed as a desirable partner to her beau, now there shall be two great friends at her side.

❧ Chapter 24 ❧

The evening of the Compley's ball arrives. I had the foresight to ensure Julia extended an invitation to Lord Dellingby, as I am sure her parents would not have dared invite him without some prompting. And sure enough, entering the assembly rooms, he can be seen standing tall and fine, conversing with Julia's papa, heightening him in my esteem.

"Miss Compley, how good it is to see you. It feels an age, and so much yet so little seems to have happened. Tell me, how do you fare? You look very well," I say, approaching my dearest, oldest friend and holding her hands.

Planting kisses on one another's cheeks, she replies, "I am all the better now you are here. And thank you for encouraging Lord Dellingby, you do me too much favour."

"He did not take much encouragement, I assure you. He was all eagerness."

"Only to accede to your whim, as you must know."

"Well, whatever the reason, he is here, and we are all ready for a fine evening. Tell me, how do you continue with Sir Reginald?"

"Slowly, I fear. He seems to show affection and reticence all at once."

"My dear, this must be remedied. There can be no reluctance to gain your hand. We must show him how desirable a partner you are."

She giggles. "Why do I suspect you are about one of your schemes?"

I flutter my eyelashes, and my fingers rest on my breast. "*Moi? Je suis toute innocence.*"

"Lady Anne, you may be all purity and goodness, but all innocence may be a little too far an exaggeration. Not that I would ever take issue, you understand, for you always act with the best of intentions and are my dearest friend. In fact, in this case, I think I must say how greatly obliged I am to you for your kind assistance."

"It is no great thing. Sir Reginald merely requires some persuasion," I tell her, smiling wryly.

We both quietly giggle together behind our fans.

"Good evening, ladies," Lord Dellingby greets with a bow.

We chorus our response and curtsey in unison.

"I do hope I may be given the honour of the first dance, Miss Compley?"

She blushes wildly. "Lord Dellingby, I could not ask you—"

"Miss Compley, I would not think you capable of being so outrageous as to ask a man to dance. I believe the question came from my own lips."

Her blush deepens as she glances across at me. Such a sweet girl to consider my feelings, but I happily nod my assent. I am not yet his wife; he may dance with whomsoever he chooses. And in this matter, our tastes agree.

I cannot help but notice the slight tremble to her hand as Lord Dellingby leads Miss Compley to the dance area. He smiles kindly upon her, and my own mouth twists upwards as he performs exactly as I had hoped.

Not long into the dance, Sir Reginald approaches. "Good evening, Lady Anne. I had not expected you or Lord Dellingby to be in attendance this evening."

"Did you not? Is it so surprising when I consider myself to be one of her closest friends?"

"Pardon my presumption. I meant no offence."

"But of course," I allow, inclining my head.

An uncomfortable silence falls about us as we watch our prospective partners dance together. Perhaps for the first time, I am thankful she is not high-born, as she would be in competition, and one cannot be entirely certain she would not be the more favoured. They do make a fine couple as they saunter across the floor.

My consolation to this undesirable pang of jealousy is that, judging by his shifting of stance, Sir Reginald feels likewise, and that was the intended outcome. I had not expected for a moment to be thus affected myself. It is really quite shameful.

"What an elegant dancer Miss Compley is," I mention, gathering myself.

"Indeed she is," Sir Reginald murmurs.

"And so sweet natured. Her voice knows no comparison. She is so much admired in town I half expect her to announce she has been made an offer any day now."

Sir Reginald's back straightens until he more closely resembles a lamppost. "Quite. And might I offer my own congratulations on your own betrothal?"

"I thank you. Pray, would you be so kind as to excuse me, I believe I see one of my friends I must speak with?"

We part ways, and I approach a lady on the far side of the room, who I have not yet had the privilege of meeting, but for the sake of an excuse, I begin a conversation which sends her into a flurry of excitement. Fortunately, from across the room this must appear to be friends being happy to see one another, so I bear her exuberance.

"Oh, Lady Anne, how good you are to notice me. I had not thought you would even see me here. And might I be so bold as to offer congratulations to one such as yourself on your upcoming nuptials?" and on she rattles.

"And how do you know Miss Compley?" I manage to ask as she draws breath.

"We only recently met in town at a ball, but she was good enough to invite me here this evening. I cannot begin to tell you how delighted I am to be here in such fine company."

Bless her soul, such grandeur of a home such as Miss Compley's seems a veritable treasure trove. Perhaps she is the daughter of a new knight, or some such. Little wonder our paths have not previously crossed.

"Pardon my asking, but we have not yet been introduced. Might I inquire as to your name?"

"Oh my. Lady Anne, my humble apologies, I should have said. Whatever must you think of me? I am quite carried away. Miss Frances Bennet, at your service," she informs me with a curtsey.

"A pleasure to meet you, Miss Bennet."

"The pleasure surely must all be mine, Lady Anne."

Straining not to roll my eyes, I enquire, "And how do you find London?"

Anything to stop her fawning over me in such a degrading fashion. She seems a dear, sweet girl, but completely unaware she is not my maidservant in her humility. Nay, not even Clément would be so cow-eyed. Her excitement overflows as she details all the parties and entertainments she has enjoyed whilst in town.

"Ah, Lady Anne, here you are," Lord Dellingby interjects.

"Lord Dellingby. I have been making the acquaintance of Miss Bennet here."

"Delighted to meet you, I'm sure, but might I beg your permission to take Lady Anne away from you so she may enjoy a dance?"

The girl's face glows red as if she were set alight and she giggles in a most unseemly fashion. "Oh, how good you are, your lordship. I would not deter the good Lady Anne from pleasure for a moment. Not on my account."

"I am much obliged," he says with a bow before leading me away.

Once out of earshot he asks, "What, might I enquire was that? What an alarming creature."

"Lord Dellingby, do not be so cruel. She was of great assistance to me."

"Was she indeed?" he asks, his brow rising.

I giggle at his incredulity. "She eased my escape from Sir Reginald who was growing irksome in his concern over Miss Compley's fine dance partner."

"Haha, was he, by Jove? My poor Lady Anne, thrown into the depths by such behaviour. Or perhaps I misjudge you, and you frequently prefer such company?"

I giggle again. "My lord, you really are too cruel. I suspect her to be the daughter of a knight, she is not so lowly as to be entirely below my notice."

"Am I to expect her to dinner once we are married?" he asks with a smirk.

"Do be sensible, Lord Dellingby," I reprimand, giving him a pointed look.

His smile only broadens. "I must ensure chef stocks a good supply of mutton."

"You are become a crowing cock."

"How you injure me. I deserve no such censure. I did not say I should deny her entry to our home."

How my breast heaves at his words, and I am filled with such warmth it must show on my cheeks. 'Our home' sounds most gratifying when pronounced by his lips.

"Might I inquire what makes you fly your colours so beautifully?" he questions.

"You may not. Concentrate now, the musicians are preparing," I tell him haughtily, which leads him to cough away what I am certain would have been a laugh.

"I am, as always, at your command, dear lady. I trust you are not too greatly displeased."

"Of course not, I do not believe it in your power to truly vex me."

He flashes a boyish grin at me as we begin to step to the music. His mood seems much improved this evening, to my relief.

"I am greatly relieved you are safe and well at my side once more," I tell him as our hands unite.

"You had any doubt as to the contrary?"

"Lord Emsby so worried me with his comment of perilous roads."

A scowl darkens his features. "The devil take him."

He looks shocked at himself. "Pray, forgive the outburst. He had no right to disquiet you so. If only he were here, he would hear so himself."

"But he is not. He and Lady Rathburn have quitted London to marry directly."

"I am sure her mama saw to it. Well, all the better. May they never quit their abode evermore."

"My lord, I find myself quite in agreement with your sentiment."

We smile our quiet acknowledgement as the dance parts us.

"I did do right by you, by allowing the continuation of your Season, did I not?" he asks, his brow furrowed as we reunite.

"There is no great hurry in our case. But nor would I be sorry to quit London."

His consideration touches my heart and constricts my throat.

"I should not even have thought to keep you here a moment longer than was strictly necessary but for the upcoming celebrations the Prince Regent is soon to hold. They promise to be a great spectacle. I confess myself eager to partake."

"Yes, Papa is to attend a dinner being held for the foreign dignitaries on the eighteenth of June, so we could not leave before then in any case. Do not make yourself uneasy."

"I find your happiness increases my own, so it is not entirely a selfless quest."

"I really am not sure when to take you in all earnestness and when you are in jest."

"It is an endeavour of mine not to remain too serious for too long at any given time."

"A fine aim in life, to be sure," I comment, smiling.

Lord Dellingby stays by my side as I seek refreshment following our turn and remains so for most of the evening. As we line up for the supper dance, I glance down the line.

With a knowing look, my head subtly nods towards the right to where Sir Reginald stands with Julia. Lord Dellingby, having followed my direction returns his gaze to mine, offering an approving look, light shining from his eyes.

"Remind me to be forever on my guard, Lady Anne, for I fear you may have more sense than is good for a man," he says, his voice low and rumbling.

"Utter nonsense. Even if what you say is true, what would be the use in my reminding you of it?"

He chuckles. "There you have it, you have proven my point most succinctly."

He touches his lips to my raised gloved hand as we meet and turn. And once more he is my Lord Dellingby, utterly returned to me as he was.

Sir Reginald escorts Miss Compley to supper, and they are seen in animated conversation. But perhaps onlookers would say the same of Lord Dellingby and myself, although that would be less surprising.

It is a strange thing to be the talk of the town, to hear mutterings of marriage whispered about you. Perhaps it is so other mamas may strike him off their list, or mayhap they take a deep interest in the happiness of others; I suspect the former.

No matter, I am once more given hope.

❧ Chapter 25 ❧

Over a week passes with Lord Dellingby coming and going. He is now a frequent visitor, but perhaps not as frequent as one should expect, but an effort seems to be being made. I am now of the understanding his father has requested him to perform some additional duties on his behalf. From the frown which flitters across his visage whenever his father is mentioned, I gather he may not be in good health, but why Lord Dellingby should feel the need to conceal this detail from me is beyond my comprehension.

Perhaps he foresees the depth of loss he shall suffer. Or maybe he fears to inherit his title before we are married, thus reducing our time of relative freedom? Or he fears the heavy burden of duty? I am sure I do not know how a man's mind works, but these seem the most likely thoughts which weigh so heavily upon him. And there would be no sense in relaying any of this to me, as what can I do to aid him?

As we attend balls, the theatre and gatherings, I do my best to be in the best of humours as this seems to remind him how to be jolly. His cares, what e'er they may be, are often seemingly forgotten during a dance or a well-timed witty comment. I suppose I am slowly learning my design; how best to support my husband once we are married. It is of comfort to note this at least is within my power.

Outside my sphere still lies Lord Beauvrais, who remains in my thoughts. I take comfort in hearing no news, as I am still as yet to hear anything. By my calculation, he should have made port by now. If his ship had been lost to the sea, I am sure to have been made aware by means of reading of it in Papa's newspaper which I've been careful to check regularly. Should anyone discover me in this task, the page is carefully laid out at the Society news, as happens now.

"Lord Dellingby has arrived for you, Lady Anne," Forbes announces, closely followed by the man so announced.

He is all smiles this morning. "Good morning, Lady Anne. How well you look," he tells me, kissing the back of my gloved hands.

Mama hurries in before we are allowed, heaven forbid, a moment of privacy. I fully accept the rules of society, but it must be said they are become rather a nuisance. Occasionally, one would favour the opportunity of a few quiet words spoken alone. Perhaps one of those delightful kisses, which have regrettably not discovered another opportunity. It is enough to make one long for a shorter betrothal period.

However, the foreign dignitaries shall soon arrive, and all will be centred on them, with much rejoicing. So, in London we must remain. One should celebrate such things, even if a dearly beloved brother has been lost to the campaign. Peace has been achieved, albeit at a high price. And the prince is keen to celebrate a century of the Hanoverian family's reign.

"Good morning, Your Grace," he greets Mama with a smile and a bow.

She greets him in kind before silently taking up her position of guard.

"I am of a mind to find some exercise and was hoping to convince you to a ride out this morning," he says, looking at me then Mama.

"On horseback?" I check, trying not to allow my excitement to show.

"If that is agreeable? I understand you have a mount."

"Mama, we have no prior engagements, do we?"

Mama shakes her head, her shoulders lowering ever so slightly with her silent sigh. "We do not."

"Allow me to dress, if you please, Lord Dellingby, and I shall be ready directly."

His response is a wide smile as he inclines his head and turns towards the door.

"Clément," I call on my way, "Clément."

I almost bump into Forbes. "Oh Forbes, please have Lady readied as soon as may be."

"Very good, m'lady," he says in his usual calm manner.

"Clément, oh there you are. Lord Dellingby is arrived to take Lady and me out for some air. Where is my riding habit?"

"I shall bring it directly."

I shrug out of my morning dress as she hurries to fetch the garment.

Clément takes great pains to be always at the ready for every eventuality, and deftly helps me into my habit, and secures my hair and hat in place herself.

"Have fun, but please be careful, my lady," Clément urges.

I shoot her a look full of curiosity that she should offer such words. Perhaps she is aware of my previous near misadventure. But there is no time to dwell on such things. Freedom beckons.

My shoes click rapidly on the steps as I hurry outside where I discover Lord Dellingby issuing orders.

"Are we all set?" I ask him, walking towards Lady.

"Almost. I hope you will forgive the interference, but you were to have only a footman in attendance."

"As is customary."

He leans in close and whispers, "It shall not serve our purpose. I am informed you have a taste for a faster pace, so have sent for a mounted groom."

"Lord Dellingby, he shall not have a livery," I reply with a gasp.

"And you think I should allow you to be disgraced? He is to borrow one, hence the delay."

"My lord, you do too much."

Perhaps he takes a liberty, ordering my servants around in such a manner. Although I am inclined to forgive him.

"Only in the pursuit of your pleasure, Lady Anne."

His warm smile melts my heart as well as all thoughts of chastising any heavy-handedness on his part. He helps me into my saddle before mounting his own steed. I quickly stifle the smile which threatens as I realise he was not prepared to take no for an answer.

The clip-clop of hooves behind signals my commandeered groom is ready. Turning in my saddle, I manage to glimpse the poor man in a jacket which is a little tight about his chest. I have to look forwards quickly before he can bear witness to my amusement.

"When you're ready, Lady Anne. I shall be right behind you."

Nudging Lady into a walk, we make our way. Or rather, I make my way, and Lord Dellingby seems to linger. Glancing over my shoulder I see him muttering to the groom. Pretending not to notice, I carry on at a slow pace until I hear his horses' hooves approach.

Lord Dellingby rides at my side as we make our way to the park.

"These busy streets must be a complete bore to you," he comments.

"Are they not to you also?"

"I have become more accustomed to them, but yes, they remain a frustrating barrier."

"I do not know how you can bear to remain so long in town."

"Until now, there was little to lure me away."

"And now, all of a sudden, you remember the charms of the country?"

He looks directly into my eyes, his brown eyes dark. "I do."

An ox and cart turn sharply in front of us, ruining the moment.

"You there, have a care," he shouts at the careless driver but is promptly ignored.

"Really, some people have no consideration," he grumbles.

"No harm is done," I tell him with a smile greater than is natural.

The incident has set my pulse racing, but now I am all concern for Lord Dellingby as a cloud seems to have taken up residence above him once again. But it dissipates as we make our way, and eventually arrive at the gates to the park. Lady starts picking up her feet, getting skittish as soon as we're through.

"Looks like she's ready for a run. Are you, Lady Anne?"

"Should we not walk sedately?"

He raises a brow at me. "Is that what you would prefer?"

I blush under his scrutiny. "No," I admit with a shake of my head.

"I thought as much. Neither of you would be happy."

"We are still becoming acquainted. She is a little high-spirited," I reply, gathering the reins tight.

His smirk is barely perceptible. "I would have her no other way. Let us make it fun. What say you to a race as far as the pond?"

I gasp. "Lord Dellingby, a race, is that...?" but he is gone before I can finish questioning his propriety.

Left with no recourse, I do the only thing possible, and kick Lady on. All too willing to oblige and show that Chestnut she's the faster of the pair, we begin to catch up. It's a chilly grey day, so there's fortunately not many to observe our recklessness.

"Yar," I urge Lady on, flapping the ends of the reins about her neck.

Her hooves thunder against the path, one two three four, one two three four. As all four hooves are off the ground we could be flying. My hair, tied close, slaps the back of my neck, the wind making my eyes water, but I trust Lady not to endanger us. I transfer the reins to one hand as the other wipes my eyes so I can properly see even so.

Lord Dellingby's horse is fast upon our heels, but we have gained the lead and shan't let up the pace now. Onwards we speed. There is nothing but her and me.

All too soon the pond looms, and we slow. One two three, one two three, we canter. Then the bounce as she trots before walking. We stop at the pond. With nobody else around, I allow her to bend her neck to slurp the water.

"I concede, Lady Anne, you are the better horseman," Lord Dellingby admits as he joins us.

Both horses greedily drink after their exertions. I look about, suddenly aware the groom did not keep up.

"Do not trouble yourself, my lady. Your man is but a short distance behind."

"Lord Dell —"

"I have no other design but to snatch a few moments of private conversation, my dear."

"Hmph!"

"If you tell me you are not anxious for the same I shall call him closer this instant."

My lips tighten together. "You are quite ungallant today, Lord Dellingby. First, you steal a head-start in a race, and now you ask me to admit to what I would not own."

"A race which I still lost, need I remind you? And I ask nothing of you but honesty. I could not remain any longer watched in my every move. Really, I know not how you live so."

"It is to be expected."

"You do not know what I suffer. How I wish I had named a nearer date for our wedding. It is not like me to be so —"

"It was Papa's suggestion, was it not?" I guess.

"It does no good to speak so. Please, forgive me for mentioning…forget what I said."

"Papa can be excessively persuasive. You should not take it upon yourself so."

"To my shame, he did not use much persuasion in the matter."

"Lord Dellingby, he would have you think so. He is far too clever. I am sorry indeed that he exerted such influence over you."

"Well, it cannot be helped. What is done is done."

"Unless we ride to Gretna Green," I reply, giggling.

He laughs. "I fear it may be a little too far for us to ride in a day."

"You see, it is a hopeless case, indeed. There is nothing for it but to remain patient," I say, shrugging, a wry smile dancing across my lips.

"It would appear so." He shifts in his saddle. "I fair almost drew Lord Alverbury's cork when he told me he'd never seen a finer filly. Fortunately, he quickly added he was in earnest and was referring to your horse, and not your good person, so his blood was spared."

I giggle at the image of Lord Dellingby striking such a blow, and to none other than poor Lord Alverbury. What a ninnyhammer to say such a thing.

"Having seen her run, I am inclined to agree with him. You have a fine horse there, Lady Anne."

"Indeed I do. I consider myself most fortunate."

"And you ride her with great grace and accomplishment." His eyes darken as he speaks and licks his lips in such a way as to make me feel uncomfortable, but I know not why it should.

"I thank you, my lord. I do enjoy a good ride."

A strange guttural groan emanates from his direction.

"Do you not agree?"

"What? Yes, a most...pleasurable sport." He shifts in his saddle again.

"Oh, see now, here's your man. I told you he was not far behind," he adds.

The tightly liveried groom tips his hat at us on his approach but keeps a respectable distance. Lord Dellingby must have paid him for his short absence. Well, it's nice to know my virtue has a price. A fine thing to leave me to the whims of the inconstant lord. I have a good mind to have him dismissed.

And it was all for nought. Lord Dellingby spoke nonsense, and still issued no more kisses. At least he could have claimed a small kiss for his trouble.

We let the horses walk on a long rein as we make our way around the park, conversing over nothing much, but getting a better understanding of one another. Like myself, he seems to relax in the saddle and becomes his natural, affable self.

"Lady Anne, I must tell you a thing which may not be to your liking, but I beg you will forgive me."

"This sounds serious. I shall listen with patience. You have my word."

"I had hoped to offer you the choice, you see. However, my father is not in good health, so it does not do to insist contrary to his wishes. But he wishes to keep Wenston Hall to himself. His reasoning is quite beyond me as there is more than enough room."

I look over at his anxious face. "Lord Dellingby, I had not expected to live there, at least not yet. It is his home, and I would not turn him out. And having a new woman in the home when he is not in good health could be nothing but irksome."

"You…you had not Wenston Hall in mind?"

"Lord Dellingby, do not mistake me for a treasure seeker. Why, Papa has enough homes should we wish to consider one of those."

"No, there is no call for that. Only, the next alternative is not quite so grand nor in such picturesque grounds. I had hoped to give you the grandest of homes."

"Pray, I am not so gently bred to expect always to be surrounded by opulence."

He snorts. "I did not say it wasn't a fine property. It has opulence enough."

I cannot help but laugh. "Do forgive me, I did not mean…oh dear."

His laughter joins my own at my terrible faux pas.

Sobering, he offers, "But my father is, of course, keen to meet his daughter-in-law, and we are promised to pay him a visit as soon as we are able on our honeymoon."

"But of course. I confess I am curious to meet with him. It is a pity he is unable to be in London."

"I wish it were otherwise. He is not half as curmudgeonly as he must sound."

"In this too, I must be patient," I say more to myself than him.

"Patience, we are told, is a virtue."

"Something only those with a surplus of the virtue can boast of. For the rest of us, it is something to be endured and striven for in equal measure."

"How gloomy we're become. What say you to a gentle jaunt?"

My response is to leg Lady into a canter. It is a lumbering, relaxing kind, not a race, and Lord Dellingby rides a pace behind. Lady snorts her pleasure, and I feel as if I could do the same. This is where I belong. What a foolish notion, but I cannot help feeling at peace whilst with my horses.

Bringing us back to a walk, Lord Dellingby rides at my side.

"Such a fine filly," he mutters.

"My lord, please forgive the question, but Lady and Rosalind will be welcome to your stables, will they not?"

"Rosalind?"

"My own horse who has been cruelly denied the pleasures of London."

Lord Dellingby chuckles. "Oh, poor Rosalind. But perhaps we should envy her. For, *hath not old custom made this life more sweet, Than that of painted pomp? Are not these woods, More free from peril than the envious court?*"

"You quote Shakespeare's *As You Like It* at me, my lord? I do not consider horses to be in much peril from court. But perhaps she is better off in the wide open fields of home."

"Is it not why she was so named? I do hope that none of us suffers the same terrible fate as that of her namesakes' father, however. Exile is such a nasty business." He pretends to shudder.

"I do so hate to press you for an answer."

"Oh, yes, yes. Who could consider for a moment of parting you from your equine friends? I rather think it would be a most imprudent way to begin our marriage, for how should you ever forgive such an attempt? Of course, you may have them brought to our home."

My insides melt as he pronounces it our home for a second time. He is not to lord it over me forever, but to share his property with me.

Lady chooses that precise moment to pass wind terribly loudly.

"Oh, I do apologise," I exclaim.

"My dear Lady Anne, I had thought the horse in error," he tells me, his look all seriousness.

"Why, Lord Dellingby," I shriek.

But his subsequent laughter gives him away, and I cannot help but join in. It is wonderful to see the light back in his eyes. He makes me laugh more than any other I have ever known. It may not be entirely proper to do so, but with him, I do not recall such sombre lessons of composure.

Regaining my breath, I manage to suggest, "Perhaps it is time we make our way back?"

"As much as it sorrows me to call an end to this excursion, I must agree with you," he says, turning his horse in the direction of the exit.

We trot up the path in the full knowledge that anything above a walk will be quite impossible through the streets.

Unwilling to part company upon returning home, I have the audacity to ask, "Lord Dellingby, you must be hungry after the exercise. Would you perhaps like to partake of a little nuncheon?"

"So long as your parents sanction the invitation, I think I should like that very much," he says, helping me down from Lady.

His horse is behind him, and we are shielded from view of the house. Lord Dellingby takes a moment to steady me as my feet touch the ground. His hands are firmly about my hips, and our faces are brought temptingly close.

Licking my lips which seem dry all of a sudden, I explain, "My knees seem all a-tremble after my ride, my lord."

"Take a moment to regain your composure," he whispers hoarsely.

His words send such tremorings through my entire body that they seem to have quite the reverse effect upon my person. My lips purse into a pout of their own accord.

"Lady Anne, I would ask you not to tempt me so invitingly, if you please. I fear for your safety when you look so," he says into my ear.

"I know not what has come over me," I mutter.

Flames seem to be engulfing me from within and there is moisture between my thighs.

"Perhaps we rode too far in this London air? Come, let us get you inside," he says, offering his support as my feet are encouraged inside the house.

I walk as if in a stupor, vaguely aware of the frustration of the missed opportunity of a kiss. I was so willing for him to take the advantage, so cleverly concealed by our mounts. But he displayed proper gallantry, and yet I cannot admire him for it.

"Lady Anne is feeling a little unwell," he tells Forbes as we enter.

"This way, if you please, my lord," he says, leading the way to the morning room, which is closest.

They settle me into a chair, which is beyond necessary, but now I feel as though I must continue with what Lord Dellingby has begun. Forbes fetches a glass of Madeira, which is welcome whether strictly required or not.

"I am not so very unwell, as you are quite aware," I tell him quietly once we are alone.

"My dear Lady Anne, your colours were flying so high I had to say something. I thought only of your modesty, I assure you. And perhaps my safety, for if your father saw you, I cannot be certain what would become of me, returning you in such a state."

"Oh, then I am much obliged to you."

"Not at all," he says, taking my hand.

"Anne, what is all this about being taken unwell?" Mama flusters as she enters.

She is silenced as soon as Lord Dellingby's presence is noticed. "Oh, Lord Dellingby, I had not realised you were here. Thank you for staying with Lady Anne. It is most considerate of you."

"I did not like to leave her, but she seems to be recovering. Merely an attack of the London air, in my opinion."

Mama narrows her eyes at him but does not pass comment. Turning to me, she orders me to dress for nuncheon.

"Lord Dellingby, shall you join us? We do not observe nuncheon with any grandeur, but you are welcome to partake in our meagre offerings if you so desire."

"That is most generous of you, Your Grace. I do not normally partake, of course. But I confess my appetite has been increased by our excursion, so would be delighted to join on this occasion, if you please."

Mama's eyes seem to bore to his very soul, so intently does she look upon Lord Dellingby. Primly, she walks to ring the bell. The poor man is left frozen to the spot, a blush warming his cheeks as though he has failed some test. But he behaved regrettably impeccably, so there is no reason he should appear so disconcerted.

Clearing his throat, he turns his attention back to me. He nods his head towards the door, a silent reminder to change my dress.

"One more for nuncheon," Mama informs the servant who hurries off to make preparations for our last minute guest.

I quickly follow the servant out of the room and seek refuge in my own. Clément is quickly on hand to put me into more suitable attire. Poor Dellingby is faced with eating in his riding clothes. Perhaps I should not have invited him in after all. Papa is sure to have been informed and will insist on joining us, thus spoiling our informal meal.

"It is beyond me how such stunning transformations are made in so short a time," Lord Dellingby admires as I enter the dining room, where all are gathered.

"Not wanting to shatter any illusion, it is no great task, my lord."

"It cannot be when there is beauty to begin with, for certain."

Mama gets a nasty tickle in her throat and emits a single cough.

"Hello, Papa," I greet, going over to him and kissing his cheek.

"You had a pleasurable morning, I trust," he says, looking at me with an inquiring brow.

"Indeed we did, Your Grace. Lady Anne behaved precisely as expected of her, and there were no incidents of misbehaving horses to report," Lord Dellingby answers for me.

Papa glowers at him. "I should be very surprised to hear otherwise. My daughter has been raised in the saddle, even talking her way into a hunt or two."

"Haha, has she, by Jove? And was at the head of the pack, I'd wager."

"True enough, she does have the ability to outride many of the chaps there."

At the mention of other men in my company, a scowl seems to cross Lord Dellingby's face, but it is soon replaced by admiration. I bow my head in acknowledgement, with a small smile.

"Well, let us not stand on ceremony, do tuck in. I do hope you are not offended by our informal ways, Dellingby. There is formality enough at breakfast and dinner. Indeed, I rarely bother with nuncheon at all, but today I make the exception in your presence."

"You honour me, Your Grace," he answers with a bow.

We eat our bread, meat, cheese and fruit in awkward silence. Lord Dellingby seems quite at a loss and makes several failed attempts at conversation. Fortunately, it is not of long duration.

Forbes comes in as we finish. "Sir Thomas Lawrence is awaiting you in the study, Your Grace."

"Ah, the sole reason I am at home at this hour. Come, Dellingby, you shall not wish to miss this. Ladies, you as well. Come, come."

We follow Papa to his lair, where the artist is indeed waiting. He seems to have been examining one of the existing paintings, which he quickly turns away from as we enter.

"Your Grace, Your Grace," he greets my parents with an elaborate bow.

"Sir Thomas, you have brought the portrait?"

"But of course, Your Grace," he confirms, walking towards a stand with a cover over, "Should you all like to see?"

"Yes, yes, get on with it," Papa tells him, wafting his hand as if flicking away a fly.

Lord Dellingby and I jostle into a position where we can see this not-so-grand unveiling. My nerves are all a-jitter. Sir Thomas had better live up to his reputation for flattery. I should not like to see Lord Dellingby disappointed in my likeness.

With a whoosh, the cover is fluttered off, and my image is displayed.

"Yes, very good. The smaller is to be delivered to Hampshire?" Papa enquires.

"It is on its way as we speak, Your Grace."

"Lord Dellingby, should you like a copy to be made?"

The man in question seems affected by the dust eschewed by the removal of the cover, for he is forced to cough before responding, "A small copy would not be out of place at Riverton House if Sir Thomas would be so obliging?"

"But of course, it would be my honour, my lord."

Papa carries on his conversation with the artist. Lord Dellingby makes use of his distraction.

"Did you not inform me the name of your dog is Prince? I suppose this is his likeness at your feet?" he checks quietly with a smirk.

"You could be correct in your assumption, my lord."

"I see. Very good, very good indeed. So long as you do not ever name any of my own hounds Duke."

"Oh, I should never go so far."

"But a prince is not beyond you?"

"It is a very different matter when one thinks of the example our Prince Regent sets."

"Ah, with that clarification I think it a most marvellous painting," he says in a louder tone upon the last two words.

"It meets your approval, my lord? I am most pleased," Sir Thomas says.

"Very much so. As fine a work as ever I've seen." The naughty man goes so far as to burst into applause.

I hardly know how to keep my countenance, so clap along with him. Thus, my smile is shown as one of admiration. And perhaps it is, but not entirely for the painting.

❧ Chapter 26 ❧

Lord Dellingby has been conspicuously absent the past two days, but Mama implores my patience as we must allow he has been busy with preparations for the ball. And as the hour is arrived for us to celebrate, I am all excitement at the prospect.

Clément seems to have taken even greater pains than normal about my toilette. My gown is blue with gold brocade along the hem, waist and puff sleeves. My lips are a touch more pink than is customary, my cheeks a rosy glow about their otherwise pale canvas. The hairdresser has worked wonders and a simple feather adorns in my hair. My reflection does indeed resemble more of a painting than reality. A flattering version of myself peers back at me.

Despite being now in June, the infamous repressible heat of town does not seem forthcoming, which I suppose is to be considered a blessing. Pulling my wrap about my shoulders, Mama and I enter the carriage. The night air carries quite a chill through the fog.

We are hardly through the door when Lord Dellingby greets us with great excitement.

"Your Grace, Lady Anne, it is my honour and privilege to welcome you this evening. Come, we have fires lit against this dreary weather," he says, leading us to the warm ballroom which has a few people occupying it already.

"We are not late, my lord?" I ask.

He whispers, "Not at all. Some of our guests were a little over-eager. It has been too long since a ball was held here."

"Ah, I see."

"Here is Lady Grainger, whom I believe you are well acquainted with," he says, steering us towards her.

"Yes indeed. Good evening Lady Grainger, how lovely to see you this evening," Mama greets with a curtsey.

As they began conversing in a most animated fashion, Lord Dellingby leads me away.

"You are full too wise to not be about a mischief," I reprimand him.

His hand covers his heart and he goes so far as to blink rapidly. "'Pon rep, I know not of what you speak."

"Have it your way, my lord," I tell him with a wry smile.

"Please allow me to take this opportunity to inform you of your exquisite beauty this evening."

"Why, thank you. You look most elegant yourself, Lord Dellingby."

"One pales into insignificance beside such splendour."

"Have a care not to be carried too far, my lord."

"There shall be no holding back once we are married," he mutters, although I suspect I was not supposed to hear, and so pretend not to.

"Oh look, Miss Compley is come," I exclaim.

"The very person I was escorting you to, so I may welcome my other guests, if you will permit it?"

"Really, you do talk nonsense. Of course you must greet your guests. Only, should I not as well, for it is our betrothal ball?" The thought had not occurred to me before now.

"Do not concern yourself. You may talk with your friends until your heart's content, for this is not your house as yet."

"Oh, how silly of me."

"Not at all. It is a most thoughtful notion. But there will soon be duties for you enough. Enjoy this time whilst it is allowed you."

It is a rather painful reminder that I shall not be much in my most beloved friend's company often. It cannot have been his intention to offend, but it weighs heavily upon my heart all the same. Not that Julia would know judging from my exterior, of course.

"Lady Anne, you are come. Felicitations on what promises to be a fine evening."

"Delighted to have you here, Miss Compley."

"Ladies, if I may take my leave?" Lord Dellingby asks with a bow.

"Yes, go, go, my lord," I allow.

A sudden urge comes over me to kiss his cheek before he departs, but I quash it within my breast and turn my attention fully to my friend.

"Lady Anne, I have such news. You will never guess, so I shall tell you. Sir Reginald has made me an offer."

"Oh, I am delighted. Congratulations my dearest Miss Compley," I tell her whilst wrapping my arms about her person, "I knew he could not resist for long."

"Thank you for your part in it."

"My dear, I did nothing at all."

"Lord Dellingby danced with me of his own accord, I suppose?"

"As a matter of fact, he did, although I sanctioned his actions, and would have beseeched him had he not done as much."

"Well, pass on my gratitude to him, for it is certain it encouraged Sir Reginald to discover his courage."

"Has a date been set? And how did you not tell me before? When did he offer?"

Miss Compley lowers her gaze to the floor. "He made his offer last week. But I confess we have been amidst commotion ever since. And I had wanted to surprise you with the news in person this evening."

"A most fitting occasion, and of course you are forgiven your secret. It is admirable how you kept it so long."

"I almost rushed to your house immediately, but Aunt Retland stopped me, reminding me of my duties."

I cannot help a momentary sneer at that woman's name. "I am sure you did as was proper."

"We are to be married a fortnight from now and are to travel home in but a few days."

"So soon? Oh, there is not sufficient time to say a proper farewell."

"Then we shall have to visit once we are both settled."

"Aye, there is nothing else for it. You must visit Lord Dellingby and I."

"There is no power on Earth which could keep me away. We are firm friends, and I am determined to forever be so," she says, holding my hands tightly in hers.

"As am I, Julia, as am I." I can say no more as tears are threatening and a lump has formed in my throat.

"Lady Anne, Miss Compley, good evening to you both."

"Miss Plimpton, good evening," Miss Compley says first.

I smile and curtsey but dare not risk words.

"Miss Plimpton, I was informing Lady Anne of my betrothal to Sir Reginald."

"Felicitations, my dear. But of course, it was always certain how it would be."

"And now we are left with only your own conquest. How fares Lord Meltcham?" I inquire, my composure back under control.

"My dear, do not *speak* to me of him. He is so slow as to be mistaken for a snail and immovable as a mountain."

"Perhaps you should dance with Lord Dellingby?" I suggest.

"What is this? Am I to be loaned out to all of your circle, Lady Anne?" he asks mischievously at my side, making me gasp.

"My lord, how you do sneak up on a person."

"Haha, I did no such thing. You were merely too engrossed in conversation to observe my approach. However, if I may be of service to Miss Plimpton, it would be my honour if she should be my partner in a dance. Although, the first at least is reserved for you, of course."

"Lord Dellingby, you are all goodness. Please, it was idle chatter and not to be taken seriously. Do not feel obliged," Miss Plimpton says, a blush on her cheeks.

He turns to her. "Has Lady Anne not informed you? I do try not to take anything too seriously. But the offer stands. Miss Plimpton, would you favour me with a dance this evening?"

For perhaps the first time in our admittedly short acquaintance, Miss Plimpton seems at a loss. "Well, if it pleases you, Lord Dellingby, yes of course."

"Now ladies, if you will forgive me, I would take Lady Anne for the first dance which is in preparation."

Giggles ensue from my two friends who both curtsey.

"Tell me, for I am curious, Lady Anne, do women ever halt in their scheming?" he asks with a chuckle, once we are approaching the dance floor.

"Not that I am aware of, Lord Dellingby," I tell him with a titter.

"And whose eyes are we turning green this evening?"

"Lord Meltcham's. He is being most ungallantly slow. Poor Miss Plimpton. She has been courted the longest of any of us, and yet an offer has still not been made."

"Lord Meltcham?" he asks, his eyes growing wide.

"Yes. You know him?"

"Why, yes. But his delay should not come as any great surprise."

"Should it not?"

"Is Miss Plimpton oblivious? His father is urging him to marry Lady Rosen."

"Lady Rathburn's hideous friend?"

"She comes with a hideous fortune."

"Oh, how can you talk of such base matters? Lord Meltcham is of a good family."

"My dear, do not force me to explain financial matters. It is so distasteful."

"But he is not impoverished, surely?"

"I do not speak of bankruptcy, of course. But their funds are not limitless, and the future must be considered."

"How vile."

"Quite."

"Well, may he be forever miserable."

"My dear, before you cast such curses, please recall as to whether you have heard of an announcement? You have not. He resists as far as is possible."

"If only I had known, perhaps Lord Emsby would have done for Lady Rosen."

"Lady Anne, you must not say so. For it is quite certain I would have had a fearsome challenger in him."

"How can you speak such nonsense? Papa and I would always have favoured you."

He kisses my hand. "I am glad to hear it. But perhaps your scheme could be adopted in a similar fashion?"

In mimicry of his own actions earlier, I place my fingers over my breast. "My lord, I am quite sure I know not of what you speak."

"Minx," he declares, laughing, "But let us consider who would be suitable for Lady Rosen. There is Lord Sudville, I suppose."

"Oh, you cannot be so cruel to that poor boy. He is far too sweet for such a bride."

"Lord Nordfield then."

"Lord Dellingby, you are not terribly good at matchmaking, are you? He would never do. But there is perhaps Lord Trunton."

"Ah, there you have it. Yes, they would rub along together nicely. I should have thought of him myself. What a clever girl you are."

"Do try to remain on the task in hand, my lord."

"I beg pardon. So, it falls on you to highlight him as a desirable partner," he says with a wince.

"Lord Dellingby, this was your idea. And it shall be more arduous for myself than you. There is no need to shudder so."

"To see you dance with such as him? I am not sure I can endure it."

"He is yet to ask, you addlepate."

"Steady on, my dear."

"I apologise. But do try to concentrate."

"Lady Anne, I bow to your superiority in the matter," he says as the musicians start to play.

It is perhaps the most uncomfortable dance of my life, as my mind mulls over Lady Rosen and Lord Trunton. He always did put me ill at ease, and now, just when I should be safe from his leer, I must encourage it. But it is for the fair Miss Plimpton, who has been so very good to me. And Lord Dellingby shall not let anything terrible befall me.

One cannot even be certain of its efficacy, for now my engagement is well known. She cannot view me as true competition for Lord Trunton's affections. The best I can hope for is a display of recommendation.

After our dance, I part from Lord Dellingby who goes to my friends, whilst I go seemingly in search of Mama. Lord Trunton is en route, and I make sure to smile at him on my way.

"Lady Anne, how well you look this evening," he says in his nasal tone, his eyes staring as if I were a rabbit and he a fox.

"Lord Trunton, I trust you are well."

"Very well indeed. I trust your intended would not take offence should I beg a dance with you? For really the temptation is too great to resist."

"There is no objection."

His smile makes me sick to my stomach. What can he be about? He knows that I am intended for another. But this is what was hoped for. Taking a deep breath, I let him lead me to the next dance. Lord Dellingby stands but a few people away with Miss Plimpton, a smile playing at his lips as he catches my gaze.

It is surprising with how so little effort Lord Trunton was lured. The power of our sex strikes me in this moment. The choice was always mine. By means of small acts of body language we display our welcome to the opposite sex, who are more than willing to take every opportunity afforded them, it seems. If I had but been fully aware from the start…but no, perhaps all has come right as is. And there is no use dwelling on such things.

Each step is agony as Lord Trunton holds a little too tightly and closely with each move. Yet I am all smiles, hoping Lady Rosen is looking on, as her foolish counterpart did before her. Ah, there she is. A look of forlorn longing is surely apparent in my creased brow and pert lips.

"You need not say. I understand. Your choice is not your own, Lady Anne. I pity you, for you should have been far better rewarded with…but I go too far. No more shall be spoken on the matter," he consoles as we part at the end of the dance.

Lord Dellingby is by my side in an instant. "Lady Anne, I am come to claim the next as promised."

"I am all yours, my lord," I reply, clinging to his arm so he may take me away before I am parted with the bread and cheese I indulged in before leaving home.

"Hush, you did very well."

"He makes me feel so —"

"We attempted too much. You are quite unsettled. Let us find you fresh air instead."

"Thank you. That is most sensible. I had not thought to be so affected. I have danced with him before."

"I am sorry for my part. Never again shall you stand up with any other but me," he tells me softly.

"I have no wish to."

He glances behind. "But it seems to have had the desired effect."

"Are people really so easily persuaded?"

"They can be when their motives are not pure and they are not on their guard. Why do you think I was always quiet and out of view at such events?"

"I confess I had believed it for other reasons than mere observation."

"Haha, as is so often the case. I know people have called me antisocial and worse for such conduct, even dull."

"But you are neither of those things."

"To hear you declare it fills me with relief. For yours is the only opinion which now matters to me."

We have ventured outside, onto the dimly lit veranda.

"How foolish. I had not thought to collect your shawl."

"I will be well without it."

"Here, have my jacket," he says, removing it and placing it about my shoulders before I can object.

"Thank you."

We walk down the steps and into the garden.

"Haha, you look fine even in my clothing. Perhaps more so, by Jove."

I gently nudge him with my shoulder. "There you go speaking nonsense again."

"But I am in earnest. I grow ever more anxious to make you my wife."

"It does seem an age, does it not?"

"You feel it too? But of course you do. Did you not tell me with your enticing pout as we stood between our horses?"

"Oh, you knew. But you did nothing," I exclaim with a pout.

"Lady Anne, it was not for lack of want. But I was not about to claim a highly improper kiss outside your father's door."

"Nobody would have seen."

"There were grooms present. But now, oh, we seem to have wandered into this enclosed area here, alone. The fountain our only witness," he says, his voice hoarse and low, rumbling delectably through me.

"So we have," I reply, a tremor evident even to my own ears.

His head bends down as mine reaches up. My breath hitches and I am all a-tremble as our mouths draw closer.

"Lady Anne," he whispers.

His mouth is upon mine, soft and supple. My lips part, but I am taken aback by the presence of his tongue. Growing accustomed to it, my own meets his, eyes closing in complete abandon.

The more I give the more he takes, and he becomes hungry in his desire. My body responds in the most unnatural way. My hips lean towards him. That warm stickiness is at the top of my thighs again.

Lord Dellingby seems hungry for more as his kiss grows ever deeper and more impassioned. As his hand pulls on my lower back, my bones seem to disintegrate and my body goes limp, but by no means lifeless at his touch.

I am lost in a sea of Dellingby, quite outside of myself, with no idea how to regain corporeal form and without any desire to do so. He may keep me here in this otherworldly existence forever.

"Lady Anne, are you here? Anne?" Mama's voice breaks through, bringing me back to reality with a thud.

"I am here Mama," I call, painfully breaking apart from Lord Dellingby.

"Quick, sit here on this bench," he whispers, dragging me over to it.

"Thank goodness for your mama, for I fear I was about to forget myself entirely," he murmurs under his breath.

"Anne, what are you about?"

"Forgive us, Your Grace. Lady Anne was feeling unwell, so I brought her outside for fresh air. It is quite well-lit here in this part of the garden. And regard, she is wearing more clothes than when we came out," he tells her with a gesture of innocence, but I see the mischief in his eyes.

He had ensured his coat was back in place upon my shoulders as we sat, for it had slipped during our amorous encounter. Oh my, what an encounter.

"So I see. Are you recovered?" she asks me.

"I think I should stay a while longer, Mama." That kiss has truly made me quite giddy.

"Very well. But here, take your shawl, I saw it next mine before seeking you out here. You may give poor Lord Dellingby back his coat before he catches chill."

"It is of no consequence. Lady Anne was my only concern," he says, shrugging his clothing back on.

"Thank you for ensuring her health, safety and reputation are intact."

"I leave her to your excellent care then, Your Grace." He bows and hurries away.

"Would you care to tell me what happened?" Mama quizzes.

"I danced a little too rigorously in the warm room. As Lord Dellingby was about to take me into the next dance I grew faint, so he brought me out here. Is the fountain not beautiful? I believe he thought it a fine distraction."

"I am quite sure he did," she says in a clipped tone.

"Shall we return to the ball? I'm feeling much better now." Excepting my still wobbly knees, which I pray will support me as I walk.

"Are you quite sure? Would you not sooner go home?"

"Mama, it was but a passing moment."

"Let me look at you before we return then."

Mama examines my lacings. "That foolish girl has tied you far too tightly. No wonder you had a fit of dizziness."

She loosens my fastenings, which is a relief whether it is required or not.

"There, much better. Now, let us return. And do not even think of running off on your own with Lord Dellingby again."

"Mama!"

"You are not married yet, young lady. And that is all there is to be said on the matter."

We remain silent as we re-enter the house together. How could she have known? I feel so guilty. And if she had not come along…well, perhaps I should not think of it. I do not know what came over me to act with such utter impropriety. Nor indeed what is so very wrong of me, for I enjoyed it very much.

❧ Chapter 27 ❦

Letter to Margaret, 25th June 1814

Dear Margie,

I thank you for your continuing letters. They bring me more comfort than you could know, for they make me feel almost as if I were at home with you, where I so long to be. And your perseverance with your lessons, despite struggling with the intricacies of the quadrille is most encouraging. Persistence is a virtue, for sure, and will benefit you greatly during your time in London.

Mama and Papa have been greatly occupied with the dignitaries visiting the Prince Regent. On the 11th of June, we all attended the opera in Covent Garden, where the prince was entertaining the allied leaders. It was only by royal request, for as full you know, Papa would not attend such a thing otherwise. I had thought myself too much on display as part of the marriage mart, but that was nothing compared to that evening. There was a great deal of pointing, nodding of heads and whisperings.

And then there was the re-enactment of the Battle of Trafalgar on the evening of the 20th in Hyde Park, of course. The Prince Regent, the Duke of York, the King of Prussia, the Czar, General Blucher and Lords Beresford and Hill looked on. I am thankful I am not to be united with any of them for they were all old and surly.

The re-enactment was an extraordinary feat. So many troops all pretending to do battle. I almost believed they were in earnest. There were large model ships, three feet in length, floating on the Serpentine. The French ones were sunk at the end whilst the National Anthem was played, receiving much cheering and patriotism. Most raucous!

It was almost a mercy when Mama and Papa left me at home with nought but Clément for company whilst they attended the other formal events. Although it has been rather dull and far too quiet. Even Lord Dellingby has been called to attend in place of his father who continues in ill health.

Is it not concerning that he is not yet recovered? I begin to wonder whether I shall be marrying a duke and not a marquess. It should be a most sorry affair if that were the case, for such sorrow would surely cloud our union. I pray for his recovery.

The tedium was broken up by the arrival of a friend. Miss Compley is already left town, but Miss Plimpton paid calls still. We were quite happy playing cards and singing, we two. With so few people about, we were able to be in each other's company longer, which was agreeable to us both.

We have been in London above two months, and I find it an excess of time. Indeed, it seems an eternity since last I saw you and home. Please do not chastise me for my longing, for you are full aware of my hesitancy in coming to town in the first instance. But, to please you, I continue to try to make the most of my time here.

There are many amusements you shall find pleasurable, and I do not mean to dampen your enthusiasm. I cannot help but want the quiet of home, and perhaps I grow more anxious for my upcoming nuptials to arrive.

On the 1st July, there is to be a masquerade ball at Burlington House for the Duke of Wellington. Lord Dellingby has persuaded Papa that we should be in attendance. I find myself anticipating this event with great eagerness. I do believe the Watier's Club is trying to outdo White's in extravagance.

The latter held a ball on the 21st June, which I hear Henry, the brother of Jane Austen attended. It is of little consequence to most perhaps, but as a fellow reader of her books, I am sure you shall join in my excitement over this. It is a pity she herself is not in town. It would be delightful to quiz her on how she conjures up her funny stories. Do such odd people truly exist, do you think?

The visiting sovereigns have now departed for the Continent, so hopefully all shall return to our usual pattern of life here soon.

Your ever affectionate sister,

Anne Frithringham

As predicted, life has already begun to settle back into what is considered normal around here. One is taken for walks and carriage rides, but Lord Dellingby is conspicuous in his absence once more. The man is infuriating. I cannot call on him, so am reliant on him to do so. Yet he remains aloof.

The kiss he gave me at our ball remains a vivid memory, but I am painfully aware it is not to be repeated. Perhaps an apology is in order? I'm not quite sure whether there was any error on my part, but perhaps I displeased him.

Hoping to find a means of escape, I retreat to the library and retrieve one of my favourite tomes, settle into the chair nearest the fire, and begin to read.

"Ahem."

I look up at the muffled sound.

"My lady, there was an item of post which I thought perhaps your papa need not be made aware of. Aher. It is marked for your attention and is prepaid from Canada" Forbes tells me with a wink.

"From Canada?" I yelp, rising from my seat a little before reseating myself. "Hm, I see, thank you, Forbes, for your kind discretion."

"Think nothing of it. Only, should anyone discover its existence, I never saw this letter."

"Of course, you saw no such thing. But I intend to keep this out of all knowledge, so have no fear."

"Very well, my lady." He bows and exits, leaving me alone.

My eager fingers almost rip the pages in my eagerness to open the seal. At last, at last, he has written. He must have gotten to his destination safely. I hold the letter to my breast in quiet thanks.

Looking at the sender information, I cannot help but laugh for the funny man has indeed written from Jane Fairley as promised, and not the Bamber Beauvrais of my youth. Oh, it is truly from him. No other could have known our secret name. Tears spring to my eyes, and it is necessary to wipe them away before I can make out the words on the pages.

Letter from Jane Fairley (Lord Beauvrais), received 28th June 1814.

My dearest friend, Lady Anne,

I trust this letter finds you in good health and you have not suffered too much concern over others. How goes the marriage mart? You must surely be promised to a good husband by the time this letter reaches you across seas more stormy than you could possibly imagine.

What a voyage I had! I was really quite ill at first as our ship was tossed and turned upon the waves. Indeed, even the memory leaves me queasy. However, I survived, and that, I am sure, is the most important thing. I alighted at and have chosen to settle for now, in Halifax, as you can see from the address here. My companion is ensuring my every need is met. I hardly know what to write, I am so fatigued. But I was determined to write to you as soon as may be. Have no fear, I am in good health and far away from any fighting.

Please be informed that I am, if not quite yet happy, at least content with my new situation.

The port is exceptionally busy. I have never seen so many ships. Life is vastly different here. There are a great many people with black skin about, which was alarming at first. But they seem as good-natured as the other inhabitants. I understand they are refugees from the United States of America. Perhaps I can consider myself a refugee of sorts also, so am able to feel some sympathy in their plight. To be chased out of one's home is quite an ordeal.

There are green rolling hills all about, which would please you greatly, as well as the large expanse of water. The town is sparsely populated, and we live more basic than our fellows back home in London, but comfortable nonetheless.

As might well you imagine, fish is popular at mealtimes. But I want for nothing, and there is plenty of choice. There are the usual offerings of partridge, pigeon and rabbit. I am promised a meal of moose and even bear at some point, which is most intriguing.

There are curious creatures about, including small grey animals, a little larger than squirrels, with wide chubby cheeks and who have the appearance of wearing a black mask. I am informed they are called raccoons. Jolly looking fellows they are. Most entertaining.

323

The weather is not much cooler than that left behind in England. The sun should warm us more over the following months, but then preparations must be made as the winters apparently get very cold indeed.

I am so recently arrived I have not much news. However, I am already making friends and am hopeful that my time here shall be a happy one. I have but one wish, and that is that the ones I love could be here also. I rather wonder if there will ever be a time when there is not an ache in my heart. But I begin to be morose and would not have you think that I am in any danger of being overcome by such things.

By the time you receive this and respond, I hope to have much more to tell you. But for now, I bid you the fondest adieu.

Yours faithfully,

Jane Fairley

Relief washes over me, and I am thankful to be sitting down. He is well, and in as good spirits as can be hoped for under the circumstances. Tears are streaming down my cheeks. I scarce know how to name the many emotions which are threatening to overwhelm me but must define some as happiness, relief, longing, heartache and joy. I miss Lord Beauvrais more than ever, yet I must be happy for him.

My heart wishes again that things had ended differently for us, although I know the impossibility of such. But oh, if only he had found it in his heart to make me an offer, we could have lived quite comfortable and he would not be about to endure a freezing cold winter. How I fear for him.

But what am I thinking? Would I prefer a life of quiet companionship over what I hope Lord Dellingby is offering? If only he would pay me a visit, bringing with him the reassurance his presence seems to inspire. And if only I could be certain of his character; he seems so changeable. Perhaps he shall not be at all the sort of husband I imagine he should be.

Enough. Ensuring all evidence of my tears have been wiped away, I remove to my room so the precious letter may be secreted away in the hidden compartment of my writing set. Before anyone has the chance to wonder where I am, I return to the library and pick up my book again, but no reading takes place. My mind is full of Lord Beauvrais and a smile sits on my lips.

Not that there is anyone to concern themselves over my whereabouts. Mama and Papa are gone to Buckingham House as the queen formally welcomes Lord Wellington. There is a great deal of fuss being made over that man. He has done the country a great service, and he is most handsome, but poor Papa does feel it so. The painful reminders of the loss of my brother George are ever present here.

My sigh echoes around the room. Lord Dellingby is sure to be at the ceremony as well. And here I am, kept at home with not a soul for company, excepting the letter from my friend, which is enough to warm my heart. I must make a reply, but what to say? It requires some thought.

Letter to Lord Beauvrais, 28 June 1814

My dear friend,

Thank you for informing me of your safe arrival. It had been a cause of consternation, as you surely discerned. Your new home sounds intriguing, and it is my dearest wish you should live happy there.

The Season continues here, and I am to marry Lord Dellingby this August. I trust this choice meets with your approval. La, how you would have laughed at me. Papa had me believing he intended me for Lord Emsby at one point, which disturbed me greatly. However, he is now married to Lady Rathburn, to my relief. Can you fathom such a fate for me? He who set his men upon a most beloved friend to be my partner? How it sickened me. All seems to be well now, however, so one must not linger upon such terrible thoughts. We must satisfy ourselves that he shall be kept miserable in perpetuity.

I shall be sure to write with my new direction once it is ascertained. Sheringley Hall seems most likely, I am told. I would ask if you are aware of any peculiarity in that family, for there are some disquieting thoughts caused by some of their actions. Sadly, your reply would arrive too late. I shall be wed to Lord Dellingby for better or for worse before I receive word. Surely there can be no great cause for alarm though.

Going to the effort of posting this letter in secret, I am certain it should contain many more words and news, but I am at a loss. There are balls and parties as ever. I miss your counsel and companionship. All the celebrations of the newly elevated Duke of Wellington serve to remind me of the loss of my brother and of you.

Pray, can I hope at all that one day you shall return? No, I must not ask it. Pardon my question. It is selfish and indulgent. Besides, I do not think I could bear it should you respond in the negative. I must content myself with being happy for your safety.

I do hope my next letter will contain happier thoughts. All will be settled by then.

Lord Dellingby did take me to Astley's which was marvellous. The greatest spectacle I have ever seen. Such fine horsemanship as you cannot imagine. Or perhaps you can. I am unsure whether you ever visited yourself. There, a happy thought.

And speaking of horses, I would assure you Lady is being well taken care of and is quite content, read spoiled, in her new home. She shall accompany me to my marital abode; have no fear. A fine note to end on.

Please do keep me updated on your progress.

Your well-wishing friend,

Anne Frithringham

✂ Chapter 28 ✄

The first of July arrives, bringing a hubbub with it. Having spent many hours in the carriage, the relief of gaining freedom is short-lived. There is such a throng of people to behold, and the noise is deafening as we enter the ballroom at Burlington House.

A great rainbow of colours assaults my eyes, and it is with some difficulty that I distinguish anybody at first. However, discovering a slightly quieter spot, I take a moment to observe some of the fine costumes. The hosts are without masks, and the Duke of Wellington is in his military uniform. All others are in masks; some grotesque, some ornate. And such an array of dress as I never saw before in my life.

Present, there are dominos, harlequins, Spaniards, Turks, Venetians, chimney-sweeps, princesses from around the globe, shepherdesses, sultans, sultanas, Circassians...

"Behold, that young chap there in green pantaloons, laughing gaily is none other than Caroline Lamb."

I jump at the sudden, low voice at my ear. My head snaps to my right, where I observe a fine Albanian. There is no mistaking the glimmering brown eyes shining from the holes in his mask.

"Lord Dellingby, a rare pleasure to see you. Fancy yourself a Lord Byron, do you?" I respond, dipping a curtsey.

He snickers. "Hardly, my dear. It was rather a lack of imagination on my part."

I observe a faint blush upon his cheeks as he casts his gaze down at himself, his hands spread wide.

"Well, it suits you, so you needn't trouble yourself."

A slight hissed intake of breath. "Lady Anne is displeased?"

I cannot help but roll my eyes. "Lord Dellingby, I wonder at your amazement."

He looks at me, his head cocked to one side.

Lowering my voice to a whisper, I inform him, "You embrace me as…soundly as you did, and then desert me. No sight nor sound of you has been noted in the interim, leaving me to think the Lord God knows what—"

His bass chuckle cuts me off.

Glowering, I have to ask, "And what do you find so amusing, my lord?"

"I had feared it was something serious. Dear Lady Anne, I humbly apologise for my absence," he says, taking my hands into his, locking my gaze with his.

"You should not find it necessary to apologise with such regularity should you practice a more constant rendezvous."

"Indeed, you are correct, Lady Anne. However, in part, it is owing to matters outside my control." He glances around the room, then whispers, "And partly, I find I cannot trust myself in your presence."

It is my turn to blush. Clearing my throat, I manage to say, "Well, perhaps you may be forgiven under such circumstances."

I attempt to remove my hands from his, but he holds firm and draws them to his lips. "You are all goodness, my lady. And might I remark what a fine Armenian you make?"

"I thank you. Rather delightful how the reds and golds of our costumes complement each other and are not entirely dissimilar," I tell him with a wry smile.

"Quite a happy coincidence," he replies with a grin.

I don't believe him for a moment and wonder which of my papa's employ he paid to gain such information. But there is no harm done, and being rather pleased with the result, I let the matter drop.

"Ah, here are your excellent parents. Your Grace, Your Grace," he bows to each.

"Dellingby, is that you?"

"Indeed, it is I, Your Grace," he says, bowing lower to Papa, whose only attempt at a costume is a mask.

"Gadzooks, and is that Lord Byron in the robes of a monk?"

"You know, I rather think it is. Somewhat of a sardonic costume for him, is it not?" Lord Dellingby replies, sniggering.

"Indeed it is, indeed it is." My papa's laughter echoes that of my intended.

"Duke, I see Lord and Lady Brandersleigh. Come, we must make ourselves known," Mama interjects.

We all curtsey and bow as Mama leads Papa away, casting a pointed look my way. I am being given privacy, but on the clear understanding I am to be on my best behaviour.

"Lady Anne, it is high time we took part in a dance. Would you do me the honour?"

"But of course."

Part of me is well aware that I am amongst other members of the *Haut Ton*, but it is hard to believe when one is thus surrounded by a heady mixture of costumes. It is all I can do not to laugh at the characters bouncing up and down. I do hope Minerva shan't attempt to join in, for I very much fear for her modesty if she should. The image in my mind is too much, and I cannot help but laugh. There is such a commotion in the room it is unlikely anyone shall notice, to my relief.

Happiness bubbles up inside me as I am whirled with perhaps a little more exuberance than is customary. The whole assembly seems to have unburdened itself of its normal confines and is livelier than one would expect. Even Lord Dellingby has a greater spring in his step.

By the time our set comes to an end, I am quite fatigued.

"Come, let us fetch you some orgeat, Lady Anne," my partner offers, and I willingly follow.

Together, we explore the garden, which has been transformed into a pretty room by means of tents. There are above 1,700 people in attendance it is said, as well I can believe as we squeeze between the multitude of whiffy bodies.

We attempt conversation but can scarce hear one another above the din. It is most infuriating. We do our best, however.

Lord Dellingby doesn't leave my side all the evening, which is pleasing. We sit next one another at supper and take part in another dance afterwards. But Papa seeks us out at its conclusion, eager to return home.

My ears are veritably ringing as we enter the carriage, and despite the frivolity, it is a relief to be away.

"Damned dreadful excuse for debauchery. Courtesans amongst us as equals," Papa grumbles as the carriage makes its way through the dark, murky streets.

My hand flies to my mouth as a squeaked gasp bursts forth. The noise makes Papa turn his scowl upon me.

"I see you are shocked. As well you should be. Such lewd behaviour."

"I did not observe any, Papa," I tell him meekly.

"Then I am sorry to have alerted you to the fact. Yes, perhaps your attention was better engaged." His brow arches at me, drawing a 'hmm' of agreement.

However, as Papa falls silent, surely grumbling inwardly, my mind starts to recount the evening. Glimpses of bodies too close to one another, hands wandering, sly looks; all this I had seen without truly seeing. Courtesans? I had never thought to be in close proximity to such. How exciting. Or dreadful, as Papa would have it. Hardly fitting company for gently bred ladies.

Deciding I care not one jot, my back nestles against the seat a little further as I sigh. Staring out of the window at nothing discernible, I wonder when Lord Dellingby shall next present himself.

The answer is discovered the very next day, as the man in question pays a call, carrying a posy of blue hyacinths. Their scent permeates the air between us in a most pleasing fashion, making me inhale deeply.

"Lord Dellingby, what a pleasure it is to see you."

Thrusting the posy towards me, he says, "Lady Anne, the honour is mine. Please accept my apologies for having been neglectful of my duties. No harm was intended, but clearly you have been injured by my actions."

I curtsey at his bow. "My lord, you took my words too much to heart. I am far too outspoken and should not have said a word."

Straightening, he looks me straight in the eye. "I am sorry nonetheless."

The impression remaining is that he would have expanded upon this, perhaps discerning my false modesty at his peace offering. However, Mama, of course, arrives in a rustle of hurried skirts.

"Lord Dellingby, how good of you to come," she tells him, inclining her head; her tone containing only the merest hint of a sneer.

"Indeed, I was offering—"

"Yes, we are well aware of your earnestness. Really, Lord Dellingby, you do take on so."

"I beg pardon, Your Grace. It occurred to me on this brilliant day that perhaps Lady Anne would wish to take a ride in the carriage?"

"How thoughtful you are. I see no harm in it," she agrees.

The sun warms my face as I turn my head up towards it as we drive along, a smile widening my cheeks.

"How good it is to have a fine day," I say, whilst harbouring the wish to be in the fresh air of the countryside.

Lord Dellingby's fingers tense into a claw before he forces them back onto his knees. Does my observation upset him so?

"Yes. Quite." His fingers drum.

"Papa says last night was debauched. What are your thoughts?"

"Lady Anne!" Mama screeches, emphasising the first word.

"Mama, I am curious to learn what Lord Dellingby's impression of the evening was."

"And you choose to ask in such language?"

My shoulders bristling, I turn my attention back to Lord Dellingby. "Ahem, do forgive my impertinence, my lord. Did you enjoy the ball last evening?"

His fingers rub along his lips which curl up on one side before he can disguise it. And there is no shielding the mirth shining in his narrowed eyes.

He clears his throat. "Lady Anne, every evening I spend in your company is one of sheer delight."

"Thank goodness some in this carriage can remember their manners," Mama comments.

With great effort, I win the fight to keep my own countenance. Lord Dellingby does not make this easy. If Mama was not present, I am quite sure we would both be laughing heartily over the supposed debauched goings on. Or perhaps the carriage roof would be raised and we could misbehave ourselves. The very thought sends my heart fluttering.

Our conversation is kept to polite pleasantries, our bodies a dignified distance apart. Perhaps Lord Dellingby was wise to keep away? I find myself itching to reach across to hold his hand. The denial is enough to drive me distracted.

"If the weather holds tomorrow, perhaps Lady would appreciate some exercise? Should you like a ride out, Lady Anne?" he asks.

Ignoring Mama's glower, I answer, "Yes, I think I should like that very much. She has been rested too long again."

❧❦

Lady behaves impeccably despite her period of inactivity. And, more's the pity, so does Lord Dellingby. Absolutely nothing occurs which Mama would disapprove of. Nor does it over the subsequent visits. He is become a more frequent visitor this week, and one of the utmost gentility.

Thursday sees us all at St Paul's Cathedral as we are all called to give thanks for our victory over Napoleon Bonaparte. Lord Wellington looks smug as he carries the Sword of State alongside the Prince Regent. The man really begins to grow tiresome. Although I am also grateful indeed that the victory was won, causing me to sing with gusto.

Seeing regimental colours makes the ache in my heart grow. Once more I feel the pain of losing George. He should never have been there. He was always the gentlest of us all. A battlefield was no place for him.

With tears welling, I look away. Taking a deep breath, I glance behind me. A few rows behind, the opposite side, a concerned nod is aimed in my direction. Acknowledging Lord Dellingby's reassurance with a dip of my head, I return my gaze to the front. It is as if he held my hand in that moment, so strongly do I feel his presence, lending me his strength.

The rest of the ceremony is completed without me embarrassing myself. Papa must be suffering and hurries us away as rapidly as may be accomplished amongst such a crowd. That is to say, not terribly fast at all, as we file out of the magnificent cathedral with its ornate arches and domes.

"Are you well, Lady Anne?" a deep voice asks me.

"I thank you, Lord Dellingby, quite well. And yourself?"

"Never better. What a rousing service that was, wot?"

"Yes, I suppose it was," I reply, but no smile can be coaxed into appearance.

"Ah, how careless of me. Lady Anne, of course you feel it keenly, today of all days."

"It is of no consequence."

"Shall I see you tomorrow?"

"Your company would be most pleasant if you may spare the time. But please do not feel obliged. I would not have you neglect your duty."

"Perish the thought," he says with a broad smile.

"I would caution you not to over-indulge me, my lord. You would not wish me to become accustomed to such attentiveness."

"Yes, I can see how a man may endanger himself in such a way. The fairer sex is liable to steal all of our time and attention and have us believe we are happy whilst about it."

I cannot help but giggle. "So long as you are sensible of the perils."

Papa veers off in the direction of our carriage, and I am forced to bid my intended a reluctant adieu. He is in good humour and I would take full advantage if but I could. Alas, for now, one must return home without him.

❧

Letter to Margaret, 22nd July 1814

Dearest Margie,

You would never forgive me if I were not to write you of every detail of the grand fête held at Carlton House yesterday. As you well know, it has been delayed for quite some time whilst preparations were made. Parliament has finished sitting this year, and only now has the event taken place. What a to-do. And it seems the lesser orders managed to winkle their way in in the interim. Ghastly state of affairs really, but there was nothing to be done.

We have been in town above a three month, and just as we should be returning to you, we are forced to tarry here a little longer.

After many hours sitting in the carriage, queuing with many others along the approach, we finally arrived at a curious row of pillars which run along the front of the house which seem to serve no purpose whatsoever. The building's exterior is a rather drab, sorry affair, so I shan't dwell on that.

It was with great relief that I learned I was able to wear a court train with my dress, without having to adorn myself in a similar monstrosity to my presentation gown. A white silk with puffed sleeves was selected, richly embroidered with gold flowers and green jewels. Completing the ensemble was a long deep green, velvet court train, similarly decorated. Ostrich feathers, of course, were worn in my hair. And Mama let me wear her emeralds.

But this was nothing when compared to the splendours of the decorations of Carlton House.

We passed through the magnificent entrance hall to a splendid octagonal room at the foot of the grand staircase. White, red and gold adorn every surface, and many fine pieces of furniture and porcelain are on display. But that is not all.

There were three temporary rooms created in the gardens, two of which housed many military and naval trophies. These were linked by covered promenades. I am not quite sure how best to describe the main room; it was a sort of temple. A large white roof seemed to float in mid-air above us, and beautiful images were chalked beneath our feet. Flowers were in abundance. The overall effect was simply breath-taking.

The supper lasted for hours, and there was every good thing available. Roasted meats, cold cuts, pineapples, strawberries...the choices seemed endless. Are you not envious? You simply must try some pineapple when you have opportunity to do so, for they are the sweetest, juiciest, most delectable thing I ever tasted. Tingles tantalise my tongue even at the memory. I even tasted some champagne; the bubbles tickled my nose in a not unpleasant way and seemed to whoosh to my head.

Amongst the two thousand guests, Lord Dellingby appeared before me and led me to dance, which made my spirits soar perhaps more than any other spectacle of the entire event. He has been far more attentive of late, and I find that the more I become acquainted with him the more he improves in my esteem. I begin to hope that not only shall I be comfortable but also happy in my marriage. Is such a thing truly possible, do you think?

We had a splendid time and strolled the beautiful grounds together. He behaved with the highest degree of respectability. It was a far more civilised occasion than the bal masqué we attended.

There you have it; my faithful account of the proceedings. I hope they satisfy your thirst for such knowledge, and you are able to fully concentrate on Miss Swanson's teachings now.

There is but one further big event and two weeks before we may see one another again, my dear sister. I am almost counting the hours until I may be reunited with you. How cruel Society is not to allow us to enjoy the Season together. It would have been far more pleasurable if that were the case.

The wedding looms with trepidation and some elation.

Your ever affectionate sister,

Anne Frithringham

Lord Dellingby certainly seems to be intent on creating a better impression and continues to be an improved companion. This evening we are to attend the theatre. I am dressed ahead of time, all eagerness to spend more time in his company.

Mama is all elegance, as is usual of course, but perhaps a little more so.

"My darling Anne, our fun times together are nearing their conclusion," she laments as she enters my room.

I wrap my arms about her. "Thank you, Mama. Thank you for having been here with me and for all that you have done."

"Oh now, we become far too sentimental," she says, breaking us apart.

She blinks her eyes rapidly, a sure sign she is fighting tears. My own fingers wipe at my eyes, causing Clément to check for smudges before we depart.

❧❧

Entering the theatre's saloon, I soon locate Miss Plimpton.

"My dear, it is a pleasure to see you," I tell her, squeezing her hands in mine.

"Lady Anne, an absolute joy. And I have such news to tell you. Can you guess?"

"Surely not. Has he..?"

"Yes, Lord Meltcham has made me an offer at last."

A rather unladylike squeal bursts forth from me. "Oh, Miss Plimpton, felicitations. What excellent news indeed."

"And I believe I have you to thank, at least in part. Lady Rosen has been removed from harm's way by none other than Lord Trunton. What a happy event that was. Lord M's father could hold no further objection and so we are to be married in two weeks."

"I am overjoyed. What a successful Season for us all. Miss Compley's absence has been much missed, but for the best of reasons."

"Oh fie, you have been far too busy yourself to notice any such thing."

"Well, Lord Dellingby's presence has alleviated any pangs of absence a little, perhaps."

"He must have heard his name, for here he is approaching," she whispers.

I turn my head and indeed see Lord Dellingby's fine form advancing in our direction, a most amiable smile sitting upon his lips.

"Lady Anne, Miss Plimpton, a good evening to you both," he greets with a bow.

We respond in kind.

"Lord Dellingby, Miss Plimpton was just informing me of her upcoming nuptials."

"I have had it myself this moment from Lord Alverbury. You are the talk of town, Miss Plimpton. I offer you my greatest felicitations."

"You are too kind, Lord Dellingby, I thank you."

As she is called away by her party, Miss Plimpton's walk is almost a skip. It is truly good to see her so happy. Hers has been a hard-won fight indeed, and I'd wager Lord Wellington himself could not succeed near so well.

                        ◦≈◦

Miss Plimpton has become preoccupied with preparations, and my only company the past five days has been my family and Lord Dellingby, and thank the heavens for him. We have been out for horse rides and walks, but nothing out of the ordinary. London seems to be starting to go to sleep following the excited clamour of the Season. Except one last event.

Today the Prince Regent has arranged for celebrations in the three parks in honour of the anniversary of the Battle of the Nile, the centenary of the Hanoverians ascending the throne and the signing of The Treaty of Paris. We are destined for Buckingham House, by invitation of Queen Charlotte. As is Lord Dellingby, to my relief. I should not like to spend an entire evening in the presence of the other nobles without his humour to make light of it.

Lord Dellingby remains a puzzle. He is so excessively jovial in some moments, yet serious and quiet in others. Of late, the jolly version seems to be the stronger, and we have had some most pleasant times together. More and more I hope for the happy marriage I never thought possible.

My looking glass reveals no great deal of difference in the reflection. But in a little over three months I seem to have changed immeasurably on the inside. How differently I perceive the world now, all too aware of the dangers as well as the pleasures.

We all seem to stand on a precipice, learning whether fate is to be kind to us on any given day. And it is not entirely a thing which is within our power to control. All seems to be chance. Perhaps Papa is wrong to dislike the card tables so much when we all gamble every day of our lives?

My thoughts continue to wander along this path as we make our way to Buckingham House. There are fewer guests this evening, but it is still busy as all of London seems to be in the streets, making their cheerful way to their own destination. Merriment ripples all around in the shouts, laughter and cheers which are heard as we go.

Despite predictions to the contrary, the weather remains dry for now. Hopefully, it shall continue fine so we may enjoy all the entertainments which have been so carefully planned.

The excitement is contagious; I can scarce sit still as our carriage nears The Mall. More military and naval heroes are celebrated in the devices displayed at the front of Buckingham House. The façade is illuminated in spectacular fashion. My eyes must be as wide as saucers upon seeing such a spectacle. My mouth is certainly agape, and even Mama does not cough it closed for she too is enthralled.

"Oh Mama, look, there is Mr Sadler's hot air balloon. Do you really think we shall see the ascent?" I exclaim, clapping my hands.

"It would be a damn silly waste of space should James Sadler not delight us all with his prowess," Papa grumbles.

Thus chastened, I settle back into my seat, returning to dignified silence. But glancing at Mama, I see in her eyes she is equally eager to witness the flight. Imagine soaring high into the sky amongst the birds. I hear he risks sky dragons in his daring attempts. How extraordinarily brave he is.

We are directed to the receiving room where a great many people are gathered. Mama and Papa are instantly engaged in conversation by one of their acquaintances. I am left seeking refuge from the din in what I hope to be a quieter corner. Naturally, this is where Lord Dellingby is also located. We both seem to have an aversion to the tremendous noise of social gatherings.

"Lady Anne, you find me all alone," he says whilst bowing.

"Lord Dellingby, I am delighted to find you so. I am willing to risk the gossip in order to be by your side."

"That's the way to be. Down with the rotters of scandal. We are to be married after all, and it cannot be so terrible a thing to wish to converse with one's bride."

"We are in agreement," I say with a smile and nod.

"I trust you saw the hot air balloon outside?"

"Oh yes, and I am most enraptured. How I long to see it ascend into the air."

"The wait shall not be too long a one, by all accounts. Are you aware that James Sadler is a pastry chef?"

"Oh, surely not. You are in jest, my lord. He is a man of science."

"I assure you I am in earnest. A pastry chef from Oxford no less."

I cannot help but giggle. "How diverting. I wonder how he discovered his ability."

"I knew you would share my amusement. It is a curious thing, is it not? From the kitchen to the sky. The first flying Englishman. Quite a dizzying feat. Whatever possessed him to fill that expanse of silk with hydrogen and take off as he does? But he seems quite accomplished at it. And it delights many."

"Hydrogen? I have not heard of such a thing. What is this that makes men fly?"

"My apologies, I had thought perhaps you knew, for I know of your love of book reading."

"Book reading yes, but I confess I do not possess the aptitude for science, having not had much opportunity to make a study of it."

"But of course. Your time has been far better used. Hydrogen is a gas, my dear. As air is a gas."

"Oh, I see." I really don't see, but having no desire to further prove my stupidity, I make a show of understanding.

Before any more can be said, we are directed outside where preparations are being made for the grand flight. The throng of people buzzes and stirs as the balloon begins to inflate. But a chorused 'oooh' sounds round as it starts to become limp again.

After quite some time, the crowd having grown restless, the balloon is finally full and lifts from the ground. The usual decorum falls from every one of us and we each gasp and cheer. Thunderous applause erupts from our hands as the balloon climbs higher above us. The large object becomes smaller to our eyes as it drifts like a cloud over our heads and far away. Awed silence falls about us briefly before we are called inside, and chatter as we go.

"A truly marvellous sight. Lady Anne, I am quite overcome. What a marvellous contraption," Lord Dellingby says at my side.

"A man in flight," I reply, my whispered words drawn out in my astonishment.

"Quite extraordinary," Lord Alverbury adds, joining us as we walk into the house.

"Lord Alverbury, I had not known you were here," I exclaim, shaken from my reverie.

He bows his head, his green eyes shining his amusement. "I hope it is not an unwelcome surprise."

"Lord Alverbury, you must know you are always welcome."

"I am pleased to hear it. Well, well, we may not see one another for some time. You are soon to leave London, I understand."

"Yes, my family is to leave in but two days, my lord. We lingered only long enough for today, which I am glad of. I would not have wished to miss the balloon ascent for anything."

"You shall be sorely missed, my dear. But perhaps your husband may permit his friend a visit once you are settled?"

"Alverbury, I could not keep you away even if I wished to," Lord Dellingby says, chuckling and patting his friend's arm.

"Ah, never a truer word, Dellingby, never truer. Is that Nordfield? I would speak with him. Pray excuse me," he requests, hurrying through the crowd.

"Ah, Lord Alverbury, always in such a hurry," I remark on a sigh.

"I rather think your keen observation unnerves him a little."

"I? But what have I said? I'm sure I was all affability. Not an unkind word has fallen from my lips towards him."

Lord Dellingby's chuckle rumbles low. "Not just now. No, not ever. You would never be meaningfully unkind. I speak of your detection of his careful watch over you."

A blush warms my cheeks. "You know of that?" I peek up through lowered lashes.

But my question is met with more delicious rumbles. "Lord Alverbury confessed it as if he were a mere boy caught stealing cake from the kitchen."

"I had no intention of shaming him so."

"Do not trouble yourself. He was merely afraid he had failed me whilst embarrassing you. He did not make allowance for your close observance of his person."

"Oh, the poor fellow. Is he so accustomed to being invisible? I only happened to notice as he appeared so frequently at the best possible moment. I was grateful to him for his kind assistance. Truly, I had only meant a tease."

"Now, do not take his reaction to heart, my dear. He is an excitable chap at times. There is no harm done."

"You know, I rather pity the man. Is that wrong of me? He seems so alone. Perhaps we should have tried our matchmaking on him? Have we been neglectful?"

"No, not at all. He will do very well when he is ready. He will not be rushed. Come, let us think of happier topics. Regard here, couples are taking their place for a dance. Won't you join me?"

Glancing around, I see he is indeed correct. I had paid no heed as to our direction, but we have arrived in the ballroom. A frown flitters across my brows as I wonder when, if ever I shall ever dance again. Lord Dellingby squeezes my hand and I force a smile.

As the music starts, my fear of never again having this opportunity pushes me to give myself entirely to this occasion. I dance with a vigour never felt before. Throwing caution to all, I laugh as we make our way together. Lord Dellingby shares my delight and laughs at my side.

I have never been happier. What a fine evening. Lord Dellingby refills my cup of punch and we stand aside together, conversing until it is time for supper. And what a magnificent display that is.

The servants are dressed finely, with gold lace trimming their livery. Silver bedecks the table in every direction, from tureens to plates. The soup is delicious, but then the roast beef is sublime. Again, chilled champagne is served in abundance. And all kinds of fruits festoon the table. And all is served calmly and quickly by the said liveried servants who are most attentive.

Conversation flows as freely as the wine, and all are in good spirits. Finally, a celebration which lives up to its name. Even Mama and Papa are all smiles.

With supper over, we begin to vacate the dining room.

"A fortnight hence I shall be happier even than I am now," Lord Dellingby decrees, his voice a little strange.

"Is that so?"

"It is. For I shall be the happiest of all men who ever lived."

"Really, Lord Dellingby —"

"For who could not be so when they can call themselves your husband?"

He's dipped too deep, I knew it! "My lord, you really do go too far."

"But I am in earnest, Lady Anne. I never would have thought I could be so eager to enter the parson's mousetrap," he says, motioning with the glass he refused to leave at the table.

His term makes my whole body stiffen as Lord Felsenworth's own reported usage of it springs to mind. That dreadful night is recalled with all too vivid clarity.

Drawing breath, I manage to comment, "Come, Lord Dellingby. Let us not lose ourselves."

"Lady Anne, might I be permitted to steal Lord Dellingby away briefly? I have this moment remembered what I wished to tell him."

"Aye, Lord Alverbury, please do."

I watch the good man lead Lord Dellingby out into the garden, presumably for some fresh air. Really, to get so foxed at the home of Queen Charlotte is quite outrageous. But I cannot help but smile as I recollect his words. He is looking forward to our wedding with anticipation. It is reassuring to know, despite the circumstances leading him to declare his feelings quite so openly.

Finding myself alone, I take a turn about the room, greeting other ladies as appropriate. Eager to avoid any other man taking me into a dance, I surreptitiously make my way towards the garden.

I barely step foot out onto the veranda when I am halted by a female voice.

"Felicitations, Lady Anne. I knew how it would be, of course."

"Your Majesty," I whisper, spinning on my heel and curtseying low to none other than Queen Charlotte.

"It warms my heart to see the young entering upon such a fine marriage."

"I thank you, ma'am."

"Yes, very well. Off with you, do not linger, child."

I curtsey again and scurry away as fast as decorum will permit. Goodness! The queen herself approves my marriage. A weight does seem to land heavily on my shoulders along with such knowledge. It is an effort to breathe all of a sudden.

"Lady Anne, you are here. How fortunate. Shall we take a turn about the garden? I find myself longing for fresh air on this fine evening."

I offer a silent smile of acceptance towards Lady Caroline de Crois. We are not well acquainted but have been introduced this Season. Keenly aware the poor girl will need to undergo this all again next year, I oblige her whim. She's bright and pleasant but has had other friends in her company, as I had mine. But now we are both alone.

Trying to take a deep breath, I follow her into the garden which is lit with beautifully glowing lanterns. Following our gentle upbringing, we keep to sanctioned topics of conversation, but it is enjoyable nonetheless, and I soon revive from my earlier shock.

By the time we near the house again I am left wondering how she has not found a husband as of yet. She is everything a man could want in a wife. How fickle men are. It is unjust to put Lady Caroline through more balls, to put her on display for their amusement. My own gratitude grows greater for Lord Dellingby.

"I wish you well, Lady Caroline."

"And I you, Lady Anne. What a pity we were not able to spend more time in each other's company."

"Perhaps I shall find the country life dull after all this and convince Lord Dellingby to bring us back next year."

"Yes, quite." Her frown speaks volumes.

"No, Lady Caroline, I meant no offence. I wished only to convey the same wish to know you better."

"I see. Well, I should return to Mama. She will wonder what has become of me."

She disappears after a quick curtsey. My palm lands on my forehead as I inwardly chastise myself for my clumsiness. I injured rather than comforted. She must think me so unfeeling and callous.

"Did your mama not warn you against wandering alone in gardens at night?"

"Lord Dellingby, I was not alone."

"No, but you are now."

"I most certainly am not. You are here," I say through clenched teeth.

"Oh dear, Lady Anne is growling. Is anything amiss?" Mirth is playing at his mouth.

"Please excuse me, my lord. I was gathering my thoughts is all."

"And I interrupted. My apologies. I shall leave you this instant." He bows.

"No, please stay."

"Go, stay, what is it I am to do?"

"Stay, if you please. Oh dear, I do apologise."

Lord Dellingby snickers.

"Oh, you brute. You knew precisely what you were about."

"I confess it. I heard your last words with Lady Caroline. What an easily offended oaf she is."

"Do not be so unkind. The fault was all mine."

"My apologies," he says, inclining his head, but still smiling.

I roll my eyes. "You are quite impossible. However, I am glad to see you so much recovered."

"Ah, there we have it. I sought you out to apologise. I don't know what came over me, but I behaved brashly, so wished to convey my sincere remorse."

"I accept."

Don't know, indeed. He must know full well he over-imbibed, but I suppose he is embarrassed enough, so let it pass.

"The fireworks are about to start."

"Oh, let us find a good viewpoint then," I urge.

We walk together, following lines of guests towards the side of the house which faces St James' Park. Gathering *en masse*, we eagerly await the spectacle. I cannot help but shuffle from foot to foot in my excitement.

We are not kept in suspense long. The first colours burst high in the sky, booming as they go. But instead of amazement, panic grips me around the waist. Clutching my stomach, I lean forward a little as I try to draw breath. Lord Dellingby immediately offers his arm for support, which I eagerly accept.

"Are you quite alright, Lady Anne?"

Gasping for air, I can make no response but to shake my head. Wrapping his arm about my back, Lord Dellingby coaxes me towards the house until we find a bench.

"You're alright, Lady Anne. I am with you. Take a deep breath."

I screw my eyes shut. What does he think I'm trying to do?

"Look at me, Lady Anne. Open your eyes. There you go. Look at me. You're quite safe." He kneels before me, and holds one of my gloved hands in his, gently rubbing it with his thumb.

"You there. A glass of wine, if you please. And hurry," he calls to what must be a servant behind us some distance.

Returning his attention on me, he lowers his voice back to a deep whisper. "Lady Anne, I blush to mention, but do you require…should I…are there perhaps laces…"

I manage to draw breath enough to tell him, "No thank you."

His thumb continues to swish over the back of my hand, which is curiously soothing. I slowly exhale.

"That's it. Good girl. Inhale now."

His eyes glisten as the light of a lantern catches them. It's almost enough to catch my breath away again, but I concentrate on trying to fill my lungs.

The servant brings a glass of wine. "Is everything alright, your ladyship? Can I be of any further assistance?"

I nod then shake my head.

"Thank you, but I think Lady Anne will be fine. We will call if we need anything," Lord Dellingby answers for me.

"Very good, your lordship."

"Take a sip of this," he whispers, holding the glass to my lips.

It's an awkward business, but I slurp a little. How unseemly. My gaze goes up to the skies as I gasp air in.

Lord Dellingby pulls himself onto the bench so he's beside me. He trails a finger down my cheek.

"There we are, your colour is returning," he murmurs, "You gave me quite a fright, you know."

He takes my hand in both of his. "I could not bear to lose you now."

"You won't," I reply, my voice rasping.

"Take some more wine until you fully recover."

I do as instructed. "Please forgive me."

"Forgive you? My dear, what exactly is it I am supposed to forgive?"

"For whatever that was. It was certainly not dignified. You must be so embarrassed."

"Look at me."

I do so.

"I could never be embarrassed of you."

A tear springs to my eye, which I immediately wipe away. "Must be the wine."

"Naturally." That playful smirk is back.

I do not think I can ever bring myself to tell him how the sight and sound of the fireworks took me back to that dreadful night with Lord Felsenworth. How all I could see was...was...I burst into tears.

"Now, now, all is well. There is no cause for tears," he soothes, holding me close.

I make no effort to break away. I should, but I don't. My head rests on his shoulder as sobs shake my body.

His hand rubs my back. "There, there. All over now. No harm done. Shhh…"

Pulling myself together, I right myself and take his offered handkerchief to dry my eyes.

"Do forgive me. What a show I am making of myself."

"Not at all. You are upset, as is perfectly natural after a scare. You finish that wine, and we will go inside to await your parents."

Screams are heard from the crowd. We both straighten our backs. What can the commotion be?

"Fire! Oh heavens, it's on fire," I hear someone cry.

This is echoed around the whole crowd in a similar fashion. Lord Dellingby, ensuring I am able to stand, leads us to the dispersing people and follow them inside.

We hear mutterings of, "Well I never, what a terrible thing."

Listening more, I glean that the beautiful Chinese pagoda which adorns the bridge spanning the canal in St James's Park caught alight as the fireworks were launched from it. What a waste of a beautiful ornament, and a sad ending to an astonishing display.

Perhaps it is this fright, or mayhap it is my mama's watchful eye which leads Papa to take us home soon after this raucous interruption. He does obligingly permit me a moment to bid Lord Dellingby adieu.

Taking him aside, I tell him, "My lord, we are to depart."

"You are quite recovered?"

"I thank you, yes. Papa is never in attendance long at these gatherings, as you are aware."

"Much to my detriment, but yes, I am acquainted with his customs. But soon we shall be united, never again to be separated."

His look is all earnestness, and my heart hammers in my breast as I gaze into his burning brown eyes. My hand tries to calm the beating but to no avail. And I find that hand being encouraged into his, and a kiss is lovingly imparted onto it.

"Lady Anne, do not mourn this parting. It shall not be for long," he whispers.

"You promise to come as soon as may be?"

"Have I not told you so? Yes, only the greatest calamity could keep me from you a moment longer than is entirely necessary."

He chances another kiss upon my hand before relinquishing it so I may curtsey out of his presence. How my heart feels as if it is being ripped from my chest so it may remain with him. But why should it be so? Is this what love is? Can it cause such pain? Heedless of my agonies, the carriage takes me away.

❧ Chapter 30 ❧

There is a great hive of activity as preparations are made for tomorrow's departure. Trunks are packed and some of our servants depart, including Forbes as he must ready our home coming. Kemp takes up his usual role as butler in this house, which seems to please him if his highered chin is anything to go by. He had been relegated to under butler in Forbes' presence, which Papa insisted upon for reasons best known to himself.

I have sought out the library as a means of sanctuary. I simply cannot be doing with the panic. Clément has taken over my room and has items on every surface. It's given me a headache.

Fearing Lord Dellingby may yet turn out to be a John Willoughby from *Sense and Sensibility*, I pick up *Pride and Prejudice* instead, which I read but once before. It may be a foolish notion, but really, how can one be certain? Nobody seems to be who they pretend themselves to be. But surely Lord Dellingby would not have gone so far as to make me an offer if he was secretly promised to another. Would he?

As I read of Mr Darcy, I draw comparison to him as well, despite his being far lower in rank. But he was sullen and quiet when he was first introduced to Elizabeth Bennet. And all turned out well there. Is Lord Dellingby truly good underneath the quiet persona? Have I not witnessed his gregarious humour when we were alone? He has certainly never displayed such deplorable prejudice.

Perhaps he will yet show himself the quiet hero, akin to Colonel Brandon. Oh fie, now I am scouring both books, seeking answers to my real life questions in amongst pages of fiction. This is what becomes of my sister's coercion into reading such frivolous novels.

Lord Dellingby is a real person, he lives and breathes, and is promised to me. What will become of me will be. There is not much to be done about it now. Ceaseless concern serves no purpose.

Thus quitting my disquietude, I take up *The Mysteries of Udolpho*, escaping into its castle where I can be assured of horrors not intended for myself. If nothing else, Lord Dellingby is most certainly not the villain Montoni. The preposterousness of the situation in these pages is of great comfort.

I remain blissfully undisturbed until supper, having travelled through France as I am unable to in reality. Herein lies my love of reading; the ability to travel to new lands unhindered by geography.

At last, after an early breakfast, we are on our way home. It was an effort to sleep last night for anticipation. A long journey lies ahead of us, but one I can happily endure. Having been in town above three months, we are now bound for quieter surroundings.

The dark, dirty houses of London give way to hedgerows. Opening the window, I instantly breathe easier as fresh country air fills my lungs.

"Anne, you will catch chill, close that immediately," Mama cautions.

I comply, but not before taking another deep breath. The sun is shining down, blessing us with its rays. How green the grass, how vivid the colour of the flowers growing along our route. Birds serenade us as if they too are celebrating our return.

"Anne, do sit still. Your constant fidgets are quite a nuisance," Papa reprimands.

Without being aware of it, my feet had been bouncing up and down as my joy increased. It is not without difficulty that I bring them back under control and sit still. In but two more weeks I shall be free of such instructions and censure. Unless of course, Lord Dellingby dislikes movement and or any form of noise. I do not imagine we shall travel much together to raise concern over that, however. Should he be difficult, I shall keep to myself. Mistress of my own domain.

My mind wanders to the possible residence I shall find myself in. What will it look like? Shall I be allowed to decorate? Are Lord Dellingby's servants compliant, or shall they make me severe as I struggle to have myself understood?

A great many household details occur to me as we journey on, and we reach our first inn ahead of expectation, I was so lost in thought.

༄

Feeling fatigued and travel weary, our carriage finally draws close to home. Even Papa's lips are curling up at the sides. The horses' hooves and carriage wheels clatter along the path through the park and up to the house.

"Welcome home, Your Grace," Forbes greets us as we exit the carriage, stiff limbs forcing our movements to be slow and deliberate.

"It is a most pleasant thing to return," Papa replies in a surprisingly sentimental admission.

No sooner have I set foot indoors when I find myself swept up in two girlish arms, with a dog barking as he darts around my legs.

"Ooooh, Anne, you're home, you're home, how I have missed your upbraiding," Margaret cries.

"I missed you too," I tell her, tears springing to my eyes.

"Very well, very well, let us in, child," Papa gently chides.

"Hello, Prince. Yes, I missed you too," I tell him as I make a fuss of the happy dog.

"You must be hungry and tired after your journey. We have a feast all ready for you," Margaret says, leading us to the dining room.

All manner of cakes, cheeses and fruit are laid out.

"Cook let me help make some cake," she tells us, beaming.

"Did she now?" Papa queries, his brow rising, not sharing her enthusiasm for such news.

"What on ever for?" Mama asks.

"I did wrong? I meant only to join in the preparations, and it was really quite fun," Margaret explains.

What a funny girl she is. But as I settle into my chair, she hands me a slice of her work.

Taking a bite, I commend her, "Mmm, this is really quite delicious."

Someone has to lend praise, I feel. Her actions may have been strange, but youthful exuberance is a wonderful thing to behold after the stuffiness which had to be endured in London.

"And here, I drew you a picture," she says, sliding it across the table to me.

"Oh, it's Gensmore Hall," I declare, clearly seeing our home depicted.

"So you can keep it with you always."

"Thank you, how thoughtful," I tell her, tears threatening again.

"Are we to be thus interrupted all of our meal?" Papa grumbles.

"Sorry, Papa," Margaret apologises, eyes downcast.

Catching her gaze as she lifts her head, I offer a thankful smile. She grins back, remaining silent of course.

As soon as Papa has finished and leaves the table, Margaret grabs my hand.

"Come, tell me all about your adventure," she implores, pulling me out of my chair.

Laughing, I follow her to the drawing room, and recount as many details as I can, leaving out a great deal which she should not hear.

"But, do be on your guard. Men can be wicked indeed, more so than can ever be imagined. Never allow yourself to be alone with them. You must listen to Mama and Papa, but nor should you follow them blindly."

Margaret cocks her head to one side, frowning.

"Papa had me believe he intended Lord Emsby for me, but he meant it as a diversion only. For he always meant me for Lord Dellingby, long before I was aware of it."

"Surely not?"

"I did not dare tell you so in my letters, but it was thus. He arranged it all without informing me."

"Papa would not manipulate so."

"I am sorry to say it, but it appears he would. It was most underhanded of him. I cannot tell you how shocked and cross I was upon discovering the facts."

"How could you be otherwise? But is nobody to be trusted?"

"My dear Margie, you cannot wholly trust even yourself. London is such a curiosity. At times you will not know up from down."

"But it all ended happily."

"That is still to be seen, is it not?"

We both giggle.

"I am sure it will be well. Lord Dellingby sounds wonderful."

"Do not get carried away, Margie. He is pleasant enough, but do not excite yourself. Did I not tell you moments ago how deceptive appearances can be?"

"You doubt him?"

"Perhaps I doubt myself."

Without warning, my sister wraps her arms about me, and I find myself sobbing in her embrace.

"Anne, whatever is the matter?"

Straightening up and wiping away my tears, I take shuddering breaths before I can make a response. "I hardly know. Oh, it has been such a trying time. I am not sure I even know myself any longer. I feel…different. I cannot explain it. And I do not know what is to become of me."

"Well, you are come back with a husband, or as good as. So, you have done what you set out to achieve, which is highly commendable. And Lord Dellingby does sound as if he is worthy of my good sister. Have a hope, Anne. Do not be melancholy, I cannot bear it."

With a rueful smile, I tell her, "You are right, Margie. I think tiredness is to blame. Perhaps I shall lie down a while."

"Yes, rest. But Anne, might you perhaps stop calling me Margie?"

"How else would I tease you?"

"There are perhaps worse ways. But must you tease at all?"

"I am your sister, it is my duty. And you should be concerned for the state of my health if I did not."

As I get up to leave, she halts me in another embrace. "I am so happy you are returned."

But not for long, I add in my thoughts alone, and depart her company.

Oh Margaret, how I wish I could tell you how close to ruin your sister came, how Lord Emsby turned my stomach, how others leered to the point my flesh felt as if it would leave my bones, how I was screaming inside whilst having to maintain a calm exterior. Only now I am safely home can all those feelings be released, and they threaten to overwhelm me.

I shall never tell you, dear sister, how dreadfully low I am brought or how fearful of my impaired judgement. You must undergo the same ordeal, and so I shall not share my fears of my life with a husband barely known to me, who may have dreadful secrets.

Safely ensconced in my room, I collapse onto the bed and cry in earnest. All the horrors, fears and terrors of the past three months revisit me in the same moment. Frightful faces leer in my head. Lord Felsenworth, glowering down with menace at the forefront. Had I ever thought him handsome? How hideous he was in that dreadful moment. Such evil intent behind such an angelic appearance. All kindness disappeared as a phantom, and his true self was revealed.

Smothering my wail with my pillow, I relive the fear as the images flood my mind as if I were still there. How my limbs were foreign to me, and there was nothing to be done to defend my honour. If Lord Beauvrais had not arrived the worst would have happened. How on ever was I, the sensible one, in that dire situation?

I know not how long the tears stream down my cheeks as the dark chasm of my memory engulfs me. My body shakes with unbridled sobs.

Eventually taking a deep breath, I remind myself that my friend did arrive to rescue me. I shall be forever grateful to him. But alas, he is lost abroad. To be so parted from one to whom I owe my life and grew up with is agony. Another calming breath is drawn, and I am forced to see that I should not be long in his presence in any case, for Lord Dellingby is leading me up north.

And his very actions mean I never have to face the terrible marriage mart again. No more parading myself like an animal at the fayre. My prize ribbon has been obtained. I have been sold to the highest bidder and must face my fate with propriety.

My hands wash over my face as I sit upright and reach across to ring the bell. I wipe away my tears with my handkerchief; silly salty droplets which have no place here. Lord Dellingby is to be my husband, and I should be feeling excited and grateful.

"Clément, I am tired but am finding it difficult to sleep. I think a little Madeira may ease the way," I say as she enters.

"Very good, my lady," she replies before dipping out of the room again.

Once the requested wine is brought, I take a long sip. Wandering across to my writing desk in a daze, I settle myself into the chair and begin to write.

Dear Anne,

You are a lady of gentle breeding. You endeavour to do all which is right and good. No harm shall befall you so long as you remain a good, faithful woman. You are no longer a girl, and no longer are you permitted pettish displays of emotion.

I pause and look at my ruddy reflection.

A fine lady must behave with the utmost decorum at all times. You are soon to be wed, and you shall be mistress of a household. A great deal has been spent on your education in order for you to accomplish the task now ahead. You are capable and willing of performing your duties.

Do not fail your family. Bear all with honour and dignity. You are Lady Anne Frithringham, pirate Captain Nobeard of the Ruby Riches, setting sail not on the Sea of Sludge, but now on the tides of matrimony.

The last brings a smile to my lips as I carefully stow my memorandum as if it were treasure. I was born a leader, and that is what I shall be. As fearless a wife as the captain of my childhood games. Captain Nobeard would not quiver at the prospect of marriage. She would face it as she must, with courage in her heart. Onwards then, full sail.

❧ Chapter 31 ❧

The new day has brought renewed vigour, and I am determined to take a tour of the grounds on Rosalind. Lady is a remarkable horse, but Rosalind remains my favourite.

"I really wish you would reconsider. What if you take a fall? And so soon before you are to marry. It would be more than I could bear," Mama implores.

"Mama, I have not taken a serious tumble in all my years. I see no reason I should do so now. The weather is fine and beckons me to take some air. You would not deny me this simple pleasure, would you?"

"Do not go above a walk then," she says, looking to heaven for strength.

"I shan't go above a trot, how is that?"

"So long as that is all, then I consent." She kisses my cheek.

"Thank you, Mama," I say, beaming and returning the kiss before running out the door.

Rosalind is waiting, and whinnies upon seeing me.

Stroking her nose, I whisper, "I missed you too, my fair Rosalind. I half thought you would have forgotten all about me."

Her nose nuzzles into my hand. As she raises her head, I cannot resist kissing her white, velvety muzzle. Walking around, my hand remains in contact and smooths her chestnut neck, which I then pat.

Once I am sure she has not taken umbrage at my long absence, I accept the groom's assistance into the saddle. Waving at Mama who is looking through the window, we walk away, Rosalind and me.

How glorious the park looks, the grass and trees greener than I have ever seen them. The stream bubbles with more vivacity than before. The birds sing with louder voice.

"Hello home," I cheer as we meander our way around.

Rosalind snorts, sending vibrations down her back and through the saddle.

"Oh, happy day," I murmur, patting her neck.

How I have missed this prospect with its trees, shrubs and undulating fields. I would remain here forever if I could. However, there is hope that my next house will be a happy one too.

Slowing from a trot to a walk, we pass into the shade. Joyous memories of George, Bamber and I arise as we ride by the glen of our playtime adventures. Those happy carefree times which seem a lifetime ago. I can practically hear our laughter as we ran about claiming new lands in our voyage of discovery. But I must journey on.

Tranquillity seeps through me as Rosalind continues. This peace is what I have been missing. London has many entertainments and much excitement but nothing could instil the feeling of calm these grounds inspire. My eyes gently close as my face turns towards the dappled sun, my shoulders rising and falling with each inhalation and exhalation. Bliss.

No earthly cares could ever reach me here. I am far removed from any troubles. There is only serenity.

As I return to the house, Margaret is about her lessons. I am now excused; the tutors' work is done. However, I pop my head in so I may say hello to Miss Swanson, our governess who is now in charge of Margaret alone.

"Lady Anne, how wonderful to see you. My, what a marvellous grown woman now stands before me. Felicitations."

"Yes, your instruction served me well. My thanks to you, Miss Swanson and to Mr Rawlinson."

A faint blush creeps upon her cheeks. "Oh, fie. The credit is all yours. I merely guided."

"Well, you have my thanks all the same. However, I shall leave you to it. I should not like to stand in the way of my sister's education."

Dash it, I had hoped they may be finishing, but saw no evidence of such. There are yet questions I hope she may answer but am unlikely to now have opportunity.

❧

On Sunday, exiting the church is as boisterous as entering, as so many well-wishers approach to congratulate me and my parents. All manner of people seem to think it appropriate to hinder my progress home. But they mean well, so I endure it with smiles and gratitude. And it is good to be amongst friends again. Here I know whom to trust.

But even amongst friends, or perhaps especially, I seem the topic of gossip.

"Such a long engagement."

"And her beau is not yet arrived. Do you think him a phantom?"

"I hear it is a fine match, blessed by the queen herself."

These and many other whisperings are overheard, despite my attempts not to listen to such drivel. My dealings should not be any of their concern, and their opinions are certainly none of mine. But their insinuations of even the merest hint of impropriety pique my pride.

"Miss Benshaw, how good to see you," I announce clearly.

"Lady Anne, how happy we are to see you back amongst us."

"It is good to be back, even for so short a time. How I shall miss you following my marriage. In but one week my husband shall remove me to more northern climes."

"I had heard as much. How frightful."

"I am quite looking forward to the change of scene. I am told it is beautiful in Derbyshire. But at first, we shall reside in Norfolk." At least, that is the most likely residence I shall choose from Lord Dellingby's descriptions. I may reconsider after viewing.

"Norfolk? Oh, how quaint."

Miss Benshaw is living up to expectation. I singled her out so I may put my case forwards at once and have all falsehoods at once contradicted.

"I shall be kept continually amused by a great many neighbours. What an extraordinary stroke of luck I should be so happily situated."

"Did I hear you declare Norfolk as your new home?" Lady Kerkham asks upon her approach.

"Indeed you did, Lady Kerkham."

"Oh, how delightful. You know I was born in the county? But of course you do. How amusing you should make my journey in reverse. You will find it the most charming county, I am sure."

"You must pay us a visit when you are next with your family there."

"I'd be only too happy to accept such a kind invitation. Tell me, where is it you shall reside?" she demands, leading me away from the group.

By the time our conversation is ended my tummy is quite filled with fluttering butterflies. Lady Kerkham has all but decided my mind upon settling in Norfolk, she has made it sound beautiful as well as entertaining; a most desirable combination in a home. Who knows how long we shall remain there, but I find myself wishing for a rapid and prolonged recovery in the Duke of Wenston's health, even more than I had hitherto.

I am still abuzz with excitement the next day and am in great need of a walk to remove some excess exuberance. My feet cannot seem to keep still.

"Mama, I am going to take some air," I tell her, standing up from the sofa.

"There are some clouds gathering."

"But they are far off yet. I shan't be long."

"Very well, but take an umbrella with you. It would not do to catch cold. A sniffing bride would be most unattractive."

"Of course, Mama."

As I reach the front door a figure appears at my elbow.

"Margie, where do you think you are going?" I enquire.

"Out for a walk with you."

"I had intended to walk alone, Margie."

My sister pouts and folds her arms at my response. "But I want to come too."

"Don't be missish. If it means so much you may come along, but don't complain if I walk too fast for your pace."

She kisses my cheek. "I shan't. Oh, this will be fun. We have not been on an adventure in so long."

"Margie, I am going for a short walk, not an adventure. You heard Mama, it may rain."

"Then we'd best be quick," she says, dashing out of the door, forcing me to run after her.

"Margie, slow down, this is not dignified."

"Have you so soon forgotten how to have fun, Anne?" she cries over her shoulder, not slowing a jot.

"Need I remind you I am soon to be married?"

"All the more reason to enjoy yourself whilst you are yet able. Catch me if you can," she calls, speeding up.

Lifting my skirts, I give chase. "You little vixen."

"Me? I am but a sweet maid. Who shall save me from the brigand upon my heels? Oh, have mercy, dread pirate."

My feet pound against the dry earth as I run as fast as my legs will carry me. We cross the lawn in leaps and bounds. Margaret is faster than she used to be. My legs burn with effort, and my lungs gasp for air. But my prey is within my grasp as we approach the treeline.

"Luck is not on your side, fair maid. There is none who can save you from your fate this day. You shall be my prisoner and held for ransom," I snarl, capturing her hands behind her back.

"You shan't get a thing from me or my family, you foul fiend," she bravely declares, falling on the ground.

"Erm…" Words fail me as Lord Felsenworth shows himself in my mind.

After all our games and adventures, how had I not seen his intentions? Of course, nothing so sinister was in our minds as children. But surely I should have had some inkling?

"Anne? Anne," Margaret urges with increasing volume.

"Pardon?"

"This is where you throw me onto your ship."

Our game no longer seems fun. Oh, sweet innocence of youth, you are lost to me forever.

"Are you alright?" Margaret asks.

"Err, yes, of course. Sorry."

"What happened to you?"

"I grew up, I suppose." A shrug accompanies my words.

"It's not quite the same without George and Bamber, is it?"

"No, no it isn't."

"Now I've made you sad. Anne, I am so sorry. I meant only to liven your spirits with some fun."

I stroke her arm. "I know you did, and it was a lovely thought."

"But badly done."

"No, do not feel as if you are in the wrong. The fault lies with others, not you."

"I never seem to do right. Everyone is always so serious and are so stern with me."

"Now listen, Margie. You are not a little girl any longer. Mama and Papa only want what is best. You are not to think they act against you. Once Lord Dellingby carries me away, you shall be next to be married. Becoming a lady carries heavy burdens. We all want you to be prepared."

"But I'm not ready."

"Of course not, but you will be. You aren't expected to find a husband tomorrow."

"Why must I find a husband at all? Can I not come and live with you and Lord Dellingby?"

I giggle. "You have not so much as met him yet. You may not even like him."

"If you do not find him wanting then surely I cannot."

We laugh at her keen observation. "Yes, if your severe sister likes him, then Lord Dellingby must be the finest of men."

"Precisely. Although, you are not so severe as you would have others believe."

"See? You are growing up already, Margie, whether you like it or not."

She pokes her tongue out at me.

Giggling, I tell her, "But there is room for improvement yet."

Giving me a playful shove, she speeds off once more, yelling, "I'm still young."

As I am gaining ground, almost upon her, a clattering of hooves echoes behind and beside us. Looking over my shoulder, I see a large black horse cantering up the driveway. The world tilts and I land with a thud on my front, emitting a rather unladylike scream.

Hooves stop beside me in an instant.

"Anne, are you alright?" Margie yells.

"She took the words from my mouth. Are you alright? Are you able to move, Lady Anne?" Lord Dellingby asks, his brown eyes coming into view as I sit up.

"I think so."

I rub my palms against one another to remove the dust.

"You're bleeding."

"It is only a graze, my lord."

But he insists upon binding his handkerchief around my hand.

"Sir, I shall take care of my sister. If you would be so kind as to continue to the house?" Margaret commands.

Oh, how I have missed that low chortle which precedes his response. "Hello there, you must be Lady Margaret."

She dips the shallowest of curtseys. "I am, and who might you be?"

I cannot help but giggle. "Margie, this is Lord Dellingby."

"Well, he might've said."

"Delighted to make your acquaintance, Lady Margaret. Or do you prefer Lady Margie?"

"I most certainly do not. Anne, you see what you have done now?"

Laughter bursts from me. "My apologies, Lord Dellingby. You see, *Margaret* detests being called anything but that. Always has done. I am afraid I have rather landed you in her bad books already."

He makes an exaggerated bow. "Lady Margaret, my humblest apologies. I had no idea of the great offence I was committing. Can you find it in your heart to forgive such a fool?"

Margaret titters. "You silly man. I would not hold my sister's crimes against you."

"You are very good."

A groan escapes as I attempt to stand during their intercourse.

"Hey there, take my arm," he insists.

Using his support, I get to my feet and dust off my skirts.

"Are you much injured?" he checks.

"Only my pride, I think."

"Not at all. I should not have approached in such a hurry. The fault is mine. I thought it would be fun to chase the chaser."

"On horseback? That was most unfair of you."

"My lady, I own my error. Are you able to walk?"

"Of course. It is time we returned to the house in any matter."

"It is a pleasure to see you." His eyes burn into mine, and his lips approach in a most enticing manner which sets me aflame.

"Anne, do not forget yourself. Lord Dellingby, I had heard tell of you being an honourable man."

Clearing his throat and without taking his gaze away, he replies, "I flatter myself I am, and would do nothing to bring your sister's reputation into question."

"I am pleased to hear it. Shall we continue?"

His breath and mine hitch as the thought occurs we could kiss. He looks away first. "But of course. Lead the way, Lady Margaret."

"After you, I insist, Lord Dellingby," she says, making her way around us.

"Ow," I exclaim.

"You are hurt. Oh, my dear. A thousand apologies."

"Nonsense. There is merely a stone in my shoe," I tell him, making a show of removing it, but really the yelp was caused by my sister's finger jabbing my ribs.

Replacing my footwear, I lead the way. Lord Dellingby's magnificent beast is being led by him. I shoot Margaret a glare over my shoulder. She answers by means of another show of her tongue.

"You are quite sure you are unharmed?" my intended checks as we walk.

"Lord Dellingby, it was only a little fall. Do not concern yourself. It is nothing and is quite out of my mind already."

"Ah, Lord Dellingby, you are arrived early. I see you have found Lady Anne already. Won't you come in? A man will show you to your room directly," Mama welcomes from the door.

She makes way for him and glowers at me in such a manner as to leave me by no means uncertain of her displeasure.

"How could I know he would arrive so soon?" I whisper with a hiss.

"Go and make yourself respectable before your papa sees you."

"Mama, I made Anne run, and she fell chasing me," Margaret confesses as I hurry to my room.

Clément makes quick work of my change of dress and righting my hair. The cool water soothes my grazed hands as she pours it from a jug. The salve she applies after makes me wince though. Really, to be thus reduced at my age; it is quite shameful. But a smile spreads as I recall running wild.

❧ Chapter 32 ❧

Lord Dellingby is mainly silent in the days which follow. Mama or Margaret are forever in our presence, and we are never allowed a moment alone. I am convinced he is as frustrated by this as me. Conversation is kept to strict social convention, and it is stilted at best.

Mama has overseen all the wedding preparations, requiring very little input from myself. I do not quite know what to do or where to be. All is unsettled and commotion.

Papa has offered respite and taken Lord Dellingby off fishing for the day, along with my brother James who has arrived with his wife, Lady Ellingsmoor, but not with their children. Caroline says they are yet too young to travel much. But it is not too great a distance in my opinion, although I keep this to myself of course. Her presence does nothing to ease the growing tension.

All we ladies are sat with our needlework in silent contemplation when male voices and laughter signal the arrival home of the men.

"What ho, sat inside on such a fine day, ladies? This will never do," Papa announces, all joviality.

"We are perfectly content, really, Duke," Mama demurs.

"Nonsense. Come, there is more than enough time to take some air before we dine."

"More? Have you not been out in the sun all day?" Mama's tone hints she believes the sun may have gone to his head.

"I assure you, the pike kept us mostly in the shade. We have been sitting most of the day and find we must now stretch our legs."

"I beg you must excuse me from this outing, for I have one of my heads. It shall clear, I am sure, with a little rest in solitude," Lady Ellingsmoor beseeches James.

None of us seem willing to contradict her, and Mama ensures she has every comfort before we depart. I do not believe her excuse for one moment but shall oblige her whim. Perhaps this is a little selfish, but I have not seen James in so long, and crave a moment alone with him.

However, he partners Margaret as Lord Dellingby takes his place beside me.

"Did you find much success today, my lord?" I ask as we amble along.

"More than I feared, but not as much as we hoped."

"Ah, the tale of anglers everywhere, I suspect."

Lord Dellingby chortles. "Decidedly so. But tell me, what of your day?"

"It was pleasant enough."

"Is this all you have to say?"

"On that topic, perhaps it is best not to say too much."

"Ah, quite so." He glances about and stabs at the long grass with his walking cane.

"Would you be upset if I leave your side but for a moment?"

"My dear, you may go where you wish. This is your house."

I look into his hazel eyes, glinting with lighter flecks in the sun. "No, there you are quite wrong."

"Is that so?"

"This is my father's house, not mine at all. But in a few days, I hope to discover mine."

"Well, is that not a fine thought indeed? Yes, you shall have your house and me along with it." His smile broadens across his cheeks as he reaches my hand to place a kiss upon it.

Giggling, I rush away from him before temptation can overpower me and fling myself into his arms like a wanton woman.

Catching up to brother and sister, I ask, "Margaret, I would beg a moment with James."

She rolls her eyes. "Fine. I should not wish to hear anything you have to say anyway," she declares, walking briskly towards my beau.

Forcing down the concern over what she may have to say to Lord Dellingby, I turn to James.

"Dear brother, how are you this fine day?"

"I am well enough. But that is not what has brought you rushing to my side."

"Perhaps not. But it is so wonderful to be with you again."

"Is it? I had thought you could not wait for me to leave this house. You were always fonder of George."

My breath catches in my throat.

"Forgive me. That was careless. I meant only to tease, not to injure."

I look at his blurred image, trying not to let the tears fall. "I did love him very much. But that does not mean I do not love you also."

"Anne, do not take on so. I already apologised. Take no heed of my foolish words."

Taking a deep breath, I try to calm myself. I wonder if he knew about George's secret. The question is on the tip of my tongue, but I do not allow it to part from my lips. If he did not, I would not disgrace George's memory. It serves no purpose.

"Well, what was it you wanted to ask me?"

With a small ahem, I bring my query back to mind. "I was wondering...curious...well—"

"My sister at a loss for words? Can this be?"

I slap his arm playfully. "Do not tease. James, the thing is, I was hoping you would tell me what it is to be married." I huff out a big breath. There; the question is asked.

He laughs at me. "Oh, the great secret? But I do not think it is me whom you should be asking."

"Who else is there?"

He lays a hand on my arm. "I can only tell you a man's perspective, which is entirely different. But from where I stand, it is a marvellous thing."

"Even with Caroline?" The question is out before it may be stopped.

He frowns at me. "And what do you mean by that?"

"Nothing. I meant nothing at all."

"Oh yes you did, you baggage," he says, lunging to prod my ribs, but I evade his torture.

We are left in a stand-off, his arms out wide as I swerve side to side, trying to avoid him.

"You're in for it now," he warns, running towards me.

I run, narrowly missing his hands. Seeking sanctuary, I hide behind Lord Dellingby. Margaret sensibly separates herself from us.

"Help. Save me," I implore.

"None shall harm you," Lord Dellingby declares.

He spreads out his arms, providing more of a barrier against the impending James.

"I have no quarrel with you, Dellingby," James calls, stopping, holding up his hands.

"Coward," I call from behind my saviour.

"But I cannot forgive that," he adds, trying to reach me.

Lord Dellingby turns his body, guiding me in a circle.

"What are you all about? Really, a little sunshine and you act like imbeciles," Mama admonishes, having walked back to us.

"Sorry Mama," James and I chorus.

"If we could perhaps continue our promenade with more decorum?"

"Yes, Mama," we chorus again and take our places with our respective walking partners.

Once we have fallen behind sufficiently, Lord Dellingby asks, "If I enquire as to what all that was pertaining would I receive an answer?"

"You must think me a complete goose."

"Not at all. You are amongst family. It is rather wonderful to see you in this light, so full of frivolity."

"You are a curiosity, Lord Dellingby. Every time I display my worst possible side you seem intent on seeing the best."

He stops walking, holding my hand to also halt me.

Stroking my cheek, he says, "I rejoice in the truth. You light up with the radiance of a thousand stars when you are thus excited."

"Oh, um…"

His lips are upon mine, stopping any more words.

With a grunt, he stops his kiss, leaving me bereft.

"Aher, please forgive me."

"There is nothing to forgive."

"Come, we are dragging behind too far. Your parents will grow anxious."

We quicken our pace until we round the bushes and catch up with the group, who seem oblivious of our absence. Dash it all, but we could have drawn our kiss out longer without discovery. I want to scream. What a wasted opportunity.

❧

We all attend church the next day like good parishioners. But no banns are read for us, as Papa obtained a common license, as we would not be in the parish three consecutive Sundays before the event. Besides, declaring our intent of matrimony in such a fashion seems vulgar. There is no suspicion of anything untoward regarding our partnership.

Lord Dellingby attracts much attention.

"Delighted to make your acquaintance," seems to be chorused from every female about us.

Have they no shame? I am promised to him. Surely, they can have no realistic designs upon Lord Dellingby?

His good nature seemingly shines through, and he is all smiles and gentility. But perhaps there is no façade or artifice, and he is truly relishing their attentions? Maybe he is plotting which to take as a mistress. I must be prepared for such. After all, is it not accepted and encouraged a man should do so? Especially one of high standing. Why am I now jealous of such a scheme?

"Just think, the next time we leave this church you shall be my wife," he addresses me.

My attention taken back outside of myself, I notice we have left the crowd and are near the carriage. It takes a moment for his words to be comprehended. All I am able to offer is a weak smile in return.

Yes, tomorrow I shall be his, to obey and serve until death us do part. How frightful.

Nervous excitement has left me trembling and exhausted. No matter what may be, tomorrow is my wedding day. Try as I might, my mind will not fully accept the prospect with placid rectitude.

As Clément prepares me for bed, I slip her a brown paper package.

"Please, I cannot risk detection, Clément, but I would have this delivered to Lord Dellingby. I had not the opportunity, but he must be in receipt of it before tomorrow. It is only a small token, you understand. I do not ask anything untoward of you."

"I will see he gets it, my lady."

"Thank you, Clément."

It is the handkerchief I stitched for him. A silly thing really, but it seems somehow important.

With my orders discharged, I get into bed. Pulling the covers up high, my fingers clutch the bedclothes as though they can hide me from my fate. Rest will not come easily, and yet it must for nobody wants a dull bride who is half asleep.

A creak echoes through my thoughts, and a slither of light creeps through the darkness of my room. A candle lights Mama's procession to my bed. My fingers clench all the tighter. What terrible tragedy has befallen to necessitate such a nightly visitation? She is dressed in her white nightgown and is more apparition than reality.

The mattress depresses as Mama sits close to my reclined body. The candle set upon my nightstand illuminates her visage in a most alarming fashion. Her cold hand seeks one of mine. She is no figment of my imagination then.

"What is it, Mama? What's the matter?" I ask, my voice hoarse with eluded sleep.

"My dear, tomorrow you are to be wed."

"Yes, Mama."

Her shoulders bristle. "Being a wife carries with it certain...duties."

My breath hitches.

"I do not mean to alarm you. You must be prepared for what is to come."

My heart thuds in my breast as if it will burst forth from its cage.

"You are not to be afraid."

"Of what, Mama? What is to happen?"

Mama clears her throat. "Your husband shall visit you on your wedding night, whilst you are abed."

She pauses, her hand patting her cheeks and forehead. "Oh dear, but this is difficult to say. Be not afraid, that is all."

"But how will I know what to do? What will he do?"

More questions would be asked, but they are silenced by her scowl. "All you need do is lie there and perform your duty."

"But—"

"That is all there is to it, Anne. Please ask no more."

Having said what she came to say, Mama exits the room, leaving me in fuller darkness than ever before.

What is my duty? How can I perform it when I know not what it entails? It is as if she has bid me perform a quadrille without allowing for even one lesson. I shall be entirely lost, left only to the whims of my husband for guidance.

❧ Chapter 33 ❧

Clément roused me from bed as the lark began its song, and has bathed me thoroughly, using the delectably floral Pears soap. The sponge was liberally applied all about my person until every inch was declared clean.

Even more effort has been exerted than usual in the application of creams. A touch more pink is now visible upon my cheeks and lips. The hairdresser has immaculately braided my hair, curled and intertwined it with flowers and feathers. The softest muslin and lace make up my gown.

The reflection shows a beautiful young bride, glowing with confidence and gentle breeding. Only my trembling fingers hint at my true feelings as Clément passes me the bouquet of herbs and hothouse flowers.

"*Très jolie*, if I may say how beautiful you look, Lady Anne?" the sweet girl remarks.

"You may, just this once," I reply with a smile.

"I was asked to give you this," she tells me, gingerly holding out a horseshoe tied with ribbon.

"Goodness, thank you, Clément." I take the offering, touched by the sentiment.

"Colin, the groom, says it came from Lady herself. We, the other servants and I, we wanted to wish you well, a small gesture of our high esteem."

"Thank you, but need I remind you that you're coming with me?"

"Yes, my lady, but the others are not. I know children would usually give such a thing, but, well, we thought you might appreciate it."

"I do, in all earnestness."

My gloved fingers pat away a tear from the corner of my eye. I had never expected such a gift. Looping its ribbon over my wrist, I grasp my bouquet and cast one last glance at the looking glass.

"Farewell Lady Anne Frithringham," I tell the girl staring back at me.

Clément frowns a moment, but then beams. "Hello, Lady Dellingby."

"Clément, what are you about? Do you wish to bring bad luck down upon my head?" I ask with a gasp.

Her hand flies to her mouth. "Oh, my lady, *non. Sacré Dieu*, I meant only to wish you well. Pray forgive me. I was carried away by excitement. You are but moments away. Surely nothing dreadful will happen. No, you will be the happiest of brides."

"I hope you are right, Clément, I hope you are right."

We hasten down the stairs where Papa is waiting.

"Well, daughter, Lord Dellingby will be best pleased."

"I hope to bring honour to you, Papa."

"You have never done anything but. There is no reason to think you shall ever do otherwise," he says in a hoarse whisper, laying a kiss upon each cheek.

I am taken aback for an instant. Praise and admiration from Papa, and all in the one breath?

"Well, what are we all standing about for? Come, let us to the church."

He and I are conveyed by carriage to the church where my future lies waiting for me. Butterflies fill my stomach, making my breathing shallow. Spots form in front of my eyes, so I take deep breaths in an attempt to clear them.

Papa turns his attention from outside to me and offers an encouraging smile. I return the gesture in between more breaths.

"No need for nerves, now, there's a good girl. Dellingby is a good man. How would he dare otherwise with me as a father-in-law, wot?" He chuckles.

Papa is laughing? My, he is in the highest realms of merriment as ever I've seen. I take another couple of deep breaths and pinch the back of my hand to ensure I am awake and in full ownership of my senses.

"I would not part with you to anyone unworthy, Anne. Come, show your brave face. Unless you mean to tell me I have raised a chicken-hearted daughter after all?"

"Of course not, Papa. It was but a passing moment. I am well."

My mask is back in place. No need for Papa to see what a goose I am being. He has the right of it. Lord Dellingby must have undergone keen observation before Papa encouraged our union. Not for my own benefit, of course, but so as not to bring the family name into disrepute. He would not want a scoundrel for a son-in-law. And he has shown himself to be a good man. I have no real cause to doubt him.

Acrobats seem to replace the butterflies inside me as concern gives way to excitement. Along with the motion of the carriage, I am feeling quite queasy by the time we reach the church.

It is a relief to feel the cool air as we walk up the small path, where Margaret is hopping from foot to foot. Mama insisted she accompany her, perhaps foreseeing our need for solitude. But now she ensures my dress is presented at its finest before we enter the holy house of God.

Thankful for Papa's strong arm for support, we make our way up the aisle to my awaiting groom, who is dressed in black and white and is all smiles.

As we approach my intended, he pats his pocket, a slight nod and smile of acknowledgement. He received my gift.

"Dearly Beloved, we are gathered together here in the sight of God," the priest starts, his words reaching me as if through a tunnel.

The whole world seems a bit of a blur. All I can see is a pair of glimmering brown eyes.

"Into which holy estate these two persons present come now to be joined…" the priest continues.

All is a mystery to me. My focus is on keeping myself standing on my feet.

"I will," Lord Dellingby's voice reaches me through the fog.

"Lady Anne Juliana Catherine Eleanor Frithringham, wilt thou have this man to thy wedded husband, to live together after God's ordinance in the holy estate of Matrimony? Wilt thou obey him, and serve him, love, honour, and keep him in sickness and in health; and, forsaking all other, keep thee only unto him, so long as ye both shall live?"

My, this all sounds most solemn. Of course it is, but it sounds so very final. I suppose it is. But to make the promise to God, who shall smite me should I not abide by this solemn oath? The…rest…of…my…life. Oh Lor', I should make my response.

"I will."

Lord Dellingby lets out a long, hard breath. I smile at him, hoping he will forgive my delay. Truly, I had not meant to cause concern.

"Amen," I hear James murmur, and Mama hushing him.

A smile spreads across my cheeks at such familiar sounds. Encouraged and boosted thus, the remainder of the ceremony is conducted without incident.

"Lord Alverbury, how good of you to come," I cry, seeing him standing guard as groomsman as we make our exit.

"Lady Dellingby," he says with a grin and a bow.

The unusual name makes me giggle. Before I can say anything further, my husband leads us outside where a large crowd has gathered. It would appear every person in the village has turned out. Rice is thrown from every direction, and their cheers border on raucous as we make our way to the carriage.

"You're all mine now," Lord Dellingby declares, his eyes narrowed and lustrous.

"I suppose I am," I whisper, doves flapping about my heart.

As soon as we are on our way, he leans in for a deep, hungry kiss. Oh, sweet merciful heaven, at last. A groan bursts from my throat, which encourages the same from Lord Dellingby.

His hand grasps my waist and pulls me to him. His tongue dances with mine as his fingers reach along my bodice and, oh, grabs my breast and kneads it. Heat engulfs me at his ministrations. My arms are about his neck in an attempt to lose myself in my husband further.

"No. Not like this. My lady, my apologies. You deserve the best I can offer," he says, putting distance between himself and my aching body.

How much more I would ask. Without any idea of destination, I do not wish to stop. But I promised only moments ago to obey, so hold my silence.

"My dear Lady Anne, I must warn you my resolve will shatter should you continue to pout so."

"Oh?" I was unaware I was doing any such thing but attempt to control my appearance better.

"Dash it all, Now I've inspired neutrality. Anne, I mean no insult. Believe me, I would do unmentionable things to you right here, but we are in a carriage. It is no place for a lady to experience…well, you get my meaning."

"As you say," I reply with an inclination of my head.

His hands run through his hair, and a small grunt is audible from his direction. He appears so diverting when cross that I cannot help but smile.

"You find amusement in my frustration, perhaps?"

"Only in your demeanour," I answer, repressing giggles in my voice.

He shakes his head. "And this is what I have married?"

I lean over and kiss his cheek. "It is."

"And do not think me ungrateful for a moment. Speaking of gratitude, I must thank you for such an exquisite gift. Such fine needlework was created by your own hand?"

"It was."

He kisses my forehead. "A most thoughtful gesture. I shall keep it about me always."

I can find no words. All I can do is smile at him. There is always to be a part of me with him, even when we are not near. It is curious how much relief and satisfaction this simple fact imparts, how much courage it lends me.

We are arrived at my childhood home already. Righting my apparel, I exit the carriage a married woman. Our guests greet us with more cheering. Congratulations flow in like rivers. Once my family join us, we all enter the dining room to enjoy the wedding breakfast.

Cold cuts, cheese and fruits are all laid out in a dazzling display. Rather too much wine is consumed as we celebrate our matrimony. I fear the cake will not be enough to stem the effects.

We even take the opportunity to dance the first before making our farewells.

"You're a fortunate fellow, Dellingby. Ensure Lady Anne is kept always happy," Lord Alverbury commands.

"I fully intend to," is Lord Dellingby's happy response.

"You let me know if he causes any trouble, eh wot. I shall visit you soon and will expect a full report," Lord Alverbury tells me.

"You will always be welcome, my lord."

"I'll miss you," Margaret interrupts, tears in her eyes.

"Nonsense. Your ears will enjoy the peace. And I expect news often," I tell her.

"I have every confidence you have a fine husband."

My sister scurries away, supposedly overcome with emotion. It is a hard parting indeed. Our relationship is irrevocably changed. And she too is becoming a young woman. It will not be too long before she is sent in search of her own husband, I think.

Many more friends offer blessings and goodbyes. Mama is the last of our well-wishers and holds me tightly.

"My darling girl, you will write, won't you?"

"Of course, Mama."

"Well, I shall not detain you. Oh, Anne, how I shall miss you."

"I shall miss you too, Mama."

Papa ushers her away. "Come, come, they must be on their way. There is some distance to be covered."

More rice is thrown as we get into the carriage which is to take me away towards my new home, away from Gensmore Hall.

Lord Dellingby pulls me close and tucks me under his arm, placing a kiss on top of my head.

"Lady Anne Dellingby, we have a journey ahead of us."

"Hmmm," I moan, comfortable in his arms.

❦

"We are approaching Fairdown Lodge," Lord Dellingby says, patting my hand to bring me to wakefulness.

Pulling myself fully upright again, my eyes adjust to the darkness. I must have fallen asleep; how mortifying. But it is quite a journey from Hampshire to Wiltshire. We stopped at an inn for light refreshment whilst the horses were rested, which added more time. It is late, and the day has been as long as it was tiring.

"What a pity it is too dark for me to see. I would so like to view the property."

"It has many things in its favour. It's closer proximity to your family being the foremost, and what it lacks in size it makes up for in charm. It is close to Bath, which may be amusing to you. However, I am quite sure you will find it too small. It is only a hunting lodge, after all."

398

We approach closer, but I can still see precious little. Only one window has candles lit. However, I make out what I can, and find it indeed lacking in size.

Taking great care, I slowly alight from the carriage and approach the waiting staff.

"My lord, your ladyship," the man I presume to be the butler greets with a stiff bow.

"Mr Dawkins, it's been an age," Lord Dellingby replies.

"Indeed it has. And how you have grown, if you'll permit me to say, my lord."

"Haha, I do hope so. The last we met I was all of, what, ten years of age?"

"I believe you were, my lord. I have taken the liberty of having some refreshments served in the drawing room. But if you prefer them elsewhere, say the word."

"No no, the drawing room shall suffice. I remember a welcoming fire may be found there."

"Precisely, my lord, and it is lit."

"Very good, Mr Dawkins. Might I introduce the Marchioness of Dellingby to you?"

"Your ladyship, it is an honour."

"Pleased to make your acquaintance." I cannot think of anything else to say and so must appear excessively stupid.

We walk through a small hallway and directly into a comfortable drawing room. The fire is indeed most welcoming but takes up a great deal too much space. Trying not to flollop, I sit on a pretty chair at a small table with coffee cups and plates laid out.

The bread and cheese are gratefully received. Glancing around, I consider how I should like to spend more time here.

"Well, how do you find it?" Lord Dellingby enquires.

I pause before replying, "It is a pleasant lodge, to be sure."

"But too small?"

"Lord Dellingby, I have only seen this one room. Ask me anew in the morning when I shall be better able to respond."

"But of course. You must be tired. Shall I call for Clément?"

The poor girl was situated next to the driver the entire journey, and a fine drizzle fell part of the way here. However, enough time has surely passed for her to recover.

"That would be most kind."

Clément appears and leads me to my room, which too is much reduced in size from what I am accustomed to.

"Perhaps best to leave that lit this once, my lady," Clément cautions as I reach to snuff my bedside candle once I'm settled.

I do not think it wise at all. What if the bed should catch alight? As soon as she leaves, I snuff the candle, too afraid of fire to heed her words.

The mattress is soft, and my eyelids are heavy. Some vague thoughts of duty float through my head as I wait in the dark. I must stay awake for whatever it is I am to do.

"My lady, do you sleep so soundly?" Lord Dellingby whispers.

"Mmmeeuuurgh?" is the only response one can muster.

"I am come for you, my love."

"Mmm?" I'm faintly aware of rolling over to face his direction.

A candle is in his hand casting light and shadows.

"My my, what a sleepy head."

"Do not tease me so."

"Come, make way for me."

"Pardon?"

"There is no need to act so coy, my dear. Come along now, I grow impatient."

Feeling more than a little bewildered, I comply. He steps nearer, candle still in hand. His nightshirt lifts as one of his knees rises to the bed as he prepares to climb in beside me.

What is that? I scream at the sight of something poking out at my face. I draw the bedclothes up tight about my face.

"What the devil?" he shouts.

His anger only serves to alarm me further. Scrunching my eyes tight against such horror, I pull the sheets over and above my head.

"What the deuce has overcome you?" he yells.

Peering out from my hiding place I attempt a response. "I...I..."

"Well, out with it. You would not have me believe—"

"That!" I manage to squeal and point before ducking behind my covers again.

"What is so extraordinary...? Wait, do you mean you have never beheld...? In this day and age...?"

"Oh, take it away, take it away," I screech.

The slamming of the door echoes around my chamber. Oh my life, what was that?

Metal and glass crashing in the hall chills my bones. It is accompanied by a loud, "I shan't be made a villain in my own home."

I do hope Mr Dawkins was unharmed in the disturbance. Perhaps he was carrying a tray of drinks? Lord Dellingby would not have struck him, surely? But he was so very angry. And I must surmise that I failed in whatever duty was set before me.

Mama should have been more explicit, for how could anything but fear be instilled upon seeing…that. It does not marry up with the outline so often witnessed in breeches. It was so much larger and hideous. I swear it was looking at me with its one eye. And what was I supposed to do with it? I would not ever wish it near me.

Shame floods through me and out of my eyes. Tears stream onto my pillow as I lie alone in the darkness of my tiny room.

∾

"I apologise for my behaviour last night," I tell Lord Dellingby as we sit to breakfast.

I have not seen him all morning, having remained in my room in case he should visit me, but he did not appear.

"I have no wish to discuss it," he dismisses brusquely.

Thus being reprimanded, I take a bite of my breakfast in glum silence.

"Matters here have been much neglected, I shall be busy all the day. Mrs Brown the housekeeper will show you around."

Oh, so silence is not strictly observed at mealtimes then. However much I may have been cheered by this fact, it is diminished by his continued severity.

"Very well," I reply, attempting to sound nonchalant.

Pausing chewing, his head lifts so he may scrutinise me. I continue with my own meal, pretending not to notice his observation.

"It is not how I envisaged our first day as man and wife." Is that a tone of apology I hear?

"Really? What had you thought it would be?" I ask, looking up through lowered lashes.

"I had hoped to have you in my arms all the day, to see to your every need personally."

Oh, that sounds very pleasing. "Well, it can't be helped."

"No, to my regret." Again, that hint of sorrow.

What does Lord Dellingby have to be sorry for? Was it not I who erred, who incited such anger by failing in my duty?

With breakfast over, my husband rises from his chair, crosses to me, and places a kiss on my cheek before bidding me, "Have a pleasant day. Mrs Brown will be able to answer any of your questions."

And indeed she does. I ask her many things as we tour the house and grounds.

"Does the family visit often?"

"No, my lady. That is, they did when the children were young. The Duke would often summer here, for he enjoyed the shooting. But then, well, it is not my place..."

"I would not ask you to divulge anything you deem improper."

"It is not so great a secret. Lord Dellingby was sent to school, and the Duke began to visit on his own."

"But they did not spend the school holidays here?"

"Pardon me, my lady, but Lord Dellingby remained at school much of the time."

"Oh, I see. Please, say no more. I have no wish to pry. I was merely surprised at such a beautiful home not being more frequently used."

The good lady smiles. "It warms my heart to know you are pleased with our house here."

"Who would not be? And the gardens are so well kept."

"We do our best."

"I understand you do not maintain many staff?"

Our talk falls to household management. Nobody from the family has visited for quite some time, and they live quite basic usually. Guilt stabs at me as I hear how they have hired in help for our short visit. I had no idea of putting anyone to any trouble.

Looking with admittedly inexperienced eyes, I see nothing untoward. The house seems to be run tolerably well. That is unfair, it is very well kept. I find myself regretting its lack of proportions. If it were but larger it would make a most pleasing home. Perhaps we can holiday here as the family used to, once we have children of our own. My, I am getting ahead of myself. One day married, and already planning family time.

Mrs Brown is so good as to direct me to the library. There is a limited selection of books, but I select one which seems of interest and settle into the armchair to read.

"Dinner shall be served in one hour, your ladyship," Mr Dawkins informs me.

"My, is that the time? Thank you."

Hurrying to my room, I call for Clément to dress me for dinner. How luxurious to remain undisturbed all that time.

"And how do you find this house, Clément?"

"It's as fine a house as —"

I hold up my hand. "Pray, do not complete that sentence, Clément. I asked a question and expect an honest answer."

"Well, err, it is pleasant, my lady. Most comfortable. And Mrs Brown seems agreeable."

"Should you like to call it home?"

"It is not for me to say, with all due respect, my lady. If you so choose, I would not be unhappy here, I think."

"Very well."

A deep sigh heaves my bosom as she leaves the room. I should not have expected any other reply. But there are no others here to consult.

I make my way down to dinner, where Lord Dellingby is already at table. He stands and bows to receive me.

"Good evening, my lady."

"Good evening, my lord."

"How was your day? How did you find the house?"

"Charming, but I must regrettably agree it is not quite of a size for a permanent residence."

He nods. "I thought you may find it so, but it was worth a visit."

"Do not think me ungrateful. I was of a mind to perhaps summer here. I understand you had some happy times here as a boy."

"Yes, yes, I think we can manage to replicate those halcyon days."

"As opposed to the other tumultuous ones, I suppose?"

"You shrew, you took my meaning very well," he replies, grinning.

"Perhaps, but it was too good an opportunity not to tease you. You have been much too serious. I do hope I am not the cause of such sullenness."

"No indeed. Far from it. It is merely estate matters which kept me from you all day and weigh heavily upon me."

"Is there anything I can do to lighten your load?"

"How kind you are. It is more volume than detail."

"Has all been dealt with?"

"I must work some more tomorrow, I am afraid."

"But not tonight?"

"No, I cannot bear one more sum, figure or proposal."

"Good."

He smiles. "You are not deterred from my company by my oafish behaviour?"

"Well, the vase and picture in the corridor seem to have been the victims of that more than I."

A blush rises to his cheeks. "You saw? I had thought all evidence to be cleared."

"It was, but I noticed where they should be."

"Lady Dellingby's keen observation in action again, wot?"

We grin at one another.

"Aher, well—" he begins.

"I thought you did not wish to discuss last night?"

"Quite right, I don't. Tell me, have you had your fill of exercise, or would you join me for a turn about the gardens after dinner?"

"That sounds agreeable. They are rather lovely."

I eat faster than is customary, anticipation building deep inside me urging my cutlery to work quicker. Perhaps he will grant me a delicious kiss and all ill feeling between us will be quite forgot. Warmth fills my loins at the very notion.

Happily, Lord Dellingby seems as desirous as I, and declines dessert, leading me outside instead. Herbs scent the air as we stroll by. Jasmine adds its heady aroma, and a nightingale sings her song.

"What a beautiful evening," I declare, enraptured.

"Yes, it is," Lord Dellingby whispers, stopping to look me in the eyes.

When I think he may kiss me he begins walking again.

"I am particularly fond of this walk down in this direction," he says, leading me down a lane of box hedging. Roses and lavender fill the beds, their heavenly scent permeating the still air.

"Yes, that should be far enough," he announces, halting.

Facing him, I stand, licking my lips.

"Oh my dear, how have I resisted your temptation?"

But before I can make an answer his lips are upon mine. Yes, a thousand times yes, this is what I have longed for too, but was unable to give voice to. He devours me, and I am all too willing.

His breathing is ragged as he pulls back. No, please do not abandon me again. But what is this? His hands are pawing at my dress. My nipples harden as they meet the cool evening air. But they are warmed by, oh my, his mouth. His mouth is upon my breasts, and I can scarce remain standing on weakened knees.

Lord Dellingby must sense my unsteadiness, as he encourages me to sit on the grass.

"Lady Dellingby, would you permit me the liberty?"

"I would permit you anything you ask, my lord," I tell him in breathy tones, my voice no longer my own.

A strange garbled groan comes from him as he brings his body close to min and pushes up my skirts. Oh my, his hand travels up my thigh. I have no idea of his intention, but I think I want the same.

A cry is wrought from my very soul as his fingers touch upon my feminine parts.

"Are you alright?" he asks, immediately withdrawing his hand, which I grab to place back where it was.

"Please don't stop."

His coat rustles as he manoeuvres to kiss me whilst continuing his rubbing motions. My body is his, acting at his demand, my hips move to meet his touch all the more.

"My wonderful wife," he mutters.

His face disappears from view as he moves down. My eyes close as he sucks on my nipple again. The mixture of this with his hand crescendos the feeling within me until it explodes in rapturous roars.

"You are exquisite," he tells me.

Words are impossible. I am lost on a sea of bliss.

There is more rustling and then his weight is atop me, my legs parting of their own accord.

"Will you permit me entry, my lady?"

"Yes," I agree without quite knowing to what he's referring, but not caring.

Oh, there is something other than his fingers, larger and rounder at my entrance. With a grunt he pushes his hips and, oh it is inside me. Oh, how odd.

A whimper leaps from my lips as a sharp pain shoots through that region.

"Shh, it's OK," he urges, pushing further.

His lips fall upon my breast and I no longer mind the pain. My back arches, causing him to groan. "Oh, my dear, ahh…"

He pulls back slightly before pursuing forwards again. His fingers pinch my nipples, making me yelp. One of his hands reaches around my back and holds my shoulder. His movements increase in pace, filling me with even greater delights. I want more.

Greedily, I claw at the shirt on his back. My hips meet his, beat for delicious beat.

"Oh, Anne," he cries, thrusting harder.

Colours burst behind my eyes like fireworks, and I fall into tiny fragments.

I am only called back by his lips on my cheek. He is now by my side.

"You are more of a treasure than I ever could have hoped for," he says, holding my hand.

"That…that was…I don't know exactly."

"That is what you could have had last night."

409

"That? Oh, why did you not tell me? I would not have caused such a fuss."

"I thought you knew."

"Now, how could I…wait, is that what Mama was speaking of when she talked of my duties as a wife? Oh dear, I am not sure I am supposed to be so…enthusiastic."

"My dear, you may enthuse all you wish."

Chapter 34

Having recovered from the shock of our outdoor adventure, I am left with a feeling of overwhelming joy. Mama had informed me to lie still in bed and perform my duty without fear as if it were an ordeal to bear, rather than the marvellous incident which occurred, and out of doors too. How terribly brazen. Surely not the behaviour expected of a lady. However, should it be repeated I would not be sorry.

Lord Dellingby has been shut away in his study all day, much to my chagrin. But he has his duties. A giggle bubbles up; I do hope his duties aren't as exuberant as mine.

"His lordship has completed his work and asks for you to join him in his study," Mr Dawkins informs me.

I thank him but feel a tightening in my tummy. A summons to the inner sanctum of man? Perhaps I have erred. Upon reflection, Lord Dellingby finds something amiss with my character and means to correct my behaviour. I should not have permitted such a scandalous act and insisted we return to the house when he became over heated last evening.

"Enter," he calls when I knock upon his door.

"You sent for me?" I ask with a curtsey.

"Ah yes, I wished to consult with you on the groundsman's proposal of turning this floral garden here into a space for growing more vegetables? He seems keen on expanding the produce. Would you mind a few less flowers?" He points to an area on a plan of the area in question

"You...you ask me for my opinion on gardens?"

"You needn't look so shocked."

"I trust you will make the best decision for all."

"Lady Dellingby, I asked for your own opinion on the matter. Should you be sorry to lose flowers?"

"My lord, we shall not be here frequently enough for me to be overly concerned over such things."

"Very well, I shall instruct him to proceed if it will not upset your sensitivities. Now, come closer, for there is another matter I would discuss."

I step around the desk. "What would that be?"

"Closer. It must be whispered," he informs me, beckoning.

Bending my ear down to his level, I ask "Well, what is so secret?"

His arms wrap about me, and I yelp as he pulls me across his lap and kisses me soundly.

"I think I might be falling ever deeper in love with you," he says, his eyes sparkling brighter than ever.

"Oh, is that all?" I tease.

My jest is answered by tickling, making me squirm, squeal and squawk as I try to escape his clutches.

"My lord, no, oh, let me go, argh," and other utterances find their way between my laughter.

When I am quite breathless, Lord Dellingby kisses me again before holding me close in a most wonderful embrace.

"I am in earnest," he tells me.

"Oh, you silly man, you have been too serious for too long, and it has affected you in the most alarming way. Come away from this business and join me at the pianoforte instead."

He refuses to join in, seemingly content to simply watch me sing and play. However, by the time the song reaches its conclusion, he stands at my side.

"Every time I saw you performing in the salons, I longed to hold you, needing to reach out and assure myself of your corporeal presence. The agonies I suffered in my restraint," he murmurs.

Bending down, his fingers trail across my cheek. "My beautiful angel."

His hand travels down to my waist, and he pulls me to my feet. My body is held tightly against his. As I lift my head, his bends to mine, and melts me with his searing kiss.

"Do not make me wait until tonight," he implores.

I incline my head. He leads me to the sofa in silence and presses my shoulders, encouraging me to sit as he shrugs off his coat. Kneeling down, he lifts my skirts.

"Oh," is all the speech I am capable of.

My heart thunders and wetness pools between my legs. Unbuttoning his trousers, the thing with the one eye looks at me again but is far less sinister. Although I tremble, it may be more from anticipation.

"The servants," I whisper.

"May go hang."

With a little awkwardness, he lowers himself and I feel him within me again. The experience is encumbered by the confines of the sofa. Lord Dellingby pushes and shoves, and although there is some pleasure, he does not send me reeling as before.

My disappointment after must show, as he apologises. "Forgive me, I should have contained myself better. You make me forget myself."

I force a smile. "I am yours to do with as you wish."

"Dash it all. I am not my father. I hold you in high esteem, I would urge you to do likewise."

He is gone from the room before I can recover. His temper rose so high so quick that I was taken aback. Holding my head in my hands, I bemoan the lack of education. Papa and Mama were so intent in preparing me for matrimony they quite forgot what comes after. Tears fall down my cheeks as I admit if only to myself how vastly different this new world is. Without any idea of how best to act, I appear to do nothing but wrong.

❧❦

It is difficult to say how long I have remained here. Having cried enough, I breathe deep and take stock of my situation. Lord Dellingby continues to be changeable and can be quite terrifying. However, he has not struck me, which is a blessing. I can and will do better by him and take care not to anger him so.

Ensuring no trace of my outburst remains, I call for some tea to revive me. It arrives with a small cake, which brings a smile to my face. Mrs Brown is most thoughtful.

Feeling fortified, I return to the pianoforte and begin to play. Perhaps my mood has not lifted so very far after all, for the songs seem quite morose. Nonetheless, I give myself to the music as my fingers depress the keys. The melody drifts through me. Closing my eyes, I sing with clearer voice.

When my eyes open, Lord Dellingby is before me.

"Please, do not stop on my account."

"Forgive me. I did not intend to attract an audience."

"I do not doubt it. But I was drawn in even so. My dear, you are not so unhappy, are you?"

"No. Of course not."

"You must not mind my blustering. You do understand I was not angry with you?"

I look away from him and towards the floor.

"Oh my dearest," he exclaims, grasping my hands up and laying kisses upon them.

"Are you truly not upset with me?"

He pulls me to stand with him and folds his arms about my back. "Do not even think it. Why would I be angry with you?"

Foolish tears trickle down my cheeks, I try to wipe them away before he can notice. "I am at a loss."

"My lady, I had no idea of injuring you so greatly. Can you ever forgive me? What a sorry start to married life you must have had with a bear like me to make you cry so."

To hide my embarrassment, I bury my face in his chest again. His strong arms bring much-needed comfort. A kiss is planted on the top of my head.

"I must take greater care of my little dove."

My back stiffens. "You called me so before. Why?"

"I cannot rightly say, it seems suiting. Do you not like it?"

"Only one other has named me so."

"Is that so? Have I cause to be jealous and set down a challenge?"

I giggle. "Not unless you intend to travel all the way to Canada. It was the nickname Lord Beauvrais issued me."

"Did he indeed?"

"Now, don't be snappish. You know he is no threat. We were childhood friends."

"Is the association an unpleasant one?"

"Quite the contrary. It makes me feel more at home."

He leans back so he may look into my eyes. "You are home."

Closing the space again, I confirm, "I know."

We sit on the sofa together, his arms holding me as I lounge against him until we need to change for dinner.

&u&

We have enjoyed an early breakfast and are even now departing on the next part of our journey. Lord Dellingby has been so good as to agree to pay a visit to Miss Compley, Lady Rohampton as she now is. She and Sir Reginald are living happily in Warwickshire by all accounts, but I long to see her situation for myself. Her happiness is of greater import than mine.

Such a dear, sweet friend. The daughter to a baronet, and now wife to one. Only now she has the rightful title of lady, as she always should in my estimation.

And to be married around the same time as me; best friends in all that we do. It is though the stars had it written that our lives should be so in harmony. I could only wish for her to be nearer. Even should Lord Dellingby and I reside in Derbyshire, she shall be some seven hours distance. Closer than her proximity to Norfolk should we choose our residence there, as is all likelihood, but still too far for my comfort. I was determined to visit when the opportunity presented itself.

I do so dislike sleeping at inns. And Sir Reginald's home is providentially en route to Lord Dellingby's papa. How I fear that particular meeting. He remains so much a mystery. One which will at least be solved soon.

A sigh breaks forth from my lips.

"Are you not happy, my lady?"

"I beg pardon, my lord. I was quite lost in thought."

"We cannot have that now," he replies with a smirk.

"Are you laughing at me?"

"I would not dare." His remaining smirk contradicts him. "Are you not happy to be visiting your friend so soon?"

"My lord, you are full aware how grateful I am to you for this kindness. Indeed, I fear it may be my anticipation which makes me restless."

"I would draw your attention to the length of the journey ahead of us."

"Yes, I am well aware of that," I retort, sighing.

"Perhaps a diversion is in order?"

"What would you propose?"

Rubbing his chin, he says, "We have the time to know one another better."

"To what end? We are already married. It is rather too late to learn of all my faults now."

He chuckles. "You mistake me, my dear. I thought perhaps you were curious as to the house we are to journey onto, and the family who resides therein."

"I would not be so impertinent as to ask about your family, Lord Dellingby."

"As you wish." Adjusting his position, he lets his chin fall as if readying for sleep. The nerve!

"But, perhaps…that is…do you think the Duke of Wenston shall approve of your choice of bride?"

Lord Dellingby looks up from under the brim of his hat. "So, you are curious?"

"Only as to his approval."

"If that was in doubt we would not have been permitted to wed."

"No, that is true. It was a foolish concern."

He leans forwards and holds my hands, looking me direct in the eyes. "My lady, my father will find you as enchanting as I do. Have no fear on that score. Only, I wished to prepare you without causing alarm. You see, he is really rather ill."

"I knew as much, else he would have been in attendance at the wedding."

"But you know not why. My father is a proud man and has not let it be widely known, but he was struck by apoplexy last year. It has reduced his capacity of speech, and his temper is shortened. This is why he lives alone. His pride will not allow others to witness his pitiable condition. In truth, I believe it is why he was so eager for my sister to marry someone wholly unworthy of her."

My hand covers my gaping mouth. "Oh my. Lord Dellingby, this is most shocking."

He squeezes my hands. "Please forgive me for not divulging all before, but he does not wish even your father to know."

"But I will know when we meet. Why on ever are we making him endure our visit? Will he not despise my very presence?"

"Quite the contrary. He was insistent upon meeting with you. I believe it may even do him some good. We are not staying at Wenston Hall. My sister is opening her doors to us. We are to visit with my father but briefly before he can suffer embarrassment. You understand?" His hazel gaze is crowned by a furrowed brow.

I nod. "Of course. Your poor papa. How he must suffer."

A kiss is planted on my hands. "How sweet you are."

"But why am I only discovering this now?"

"My lady, as I explained —"

"Yes, he demands secrecy. But did you not think I could be trusted to keep silent?"

"We have not been alone for sufficient time to allow for full explanation, my dear."

"The past few days —"

"I have been somewhat preoccupied."

"We had the entire journey to the Fairdown Lodge. Surely there was an opportune moment then?"

"And spoil our wedding night?"

"And what is so very secret? He cannot help his condition."

"There are…unfortunate consequences. He hides himself away, refusing to see anyone. His concealment commanded my own. I perhaps took it too far and apologise for that. I had so wanted to tell you sooner but felt it would be a betrayal of his trust. Does it alter your opinion of me?"

"That you have an infirm parent? Of course it does not. That you saw fit to keep it from me? It does pain me."

"I understand."

His looks are so crestfallen that my cheeks burn in consideration of my words.

"Forgive me. I spoke far too bluntly. Please allow for the shock of your news. It was wrong of me."

"Am I thus forgiven my secrecy?"

"If I am forgiven my sharp tongue."

He smiles and leans across to kiss my cheek. "You truly are an angel."

Well, I must allow it is most assuredly a lot to think on, and that it will while away some considerable time. Lady Isabella was not in favour of her marriage partner, and that is why she fled to London. Her papa who has perhaps lost some reason may have been persuaded by her valiant brother; that was surely her hope.

Poor Lady Isabella, to be passed from a sick papa to an unworthy husband. I wonder what the objection is.

And poor Duke Wenston; to be struck down so. He must be of a strong constitution to survive such an attack, but at what cost? Fearful of enquiring, I remain silent, but there are many questions to ask. Is the duke bedridden? How does he make himself understood? Is he of sound mind? Is there hope of better recovery?

Having left it so long to inform me of the details of Lord Wenston's illness, perhaps Lord Dellingby should have waited until we were on our way to his house? Now I shall be worrying during our visit with my friend.

But surely the duke cannot be so terribly affected if he wishes to meet with me. What is there to be afraid of? He is not a monster. No, he is no more to be feared than before. Less so, for now he is to be pitied. To be thus affected by illness as to secrete oneself entirely must be a miserable thing.

"Lord Dellingby?"

"Yes, my love?"

"No, no matter."

"Please speak whatever is on your mind."

"Before, you said you didn't want to be like your...no, it is too much to ask."

He had hung his head but now lifts it enough to raise his eyes. "You would know why I do not wish to be like him."

"Yes. No. That is, I am curious, but please, you need not make a reply."

"It is a delicate matter." He winces.

Placing my hand on his, I tell him, "Say no more."

"No, I wish you to know. You need to. For should you suffer the same you must tell me. Fairdown Lodge is not large. When I was there with my parents, I bore witness to my father's...over zealousness with my mother. She cried after, physically hurt, I believe. We never spoke of it, of course. And nor were they aware of what I saw. I have reason to suspect it was not a one-off occurrence. Then the other day, in that house, I feared I had hurt you. I would never cause you harm. You must tell me if I do. Promise me." His speech is urgent, his eyes fixed upon me, unblinking and narrowed.

"I promise."

"You do not know my relief to hear you say so. I would not have you made miserable."

"And it is of great relief to me to hear of your concern."

"You are not so surprised, surely?"

"It is not every husband who would consider the feelings of his wife, Lord Dellingby."

A rueful smile crosses his face. "That may be, but few are fortunate enough to be married to a wife as treasured as you. Have I not told you I love you?"

"You did."

"But you did not believe it?"

"Of course I did. But perhaps only now do I appreciate the full meaning."

With some effort in the bumping carriage, he changes seats so he is next me, and wraps an arm about my shoulders, squeezing me close.

"Could I perhaps persuade you to remove your splendid bonnet?" he asks, removing his own hat and throwing it onto the opposite seat.

Untying the ribbons, I carefully follow suit. His fingers lift my chin gently up until my gaze meets his. He licks his lips, and my breath halts in my breast. Bending down, he places a soft, lingering kiss upon my mouth.

"I love you, Lady Dellingby," he declares, his brown eyes shining.

I cannot take my gaze away. A warmth spreads throughout my person. "I love you too, Lord Dellingby."

His intake of breath is drawn in quickly and is released on a moan. His next kiss is not dainty and sets me aflame. A small groan escapes my lips.

"What do you do to me?" he asks.

"I am quite at a loss," I tell him with a smirk.

"Come to me, my mischievous magpie."

He guides me to place my knees either side of his as I face him; a most outrageous position to be in, but one that is welcomed. My nether regions are calling for him, thirsty for his delectable organ. I do hope it is not wicked to be so eager for my husband. But there is no arguing with this desire he creates.

Lord Dellingby deftly undoes his breeches and lifts my skirts, giving him, oh, sweet access to where he is most wanted. His head is buried in my bosom as his hands clutch onto my back.

"Please tell me you are not hurt like this," he whispers.

"I am not."

"Oh, thank the heavens."

He groans as his hands grasp my buttocks and help raise me a little. I slide back down, the bumping of the carriage adding to the rise and fall.

Exaggerating the motion, again and again, I repeat it. There is a deep-seated need which only grows.

Wriggling, I try to gain momentum and become frenzied in my desire. My husband reaches a hand to rub my parts.

Lord Dellingby urges me to cry my release into a cushion as it becomes all too much. My soul flies through the heavens as I come apart, no longer in control of myself.

On, our journey continues, my final destination not yet reached. Stirrings rise up once more, and crescendo as we bounce along in delicious union.

Urgency builds, pushing me to rise and fall with greater speed. A hot friction intensifying. Oh, sweet mercy, but I would take more.

My husband pushes from his seat and holds my waist, assisting my frantic rhythm until I burst like a firework.

Lord Dellingby clenches his eyes shut, his jaw tight. A low groan rumbles from him as he thrusts but a few more times, his face falling once more into my bosom.

"Oh, my beautiful wife," he whispers at last.

"My amazing husband," I reply, bending down to kiss him.

"Come, make yourself comfortable," he urges.

I adjust my position so my legs are across his lap. He wraps his arms about my waist. My cheek nestles near his shoulder. I am held, safe and secure and sigh deeply in my contentment.

"Mmm, what a delightful sound," he murmurs.

I giggle. "What? My inelegant sigh?"

"My dear, it is the most glorious sound I ever heard for it signifies your happiness."

Oh my, there are apparently further depths to my love for this man. I had never hoped for such utter joy with my marriage partner. I sought only comfort, to not be mistreated or reviled. But Lord Dellingby is so excessively kind and generous. Such a wondrous man was beyond my comprehension.

A tap on the carriage roof stirs me. I must have fallen asleep. Lord Dellingby squeezes my waist.

"We must be near our first stop. Time to look respectable," he announces, head nodding towards our discarded hats.

I giggle, recalling the wild behaviour of earlier. Growling echoes in the confines of the carriage.

"And time to replenish our other appetites," he adds, waggling his eyebrows.

"Lord Dellingby, it is not terribly gallant—"

"The temptation to tease was too great."

His mirth is infectious, it seems, for I cannot be cross with him. As the carriage stops and we alight, we are both in good spirits. He leads me into the inn where we refresh ourselves and indulge in a little food and drink.

The horses are changed and waiting when we go back outside. I eagerly regain my seat, pulling Lord Dellingby's hand to ensure he sits beside me again.

Our journey is long, but not unpleasant. More and more, I consider myself fortunate to be in Lord Dellingby's company. Our discussions are light and remain jovial. And when I cannot fight fatigue, my husband encourages me to sleep and does not criticise. In fact, he joins me in my little naps.

The carriage pulls up to the home of Sir Reginald. It is a fine stone building, and all I hoped for my friend. A most happily proportioned abode with a pleasant aspect.

"Lord and Lady Dellingby, what an honour it is to welcome you to my humble home."

"It's our pleasure to be here," my husband answers for us, bowing smartly.

"Won't you come in? You must be tired. Have you been travelling all day?" Julia asks.

"Thank you, we have," I reply, perhaps out of turn, but she's my friend so am emboldened.

"Lady Rohampton, I must congratulate you on a beautiful home," I tell her as we walk through the entrance.

Indeed, it is tastefully decorated in pastel tones with touches of brass and a few large flower-filled vases. Our outer clothing is swiftly collected by their servants. Yes, a fine domain for Miss Compley as was.

"Thank you. Come, I will show you to your room myself, for I am eager to have your opinion of it."

We peel off, leaving the men to discuss whatever it is they do when not in our company.

"It is so good to see you," she says, embracing me.

"Now, tell me, are you truly as happy as you appear?"

"Oh yes. I am most happily situated. And now you are here there is nothing lacking at all."

"I only wish it could be for longer, but Lord Dellingby's papa is most insistent on our earliest possible arrival."

"We shall make the most of the few days we do have. And perhaps you shall make it back before too long."

"I do hope so."

"And you? Are you happy?" she enquires, leaning forwards a little and taking hold of my hands.

"I am, very. Who would have thought someone as unromantic as I could find love?"

Her eyebrows verily shoot off her forehead. "You speak of love? Lady Anne, is this truly you?"

We both laugh. "Yes, it is I. I can scarce believe it myself."

"And within days of marriage. Oh, felicitations indeed." She hugs me again.

"Should Sir Reginald enquire, this room is most prettily done and meets with my approval."

"I am sure he'll be pleased to hear it meets your approval. I'll leave you to change for dinner. We thought you may be happy to dine early after your journey."

"You are most kind, thank you."

Clément emerges to assist me. My cheeks redden as I silently hope she did not hear what happened in the carriage. Hopefully, the noise of the horses and wheels were sufficient to disguise any other sounds. Of course, she says nothing of it as she goes about her duties.

Feeling far better for a quick wash and a change of clothes, I make my way to the drawing room where the others are awaiting my arrival. I accept an offered glass of wine, its ripe notes further refreshing me.

We have a most pleasant evening and are treated to every hospitality. Sir Reginald promises a tour of his grounds tomorrow, which I am looking forward to.

I retire in the small hours, marvelling at the fortune of Lady Rohampton and myself. I should never have been able to sleep easy again had we been deceived by Sir Reginald.

How on ever did such an agreeable man fall in with the likes of Lord Felsenworth? Perhaps his very nature allowed some oversight there; eager to see goodness in all. However it was, all I can say is it's a most pleasing thing that he is so amiable and makes my dearest friend happy.

To my vexation, Sir Reginald takes only my husband out on horseback to survey his property. Lady Rohampton and I must be content with taking a turn on foot about the walled garden, which is brimming with herbs and flowers.

"Oh, is that alstroemeria, Lady Rohampton? I thought I saw some in the house. How fortunate you are."

"Aye, Sir Reginald assures me that the gardener here is one of the best in the county. His mama was keen on floral decorations, I understand."

"You are most fortunate. To take the air in such scented surroundings must be of comfort."

"Indeed. Every care has been taken."

"I am pleased to hear it."

"I wish the same for you."

"I must confess at growing anxious to view my home. To think I've not seen it as yet. But I have every hope it shall be a good one."

"It is sure to be so. Lord Dellingby seems pleased, as well he should be. For who could want a better wife?"

"You give me too much credit. You always have. But I thank you," I tell her, linking arms and gently nudging my hip to hers.

We both giggle.

"And I am sure he will be even happier with his heir."

I gasp. "Lady Rohampton, such discourse. But nothing would bring me greater pleasure than to oblige him with a beautiful boy. It is our purpose, is it not?"

"Quite," she replies, biting her lip.

"Come, motherhood is not to be feared. We are told it is a great privilege."

"I am sensible of that. It is merely that I hope I shall not disappoint in that regard."

"It is too early to become gloomy over such things. You have no reason to doubt your success."

"You are right, of course."

"I wonder which of us shall write with such news first."

"I wager ten shillings it shall be you who does so."

"Lady Rohampton, I take you up on that wager, for I am sure to win. You shall surely pip me to the post."

Laughing, we shake hands upon it. Our silly wager seems to offer my friend hope, and as Papa is no longer in control of what I do, there can be no reproach to our game.

❧

Our husbands must have found some sport on their excursion for the hour is late when they return. We do not set eyes upon one another until we sit to dinner. However, Lord Dellingby is so full of smiles that I forgive him the instant his glimmering eyes are set in my direction.

"Your day was an enjoyable one, I trust, Sir Reginald?" I enquire as our soup is served.

"Lady Dellingby, I am only left with the regret at not having had the opportunity to be in the company of Lord Dellingby more whilst we were all in London."

I smile but cast a side glance towards my husband. "Is that so?"

"Oh yes, we are become firm friends inside of a day. I am holding Sir Reginald to his promise to bring his marvellous marriage partner to visit us as soon as we are settled. I trust this would meet your approval?" Lord Dellingby replies.

"Yes, very much. What joyous news. There, Lady Rohampton, we shall not be parted long at all. And you must stay as long as you desire."

"Have a care, for we may never leave with such a request," my friend cautions.

We all laugh at this witty observation. If only such a thing were possible. But I am given hope that we shall be frequent visitors. Lord Dellingby is amiable, but only to those deserving of his distinction. It delights me to know that Sir Reginald is amongst that select number.

After a fine supper, we retire to the sitting room all together. The men must be aware of their neglect, although it is no such astonishing a thing as all that. But they are new husbands, and presumably still fixed on making a good impression. How funny, when I would have supposed the reverse to be true.

"What an oddity of a pair we are matched with, to be so attentive," I remark to Lady Rohampton in a moment when the men are out of our hearing.

"Most fortunate. They are surely the best of men."

Had anyone informed me such a thing could be before I was married, I should have scoffed. It was my belief in the baseness of all men which had kept hopes of romance from my heart. All grown men I had encountered were stern and dismissive.

It was fully my expectation that Lord Dellingby, no matter how agreeable before marriage, would prove himself to be like all others. Perhaps I have treated him accordingly? We have experienced some minor disagreements, but does the fault for these lie entirely with him?

Did he not take my fancy from the beginning, not only from that night when he so kindly came to my aid? I allowed others to cloud my judgement. The distance of his home dissuaded me from considering him properly at first, as well as my miscalculation of his age. And how foolish that all now seems.

Maybe I should allow he is, in fact, agreeable by nature, and not be quite so guarded in my behaviour? Astonishing thought.

The flow of wine and easy conversation seems to lend itself to my new demeanour. Lady Rohampton and I are each encouraged to take a seat at the modest pianoforte provided by Sir Reginald.

Eventually, we retire to bed, and a smile remains upon my lips as Clément disrobes me.

"I have had the most extraordinary day, Clément."

"I am pleased to hear it, my lady."

Sighing deeply, my head sinks into my pillow. Contentment warming me as my eyes close. A peaceful slumber opens her arms unto me. But a soft knocking at my door brings me away from such soft promises.

"Are you yet awake, my lady?" my husband's voice whispers.

"I am," I murmur.

With a creak the door grants entrance to Lord Dellingby.

"Is anything amiss?"

"No. Why should it be? I merely thought I may pay you an evening visit."

I blush as the realisation of his words hits me. "Here? Now?"

"I have made merry today, and yet wish to be made merrier. But we had perhaps best attempt silence."

I cannot help but giggle a little at his announcement. Not able to find words suitable for such an occasion, I merely peel the bedclothes from my person. The candlelight shows his eyes in deepest shadow before he places it carefully down.

With a rumble like thunder, Lord Dellingby enters my bed. My nightgown is deftly hoisted by his hands. Tingles run through me as his weight bears down upon me. My eager legs spread wider for him, seeking his presence.

His body surges forward and back, filling me with his manhood and my own desire. My whimpers are hushed by his hand over my mouth, and I try harder not to utter a sound. But it is a hard task when he inspires such inexplicable joy. Such delectable sensations of fulfilment are not easily hushed.

My hips rise and fall, urging him onwards. Such actions are greeted with his low rumbling groans.

"Oh, what you do to me," he whispers, his voice hoarse, "I beg you would do more."

Not wishing to disappoint, my hips are given free rein to do as they please. And please us they do. Lord Dellingby's face disappears into my pillow to quiet the moans which are forced from his lips. I am left pulling my lips tightly together to stifle my own sounds of pleasure.

His lips are brought up to place kisses upon my face. Our pace quickens, silence made impossible as he takes me into the abyss which I now welcome so willingly. Knowing we go there together gives me courage, as we travel the delights of some other world beyond our own. Is this heaven?

Our breathing laboured, we still and cling to one another momentarily in the afterglow of bliss. He plants a kiss upon my forehead.

"I had best return to my chamber lest we give ourselves away entirely."

"It is cruel for a man and wife to still be able to inspire scandal," I moan.

Getting out of my bed, leaving me cold and bereft, he kisses my lips quickly. "Indeed it is. Perhaps it may be different in our own home some nights?"

"Then take me there without delay."

"If but I could," he concedes, departing with one more kiss.

❧

The next day is equally as enjoyable. How I wish we could remain longer. But I fear displeasing the Duke of Wenston and must depart on the morrow.

Holding onto the hope of being reunited with Lady Rohampton again soon, I find my seat in the carriage the next morning. Lord Dellingby squeezes my hand as we are pulled away but remains silent. It is for the best, as I do not think words would be easily found.

Another long journey is upon us, but no brazen activities occur on this occasion. My heart is too heavy from taking leave of my friend and my nerves too frayed at the prospect of meeting my father-in-law. I wonder how invalid he is, and whether there will be any misunderstandings caused. Did Lord Dellingby say his papa walks with a cane, or does he use a Bath chair?

Lord Dellingby too seems deep in thought, perhaps worrying how we shall find his father; whether his health has improved or declined since their last meeting. It must be a terrible concern.

For all his sternness and taciturn disposition, I love my papa, and would be most injured should anything untoward befall him. I am left thankful for his excellent health.

Silence hangs between us for most of the journey, to the extent it is almost deafening.

Again, we arrive late in the day. The mansion looms large and magnificent in the twilight.

"You are pleased with this prospect?" Lord Dellingby enquires.

"It is difficult to say with all certainty in this light."

My smile gives me away though, for he presses further. "But what you can make out does not displease?"

"Lord Dellingby, of course it does not."

He grins like a little boy. "I am relieved."

I smile back at him and issue a regal nod. One must not appear too keen at such obvious wealth. The estate is large indeed. The carriage rattles along a fine, long path, which winds around the lake situated in front of the house. A great fountain spurts from its centre. The residence itself outdoes even Papa's in stature.

The butler stands on duty to receive us.

"Your lordship, welcome home. His Grace wishes me to convey his deepest sorrow at not being able to receive you this evening. He has been forced to retire early."

"What the devil? Is he well? We have travelled all this distance…" he trails off, turning aside, his fist at his mouth.

"Pardon me, your lordship, but His Grace has been growing more tired more easily of late. I assure you he stayed as long as he could. Please, do come and partake of some light refreshments before departing again."

Lord Dellingby hisses out a breath and rolls his eyes. "No. No, we shan't come in. I shouldn't like to intrude if the Duke is already retired for the evening. We shall return tomorrow morning."

"Your lordship, please, I implore you not to think ill of him for this inconvenience. It was most irksome to him. He has been so looking forward to seeing you. Forgive me if I say too much. But he truly intended no insult."

My husband bows his head, and the servant receives a pat on the shoulder. "You are too free, but it was with the best of intentions. We shall return tomorrow, all the better for a restful evening, I daresay."

"Very good, your lordship."

Despite his outward appearance of calming after his outburst, I note Lord Dellingby's footsteps are still somewhat heavy.

"Damned inn, if they had been quicker and not delayed us so long, we would not find ourselves thus turned away from my own father's door," he grumbles.

I reach out my hand to his, tentatively. "My dear, you should not wish to make your father ill exerting himself for our sake?"

"Of course not," he replies, slightly less gruffly.

"And are we not both tired too? Perhaps this all works out for the best."

His smile is crooked and wry behind this thumb. "Perhaps you are correct."

"Perhaps?" I shriek in mock indignation.

"I cannot always have you in the right. I would lose all control of my own house. Besides, to admit you are right is to admit my wrong. Perhaps it was foolhardy to attempt such a visit after our journey. But he was so insistent upon seeing you. You are not too disappointed?"

"Lord Dellingby, less of this foolishness, if you please. Where do you find the insult in a sick man taking to his bed?"

"When you phrase it in such a way you make it impossible for me to deny my overreaction." He hangs his head.

"Oh no, for you are disappointed not to see your father after such a long separation. No, it is to be commended, not condemned that you feel it so keenly."

He looks up, and I ignore the moisture in his eyes. "I knew marrying you would be the best decision I ever made."

He lurches forwards to kiss my cheek. With a small smile, I point at his vacant seat, which he lowers into once more.

Washing his hands over his face, he exclaims, "My dear dear lady, what have I done? I was in such haste to depart I thought not of your comfort. I committed us to a journey of a further hour without so much as offering you any respite when there were refreshments awaiting."

"What is one more hour when we have travelled so far?"

"You are too kind."

Indeed I am, for there is a thirst upon me, but the mention of that would wound him, so the complaint remains hidden within my breast. We could have partaken in a little wine and cheese before continuing without any inconvenience to anyone. But his wounded pride got in the way. Not that I can blame him. Perhaps I would have felt the same in his situation. And it is not as if I shall die of thirst.

It is quite dark when we reach Lady Isabella's house, but she comes flying down the steps to greet us.

"Oh brother, you are come," she squeals, throwing her arms about him.

Lord Dellingby takes a step back to steady himself. "Yes, yes, we are come."

She looks across at me. "Oh, Lady Dellingby, how pleased I am to see you both."

I find arms flung about my person.

"It is a pleasure to be here, Lady Longland," I tell my over-eager sister-in-law.

"Oh, but you are early. I had not expected you for another hour at least."

"Let us explain over a brandy," her brother implores.

"Of course, pray forgive my exuberance. I am just so happy to receive you."

We are led indoors, but my stomach tightens. They have always shown themselves to be close as brother and sister, but this enthusiastic welcome seems excessive. I fear she is not enjoying the same felicity in marriage as myself. Where is her husband? He is conspicuously absent, but of course, I'm far too polite to inquire.

"Lord Longland is away from home at this hour. He should be back soon. For, as I explained, we did not expect you so soon."

"Out on important business, of course," Lord Dellingby says with a sneer.

"Only the most urgent business would call him away at such a time."

I leave the explanation of our untimely arrival to my husband, and sip my wine in contemplative silence, happily watching them converse. Lady Longland still seems happy in our presence, but her eyes cannot fully conceal the sadness contained within. I grow increasingly worried for her as time goes on.

It grows late, and we have not yet dined. I am sure Lord Dellingby must be as famished as I. But Lord Longland is not yet returned home.

"Sister, we have waited long enough. Pray, let us begin dinner without that husband of yours."

"But he will be so angry if we start without him."

"Then he should have returned at a reasonable hour. You cannot be expected to keep guests waiting so long. It is beyond reason. We have been travelling all day. Come, let us make a start. I shall bear the consequences."

Looking pensive, Lady Longland calls for dinner, and we amble into the dining room. Not until halfway through the second course does the master of the house make his appearance, and it is somewhat dishevelled even then. His hair is unkempt, his coat unbuttoned, and his gait unsteady.

"You have begun without me?" he bawls, his words slurring.

Lord Dellingby stands to bow. "Lord Longland, greetings. Please forgive my interference, but we were terribly hungry after our travels. After a wait of considerable length, I could resist no longer, and urged this dinner service whilst the meal was yet warm."

Lord Longland squints and peers at my husband, a frown darkening his beady brown eyes. Not like the full hazel orbs of the one I love. The men appear of similar height and build, but Lord Dellingby is currently standing upright and the higher of the pair. Lord Longland is clearly inebriated, for shame.

"You think yourself so much grander than I that you enter my home and dine without me?"

"Forgive the insult. It was not intended as one. But we waited for you beyond respectability." Lord Dellingby's tone is low, firm and brooks no argument.

To me, it seems somewhat foolhardy to chastise a man who is clearly already upset. Our host's fists are clenching at his sides as if readying to strike a blow. Is he quite out of his senses altogether? He glares at Lord Dellingby, fire blazing from his eyes. A challenge which is met with equal ire.

"My lords, please, this is hardly necessary. Lord Longland, we are not so far in as to inconvenience you. Look, here is your dish now. It really is quite delicious. Please, won't you join us?" I try, desperate to avoid the brewing dispute.

440

His glower gets turned upon me, making me shrivel in my chair a little. Distraction usually worked on Papa. But then this man knows me not, so perhaps my interference only fuels his animosity more. Oh Lor', I was trying to help, but matters seem to be worsening.

"Lord Longland, might I introduce my worthy wife, The Marchioness of Dellingby? Who happens to be of the same opinion as me. The tongue is really tender, superb. Come, won't you partake and see if you don't share our high regard for your hospitality?"

"Lady Dellingby," he grumbles, almost falling as he bows.

With a thud, he lands in his chair at last. Lord Dellingby turns back to me and rolls his eyes as he takes his place. His hand finds mine under the table and gives it a squeeze before taking up his cutlery.

"It is tolerably well, I suppose," Lord Longland concedes around a mouthful.

The air is still thick with tension and could be cut with my knife, but I let it fall through the tongue on my plate instead. Silence reigns, thick and heavy as we all struggle to swallow our pride.

If I were a man, Lord Longland would have heard just how rude I find him. He is both late and foxed. Instead of apologising, he has the audacity to remonstrate with our behaviour. Does the man have no idea of decorum? Oh, but if he could taste of my fist. Perhaps I should have let Lord Dellingby continue and allowed him to perform what I am unable to? But then we may have been turned away from two houses in one day, and that would be unthinkable, however tempting.

A loud belch reverberates around the room. Lord Longland makes no apology. I give no outward acknowledgement but inside, my stomach churns. Can this man make himself any more abhorrent? I hope this is a one-off but Lady Longland's reaction, or lack thereof seems to suggest otherwise.

How can a lady such as her, bright and exuberant, be so cowed? I shudder at the supposed answer. I glance across the table at her but am faced with a barely perceptible shake of the head.

Lord Longland has so angered me I could spit. Once we are through with visiting the Duke of Wenston I hope to be able to catch Lady Longland alone and discover the truth of the matter. Not that I have the faintest idea what to do if she confirms her sorry situation. But still, I wish to find a way of being of assistance.

For now, we must suffer in silence to the end of this arduous meal. All pleasure has been removed from it. All turns to ash in my mouth under the watchful gaze of Lord Longland.

It is a great relief when we reach its conclusion and the door to the drawing room is opened. Unlike in the house of my friend, the men stay firmly in position. Guilt pulls at my stomach, leaving my husband alone with such a man. But my duty is to repair to the room through the doors with Lady Longland.

Any hopes of discovering more, which were not high to begin with, are completely wiped away by the false brightness presented by my hostess.

"Lady Dellingby, sister, how glad I am to get you to myself at last. Please forgive any abruptness. I understand Lord Longland has had a weary day of it. You understand, I am sure," she says, her eyes narrowing as they are cast towards the servant in the room.

Taking the hint to say nothing in his presence, I merely reply, "Of course. I pity the poor man for his distress. Hopefully, it shall be of short duration."

"I am sure it shall. Now, tell me of your news, for you must have plenty to share. How do you find the scenery up here in the north?"

"If you insist, I shall tell you, but I fear it is not as near exciting as you presume. Most of my married life thus far seems to be spent in a carriage. But what I have seen from the window is most pleasant indeed. And your brother is so thoughtful."

We fall into pleasantries, easily conversing over topics suiting to our station. To all outward appearance, we are two happy ladies, and no worry creases our delicate brow.

Letting out a yawn, I excuse myself from behind my hand.

"Oh, but I keep you up late in my eagerness to be with you. Lady Dellingby, allow me to show you to your room myself, for I have been most neglectful."

We go up the stairs side-by-side and close the door behind us upon entering my room.

"I cannot tarry long. Pray, there is much to discuss, but we must be on our guard. At the earliest opportunity, suggest a turn about the garden. It must not come from me. You have a keen interest in seeing different designs, of course, for you may refresh your own flower beds soon. But I must be wary, even then," she implores in a whisper.

"Of course," I whisper back.

"Oh, that's where it is. Thank you for your kindness, Lady Longland," I declare more loudly.

She bows her head in acknowledgement and smiles ever so slightly. My heart aches at the sadness still within her eyes. Why could Lord Dellingby not have stopped this marriage? Lord Longland must truly be a tyrant.

Chapter 36

Lord Dellingby and I take an early breakfast, happily alone. I suspect Lord Longland will be late rising, and his dutiful wife will await his presence before chancing to emerge herself. We are unusually quiet, neither wishing to disturb the silence. There is nothing I have to say that these servants should hear in any case.

A sigh whispers from my lips as I take my place in the carriage to be transported back to Wenston Hall. The short distance is a relief; there is yet time to collect myself, readying my introduction to the Duke.

"Quite an eventful evening," Lord Dellingby mutters with a sigh of his own.

"Not quite the reception I was expecting."

"No, nor I."

"Was the earl still cross?"

He laughs. "In truth, he soon fell asleep where he sat. I retired to my room in haste, glad of the excuse to be rid of his company."

"My poor husband. What a brute that man is. And how thankful I am to find you quite the reverse."

"I am glad you find the comparison favourable."

"Lady Longland begs to converse with me. I must ask you to distract him, if you can bring yourself to do so."

His brow furrows. "She asked this? Her distress must be great indeed. Yes, I shall do as requested, my lady. She is a dear sister, and I would have her more happily situated. You must discover her condition and share it with me. Do you give me your word in return?"

"Of course."

"The man is a brute, as you say. That much is clear. But I will do all in my power to protect her should he prove too much so. It is a precarious position, for he will not gladly receive any interference. What a man does in his own home is a private matter. Do not put yourself in harm's way."

"I shall tread carefully."

"I have every faith in you," he declares, holding my hands in his own.

Leaning back upright, he adds, "Now, let us hear no more of it for now. You have a different but no less arduous duty ahead."

My lips tighten into a thin line as I bow my head, the feather in my hat bouncing as I do.

The house is even more impressive in full daylight. Lawns of the lushest green surround it in all directions, trees framing it majestically.

"Is the duke more receptive to visitors this morning?" Lord Dellingby asks the butler as we alight.

"Certainly, your lordship. Right this way, if you please."

We follow him into the house. Black and white tiles lie underfoot, with grand golden staircases to the left and right of us and a colourful fresco above our heads. Faces look upon me from large portraits on every wall. Sculptures stand beneath them, also standing in judgement of their newcomer.

My shoes click on the hard floor as we make our way through. Ancestors peer down from their wall dwellings in the long corridor. I am thankful for my schooled mask, for it hides my inner misgivings. How I tremble under such speculation. How daunting their presence.

We are shown into a darkened room, the full length red curtains shut against the sun. A man rises slowly to his feet as our names are called. He is a little shorter than Lord Dellingby, but I am prone to attribute that to his withered stature. He is rather thin and frail, yet sturdier than I had thought.

It is almost a disappointment not to find him some chair-ridden gargoyle after all. His face hangs a little more on one side, and he is propped up by a cane. Perhaps the duke appears a little older than his years, but he is no monster to be kept hidden out of sight. Indeed, it is a wonder what all the fuss is about.

"Welcome, my son. Lady Dellingby, a delight," he greets, with an attempted bow.

Yes, he is unsteady, and his words are somewhat garbled. But still hardly an invalid. I curtsey back.

"Your Grace, it is an honour to meet with you."

"The pleasure is mine. Come, sit. I cannot stand long. Forgive the dark, won't you? The light, you see, it hurts my eyes."

I understand him with a little difficulty. It is obviously a long speech for him. I bow my head to show my understanding.

"My boy, my apologies for not receiving you —"

"Pater, do not make yourself uneasy. Of course, I was disappointed, but it is perfectly understandable. We were so looking forward to seeing you. But here we are now, so all is well."

"Very good, very good. Where the blazes is Jacobs? I ordered immediate tea." He bangs his cane on the floor three times in quick succession as he speaks.

Perhaps alerted by the noise of his master's cane, the doors open to a servant bearing a tea tray.

"You take tea, I trust?" he asks me.

"I am most fond of it, Your Grace." Truthfully, I prefer wine, orgeat, coffee or hot chocolate in that order, but one must not seem ungrateful.

The hot beverage is refreshing, I have to admit. It is rather warm in here; the fire is well lit. The day is a little chilled, but the roaring fire in the closed room seems excessive.

"I knew your father of course. Long time ago now. We were at school together, did he tell you?"

"He did." Not, I finish in my head, not having the heart to press for a full explanation.

Of course, being school chums would explain Papa's enthusiasm for my match. I had suspected some former acquaintance but had no inclination as to its origin. That would have involved Papa speaking more than three words together to me, and not in the process of reprimanding.

The Duke asks me inconsequential questions with some considerable effort. He is quite chatty for one so confined and who has difficulty getting himself heard. But he seems a jovial sort. Not the severe patriarch I'd expected at all. Such a pity I shan't have the opportunity of spending more time in his company. I think I could grow to like this man exceedingly well.

Our conversation is interrupted by a rather unsociable squelching parp sound, and my heart sinks for the poor duke. The accompanying stench leaves little room for doubt of his soiling himself.

Before he has chance to utter a word, I interject, "Lord Dellingby, we have been here all this time and you have not yet shown me the gardens as promised. It is really quite neglectful, you know."

"Yes, they will be best seen in this light. Pater, I beg your indulgence in allowing me to take my wife on a short tour now."

"If you must," is his response with excellent feigning of being put out.

We quickly exit the room, Lord Dellingby leading me outside. I take a gulp of fresh air. The smell of excrement was overpowering. Not that I blame Duke Wenston, he can clearly not help it. The poor man; I see now why he is not much in the presence of others.

"Thank you, my lady."

"For what? I am quite sure I haven't the faintest idea of what you speak. Silly man. Now, are you going to show me these gardens or not?"

His smile is broad as he bows. "As my lady commands"

As we walk, I am given a commentary. "It is my understanding that your tastes are more for the florals, so I hope you shall not be too disappointed. Our estate houses more wilderness and greenery than perhaps your inclination would favour."

"Lord Dellingby, how anyone can consider your home anything but beautiful is quite astonishing."

"You are in earnest?"

"What a question. Of course I am in earnest."

The grounds are extensive and stretch out for miles. I think I could be content to aimlessly amble all day here. There is a rather fine water cascade which draws my attention for some considerable time. Lord Dellingby patiently waits in silence at my side.

"So sorry. I had no idea of place or time," I apologise, coming out of my reverie.

"Not at all. It was rather charming to see you so calm and content."

"The fall of water somehow diverts one."

"Indeed. There is a bench just yonder, for my mother found the same solace here. Had you wished to spend a minute longer I was about to offer it."

"We should perhaps return to your father…" I was about to add that he should have had enough time to attend his needs but manage to stop myself.

"Yes, he will wonder where we have gone. We wouldn't want a search party sent for us."

We laugh at the thought as we head in the direction of the house. The gardens are simple yet beautiful. Great care is clearly taken over them. A longing to spend more time here sweeps through me.

Shouting reaches our ears as we near the room we left the Duke in.

"Where is she? Where is she?"

"Your Grace, she is unavailable at present."

I rush in. "Your Grace, my apologies if we were too long in your beautiful gardens. We are returned now."

"Not her. Who is she?" he asks.

My blood is frozen.

"Begging your pardon, your ladyship. He means nothing by it, he gets confused sometimes," a servant explains.

My feet are rooted to the spot. The charming duke is crazed in his distress, his arms are flailing as he continues to rant.

"Perhaps we had better make our departure," Lord Dellingby offers.

"He has been so much better of late. My apologies, my lord."

Taking hold of my arm, Lord Dellingby leads me away, tears forming in my eyes. They refuse my control and fall down my cheeks before we reach the carriage. I reach for my handkerchief as we hasten outside.

"Seeing the Duke thus must be quite the shock. I am sorry it causes you such distress," Lord Dellingby offers as he helps me into the carriage.

"What is my distress to what your own must be? Your poor papa. He was so nice to me..." I cannot continue for fear of sobbing.

"It is a heavy burden, I confess it. One can never tell what mood he will be in. I am glad you saw him in good spirits at first. Perhaps now you understand his desire for privacy?"

I nod. "I do. Oh, I understand."

In vain I try to dry my tears, but they are so willing to depart my eyes that my handkerchief is quite sodden by the time I bring them under control.

"What a goose I am," I declare on a half laugh, looking out of the window.

"Not at all. Your sentiment does you credit. I am touched by your sympathy." His own voice is a little hoarse.

"Well, what delights do you expect are in store for us this evening?" I ask, desperate to change the topic.

"Haha, perhaps Lord Longland will have discovered a modicum of modesty in our absence and we shall be treated to a fine evening in reparation of the last."

I laugh at that. "You do not think it likely."

He laughs with me. "No, not at all, but it is a happy thought."

"Oh yes, fancy Lord Longland sitting serenely in a chair, admiring his wife at the pianoforte."

"Or better yet, playing upon it himself."

"Oh, now that really is beyond all belief."

Lord Dellingby skips his hands in the air and sings terribly out of tune, making us both guffaw.

"Oh, Lord Dellingby, you are a wit."

He waggles his eyebrows. "Never too serious too long. Wait, what is that in Latin? I may change our family motto."

It feels good to laugh, even at such absurdities. The past day has been most taxing, and it is not yet at an end. Having met with his papa, we need stay only this one last night before finally setting out for our own home.

❧ ❧

"Good afternoon, sister," Lord Dellingby greets as we happen upon her in the drawing room.

"Good afternoon, Dellingbys," she replies with a small smile and curtsey.

"Where is that husband of yours, eh?"

She puts a delicate finger to her forehead and swishes it into the air. "Shooting something, I imagine. I've heard gunshots for the past hour at least."

"Jolly good. In which case, I shall repair to the library. Hopefully, there is something left of the newspaper I have not had chance to read today."

"You'll find it quite untouched I'm sure," she mumbles aside, and so quietly I believe we are not meant to hear.

Lord Dellingby bows his way out of the room, leaving us alone. I remain standing.

"Lady Longland. I have been too much in that confounded carriage of late. Might I request the honour of your company as I take a turn about your garden? The day is yet fine, and the fresh air is much needed."

"Your poor dear, of course you are fatigued by so much travelling. It is good you should ask, for I am eager to show you our delightful flowers, knowing how fond you are of them."

"Indeed I am. Shall we?" I ask, offering my arm.

She takes it, linking us together like the oldest of friends. Our conversation is kept modest and polite until we find ourselves quite alone and surrounded by fine herbal fragrances and low boxed hedging. There are no high walls in this area for anyone to hide behind, which must be part of Lady Longland's design in bringing me to this spot.

"Thank you for your discretion, my dear Lady Dellingby. How proud I am to be able to call you sister. You do not mind it?" she says, her voice low despite our solitude.

"Of course not, it brightens my heart to have another sister, especially being so far removed from my own."

"And as a sister, I am able to place all my faith in you, am I not?"

"You already know you may, else you would not be here with me now."

We walk around in slow circles, my companion pointing now and then.

"It is true. But what I have to say must go no further. Indeed, I know not why I share it, but I may burst otherwise. But nobody else must know."

"My dear, you put me gravely ill at ease."

"Are you yet aware of the true purpose behind my visit to London?"

"I confess you made me curious and surmised it must have been to implore your brother's intervention. You were against this marriage, were you not? Do not blame your brother, he has said not a word. This is pure conjecture on my behalf. Please correct me if I am too bold or am in the wrong."

"I am forever watched here. There is not even a moment of peace. I shall be blunt to make best use of our time alone. But yes, you are indeed correct. I applaud you for being so astute. I had not been in favour of Lord Longland from the start. He had shown himself as coarse, high handed and abrupt. Alas, my brother's pleas fell on deaf ears as Papa, it pains me to say, is not in full capacity himself. You have seen so yourself, I think."

"I admit I have. Such a sorrowful thing to happen to the Duke."

"But none of us could have imagined just how vile a man they were marrying me to. Papa is insensible perhaps but has never been cruel. He merely was intent on an eligible match that would not take me too far from home, for I fear he has grown dependent on me during his darker moments. As dreadful as it is to see Papa suffer so, the times I am called to his side are a respite from my life here."

"It is not so very dreadful here, surely?"

"Sweet sister, you do not doubt me? I blush to tell you, but he was so excessively forceful in the performance of his marital duties that the suffering lasted for a full day after. He seems to despise me and is interested only in creating a son and heir."

My brow creases as I think on the comparison to my own sweet Lord Dellingby, so concerned when he thought he may have hurt me at all. I can say nothing.

"And if that were but all, perhaps I could withstand such torments, for they are surely short-lived. As soon as a son is born he should forget about me. But the man is so violent. He frequently absences himself, sometimes not reappearing for days until I am left to wonder if he has been left to die in a ditch. Regrettably, he does emerge, usually dishevelled and wreaking of alcohol and perfume. I can be in no doubt of his purpose in these disappearances."

"This is shocking indeed."

"I had thought perhaps he would discreetly take a mistress, but he seems to revel in his unruly behaviour. It is beyond disgraceful."

"Indeed it is. How can he behave so?"

"And yet there is worse. For when he does come home of an evening of drinking, gambling and the Lord knows what, he is in the worst of tempers. He declares me a bad luck charm and beats me for it. The servants fear him so that they dare not offer assistance, for his wrath should be turned on them. I have seen as much."

My hands fly to my mouth as I gasp.

"Lady Dellingby, quickly, smile, that was merely a look of amazement at these flowers here, for surely they watch from windows," she reminds, pointing to a flower.

I nod slowly and force a smile, leaning forward to inspect where she pointed. Such deceptions are unbecoming. Is Lady Longland really so closely watched, or has she begun to lose her wits at the hands of such maltreatment? Either way, compliance is the best course of action.

Standing upright, I look at her, and notice bruises under the shawl which has slipped. My stomach turns whilst a cloud descends.

Walking on, and turning my head, I say, "Lady Longland, your shawl. My apologies, but I must make mention, was this the hand of your husband?"

She pulls her shawl closer. "Yes."

Her single word answer is simple, direct and all the more shocking for it. We walk further away from the house and into an open area of grass.

"Tell me, what can I do?"

"Do? What is to be done? I am married. I cannot escape without scandal."

"You are to endure such repulsiveness in silence?"

"Of course."

"But why tell me if that is the case?"

She blinks a tear away. "Because should he go too far, should my life end, I would have someone know the truth."

My intake of breath is short and sharp, tears spring to my own eyes. "Lady Longland, no."

"No sentiment. Not for me."

"Well, I am sorry, but you have it all the same. Lady Longland, you declare sisterhood, yet expect me to stand by and allow this?"

"You must."

"I must do no such thing. There must be ways. You are sometimes called to your father's side, so you are allowed some freedom?"

"No, one of his servants always accompanies me."

"What does he mean by it?"

"To ensure I do not flee."

"But he has so little regard for you."

"My person perhaps, but not my status."

"Yes, he does seem to begrudge not being made higher than an earl. But I digress. How can we be of service? Might you come and pay a visit with us perhaps?"

"He would never allow so long an absence."

"It is trying indeed. You must at the very least, write to me should things escalate. As we have set the precedence for floral arrangements, you might perhaps use them as a code. Yellow roses for increased concern, pink dianthus for an emergency, and I shall create some reason for your immediate presence. Surely should your brother take ill you might be allowed to pay your respects."

She kisses my cheek. "Lady Dellingby, you are so clever. Although, if there is occasion for pink dianthus, I may not be able to write at all. But, if he grows beyond my forbearance, I promise to try."

"Lord Dellingby would never forgive me should I sit idly by and allow disaster to befall you. I would never forgive myself."

"You truly are angelic. My brother has sincerely made the happiest of matches."

Trying my best to appear as an amused lady, I return to the house arm-in-arm with Lady Longland as if nothing serious had passed our lips, a plucked helenium flower twiddling in my free hand.

The hunting must have gone well. Either that or Lord Longland has realised how shamefully he behaved last evening. For he enters the house whistling cheerily as if he never uttered so much as a cross word.

"Ah, Dellingby, there you are," he bellows like a hunting horn.

We hear no more, as he surely enters the library to assault my husband's peaceful solitude. Unable to go to his aid, I continue with my needlework. Out of the corner of my eye, I notice Lady Longland stiffen and pause in her stitch but am forced to make no remark. One observes naught.

Having changed for dinner, we all convene in the drawing room. All being accounted for, we enter the dining room. I stifle the rising bile as Lord Longland oozes himself into the seat next to mine. Every bit of my restraint is applied in repressing a sigh. Somehow, I manage a polite smile.

"How are you this evening, my lord?" I enquire with all good grace.

"Tolerably well. Your introduction to your father-in-law went well?"

I wonder if he could appear any more obnoxious. My dislike for him curiously increases with his efforts of pleasantry.

"Very well, I thank you."

"Ah, good. Can't stand the man myself, of course. Odd fellow, quite out of his mind. I avoid him at all costs. I urge you to do likewise, for your own good."

How dare he? Poor Lady Longland and Lord Dellingby are visibly shaken by his condemnation. Their anger makes me bold.

"I found him quite the contrary, my lord. He was most pleasant. As affectionate as my own papa." My tone is overly sweet and my eyelashes flutter.

His eyebrows near shoot off his head as he almost spits out his soup.

"Is that so? How curious. He must have had a moment of clarity. But how could he not with such a fine woman before him?"

My skin crawls as he leers at me.

"It is a great pity we shall be removed so far. But it cannot be helped."

Lord Longland makes a scoffing noise.

"Did you find anything of amusement in the newspaper, Lord Dellingby?" I enquire.

"A great deal, but not much you would wish to hear, I fear. A great deal too boring for your feminine charms. Am I right, Lord Longland?"

Oh, what a clever man. He has picked up on my opportunity to make the detestable man squirm a little.

"Err, of course. Not much for the gently bred ladies at all," he blusters.

It is sufficient to place him on a wrong footing. He halts his leering and continues his meal in sullen silence. I would never have expected to want such a thing, having detested Papa's own quiet meals, but now perhaps I see some sense to them.

"Can I top up your wine, Lady Dellingby?" Lord Longland asks as the next course arrives.

I nod my assent. But what new calamity is this? As I push my glass towards him, he reaches out and our hands touch. Instead of pulling away, or allowing me to do so, he puts more weight down upon it. It is with some difficulty that I free it from his grasp, and I cannot help but gape a little. Such audacity. My appetite is quite lost.

"I do hope you found some inspiration in our grounds today?" Lady Longland asks me.

She is clearly trying to let Lord Longland know of our stroll, showing she has nothing to hide, thus avoiding suspicion. A cunning ploy.

"Oh much. Lord Dellingby, I fear your sister is going to put you to great expense should the grounds of Sheringley Hall not be up to scratch."

He snorts. "My dear, I would have saved you the trouble, for I am sure you will not find them wanting."

"Well said, Dellingby. Keep her in her place, wot? Can't have the ladies riding roughshod and changing everything, can we, eh?"

How did he turn a teasing remark into something so sordid? Hateful man. To my astonishment, Lord Dellingby does not jump to my defence.

As soon as the men's gazes are turned towards their food, Lady Longland pulls a face at me to show her sympathetic disgust. I hide my smile behind my loaded fork.

Having received no response, the dullard clearly thinks he must enlarge upon his point. "No, my dear, you settle on keeping Dellingby here well fed and yourself in whichever lace best pleases you. Can't go wrong then."

My knuckles turn white as they grip my knife. How I could stab him with it. However, I genteelly place it on my plate, out of harm's way, and take a sip of wine. Taking a deep breath, I muster a smile.

"Such sage advice. Thank you, Lord Longland."

His grumbling noise is so full of self-satisfaction I would smack the grin from his face. Lord Longland, it must be said, inspires the deepest and most alarming tendencies to violence.

There is a great deal of food left on my plate, as I am unable to manage another mouthful. Not even the desserts can tempt me. Our host, of course, appears oblivious.

"I say, it's been a jolly good day, and we so seldom get company here, what say you to a song, Dellingby?"

"It seems a splendid notion. Lady Dellingby has a voice to rival the sweetest songbird."

Inwardly, I cower. Why would he present me so grandly? I feel as if I were a blancmange offered for Lord Longland's delight. He is already salivating.

We all repair to the drawing room.

"Guests first," Lord Longland pronounces, pointing me to the pianoforte.

Really not convinced I can find my voice, I entreat the aid of Lord Dellingby. "Won't you accompany me, my lord?"

"You wish me to sing?"

"Indeed, for you have the finest voice of any of us."

"You give me too much credit. But if that is your wish, who am I to decline?"

We select a piece, which I play whilst he sings. His voice is every bit as deep and melodious as I remember it. It lifts my spirits immeasurably. A thing of pure beauty amongst the turmoil.

Lord Longland bursts into applause at our completion.

"Jolly good. Never knew you had it in you, Dellingby. But you know I cannot be satisfied until I compare your voice with that of Lady Dellingby. I am all eagerness."

I am left on my own. If it were not so wholly unladylike, I would be wearing a scowl. But civility prevails, forcing a smile. I sing "The Baffled Knight" whilst presuming the symbolism of protected maidenhood and its sanctity may well be lost on Lord Longland. Even so, it gives me cheer.

Lord Dellingby rubs his upper lip with one long finger whilst he listens in earnest, a slight frown creasing his brow. I do hope he does not think my barbs are aimed at him. My gaze is thrown more pointedly at my foe for an instant to allay his concern.

Lady Longland listens with a pleased smile, as if in awe of the song. But her intelligence must leave her in no doubt of my devious intent. I persuade her to join me for one of the sweetest duets which e'er was played, I wager.

Her husband seems to appreciate our efforts. Perhaps we have impressed upon him her more sweet, delicate nature. I can but hope. He refuses to play or sing but reads a rather dull, bawdy poem instead. I applaud as expected whilst inwardly groaning.

The evening is endured to the best of my ability, with polite smiles, comments aimed to appease the foul beast and more wine than is customary for me.

"I do hate to be the one to spoil the fun, but Lady Dellingby and I have an early start tomorrow. I bid you goodnight," my husband declares, standing.

"So soon?" Lady Longland whimpers.

"I am afraid we must. But it is with a heavy heart we make our farewells. However, we invite you to our home at your earliest possible convenience."

"You are most kind, brother," she says, holding his hand to her cheek.

As Lord Dellingby climbs the stairs with me, he whispers, "Lock your door."

My mouth gapes for but a moment. Yes, he has borne witness to the overly familiar looks from his brother-in-law. What a term to be used on such a man.

Lord Dellingby places a gentle kiss upon my hand before allowing me to enter my chamber, and aways to his. The door is locked the instant I am inside. I can undress myself this one evening, having no desire to be in the presence of any other person, not even Clément. She has left a bowl of water on its stand, which I eagerly rub myself down with. The unhealthy looks from our host have left me feeling sullied.

I hasten to bed, snuff the candle and pull the sheets up tight. What a terrible day. Only now do I allow myself to think upon it. Poor Duke Wenston; so terribly afflicted. He was so agreeable and engaging when we first arrived. Lord Dellingby has clearly paid close attention to the good example set him. Although, what I was told regarding his rough treatment of his wife now springs to mind, making it difficult for me to marry the two sides of him together.

Then the attack of mania; so violent and confused. Pity bears down upon my heart, making it heavy as iron. Surely, he was no Lord Longland, even in his darkest times. Even now he is not; that much is clear.

And what of Lord Longland? So terribly vicious and unfeeling to his wife, and lecherous towards me. Vile, hateful man. Those bruises on Lady Longland's neck; how far do they reach? Did he attempt strangulation? Did he strike her? And how many times?

Tears spring from my eyes as I feel such dread for my dear sister-in-law. How much more can or will she withstand? No woman should ever be made to suffer thus even one single time. We have so little say in our lives but do our best to please. Yet we are scolded, punished and even beaten for any perceived misdeed. How are we to blame if our husband is of bad character or suffers a loss at the gaming tables?

Lord Dellingby extended an invitation, carefully to her without insinuation to Lord Longland. I do hope she will make the journey by herself. Surely nobody can blame a woman for visiting her brother and new sister-in-law? We shall have to make it of long duration.

Dear God above, please show mercy, and leave Lord Longland lying in the ditch on his next outing. Let Lady Longland live in freedom from cruelty. My sob is muffled in my pillow as my body shakes with the effort of my tears. My breath halts as a knock sounds upon my door.

"Who is there?" I call, trying to sound normal.

"It is I, Dellingby. Will you allow me entrance?"

I rush to the door in darkness and fling it open.

"My dear, are you quite well?" he asks.

I look at the floor, still swiping away the last traces of my tears. "Yes, quite well, I thank you."

"But you are distressed." It is not a question.

Unable to formulate a verbal response, I shake my head in an attempt at no. His finger encourages my chin to lift, and I find warm eyes searching mine in the light of his candle.

"The lie is clear upon your face, but I shall not press you for answers you are unwilling to provide. I merely wished to inquire how you're faring following this distressing day. I have my answer, and shall, of course, leave you to your solitude if that is what you desire."

He turns to leave, but I grab his hand. "Please stay."

Turning back to me, he gives a small bow. "As you wish."

The door is closed. I look about me in the surrounding darkness, unsure how to proceed. My hand is squeezed by that of Lord Dellingby's.

"It pains me to see you like this. Tell me, is there anything I may do to bring you comfort?"

Pulling his hand, to encourage Lord Dellingby to follow, I go and sit upon the edge of my bed.

"There is much I would say, but I have given my word to the contrary," I confess in hushed tones.

"Of course, I would never ask you to break a trust."

"And I thank you for that. But truly, there is so much concern in my heart I am unsure whether concealment is truly the correct course of action."

"This does not pertain to my father then?"

"No."

"My sister?"

I nod.

"She has informed you of the details of her situation?"

I nod again.

"My lady, if my beloved sister is in peril, I would urge you to speak. If there is anything within my power, it shall be done."

"I am sensible of that. But I truly do not know what there is to be done," I tell him, wiping away a fresh tear.

"Is it truly so terrible?"

"It pains me to admit it, but yes. Oh, Lord Dellingby, it is far worse than I had feared. But what is she to do? She said herself how irreversible her marriage is."

"You have said enough."

Bringing his hand to my cheek, I implore, "Please. Please, Lord Dellingby, do nothing rash. I fear worsening her situation above all else. And she must not know I betrayed her secret. She has promised to write should matters worsen."

"How did Pater ever admit his daughter to such a fiend? I will not stand by and see her harmed."

"I fear we must."

"No."

Oh, he will fight with Lord Longland and his revenge shall be taken upon his wife. Disaster shall surely follow.

"No? So blunt?" I check.

"Fear not. I shall ensure it appears the discovery is all mine, but I will have this out with Longland in the morning. He cannot be allowed to continue with his conduct unchecked."

Seeing the determination in the firm set of his jaw, and glower in his eyes, I concede, "Perhaps her shawl shall slip a little as it did today? You see how she wears it continually? It is not due to the chill alone."

With as grim a face as I have seen upon him, Lord Dellingby nods before marching out of the room. My hand flies to my breast. Dear Lord above, please do not let this end badly. Make Lord Longland see sense. How I fear becoming embroiled in another duel.

∾

Lady Longland and I are seated at the breakfast table, awaiting our husbands' presence the next morning. I slept not a wink all night, and no amount of Clément's' efforts can fully conceal the fact.

"My dear, you did not sleep well?" my kind companion asks.

"It is so obvious? I confess I did not. Please do not make yourself uneasy, for it was due in no way to any lack of comfort."

"I am glad to hear it. But yet a sense of responsibility does not escape me." Her face is forlorn, and my heart goes out to her.

My hand reaches across to hers. "Please, do not take it on so. Yesterday was rather much for me. Your papa, the Duke of Wenston inspired my deepest sympathy."

"Then I must thank you for feeling his condition so keenly. He was the kindest of papas once. It is cruel he should end his days thus."

We may have all the appearance of speaking of her papa, but the gentle jostle of her hand in mine suggests her understanding that we could just as easily be speaking of herself. Do I not believe father and daughter alike are worthy of my pity?

My shoulders hunch and my eyes scrunch as raised voices carry to us at table. The conversation between the marquess and the earl has clearly grown heated. Lady Longland's mouth forms an 'o' of concern, her eyes wide.

"I thought it curious my brother did not accompany me in here. We passed on the stairs, but then he turned a different direction from the one he intended, I think. His destination is now revealed."

It is my husband whose words are first loud enough to distinguish. "I have seen the bruises beneath the shawl she tries so fervently to conceal the evidence with. Do not continue to deny it."

Please do not allow a duel, please do not allow a duel.

"Perhaps we may be forgiven for beginning without them," I suggest.

Lady Longland hesitates but then gestures to a slice of plum cake. I transfer it to my plate and pour some hot chocolate. Whatever comes of this meeting, my full strength shall be called upon. Besides, eating a good meal brings comfort when my nerves are set so on edge.

"You come to me in my own home and tell me how to act? How very dare you?" Lord Longland rages.

"I dare when my sister is made to suffer at your hand. Blood claims my duty. Need I remind you she is the daughter of a duke? Surely there is no need when that is clearly the sole reason you married her. Her rank so far outstrips yours it should make your head spin. The honour she bestows upon you should leave you prostrate at her feet each and every morning."

"You go too far, Dellingby." It is a growled threat.

"Not far enough. Have you heard a word of what I have said? You stand there, denying all that is obvious to any casual observer, and bring further shame upon yourself. Where is my fault in this? Can I have your word, Lord Longland, that you shall not lay so much as a finger of harm upon Lady Longland?"

"Why should I make you any such promise? Who are you to me?"

"I…am…your…brother-in-law and would have thought myself worthy of some notice."

"What would you have me do? Bow and scrape to the marquess who so nobly enters my home to give me a dressing down?"

"I came in here hoping to reason with you, to appeal to your better nature. Anyone worth a jot would see the fortune of your situation. There are princes who would be humbled by such an alliance. But not the mighty Lord Longland. I see full well you will not acknowledge such. My breath is entirely wasted. Lord Longland, I take my leave, we shall leave directly."

Angry footsteps sound across the floor and grow louder as they approach. I have managed only a couple of mouthfuls and one sip of my breakfast. Yet gratitude fills my heart as there has been no mention of retribution or demands of satisfaction, although they were surely held in the next breath.

"Lady Longland, my apologies to you. Lady Dellingby, we leave this instant if you please." His voice is still louder than usual, and his entire frame is taught with tension.

Without a word, I get up from my seat, kiss my sister-in-law on each cheek and take my leave, whispering a reminder of her promise to write to me.

Oh, Lord Dellingby, I do hope you have not succeeded in plunging your sister in greater danger with your well-intentioned lecture. Perhaps a duel would have been preferable after all? End the miserable fellow and remove all chance of harm.

The carriage is already waiting outside, loaded with our trunks. The horses are already stomping their impatience as they stand in their harness.

"My dear, go ahead, I shall be with you in but a moment," Lord Dellingby urges.

I cast a look of query in his direction but receive no response. All that is allowed is for me to obey.

Disturbingly. considerable minutes pass before the carriage shakes to my husband's entrance.

"Away, fast as you please," he commands.

As soon as he is seated, we depart with a lurch.

"Lord Dellingby, after such heated debate, what could you possibly have to be so amused about?"

"My lady, that is knowledge best left entirely to my own keeping."

My head tilts as I peer at him. He is clearly up to some mischief. How infuriating he refuses to share when I have been so open with him.

He rolls his eyes. "Suffice it to say, Lady Longland shall be safe from harm for now."

"But how so?"

"I shall not be drawn out."

"Well, you seem very sure, so I must thank you for your intervention, I suppose. But Lord Longland seemed so terribly angry it is beyond me how you achieved such a feat."

Lord Dellingby's finger rubs along his mouth, his eyes sparking lightning. Indeed, I must trust in his success, however it is brought about.

Hope swells my breast as we journey on. Our destination today is not quite home as it is above a day's journey. Lord Dellingby has arranged a night with one of his cousins en route, which spares me a night at an inn. Once I have then had the opportunity of seeing my prospective home, we are bound for Yarmouth to visit with an aunt of his. I begin to wonder if there are Dellingbys scattered all about England.

ᖇ Chapter 38 ᖇ

After many more hours of travel, we arrive at the home of Lord Dellingby's cousin at a reasonable hour through a fine drizzle.

We are ushered into the house swiftly and are shown into the drawing room. The entire family are there to receive us.

"Henry, so good to see you, my dear fellow. How do you fare? You look very well," a rather jovial man greets, grabbing my husband into his embrace.

He stands a little shorter than Lord Dellingby, and a little stockier. They share the same hair and eye colour. The family resemblance is apparent, particularly in the long, straight nose.

"Thomas, good to see you too," he returns, wrestling himself free of his cousin's grasp, "Might I introduce my wife, The Marchioness of Dellingby, to you?"

"Certainly, we are overjoyed to receive you, Lady Dellingby. You shall always find welcome here." I am spared a hug, but my hand is firmly grasped and patted as I curtsey my greeting.

"Indeed we are, Lady Dellingby, do come take a seat. You must be weary after your journey," a woman calls from a sofa, patting the cushion next to her.

"Lady Grungate, a pleasure," I say, awkwardly taking my appointed place.

A baby boy rests in her arms, whilst a twin boy and girl squabble behind us, and an older boy scolds them. It is quite raucous.

"Never mind them, my dear. They are forever at one another's throats over some nonsense," Lady Grungate tells me with a wave of her hand.

"Would they perhaps not be happier in the nursery with their toys?" I offer.

"Lady Dellingby, I warn you that you are onto a sorry footing there. I have often suggested this myself, but my good wife is so attached to our cherubs she is loath to be parted from them," Lord Grungate informs me, grinning.

"Then I shall make no further mention of it, for Lady Grungate must know best in this matter, I feel."

She leans herself forwards a little. "Thank you, my dear. I knew the instant I set eyes upon you how sensible you must be."

Turning her head, she adds, "Lord Dellingby, you have found yourself a fine wife, and I must congratulate you."

Lowering her voice conspiratorially, she turns her attention back to me, "He has taken his sweet time about it. We were forever urging him into marriage, but he would not be rushed. Lord Dellingby insisted he was in search of someone special, a lady who would best suit him in personality and wit, and not in name alone."

A smile spreads across my face as I glance at him from the corner of my eye. "Did he now?"

There is a pink glow upon my husband's cheeks.

"Oh yes, he was most particular. What was it he said, husband? It was rather touching."

Lord Grungate touches his fingers to his chin. "Let us see now. 'Lady Dellingby shall be the finest of women, the best in the land. For she must be strong of spirit to withstand my whims, yet gentle enough to be a balm to my tempers.' Yes, I believe they were his words."

I cannot help but laugh, whilst Lord Dellingby is left clearing his throat, blushing wildly. "I may have said something of the sort. But you forget I added that she must also be beautiful."

"Well, Lord Dellingby, I no longer wonder at your reticence. However, I do wonder at you finding anyone who matches up to such lofty ambitions."

He approaches and strokes my cheek. "But I did."

"Ah now, is this not a wonderful sight, husband?" Lady Grungate cheers.

"Oh, come now, let us finish with this nonsense. Lady Grungate, you have not introduced me to your delightful children," I declare.

"Georgie, bring the twins here," she calls, not looking behind her.

The beautiful boy with bright blond curls, taking after his mama in hair colour, drags the two younger children by their hands until they stand in front of us. A pair of big brown eyes look at us, a cheeky smile playing about his lips.

"Lady Dellingby, this is George, my eldest."

My breath skips as the name echoes in my heart, calling to my own brother. The use of first names is also most shocking, bordering on scandalous. Whoever heard of such a thing in a house like this? What can they mean by it? There is clearly no insult intended, yet it shows an utter wont of manners.

"Delighted to meet you," I tell him, bowing my head.

I am rewarded with a smart bow from the boy, who I would put at around six years of age.

"And these you see here are Harvey and Harriet," she nods in their direction.

The four-year-olds giggle shyly and wave.

"How do you do?" I ask, which receives more of the same.

"They are simply darling," I tell their mama, my hands holding my heart.

"Thank you."

"Very good, continue to play nicely," she adds to the children.

"And this is Ludlow," she whispers, gazing upon her babe in arms, who continues sleeping.

"What a fine family," I admire, looking towards our host.

"You find me the luckiest of men," he says.

"With respect, I must dispute your case. Perhaps the second luckiest," Lord Dellingby tells him.

Inclining his head, he responds, "Perhaps. But mayhap we are joint first, wot?"

"I think I can agree upon that."

The men chuckle together, and I try to disguise my rolling eyes. I have not heard two words of sense spoken together since we arrived. Although, seeing Lord Dellingby so relaxed has its charms.

"Thank you for permitting us to stay the night. I regret it is not for longer on this occasion, but you must understand poor Anne's eagerness to see her own home," Lord Dellingby says.

Anne? Did he call me Anne? In company? Honestly, this lackadaisical familiarity can go too far.

"What? You mean to tell me she has not yet seen her own house? Oh, you poor dear. Your nerves must be in shreds. You have been married above a week. Well, have no fear, for Sheringley Hall is one of the finest estates you ever shall see," Lady Grungate shrills.

"And you are of course welcome to visit once we are settled," Henry, err, Dellingby offers.

Oh Lor', this is become contagious. With such a young family, surely they will not be too eager to attend upon us.

"You are too kind. You will not be able to keep us away. The children so love it there."

I do not know which is the more astonishing; Dellingby playing good Uncle Henry, indulging his nieces and nephews, or that the family all travel together. My stomach tightens. Oh Lor', what if he expects me to be a mother like Lady Grungate?

"Lady Dellingby, are you quite well?" the Mama enquires.

"Why yes, it is a little warm today, and I am perhaps tired after travelling."

"Oh, and we have not so much as offered you refreshment. Benson, some tea, will you?" she commands the nearest servant.

"Do forgive my neglect, my dear. It is all owing to our eagerness to meet the wife of our cousin, I assure you."

"There is nothing to forgive, Lady Grungate."

"Won't you please excuse us? I think perhaps I should take Lady Dellingby for a turn in the gardens whilst the tea is prepared," my husband says, rising to his feet and offering me his hand.

I willingly accept.

"Of course, of course. Too much sitting is bad for the blood," Lord Grungate states.

Lord Dellingby sedately walks me through to the lawn out the back of the house.

"I thought you may require a moment of peace. They can be somewhat boisterous, perhaps I should have warned you," he says softly.

"Some warning may have been favourable. They are wonderful though, do not think me unaware of their generous nature, *Henry*," I say, emphasising his name.

"Haha, yes, they are the most informal, eccentric family you shall ever meet, to be sure. But do allow for their excitement in meeting you."

"I am but myself."

"And all the more wondrous for it. Thomas and I were practically brothers growing up. We'd often spend our entire summers in each other's company. I was glad of the male company."

"I am glad you had someone like him."

"They will be calmer once they get to know you better. And you know, once they are at the hall, the children are mostly left to run amok outside. Having lost their first child in its infancy, Lady Grungate finds the need to be much in their company."

"It must be of great reassurance."

"It is good you appreciate her delicacies."

We walk in the chill air, arm-in-arm. The rain has stopped, but more is threatened in the clouds. It is respite enough for me to collect my thoughts.

Tea is awaiting as we re-enter.

"You have fabulous timing, my dear," Lady Grungate remarks.

I take the offered cup of tea.

"The children are gone to the nursery to enjoy their treats."

"Oh, well, I am sure they will be grateful for that."

Their disappearance has left a gaping chasm, an eerie silence in the room. How odd that I should feel it so.

Our husbands do not retire, as I expected, but remain with us and each take a cup too. Our conversation falls into pleasantries as we become better acquainted. An ease falls about me and I sit back in my chair, almost slouching.

The children bound back into the room in the afternoon, but without their youngest sibling. I do hope the prolonged absence is not on my behalf.

"Mama, Mama, we had jam tarts," George informs us, his eyes sparkling with joy.

"Did you, my dear? Fancy that. What a fortunate boy you are."

"I ate three all to myself."

"Gosh, what a great many. You make sure you still eat your dinner, like a good boy."

"I will," he agrees with a vigorous nod.

"I do not doubt it. Now, go play," she says, leaving a kiss on his forehead.

My breast swells with the love all around me. What sort of a mother shall I be when my time comes? Perhaps Lady Grungate sets a better example than first appearances would show.

Once dinner time arrives, the absence of the children runs through me like a cold hand once more. How sentimental I am become within an afternoon.

We are treated to all manner of good things at table and our conversation continues. No awkward silence, no arguments; it is a fine and rare thing.

After dinner, the men accompany us to the drawing room. It is no longer a surprise. I am becoming accustomed to this excessively close family and their way of living.

My cheeks are hurting as I retire to my room at last. I do not seem to have stopped smiling for hours. How freeing not to be forced to conceal one's emotions, especially when they are such pleasant ones.

"And how do you find it here, Clément?" I ask as she prepares me for bed.

"If I may say, my lady, it is a rather unusual household."

"Have you been treated well?"

"A little too well. They overfed me," she says, patting her tummy.

"Oh, we cannot have that now, can we?" I say with a smirk.

"Not that I have ever been wanting in your care."

"Be easy, Clément, I took your meaning."

"I shall be glad when we get to Sheringley Hall."

"You feel un-homed too? Of course, you must. It is all a little unsettling, is it not?"

She nods mutely.

"Almost there now."

She tries a smile. "My apologies. What are my problems? I spoke out of turn."

"You did no such thing. I made the enquiry. Come now, I like to know you are happy."

"Well, I hope you find the hall to your liking, my lady."

She makes her exit. The poor girl was quite at odds this evening. Perhaps she is weary of travel also. My own fatigue sends me almost immediately into a deep slumber.

The next morning, we pay heartfelt farewells to our hosts, but with promises they shall soon visit. I welcome the prospect. It is nice to have such friends. They may be an oddity but are so obliging as to overcome any possible objection to that.

And then we are away, to what is hoped to be my home.

Not long now, I keep reminding myself with each passing mile. I heartily believe that this property shall be the best ever beheld if for no other reason than the fear of enduring further travel to discover any alternative.

My hand keeps smoothing my bodice and skirts. It must be driving Lord Dellingby to distraction, for eventually he grasps my hand.

"My dear, you look wonderful, and all shall be well. I have every confidence."

His smile is reflected in the depths of his hazel eyes to such an extent that I'm inclined to believe him. What is there to worry about, after all? There is no family to impress. Lord Dellingby deems Sheringley Hall a delightful home.

Perhaps it is not the building itself which does not allow my heart to slow to a sedate pace. Rather the ownership of such. It has all been well and good being the dutiful wife of a marquess whilst visiting, but now I am to lay claim to an entire household, and ensure it is run as is expected.

It has surely been run admirably well without any interference from myself thus far. But there lies the rub. What if my way is not conducive to those of the staff? What should I care? They shall have to adapt. But then what do I know? I am new to all of this, after all. They are the ones who may claim experience. Oh Lor', what am I to do?

My hand gets another squeeze and a little shake. "Not far now."

It is as if he read my thoughts. Well, it is far too late to turn back now. Myself and the staff are about to discover just what sort of lady of the house I am. Having studied domestic manuals, some of which are in my trunk, surely this is not impossible. But how my heart sinks when I think upon my lessons in mathematics; this is not my area of expertise, and yet shall be perhaps my most utilised.

Mama has copied out some recipes which she knows I am fond of, and some which may prove useful when guests visit. I hope to equally impress the cook with my knowledge and demonstrate I cannot be deceived. Firm but fair, that is to be my approach.

My ears are thundering with the sound of my heart as the carriage pulls along the approach to the house. So much for it being small, as Lord Dellingby had indicated. My hopes had been raised of perhaps being introduced into my new duties gradually. It is not a great deal smaller than Wenston Hall, nor even Papa's Gensmore Hall, from what I can see. There is no great lake in front of the property, but that does not diminish its grandeur.

There are trees and grass enough to satisfy my tastes, but perhaps a few too many pillars. Oh Lor', this could be a challenge. Taking a deep breath, I try to remind myself of my schooling and breeding. Clearing my throat, I stiffen my back, preparing myself for the all-important first impression.

"I say, does the driver remember we are still aboard?" I ask as the carriage veers off, away from the house.

"He has his instructions," Lord Dellingby replies with a knowing smile.

My brows furrow at him, but my question remains unspoken. He is up to some mischief. I do hope he does not seek to amuse himself by showing me in via the servant's entrance; my humour does not extend to such liberties.

The carriage swoops round and comes to a halt...at the stables. Lord Dellingby helps me down.

"I imagined your first priority may reside here," he tells me, still grinning.

A whinny reaches my ears, making me look around.

"This way, if you please, your ladyship," a proud groom says, indicating the entrance.

A brown head with a white blaze peeks from a stall.

"Oh, Rosalind," I cry, making a goose of myself, stroking her nose.

"And Lady, hello Lady," I call, as her white face emerges from the next stall.

Hooves stamp and whickers are cried as I make a fuss of each beloved horse.

"Lord Dellingby, they are here already. And not to tell me. What a wonderful surprise."

I wipe a tear from my eyes as subtly as one can.

"I thought it may feel more like home if they were here. And I knew you would like to see they are well cared for," he tells me.

"That they are, your ladyship. Most particularly cared for, if I may be so bold," the groom adds.

"Thank you…oh dear, we have not yet been introduced."

"Lady Anne Dellingby, this is our head groom, Arthur."

He duly bows, doffing his cap.

"Well, Arthur, I am pleased to meet you. I daresay we shall see one another a good deal. I suppose Lord Dellingby has made you aware of my fondness for horse riding."

"Indeed he has, Lady Dellingby. He sent word that these horses were to be especially cared for, and always at the ready."

"Perhaps not always, but I do appreciate your careful attention. They seem well pleased."

"I'd wager that is more due to your arrival, my lady. I've not seen them so happy."

"Yes, yes, very well. Come, we cannot live in a stable. My lady, if you would accompany me to view our own living quarters?" Lord Dellingby interjects, offering his arm.

"Of course, my lord."

Really, he grows too impatient. He cannot reunite me with my horses and not expect me to fuss over them a little. Of course, my smile is all politeness as he leads me away.

"The carriage is still here if you care to use it to transport us to the main house. Or would you rather walk?"

I try to imagine the distance, and what state I would be in walking so far.

"I think the carriage on this occasion, if you please."

Once we're back inside, he glances across at me. "He was becoming too familiar. It is not to be encouraged."

"Whatever you say, my lord. I am sure you know best."

His eyes flicker back towards me as his head turns towards the window.

"Ah, good, the household are at the ready."

The entire staff seem to be lined up outside. Oh Lor', here it is, the moment of truth.

We exit the carriage and are greeted by a rather severe, smartly dressed man.

"Your lordship, your ladyship, welcome home," he greets, bowing.

"The Marchioness of Dellingby, this is my steward, Mr Baxter."

"Pleased to make your acquaintance," I say with a shallow curtsey as he bows.

"And this is Mr Edkins, the butler," Mr Baxter says, indicating the next in line, as we make our courtesies.

"And Mrs Hinchley, the housekeeper."

Before me stands a short, stout, weathered lady, her face well lined, but with brown eyes shining with sense. Her grey hair is worn up in a bun atop her head, which seems to indicate a smart orderliness which I admire.

"Good afternoon, Lady Dellingby. I have taken the liberty of having some refreshments set out when you are ready."

"Most thoughtful. Thank you, Mrs Hinchley," I say with a smile and curtsey.

We make our way down the line, with many names being announced, heads bobbing up and down all the while. I shall never remember all of these names, there's far too many. However, I strive to commit to memory all the main people. Perhaps I can fudge the rest until we become better acquainted. Although, surely there will be some whom I never see again at all.

We finally make our way to the front door, which a footman opens for us. Mr Baxter follows behind.

"Your lordship, would her ladyship prefer a brief tour now or wait until you have taken tea?"

"I think tea will be first, thank you, Mr Baxter."

"Very good, my lord."

He bows and vanishes away. Lord Dellingby leads me to the drawing room.

"Tour indeed. I have been here before," he mumbles.

"I am sure he meant to pay a kindness to me. Come, these cakes look delicious."

He takes the offered plate from me and raises an eyebrow as he looks sidewards at me.

"Perhaps you have the right of it."

Silence seems the better path to take. We are both surely tired and hungry.

"Well, what is your impression thus far?" he enquires after eating his cake.

"I am sure we shall be most happy here."

He sighs and leans back in his chair, almost spilling his tea. "Good, good."

Once we have emptied our cups, Lord Dellingby declares, "I will go in search of Mr Baxter but must keep him to myself. I will ensure Mrs Hinchley is sent to conduct your tour."

I stand and curtsey, allowing him to leave me. Alone in the large, bright room, I walk around, looking at the paintings and furnishings, my fingers running along the back of the sofa. Yes, a most pretty room, which I shall be happy to spend time in. I cannot even see any immediate need for any redecoration. The pale duck egg blues and creams are rather pleasant.

Walking over to the windows, I see a fine aspect of the park. My fingers are itching to grab the reins, both metaphorical and physical, but mostly those of my horses. At the earliest given opportunity, I shall ride across the land. Too long I have been cooped up in close confinement.

"Hello, your ladyship. It is a fine view, is it not?" a female voice calls from behind me.

Turning, I agree, "Yes, most pleasant, Mrs Hinchley."

"Well, I understand you would like to be shown about the house. It is my pleasure to do so. It has been too long since I was able to show off Sheringley. But you must be tired after your journey, so let us satisfy ourselves with the necessary today, and tomorrow we shall investigate fully. What do you say?"

"A most thoughtful idea," I placate.

She prattles on happily, divulging as much information as she can think of as we go about each room. One of the highlights for me is the beautiful blue Axminster rug in the music room. I suspect many hours may be spent in here.

The walls are kept cream, allowing the blue carpet and chairs to sing out. The pianoforte is exquisite and makes my fingers fidget in their longing to play such an instrument. Both a harp and a harp lute are happily located here too. I am spoiled for choice. The paintings I shall make a study of later.

Continuing our tour, we pass the study.

"The master is about business already in there," she whispers.

Anybody may be mistaken for Sheringley Hall belonging to this woman, she is so proud of it. She is friendly yet not too forward. Most importantly, she seems keen to take my orders.

"Dinner tonight shall be simple fare, I'm afraid. I was not sure what your tastes ran to, so have kept it plain. But tomorrow morning, first thing we shall sit down together and form plans what to do going forwards. Then cook can make a start whilst we get you introduced to the estate."

"Thank you, Mrs Hinchley. It is a great relief to find you so agreeable," I let out without meaning to.

Her cheeks wrinkle more as she smiles. "Likewise, my lady. Right, well, here we are at your room. I shall leave you to dress for dinner and bid you a goodnight."

"Goodnight, Mrs Hinchley, and thank you."

With a deep sigh, I flollop onto the bed. Phew, that was quite some tour for a basic one. Time has quite disappeared. The house is large and tastefully decorated. Yes, I think we may be happily situated here. My fingers are stroking the bed coverings in little circles when there is a knock upon my door.

"Enter."

"Evening, my lady," Clément greets.

"Clément, hello. Tell me, what is your room like? Does it suit? I have not yet seen the servants' area."

She smiles. "Oh yes, my lady. It is a pretty home, is it not? *Très jolie.*"

"Yes, it seems we have a delightful home, Clément."

"Pleased to hear it, my lady."

"But you will tell me, won't you, should you hear anything ill spoken below stairs?"

"But of course. Not that I should expect any such thing. You are too good to be spurned. And I would put anyone right who should utter such horrid words."

"You are very good, Clément."

Perhaps this is asking too much, but I must have eyes and ears about me. I will not be censured or be spoken against in my own home. The servants must respect me from the outset.

Dressed for dinner, I make my way down to the dining room, managing to not get lost. Golds outweigh the blues in this room, making it the more opulent when compared with the drawing room. As in there, a chandelier shines down, but again, this is grander here. The large gold framed looking glass above the fireplace reflects the beautiful tapestry on the opposite side.

A faint smile spreads across my lips as I spy a pair of Blue John vases. What a beautiful, sentimental touch; bringing a piece of Derbyshire here to Norfolk.

My husband beams as he stands from the table and beckons me.

"Good evening, Lady Dellingby," he says, placing a kiss upon my cheek.

"Good evening, my lord. You seem all cheer."

"That I am. There are not as many urgent matters as I had feared. Mr Baxter has been managing most admirably. I hear you enjoyed your afternoon."

"Well, news does spread rapidly here."

"Not at all. I happened across Mrs Hinchley on my way down. I asked her what your impressions had been."

"That was quite cruel of you, to put the poor woman on the spot. Especially when you need only ask me, and you know I shall tell you the truth."

"Ah, but then I would not have heard her wax lyrical about what a splendid young wife I have."

I giggle. "Did she now?"

"Indeed, I had a job to stop her singing your praises."

"Oh now, you go too far again. But I am gratified to know she holds me in high esteem. It makes life so much simpler, does it not? I happen to find her just as agreeable in return."

"So, you really like Sheringley Hall?"

My grin spreads clear across my face. "I do, very much."

We remain quite animated throughout the entire meal. It must be an excess of exercise or some such. I feel quite giddy by the time we quit the dining room.

"Will you take a turn about the gardens with me, whilst I partake of my nightly cheroot? It is such a fine evening."

"Why, yes, I have not yet stepped outside."

"Good heavens, where did Mrs Hinchley take you?"

"We spent a great deal of time in each room. She was most willing to impart the history of each artefact and ornament."

"By Jove, what a bore. Well, let us take you out of doors now, and make up for it. There is yet enough light for you to see tolerably well."

He lights his cheroot and puffs as we make our way out of doors. I waft the smoke away with my hand as it makes me cough. He transfers it to his other hand and takes a step away.

"Does my smoking disturb you?"

"Not at all. I merely ingested a rather large amount at once." My eyes are watery with the effort of not coughing more.

Breathing deeper as we reach the outside, the scent of jasmine reaches me. My feet take me towards its source. It doesn't take me long to discover the archway covered with jasmine, and it leads to some delightful flower beds.

"Oh, Lord Dellingby, you had need only make mention of this garden alone and I would have agreed to live here."

"You think I am unaware of this, perhaps? But I wanted to make sure you were happy with it all and not only some flowers which may be planted anywhere."

I look at the grass below my feet.

"There, there, no need for bashfulness. You know how I like to tease. You are not truly affronted?"

"No. Merely, when you put it that way it does sound rather foolish."

"I could never think you foolish."

My eyes shoot up to search his at his sincere words.

"My dear, you surely know by now that I admire those brains you so sweetly tried to hide."

"But—"

"Shh now, you may have hidden your true self from others. But you should be glad you did not succeed with me. Let others have their stupid wives. You are to help me run my household. And your spirit matches even my own in liveliness. Who wants a dull companion? Not I."

Before I can make my reply, his lips are upon mine. The taste of tobacco fills my mouth, but when mixed with his brandy, it is quite pleasant. He stubs out the remainder of his cheroot with his foot, and his hands pull me towards him, so he may kiss me more fully. His tongue meets mine in a wondrous union.

Clearing his throat, he steps back a little. "Do I make myself clear?"

"I rather think so."

He chuckles at my dazed expression and takes my hand. "Come, explore your flowers."

My body may be led around the gardens, but my head takes barely any of it in except for a passing recognition of their beauty. There is a yearning, deeply seated, and yet I know not how to request relief.

Happily, Lord Dellingby comes to my aid. Getting close, he whispers next to my ear, sending shivers all throughout me. "Do you object to being wild and free, my lady?"

"No…no objection," I stutter, pawing at his upper arms, trying to steady myself.

Secreted within the confines of the walled garden, he lies me upon the grass. Lying next to me, he regains our kiss, and drags it down along my neck, wrenching a gasp from my lips.

His hands push my dress out of his way, and his mouth finds my nipple.

"I would show you how enraptured I am by your very being," he whispers into my bosom.

I can only murmur nonsensical grunts in return.

Pushing my skirts up, he brings his body atop mine.

"With my body, I thee worship," he whispers, entering in where the ache was.

Oh, how much I desired this. My neck arches, my moans of pleasure are directed towards the stars. Perhaps I should give some thought as to our location, but all I truly know is I am grateful for his presence.

His hands cup my breasts, as his tongue explores each one. His mouth travels back up to suck on my neck, his hips rocking, our bodies grinding. My hands clasp his buttocks in my desperation for ever more, my feet kicking out.

He grunts as he pushes himself further within and then back out. I whimper, wanting him to bury himself inside forever. All thoughts of ladylike behaviour are a distant memory as I wriggle beneath my husband, clawing onto him, crazed with need.

"My love, show me what you need," he urges, twisting us about, resting me atop him.

All sense is abandoned, as my body demands his. The friction between my legs grows and grows; warming, heating beyond all…thought, my inner voice whispers as it travels in black nothingness, lit only by stars.

Lord Dellingby grabs my body to his and regains his position on top. My legs are resting upon his shoulders, my muscles limp and free to his will. Pleasure bordering on pain fills as he surges forward. My hands clutch into my disarrayed skirts, trying to find something to anchor me. A few more thrusts and he is spent, raising grunts from us both.

I bring my legs down and to me as he withdraws.

"You are not hurt, my love?" he asks, all concern.

"Not in a bad way."

"My dear, you should've said."

"Lord Dellingby, it was not in a bad way." How does one explain the sensation? I cannot.

He lies down at my side, his hand over my waist, and I curl against him. We remain only so long as it takes to regain our breath.

"This is becoming habit," I tease, righting my clothing and hair.

He smirks. "An unwelcome one?"

I slap his shoulder, smiling. "You know it is not."

As we stand, he holds my body close to his and kisses the top of my head.

"Welcome home," he whispers.

❧ Chapter 39 ❧

Phew, finally, a chance to review my correspondence. There were letters awaiting my attention here, but I had neither time nor concentration enough to read them until this morning.

There is one from my sister, urging news. I had intended upon writing her letter this morning in any case.

I recount all the details of my journey I am at liberty to and add my hopes of finding the dowager countess, Dellingby's aunt, not so formidable as expected next week.

As my signature goes onto the page and is blotted, Mrs Hinchley knocks upon my door. We discuss meal choices in great detail, making me desperately ready for breakfast.

It is of great relief to discover a good spread laid out when I enter the dining room. Lord Dellingby smirks across his cup at me.

"How fare you this morning, wife?"

"I am very well, I thank you, my lord."

He eyes the pile of food upon my plate, his grin seemingly irrepressible.

"What have you planned for the day?"

"Mrs Hinchley is to complete our tour, and then there are accounts to be gone over."

"Ah, The Grand Tour in our own home. Sounds thrilling."

"Probably as exciting as your day's prospects."

"Quite so."

The look of mischief continues to pass across his face, lighting up his eyes. It is upon my mind to quiz him, but such things are best left unsaid. It would not do to spoil his good humour.

We part ways once our meal is over. The large breakfast was much required, as the tour is extensive, and takes some considerable energy. Mrs Hinchley has no compassion for my previous exertions. Perhaps tomorrow I shall refuse to leave my bed and remain in safety. Perhaps I could remain there for the remainder of the week, which is what I could best benefit from. But alas, duty calls.

"Ah, Arthur," I greet as we reach the stables.

"Good morning, my lady," he returns, smiling broadly.

"Mrs Hinchley, I would check up on my horses whilst here."

"Very good, my lady," she returns as if she expected nothing less.

Breathing deeply of the smell of hay and horse, I enter the stable block and approach the stalls.

"Arthur, where is Rosalind? Is she well?"

"Well, my lady, if you please, you will see Lady is inside the next."

"Yes, I can see that," I say, walking over to stroke her nose, "But my question was regarding Rosalind."

The groom squirms a little. "She is very well, my lady. If you would permit me to show you the rear of this block?"

Well, this is a little alarming, and highly suspicious. I am grateful for Mrs Hinchley's presence. Perhaps Lord Dellingby was wise in his correction of this man's forward behaviour? Ensuring my companion is with me, we follow the groom, whose head is shaking from side-to-side.

Lo and behold, who should we see, but Lord Dellingby himself sat astride a horse, with Rosalind alongside standing ready-saddled.

"Good morning, Lady Dellingby," my husband calls, doffing his hat.

"Good morning again, my lord. But what do you mean by this? I am hardly dressed for horse riding."

He nods his head towards the stable block. "Your maid is awaiting you in the last stall, I believe."

I gasp. "Lord Dellingby, you do not mean for your wife to get dressed in a stable?"

"Well, if you would delay by returning all the way to the house…?"

My mouth hangs open and my hands thump my hips. I make a complete ninnyhammer of myself as my mouth works to form words but in silence. Argument is willing but can find no sound basis.

Stomping into the stables, I hear his chuckle behind me. He could have warned me so I could dress appropriately before coming all the way out here.

Clément works incredibly quickly in the semi-darkness of the stall.

"I am sorry Lord Dellingby dragged you all the way out here," I tell her.

"It is nothing, my lady. It is quite pleasant to see some more of the estate. And to assist you in doing something you enjoy so much is no great burden."

Yes, it is. But I sigh deeply, having to admit to myself that Lord Dellingby was acting in thought of my pleasure. It was generous of him to interrupt his own day to assist me. Yes, he could certainly have gone about it in a more considerate fashion, but he surely meant well.

Lord Dellingby's brow is furrowed as he looks down at me as I approach. His mount is pawing the ground with his hoof. The poor beast; how long has it had to wait? Rosalind looks equally as anxious to be away. I pat his horse's shoulder and smile up at its rider.

"Jolly good, shall we away?" he asks, smiling back.

"What a splendid notion," I reply coquettishly.

"You're a very naughty man, not to warn me," I reprimand Arthur jovially as he helps me up.

"My apologies, my lady." His smile gives him away.

"Right, tally ho," I call, laughing and kicking Rosalind on.

Lord Dellingby is surely rolling his eyes, but I cannot see, for he is aft as Rosalind and I charge off.

"Lady Dellingby, you know not which direction we take," he cries.

"You had better catch up and show me then," I yell over my shoulder.

Having reached soft ground, we are at a canter already, surging in flight. Oh, how good it is to be so free once more. Too long I have been confined in stuffy carriages and houses. My husband is a fine horseman and is soon by my side.

"Let us pace ourselves. It'll not do to tire the horses before we begin," he states, slowing to a walk.

Rosalind is duly slowed, and stretches her neck, giving it a shake. I pat and rub her neck, which is answered with a happy snort. Poor girl, she has been likewise limited.

As we walk on, Lord Dellingby points out places of interest. The park is extensive and takes a good deal of time to view.

"I had thought you would prefer to complete this tour atop your faithful horse," he says as we go.

"You were correct, my lord. I thank you for your thoughtful generosity. You surely have more pressing duties to attend to."

"Nothing which cannot wait until the lady of the house is satisfied," he returns with a wink.

There is a lake for fishing, farms dotted about, and a good many trees and hedges. All seems to be in good order. It seems the estate needs no master at its helm to run itself. This is somehow unnerving more than comforting.

"It is almost as if we are intruding on the way of life here," I note.

"Not at all. Servants are never happier than when they have someone to fuss over, I assure you. They muddle through tolerably well without us, granted, but our presence gives them a purpose for doing so."

"I suppose that must be so."

"Come, you are not going to make yourself uneasy about being in your own home, surely? Such squeamish issues are not worth your notice."

"Quite. But it is all so new still."

"Before the week is out you will be ordering everyone about as assuredly as if they were your old Forbes."

My cheeks burn. "For shame, Lord Dellingby, that you should notice such things."

"I warn you I am exceedingly jealous, and he was most fond of you."

"Oh fie, Lord Dellingby, not in any uncommon way. He looked upon me almost as a daughter, I believe. Is that any great peculiarity, given I was daughter of the household?"

"The entire household, eh?"

"Lord Dellingby, you know full well my meaning. Do not tease so."

He chuckles. "Poor Forbes. I am convinced he would do whatever you ask, no matter how outrageous."

I giggle. "Yes, perhaps he would. He was a most advantageous ally."

"But you had no great enemy in your own home?"

"No. But Papa's temper…well, it is not proper to speak of such things. I have not the faintest idea how we stumbled across such a topic."

To avoid any further foolishness, I nudge Rosalind back into a canter. We race some considerable distance. Our horses are in quite a lather by the time he declares me the winner. A most gallant gesture, for he could certainly have overtaken if he had the mind to. I laugh and cheer, pretending not to be wise to this fact.

The horses are given a long rein as they saunter towards home. For home it is truly becoming, albeit slowly. But one does rather get the impression of settling here very well indeed.

Lord Dellingby came to my room last evening, and I am forced to lie in bed longer than anticipated this morning; fatigue pulling me into my mattress further when Clément came to open the curtains.

When Mama spoke of marital duties, I had thought it would be a one-time event, but we seem to be forming a habit of joining together. Not that there is any complaint from me, of course. It is rather enjoyable, and to be encouraged.

Now that I know the layout of the estate, it is time to become acquainted with the finances, more's the pity. My eyes are sore with numbers and my head aches from determining the accuracy of such.

Rubbing my temples, I breathe in deeply in an attempt to clear the fog. I am saved by a nuncheon, for I am to expect callers this afternoon, now word has been put out in the paper of our arrival. One must fortify one's self for such encounters.

Sure enough, at just gone three, Lady Winterthorpe is shown in.

"Lady Dellingby, how wonderful to meet with you at last. Your arrival has been greatly anticipated," she greets, curtseying.

"Lady Winterthorpe, it is a pleasure to meet you too. Thank you for coming to call. I shall be sure to return the favour as soon as is possible, but you know we are to depart for a bridal visit soon."

"When you are so recently arrived?" she asks, her voice shrill.

"Why yes, it could not be helped as Lord Dellingby's aunt lives further east, and we travelled from the west. But thereafter I hope to remain some time in the vicinity, for I already find it a delightful residence."

"I am very glad to hear you speak so well of our area. We take great pride in it, you know. And you shall be kept busy, as we form quite a number hereabouts, and there will be many balls and parties."

"So I understand. And of course, once we are more settled, we shall hold a ball here."

"Lady Dellingby, I can see we shall get along famously. We are fond of such lively entertainment. The city folk of London fancy they are the best amused but let me assure you, we challenge their belief."

"And yet, we must also boast at being able to breathe freely," I say with a small giggle.

"Oh, my dear, I see you share the same opinion. It is quite dreadful is it not? In town one struggles to remain on one's feet whilst taking daily exercise. Yes, you shall be most joyously received," she says whilst fanning her face.

Lady Winterthorpe remains for twenty-five minutes. She seems a little enthusiastic for the high life, and I cannot as yet fully trust her intentions are pure. She is surely the first of many to pay their respects whilst judging my character. Although she may speak words of welcome, one must wait and see if these words are followed by action.

Two more callers succeed her, and I am kept talking all of the afternoon. I am so weary over dinner I can barely keep my eyes open.

"Lord Dellingby, I beg your forgiveness, but I think I shall retire early this evening," I say, breaking the silence which engulfs our evening meal.

"You do look somewhat fatigued. Are you well?"

"Yes, quite well. It is merely that my presence has been much in demand this day."

"But of course, I shall not detain you a moment longer. As soon as we are through here you must find your chamber, where I hope you will find a peaceful slumber."

"Thank you, my lord. Your generosity and thoughtfulness always do you credit. And I believe sleep shall find me the moment I reach my bed."

True to his word, he allows me a hasty exit and does not come knocking at my door. Guilt briefly washes through me, constricting my heart. However, all is soon forgot as my head melts into my pillow and dreams claim my attention.

≈✥≈

We are attending church today, being a Sunday. Upon arrival, it is most pleasing to see one's servants accommodated in a box pew, and that we have our own pew in a gallery. Our presence, of course, attracts much attention and speculation. It is with this in mind that Clément dressed me in my finest bonnet and pelisse, for first impressions are more worth the effort.

My attention during the sermon is captured by the parson, Mr Woodburn, who rouses one greatly with his preaching. One cannot help but feel chastised. I am sure the blush on my cheeks must be evident. Fornication surely does not apply to we married women, but perhaps my exuberance for my duties could be called sexual immorality? I am determined to behave with less frivolity and more propriety going forwards.

We greet those amongst the congregation with whom it is appropriate to do so and promises for calls are made. I shall never have a moment to myself, I can see it. However, upon congratulating Mr Woodburn on his sermon, I find myself being introduced to Dr Deacon. It is most gratifying to know one has a physician at one's disposal. I suppose it is owing to the number of gentry in this area that one has been found. I believe these two gentlemen could be interesting dinner guests; they both seem to have deep wisdom.

Lord Dellingby and I soon extricate ourselves and head home for a leisurely afternoon of reading, he in his study, I in the library.

However, my studies are interrupted.

"Lady Dellingby, I must confess my ailment, for it seems I cannot be parted from you without great distraction. And, at present there appears nothing demanding enough to occupy my thoughts," he informs me, leaning down so he may stroke my cheek with his fingers.

"Lord Dellingby, you are incorrigible. And after that fine sermon this very day too."

His response is to kiss my mouth most firmly. Forcing myself not to give in, I pull away.

"I am in earnest, my lord."

He frowns. "You are? But why? Are we not married? There can be no fear of God here."

"But, my lord, is such behaviour not excessive?"

He seats himself upon a nearby chair. "My dear, you have been most gently bred, and it is to your credit. But I would urge you not to take such sermons so much to heart. There can be no wrong-doing between man and wife. Besides, if I were bolder you may hear tales so shocking it may have you reconsidering your opinion on pre-marital indiscretions."

My mouth is agape. "My lord, you do not mean to tell me that you would condone such behaviour?"

"My love, you must not doubt I have committed such sins myself, but merely so I could serve you better as a husband."

I am left agog.

"And some amongst your own acquaintance were not so observant of their morals."

"Lord Dellingby! You cannot mean to say…you…with…no, I shall not hear it."

He chortles. "Be easy on that account. Of course, I have not lain with any of your friends. What do you take me for? However, I have it on good authority from others."

"Oh, men brag about many such falsehoods amongst each other, I am sure."

"You may choose to disbelieve it if it makes you happy."

"You mean you believe such scandalous declarations?"

"Would it be entirely indiscreet for me to make mention of Miss Plimpton's efforts to secure her husband?"

"She…?"

He grins. "Have I shocked you? I can see I have. She was most determined to claim Meltcham despite the opinions of both their fathers. Quite why she should be so set upon him is beyond me, but there it is."

Lord Dellingby shrugs, all nonchalance.

"I cannot believe it. I know she is a little modern and forthright, but this?"

"Oh, my dear little dove, how much you would swoon had you but opened your eyes and truly seen all about you."

"About me?"

"Certainly. You attended balls and parties where had you but glanced behind pillars and into corners you would have blushed to bear witness to the goings on of those in attendance."

"Surely not."

"You doubt me?"

"Of course not, not if you tell me you are in earnest."

He moves forward and kisses my forehead. "I am in earnest. And here lies the supposition you may also have indulged, if you can ever forgive such a notion. It is so commonplace, and I had feared your intentions were directed...well, perhaps it is best not to make mention of the past."

I stare at him through misted eyes. "Am I so very naïve?"

"Unspoilt, virtuous and beautiful," he whispers, pecking my lips.

"At least until you were properly wed," he adds with a wink.

Taking a raspy breath, his mouth sinks onto mine, his gliding tongue leaving no trace of thought except for one: him. When he is so attentive my mind is no longer my own, my body takes control and demands him.

"It is my privilege to educate you in the leud ways of life," he says, his voice rumbling right through my person.

Lord Dellingby has his not-so-wicked way with me in the library, surrounded by knowledge which sees not. I am left wondering how such delights could ever be viewed as anything other than holy and dismiss the sermon as being wholly without foundation. For surely there can be nothing amiss when one is left feeling so complete.

❧ Chapter 40 ❧

A letter has arrived this morning from my sister-in-law. Anxious about her situation, I sit down to read it immediately.

Letter from Lady Longland, 26th August 1814

To the Marchioness of Dellingby,

Be not alarmed upon receiving this letter from me, for I have glad tidings for you. The distressing nature of the conversation between our husbands brought about a faint shortly after your departure. My maid had the foresight to become most concerned, having noticed what I had failed to. A doctor was called to confirm her suspicions, and it seems, in short, that I am in the family way.

I know you will join with me in celebrating such wonderful news and shall not mind such vulgarities in a letter. And you know, it has lifted my spirits so that all seems brighter. What a laugh, the grass seems greener and the sun seems warmer. I have quite lost all sense in my happiness.

Now, tell me by means of reply how you find Sheringley Hall. I always enjoyed my time there and wished we were able to remain longer. We so seldom had opportunity, alas. It is wonderful knowing you may make a wonderful home of the place. I do hope to pay you a visit soon, all being well. How terrible I am to impose myself, but you have already been so kind as to extend the invitation, so there can be no offence in my making mention of my anticipation.

This is but a brief letter, as I had only this news to convey, but it seemed urgent as I picked up my pen. Perhaps you will laugh at my impulsiveness. I beg your forbearance.

Yours faithfully,

Isabella Longland

I do not quite know what to make of such a strange letter, but I am sure there is more to this than I am acquainted with. Determined to learn more, I march straight into the study.

"Lord Dellingby, I must speak with you."

He looks startled then annoyed, as his brows lower into a scowl. "Lady Dellingby, what do you mean by coming into our company in such a manner?"

His gruff response is most alarming. Then my eyes turn towards the other man in the room.

"My apologies, Mr Baxter, I was unaware Lord Dellingby had company."

"No offence taken, my lady," he assures kindly.

Turning back to Lord Dellingby, I tell him, "But I must beg a moment of your time, if I may."

"There is nothing that cannot wait," is his rather rude response.

Waving the letter which remains in my hand, I insist, "But I have received word from your sister, my lord."

"Ah, well that is quite a different matter. Pray excuse us for but a few moments, Mr Baxter."

"Very good, my lord," he says, bowing and exiting the room.

"Now, kindly tell me what is so urgent as to cause such a disturbance."

"My lord, I do not understand quite why I am met with such abruptness, but your sister, The Countess of Longland has written to me with the most astounding news. She says she is in the family way."

"Is that all?"

"You are going to deny any prior knowledge?"

"My dear, how could I know of such things?"

"Argh, Lord Dellingby, do not think me so stupid as to believe such an announcement. This is your doing, and it may place her in ever more danger."

He rolls his eyes and then taps the desk with his fingers repeatedly before smoothing it. "Lady Dellingby, it was my belief it was safer for yourself not to be in possession of full knowledge. My error was forgetting your thirst for truth. Yes, I spoke with one of the servants I believed to be cowered yet trustworthy. I had it arranged that Lady Longland should make a show of a faint and that a doctor would be sent for to confirm the happy news."

"But why?"

More eye rolling. "For the Earl of Longland shall not wish to risk harm to his heir. She will be safe."

"Until he discovers the lie and his wrath is increased all the more."

A deep sigh comes from him. "My dear, it is a very real possibility that she is in fact with child. My sister is a married woman, in case I am in need of reminding you. And the doctor was well paid to, err, ensure the chances."

I gasp shrilly. "Lord Dellingby! Of all the vile actions. You cannot seriously be in earnest. Do you truly mean you would allow such a dastardly act, nay, actively encourage it?"

"Now you see why I was loath to inform you of the particulars. The earl, of course, must never know. If she is indeed in the family way, he must be in no doubt the child belongs to him."

My hand rubs my stomach. "But of course. That much is plain. But it is all a little sick-making. How utterly distasteful."

"My dear, I would rather she bore the child of a footman than that scoundrel."

"Lord Dellingby, you go too far. But I cannot say I am wholly against your opinion."

"You see the sense of it?"

"Why, of course, she was in great need of protection, and you have done what you could without compromising the show of honour. Although I cannot approve of the method. And what if she fails to produce a baby? He is no fool."

"My lady, you try my patience. Women lose babies all the time. Blood is readily obtained for her bedding should she not begin to show at the appropriate time. And if she now carries the other man's child, well, some pregnancies are known to tarry."

"Oh, please spare me any more mention of such issues. I thank you for your candour." I curtsey and stomp out of the room.

Mr Baxter passes me on his way back to the study and bows his head. I do likewise whilst not breaking my stride.

"Clément, some wine, quickly. And my smelling salts," I call as I find my room.

Slumping down into my day chair, I do my best not to swoon. Really, it is too much. What monster have I married that could even consider let alone put into practice such a scheme?

Clément is wafting the foul-smelling salts under my nose which scrunches against the pungent bottle. Meurgh! As soon as she sees me recoiling, she begins working the fan.

"Are you well, my lady?" she keeps asking.

Eventually, I am able to make my reply, "I am revived, thank you, Clément."

Taking a sip of wine, I ensure my senses are all returned.

"What a thing to happen. Can I get you anything else, my lady?"

"No thank you, Clément. I believe the danger has passed," I tell her, patting her hand.

She really is a marvellous maid. I cannot fathom what I should do without her.

It takes some time to deliberate upon all Lord Dellingby informed me of. The more I think on it, the more the sense is revealed. But it is all so underhand and vulgar. Having not met with her doctor, I can only hope he is at least a reputable physician and not some lowly surgeon, or heaven forbid an apothecary. No, surely it was a physician. I am certain they will have one nearby. Oh, Lor', I do hope he was not old or repulsive. No, I cannot bear to ruminate upon it.

The rest of the day, as I attempt to concentrate on my duties, however, the unwelcome thoughts keep returning. At dinner, it is quite an effort to partake of anything whatsoever.

It is a terrible duty the next day, as I visit the poor, elderly and sick in the village. Not that the duty itself is irksome. I am glad to do it and used to accompany Mama sometimes as she did the same. The estate has ample supply of provisions which may assist them.

Mrs Hinchley accompanies me, as she has been undertaking this errand in the absence of anyone in the house. Upon our rounds, we meet with Dr Deacon. My stomach turns as I curtsey, and the image of him impregnating anyone leaps into my mind. However, it is soon overcome as he talks of his work, which happily concentrates on the sick.

He had not been visiting the poor, of course. Perhaps they are better off for that, though. I have heard such dreadful accounts of these medical men that I am rather suspicious of some of their methods. I do all within my power to avoid the need of calling upon their services. Still, Dr Deacon seems learned enough; perhaps his assistance may prove useful should I ever require it.

The next couple of days are much taken up with calls and household matters. It's quite exhausting, and I am not yet settled into a routine. And now we are about to depart once more, and this time we are destined for the Dowager Countess Mettingford. She was married to Lord Dellingby's uncle on his papa's side. He passed away a few years ago, leaving his son to inherit, along with his wife. So, the old countess moved away, choosing a cottage by the sea instead of remaining in the house with her son.

The journey from Norfolk to Great Yarmouth is only around four hours, so is no great burden.

"Do calm yourself, my dear. My aunt is not so eager to find fault with tiny details," Lord Dellingby mutters as I smooth my skirts for the umpteenth time.

It cannot be helped. I am so eager to make the best impression. All I have heard is how fearsome she is.

"Ahem, my apologies."

Doing my best to still my hands, I try gazing out at the view from the window. Lord Dellingby breathes in deeply.

"Ah, we are close," he announces.

The sweet, salty aroma drifts tantalisingly through the window. The Countess' house is situated very close to the sea. It is most exciting, for I have never before been to the seaside.

The sun glitters upon the softly undulating waves that I can see from the clifftop as the carriage rumbles on.

"Beautiful," I whisper.

"Quite."

I start a little, having not expected a reply, having not fully intended to speak. I look across and exchange a smile.

The carriage pulls up to what cannot in all seriousness be called a cottage. Even to my eyes, this house is larger than that. Admittedly, it is a great deal smaller than the Hall but is similar in size to the Fairdown Lodge. A fine residence for a lady on her own.

A magnificent lady greets us as we are shown inside. Her clothes are fine, and much care has clearly been taken over them. A mob cap with a great many frills and much lace adorns her still brown hair.

In my mind, I had seen her as being more advanced in years and had therefore anticipated a withered, greying woman. Now I realise my foolishness, as she is not much older than Mama. This clearly makes sense as she is an aunt, not a grandmother. I suppose it was the manner with which she was spoken of that gave me the impression.

I suddenly feel dowdy in comparison but refuse to allow my hands to adjust my apparel, no matter how sorely they are tempted.

"Aunt Mettingford, how good it is to see you," Lord Dellingby greets with a smart bow.

"Nephew, it has been a good deal too long since our last meeting."

"Well Aunt, I hope you will forgive my negligence once you have met my wife. Might I introduce the Marchioness of Dellingby to you?"

"It would be a disappointment if you did not since that is the purpose of your visit."

Looking at me, her keen, brown eyes travel the full length of my body.

At length, with a nod of her head, she says, "I am pleased to meet you, Lady Dellingby. I have heard a great deal about you, and none of it has done you full justice."

"I thank you, Lady Mettingford, you are too kind," I reply with my deepest curtsey.

"Now, do not spoil it by toadying, girl, not when I am inclined to think well of you."

"Very good, my lady," I return, inclining my head, and the hint of a smile showing.

My goodness, she is bold indeed. It is hard to know what best to say, for too much is clearly going to be as bad as too little. But I admire her forthrightness. I am sure to know the instant I cause her displeasure or amusement.

"Well, I cannot stand about all day, do take a seat," she declares, sitting herself onto a chair.

Without even having to call for it, a tea service is brought in to us by a smart looking woman.

"How fares your papa, Dellingby?" she asks over her teacup.

"Alas, not much improved. In all honesty, I fear he may be worsening."

"I am sorry to hear it. You should have him brought to the seaside. It has done me the world of good. Lady Dellingby, during your stay, I hope you shall join me in the bath house, for it will set you up for all that is yet to befall you."

"I should like that very much, thank you, my lady. To my regret, we were not at Fairdown Lodge long enough for me to venture into Bath."

"What? You were so close yet did not so much as partake of its waters? Nephew, what were you thinking of? You have deprived poor Lady Dellingby of a great delight and good health."

"Indeed, I hope soon to return to remedy the omission, Aunt. But we were in haste to make our journey up to see Pater," Lord Dellingby explains.

"Well, make sure that you do."

She turns back to me. "It is a delightful town, and the assembly rooms there are one of the finest you shall see. In fact, if you set a date for your excursion, I have a good mind to accompany you. It has been too long since I was there."

Oh Lor', all those hours stuck in a carriage are bad enough without having to fear the derision of your travelling companion.

"It may not be for some time. I have had but one week at home at Sheringley, and there is much to be done."

"I do not envy you a jot. The setting up of one's household is a tiresome task. I hope that at least your staff are proving themselves useful."

"Oh yes, the housekeeper, Mrs Hinchley has proven herself most reliable already. And I my own maid has remained with me, of course —"

"Yes, yes, I am sure they are all very good. A simple yes would have sufficed."

Oh Lor', I have upset her.

"You own house seems most pleasant," I try.

"One makes do."

"It must be wonderful to be so near the sea."

"I find it beneficial to my health. Of course, I insisted upon a house high up. It smells too much of fish down in the town, but one cannot hold it against them. They must make their living by some means."

"Quite."

Once we finish our tea, the countess announces, "It is time for my afternoon airing. I invite you both to join me for a short walk along the cliffs here. I cannot bear to be indoors all of the day."

"A trait you share with my good wife, Aunt," Lord Dellingby supplies.

"Is it now? I confess I am surprised. Young ladies today always seem preoccupied with a pale complexion, which I note the marchioness boasts herself."

"My mama always made sure I was well covered when I ventured out," I explain, despite not having been directly addressed.

A glower gets thrown my way. "Well, it was thoughtful of her, I suppose. Shall we?"

Without waiting for a response, she stands and walks out of the room. Our pelisses and bonnets are instantly supplied. I see Clément has managed to change my travelling one with one more fitting for such an occasion.

Suitably wrapped up, we venture out, Lord Dellingby in the middle, a lady on each arm. As we round the corner, a great gust of wind catches us, and it is a good job my bonnet fastenings were so closely tied, else it would have flown clean away.

"Wonderfully bracing," Lady Mettingford declares, walking with even more purposeful strides.

She sets the pace, and it must be said, it is as fierce as the woman herself. It seems everything has a purpose in her life. Although I am inclined to think her concerns over health are wholly unwarranted, for she seems to be the most robust of us all.

The noise of the wind means conversation is difficult without raising one's voice to an unseemly level, so we remain mostly silent as we take the well-trodden path. The view is stunning, even when viewed through watery eyes. The bustling town can be seen in the distance. And there is a great expanse of sand, with waves washing up onto it. Gulls cry their piercing "caw caw caw" as they glide above us.

If I were a lady living by myself, children grown and married off, I do believe I should like to live in such a place. But I am yet to discover the opportunities of socialising. Perhaps it is too confined and unvarying. I cannot imagine many of the gentry choose to live so remote. It is tiresome having to be too much in company, but it should be terribly lonesome to be without it entirely.

We have not been gone a full hour when we return to the cottage, as the countess insists upon calling it. The walk does indeed prove invigorating. I feel in full health as we return. Perhaps there is something in her recommendation. However, my cheeks are chilled and ruddy, I note, passing a looking glass.

"What a fine promenade that was," I declare, removing my bonnet.

"It was adequate," my hostess replies.

Oh Lor', am I not even permitted to compliment her choice of activity? Her forthright manner is rapidly becoming more irksome than admirable.

We remain talking quietly and modestly until it is time to dress for dinner. Clément is most attentive. She surely also noticed the meticulousness of the countess.

Approaching the dining room, I overhear my companions' conversation.

"So, you see, Aunt, how Lady Longland would appreciate the womanly cares of one such as yourself."

"Well, I am the nearest thing the poor girl has to a mother."

"Pardon the intrusion," I say with a curtsey, not wishing to dally and be caught in eavesdropping.

"Not at all, girl. We were discussing the merits of another female's presence when one is in a delicate state. I am rather inclined to agree with Dellingby, that I should stay with his sister so long as she requires it. What say you?"

"I think it a superb notion," I reply, marvelling at my husband's manipulation.

Surely, not even the earl could stand against so formidable a character. She would brook no insubordination. A better guardian for my new sister could not be found should one search throughout the entire country. Yes, a fine plan, which perhaps should have occurred to me.

"Then it is settled. I shall travel with you when you return to Sheringley. You know my eagerness to see the old place. And then I may travel safely on to dear Lady Longland. Such a sweet girl."

Oh Lor', I am sure that the Hall is not yet fit for her viewing. How many faults she shall find. But it cannot be helped. She is determined to set out at the earliest opportunity, and I would not delay a protector for Isabella.

With my bathing suit made and ready but a couple of days after, the countess and I make our way to the bath house. It is not with a little trepidation, for it seems a curious thing to do, let alone in the company of one's husband's aunt.

It is with great relief that I am led to a well-partitioned room. Goodness heavens, but I am forced to wear long trousers beneath my gown, which itself is loose about my top. A girl is on hand to assist me into the large tub.

"Oh, it's warm," I cry as my toes enter the water.

"Goodness, are you in already?" the countess enquires from the other side of the screen.

"Not quite, merely a toe. I had expected sea water to be cold."

"Tsk, silly girl. If one wished for cold sea water, why not simply walk into the sea from a bathing machine? No, it is far too brisk even for my tastes. This is far more civilised."

There is even a lit fire nearby, warming me further. It is all rather pleasant as I wallow in the warmed water which has herbs added. My eyes close as my thoughts drift away.

A waitress brings a glass of water to me, which I almost spit out.

"The seawater in these parts has many great benefits," the girl reminds me, thus forcing me to swallow the vile concoction.

It would not do for the countess to be alerted to the fuss I long to make. I fail to see how this can be of any benefit, but I have been assured by so many that it must be. Not that I felt in the least unhealthy before. My constitution is a strong one. However, one must appease one's relatives.

I stifle a giggle as I hear a disgusted, "Eurgh," from the other side of the screen. Of course, I venture no comment. There was nothing to hear, surely.

At the allotted time, warm towels and robes are brought in. I wonder if there is a way for Clément to provide such each day; it is rather sumptuous.

Dressed in our day wear, Lady Mettingford leads me into the assembly room, where I'm pleased to receive a proper tea. It doesn't fully remove the salty aftertaste which still lingers, but it helps.

"This is The Marchioness of Dellingby. You know my nephew, of course. They are recently arrived at Sheringley Hall, but have condescended to pay me a visit," and other such announcements are made to those amongst the countess' acquaintance.

Oh Lor', it is almost as if I am back on the marriage mart, I am so paraded. But she must be pleased with me to boast so magnificently. And the raising of eyebrows is surely a sign her friends are in approval too.

The good lady even confides to some of her forthcoming visit to her niece. Poor Lady Longland cannot be informed herself as yet. But then I daresay that the countess needs no invitation or acceptance, she will arrive and there can be no argument made.

In the carriage, on our return to her house, I venture, "Lady Mettingford, you must allow me to thank you for such a remarkable experience. What a wonderful day you have provided me with."

Her only response is a slow dip of her head with the barest hint of a smile.

☙ Chapter 41 ☙

Having spent time with Lady Mettingford, I conclude that she is as kind as she is fierce. It is perhaps a little disguised by her outer prickly demeanour, but her heart is full. This is the thought which keeps repeating as we all journey to Sheringley together, mostly in the silence her ladyship is partial to.

Mercifully, she seems to keep her opinions to herself as we enter my marital home. I sent word ahead, so the staff could ensure it was gleaming more than ever for our arrival. They have performed their task admirably well.

She stays but two nights, but they are perhaps the most taxing of my life. Every moment seems full of opportunity to show my total inadequacy. My nerves are in tatters by the time Lady Mettingford departs.

"Lady Dellingby, it is clear to me that you are a most accomplished young lady. Sheringley Hall is in good hands, which is most gratifying. You have it in good order in so short a time, which is no mean feat. Carry on in this vein and you shall be handsomely rewarded."

"Why, thank you, Lady Mettingford," I reply, my breath catching.

It is a wonder I do not swoon on the spot I am so taken aback. High praise indeed, which I was sure would never be pronounced from her lips. Goodness!

"Do close your mouth, dear. It is most unbecoming."

"Dellingby, you take good care of her now. She is a rare find. I hope you are sensible of your good fortune," she tells my husband.

"Indeed I am, Aunt."

"Very well then. I bid you both adieu. I shall be happy to return on my way home, when e'er that may be."

"Indeed, your stay with Lady Longland may be of considerable duration, I fear. But you are most welcome at any time, Aunt."

With her customary head tilt, she turns and glides out of the door and into her carriage. As soon as our door is closed behind her, my shoulders slump and a long breath whispers out. Realising my error, I immediately pull myself up but laugh as I realise Lord Dellingby is the precise reflection of me.

"Oh, my lord, what a reaction to such a fine lady."

"Quite dishonourable. But, by Jove, she is a most trying woman to be much in company with."

"I cannot, in all honesty, wholly contradict your opinion, my lord."

He accompanies me into the drawing room and we both slump into our chair with more sighs. Lord Dellingby calls for wine.

"I have received word Lord Alverbury shall be arriving the day after tomorrow."

"That will be a welcome change for you," I reply, secretly cursing his arrival.

Am I to have no time to myself to truly get to grips with my household? But, as Lord Dellingby's friend, I imagine they will amuse one another, leaving me to some peace during the day.

Trying to recall his choices at suppers we attended in each other's company, I plan our meals accordingly once Lord Dellingby departs to his study. And promise to make a more concise note of his preferences during his stay.

I also plan a dinner party for Saturday, which is something I would have done even if Lord Alverbury were not to be with us. However, it coincides nicely. His presence will surely be a reassuring one as I become better acquainted with our neighbours.

⊷⊶

Goodness me, but Lord Alverbury is even more morose than ever when he arrives. It is a relief when Lord Dellingby takes him off for some shooting the next day. One is somewhat concerned he may turn the gun upon himself, but I trust my husband shall prevent such a catastrophe befalling him.

My time is much taken up with book keeping and discharging duties. The guest rooms are all prepared, in the event anyone else descends upon us overnight. Menus have been selected under the care of Mrs Hinchley and staff are fully organised.

Our dinner conversations are subdued. I am certain Lord Dellingby has discovered the source of Lord Alverbury's distress but has not disclosed it. Therefore, it is quite impossible to know which topics to avoid. Hence precious little being talked of at all.

However, in front of strangers, Lord Alverbury wears his socially acceptable mask once guests start arriving on Saturday. I suppose it is quite flattering he is comfortable enough around me, certain of our friendship, that he shows his true feelings at all.

Lord and Lady Winterthorpe are amongst us this evening, which is pleasing. Her husband seems as lively as she does and proves himself a great wit. Lord Dellingby is soon sparring with him across the table in games of words and amusing tales.

Having carved the roasts of meat, Lord Dellingby begins his toast. It is his first in our home, so he goes on at great length about the honour of being so happily situated and toasting each person at table. I am quite merry by the time the wine glasses are put down.

Looking around, the candlelit faces are all smiling or laughing. And the plates are emptied. A small sigh of relief escapes as my efforts are rewarded by murmurs of satisfaction. A hubbub echoes around me as small groups carry on their own conversations.

Lady Winterthorpe leads us ladies into the drawing room once the meal is completed. Small samples have been carefully arranged should any lady wish to pick up some needlework, having neglected to bring any with her. However, these are left untouched as we all converse together.

The ladies, although having met with me before, seem eager to learn more, and ask as many delicate questions as convention will allow. And I answer them all, but also fit in some questioning of my own, for I am as eager to know them better in return. I am duly informed of local news and which are the best warehouses hereabouts.

Following our sumptuous meal, I seem to have won the majority over already. It is of great comfort to be so easily accepted amongst the society of these fine women. For fine they are; such good manners as I had not thought to expect outside of London.

We are still conversing happily when the men enter the room.

"Shall we not have some music?" I ask, looking towards Lady Winterthorpe.

She plays the pianoforte with considerable skill but does not sing. I suspect this is owing to her skill being focussed upon playing and having neglected her voice. Perhaps an uncharitable thought, but it refuses to be suppressed.

Next, I am encouraged to perform, which I do with as much fervour if not more than when I was in London. Now it is for the benefit of my new friends, and not the men present, however. The ensuing applause confirms I did not disgrace myself.

As the evening progresses, there are even some duets. Lord Dellingby leads me to sit at the pianoforte for him. Warmth fills my heart and makes my cheeks glow as my soprano blends with his baritone voice, carrying me away into a dream. My eyes are misty as I gaze into his brown orbs, which reflect the candles about us. How I love this man beside me; it is almost overpowering.

Having quite forgot where I was, the thunderous applause is alarming.

"Quite beautiful," I hear someone declare.

"I am enraptured," says another.

Lord Dellingby squeezes my hand and places a kiss upon it as he leads me, blushing, back to my seat.

"That was quite the most extraordinary performance I ever beheld," Lady Winterthorpe whispers to me, one hand at her breast, the other wiping away a tear.

My own hand goes to my décolletage. "Oh really, you give me far too much credit."

"No, you must let me profess it. Never have I been so moved."

"Thank you, Lady Winterthorpe."

The next player begins, and we fall into silence, so we may observe respectfully. The fires roused by song are still aflame between my legs, and it is most uncomfortable to be thus indisposed in company. There can be no relief in the foreseeable future.

Looking across at Lord Dellingby, I see his eyes directed towards me. He inclines his head, smiles, and returns his attention to the performance. Perhaps he feels it too. Confound this longing.

The rest of the evening is pleasant, if not a little uneasy. I believe new friendships have been forged. A fine home, a good husband, agreeable friends; I would never have believed such fortune could befall me.

Once our guests are gone and I am able to retire to my bed, my fortune continues. Presumably once Lord Alverbury declared his inclination to retire, Lord Dellingby arrives in my room. He shows me with his body how much I am loved, and it is the greatest compliment of the evening.

෧෫෩

The house feels almost empty once Lord Alverbury leaves us, giving us each cause for continued concern. He is still without a wife of his own, which I am sure would give him distraction if not comfort. Perhaps I may find someone suiting once I am more in Society here; I shall endeavour to do so. He is such a kind, gentle man, and should not be left in such melancholy.

Having been put in mind of gloomy thoughts, I write to Lord Beauvrais in Canada, wishing him happiness and health, and updating him of my own situation. I do hope he is settling in nicely. It still grieves me to think of him so far away.

My life begins to fall into routine as the months pass. Calls and balls, finance and governance…it is an endless stream of people who fill my life. Appearances, visits, charity and patronage are all time-consuming. All the while I am observed and commented upon, for good or ill. And I grow increasingly tired. Horse riding lessens as time and energy do not permit as much as I should like.

Lady Kerkham and her husband visit from Hampshire as promised when last I was there. It is heart-warming to see a friendly face from home. We take the carriage and take a tour of beauty spots she is anxious to show me, which is most pleasing. And we have a fine time together.

I receive word of Lady Longland's progress. In her own words, she is now *grosse*, which is fortunate indeed. And Lady Mettingford is clearly performing her role of protector with alacrity, for the tone of my sister's letters is noticeably more cheerful.

Also, Lady Rohampton has sent word that she fears I will win our wager, so I am to take it she is now breeding. It is enough to make one slightly envious, as well as happy, of course. Such wonderful news, even if it has kept her from visiting.

Her accoucheur has recommended a lowering diet, but it seems not to be calming her bouts of morning sickness. Despite the plethora of fruits and vegetables, she declares herself much wearied. Indeed, this is evidenced in her handwriting, which has a distinct shiver to it. It is most concerning, and I long to go to her.

However, I am grown so weary myself that I cannot stir from my bed today. Lord Dellingby has insisted upon the attendance of Dr Deacon, which I am sure is highly unnecessary, but one cannot argue.

After some impertinent questions, and deplorable examining after checking whether I would take a pain, he declares I am in the family way. I confess I had not considered this may be the cause. Exhaustion from all my many duties seemed the more likely. But he is certain in his pronunciation of my condition and recommends staying abed whenever thus fatigued. It is most inconvenient, but I promise to follow his instruction.

Oh Lor', three women all carrying babes. God has been very good to us. Tears of gratitude trail down my cheeks. Naturally, they are swiftly dealt with.

Not long after the doctor departs, Lord Dellingby bounds into my room, sits upon my bed and holds me tight in his arms.

"Oh, my beautiful wife, is this true? You are…carrying my child?" he asks, his face beaming.

I nod. "It would appear so, my lord."

"My clever, beautiful, lady."

"Lord Dellingby, do calm yourself, if you please. It is not yet here."

"No, I am not to be mollified. I am the happiest of men," he says, squeezing me again, and kissing my forehead.

❧

Winter draws in and we all seem to begin a sort of half slumber. Parties are still attended, of course, but are not so plentiful as we concern ourselves with travel in inclement conditions.

News reaches me as I am in most need of amusement.

Letter from Lord Beauvrais, received 6th November 1814

To the Marchioness of Dellingby,

What a fortunate alliance you have by now made. You cannot fathom how happy such news made me, especially as it so soon followed a pang of heart. That your papa ever sought to have you believe you intended for Lord Emsby is dreadful indeed.

You are correct, he did set his men upon me when I left London. But you seem ignorant of the full reasons as to why. May God help me should such details be discovered by any but your eyes, but I am so far removed geographically, I take the chance in the hopes of enlightening you as to particulars.

You must have thought it odd indeed that he was so incensed by rumours of a mere duel, and one seemingly so wholly unconnected with himself. It was, of course, the merest excuse he could discover of exacting revenge upon me.

Some years ago, he made advances to…a mutual friend of ours. Those advances were obviously rejected, for who could welcome such from so foul a creature? He was most embarrassed to be flung aside. Here the seed of resentment was planted.

That seed only grew upon his discovery of that friend's attachment to myself. His hatred was given too much attention but had no means of escape. Our friend's demise did nothing to extinguish such flames. Indeed, I believe he lay the blame at my door for such, which fanned his ire all the more.

Had I thought for but a moment he would ever so much as insert himself into your presence, I should have sought you out and provided this explanation. Pray forgive that I missed this detail out of our dialogue. I was not in full presence of mind, you may recall. Perhaps I should have noticed and informed. But all that is left is for me to beg your forgiveness.

I am greatly relieved his marriage shall serve as a constant thorn in his side. May his suffering be of long duration. Truly, a more hideous beast never before roamed the land.

By the by, his men were soon informed of the true nature of their employer and championed my own cause. They left us at Halifax, seeking other towns for employment, and I have reason to believe they continue well.

So, there you have it, my sincerest, deepest felicitations on the far better man who has become your marriage partner. What I know of him, Dellingby is an honourable man. A little quiet perhaps, but you shall soon remedy that with your vivacity, Little Dove. I venture to foretell a most prosperous alliance and that the two of you shall rub along most happily.

Things continue well here. I have taken up enough paper, so shall say no more than that I am content.

It is with some relief I am now able to at least sign as myself, with continued affection,

Yours faithfully,

Beauvrais

Well, there I have it, an explanation of the extreme reaction of Lord Emsby. What a vile man he is. Oh Lor', but poor Lady Rathburn, I feel sorry for her. Whoever thought that possible? To be married to a man who cannot return any possible affection she may have for him. Oh well, she is not likely to feel much, it must be supposed. There was no great attraction except for his rank, and she has that. Perhaps only that. Oh dear.

The days grow hazy as I try to keep up with all my obligations. Mrs Hinchley proves she is worth every penny of her wages and takes a good deal off my hands. She almost goes so far as to forbid me from visiting the sick, but I am happy to allow her to take that duty on, for it cannot be a good idea for me to do so at present.

I celebrated Christmas and turned eighteen whilst resembling a prize turnip. It makes a change from the prize pig I was last year, all things considered. Having been given away like a breeding sow, one is now fulfilling the expectation.

My own accoucheur has put me on a strengthening diet, which includes the addition of claret. It is a pleasant medicine, so am taking the advice well. The removal of stays is also another happy adjustment to my predicament. Although, when one is attending functions, it feels perfectly brazen to go without such things.

This evening, we are attending a performance of *The Duenna* by a touring opera, which is most pleasing and has brought great anticipation to all my circle. Clément ties my dress more loosely and inserts more feathers into my hat, apparently to draw more attention upwards. A bourdaloue is also in my reticule, owing to my increased need for such things. I am assured an increase in urination is a healthy sign.

My spirits are invigorated, and my health revived. Lord Dellingby's head is held high as he leads me to our seat at the opera. There is a buzz of excitement in the air, along with much chatter. It puts me in mind of those days spent in London with Mama. How long ago they seem, and how I miss her. However, we shall soon be reunited so she may assist with my confinement.

The first act and scene start dark and dramatic, seizing my entire attention. I am brought to laughter several times throughout it is so diverting. Lord Dellingby only need nudge me back to wakefulness a few times. Each time he does, I look into those smiling eyes of his and count my blessings for such a husband. He does not censure my fatigue, and only gently teases from time-to-time.

It is a splendid evening, which my friends enjoy as much as I do. We are all achatter for a good while after, exalting its merits, and conspire to find ways of inducing more performers to visit us.

I have kept busy as long as possible over the seemingly endless months, but as my time draws near and I grow increasingly *grosse,* Lord Dellingby accompanies me to London. The distance is great, and I could happily forego it, but a lady is expected to undergo such things. So, armed with my birthing dress and Clément, we make the journey. I consider myself fortunate to have had the foresight not to plan my confinement during the winter.

It is an enormous relief when we finally arrive in one piece. Although, quite how the baby was not brought about by such carriage driving is beyond me. A birthing bed has been constructed in the lying-in chamber, which I quickly inspect before heading to my own room. There is no need for it today, and in all honesty, the sight of it sends shivers of absolute terror through me.

Lying in bed, I think upon the success of Lady Longland. She gave birth to a baby boy one month ago, making Dellingby an uncle. They are doing fine, I hear. It grieved me to not be able to pay them a visit, but really, I have been both busy and unwell, not that you would know it to see me, of course. Like all things, my discomfort has been concealed, and only Clément has borne any real witness to it.

But still my tears fall. Am I truly capable of bringing another person into this world? How is such a feat even possible? It must be so, for women do it all the time. But how? And the knowledge that not all mothers survive the ordeal rings like a bell in my head.

We attend all the usual functions, of course. However, dancing is prohibited by both my size and marital status. It is more amusing to stand and observe in any case. Was it but one year ago I was one of these girls? It is incredible to think it possible. How fast the time has gone, but how different I feel. It is but yesterday and yet an age away.

They are much to be pitied. How eager their smiles and attentions, these silly young ladies who cannot have any notion of what they are truly courting.

"You remain the belle of the room," my husband mutters at my side.

"Flatterer."

"And the most wondrous. For you have succeeded where they are yet to tread."

"Lord Dellingby, you are become quite vulgar," I admonish but smile despite myself.

Infuriatingly, we are separated. His friends take him off to play cards. And mine demand conversation, but not before I find a sofa to rest upon.

It is amusing to discover the young girls in attendance are sporting a slightly higher line of gown upon their bosom, more in the style for which I was censured last year. Beware the gossips of envy, for they are false whisperers.

My condition attracts many glances, and yet no questions arise. The girls must all burn with curiosity but are not permitted such impertinence. Hiding my smile behind my glass, a sense of satisfaction in holding a secret passes through me like water. For pity's sake, now I must relieve myself again.

Walking back to my perch, I note all the mamas pushing girls this way and that, gossiping with one another, presumably exchanging details on the most eligible present. Oh Lor', it strikes me that all too soon I shall be amongst their number.

Shall I too look upon the marriage mart as they do, locating the best match for my daughter? Or shall I be trying to protect my son? Of course, in that instance, I should not be present at all, but already I would like to be. Who else would be best to keep my boy away from fortune hunters?

"Lady Dellingby, you are as serious as ever," someone says.

As the brown-haired figure rises from its curtsey, I see a familiar face and attempt to stand. It is one I met for the first time but a year ago. Lady Meltcham, formerly Plimpton, puts a firm hand on my shoulder.

"My dear, you are in no condition to be forever rising and falling. Here, let me sit beside you."

Grasping her hand tightly as she sits, I exclaim, "It is so wonderful to see you. I had no idea of you being in town. How have I not seen you until now? You were not hiding from me?"

She giggles, but her eyes do not reflect her merriment. "Of course I would do no such thing. I discovered you would be here this evening, and simply could not stay away, so you see, quite the reverse is true."

"Then please explain yourself."

"Lady Dellingby, we are old friends, and I know I can tell you anything, but perhaps explanation would best wait until tomorrow. May I call upon you?"

"You know very well you are always welcome."

Before we can discuss anything further, supper is called, and my friend vanishes into the crowd like a wisp. Lord Dellingby soon replaces her and leads me to the dining room.

There is far too much on offer which I know I should not have, but how can one resist such temptation? I partake in a little of my favourite things and enjoy them most heartily. There is no accoucheur present to tell me anything to the contrary. Although, my man here in London is far more reasonable than the one I left behind in the country.

Seeing me delight in these simple pleasures, Lord Dellingby smiles his approval.

"It is good to see you so happy," he comments.

"Thank you. It is most satisfying to feel it too."

I take a sip of claret before asking, "Have you had much luck this evening?"

"Oh yes, quite. Poor Meltcham looked quite distraught at my win."

"Lord Dellingby, you have not taken money off our friends?"

"Taken? The very notion. My dear, it is what happens when one plays at the tables."

"I do wish you wouldn't."

"I'd wager even your noble papa could not remain away from it entirely. I'm in no danger. Do not worry about such trivialities." He plants a kiss upon my hand.

"Well, so long as there is no harm in it, I suppose you must do what you must."

His answering smile is wry and wonky, his eyes shimmering.

"You need not look so pleased with yourself. You know full well I remain uncomfortable with gambling."

"Yes, my love. As you know I would not do anything to vex you, at least, not without great cause. So, you saw Lady Meltcham?"

"Aye, all too briefly, but she has promised to pay me a call tomorrow. Although, I do not see her here. She did seem to depart quite swiftly."

"Hmm…"

"And what do you mean by that 'hmm'?"

"Nothing, of course, my dear, nothing at all."

I am brought into another conversation the other side of me, and cannot press further, which is most irritating. Not that I suspect I would glean much more from Lord Dellingby on the matter.

Fatigue draws my evening to a close after supper. It is surprising I remained so long, and our hostess commends me on my attendance at all as we take our leave.

≈୬ও৯

The next day, Lady Meltcham is good on her word and calls on me.

"Now, will you not tell me more?" I ask, the pleasantries completed.

"Ever forthright, my friend. Yes, there is no denying my situation, and I must share my woes with someone."

"Oh dear, you do sound most serious. Had I thought any great wrong had occurred I would never have dreamed of pressing for information."

She places her hand upon mine. "I know you would not."

Her eyes reflect such sadness it is as much as I can do not to cry, and yet without any idea as to why.

"You see, we were quite mistaken with Lord Meltcham."

"My dear, is he unkind?"

"Worse. He is in quite deep."

"No, but his family…?"

"His papa has cut all ties, at a loss what to do with him. He had warned him several times, for he had bailed him out of his debts repeatedly. But still he continues to gamble, even now. We are forced to creep about town, attempting to avoid creditors at every turn."

"Lady Meltcham, this is most shocking. What can be done? Tell me, how much did he lose to Lord Dellingby last evening? Let me at least make reparation for that."

She lowers my pleading hands. "You are too good. But it will not be near enough. It is quite hopeless."

"But what will you do?"

"We are to leave town without delay and must make our own way in the world. Lord Meltcham had hoped perhaps last night would prove an opportunity to regain some of his standing, but he lost what he already did not truly have. It was our last hope."

A dainty yet dirty handkerchief is raised to her eyes.

"No, I cannot accept it. There must be something that can be done," I declare.

"My dear friend. I have come to accept we are quite ruined. It helps not that it was all of my own doing."

"It was no such thing."

"But I forced Papa to accept him as a son-in-law. Even his own father tried to intercede but I would not listen to reason. If they had explained their full reasoning I should still not have heard, for I was blind to all but his goodness."

"I am sure they were not explicit as to their concerns. But will your papa not come to your aid?"

"He will accept me back into his house, but not him. How could I live without Lord Meltcham?"

"You still love him?"

She nods, her tears dripping down her cheeks. "I do. It is impossible not to, despite all."

"Let me go to Lord Dellingby and ask for his assistance."

"No, you must do no such thing. This is not his problem to deal with. It would be a disgrace to even ask."

"At least let me provide you something from my own pocket then. I have ten pounds I can give you this instant. At least it will keep a roof over your head until you find a remedy."

"He will only gamble it away."

"Then do not tell him."

"He knows all."

"Dear dear Diana, how can I let you leave my house in such a state?"

"And yet you must. I came only to inform and to bid my last adieu. I could not leave without seeing you when I learned of your being in town."

"Perhaps you should head for Canada like Lord Beauvrais?" I scoff.

"You know, that may be a sound idea. We can start anew. Nobody will know us there."

"Lady Meltcham, I was not in earnest."

"No, I am aware of that. But yet the idea has merit."

"The voyage is long and arduous. And I cannot lose another friend so far."

"You must consider you may lose her entirely if she stays."

I embrace her and allow my own tears to fall at last.

"You cannot be brought so low. It is too shameful. Go to your papa. Make him understand. Tell him what you told me."

"Perhaps," she says with a rueful smile.

"Please try. For me. And let me know how you get on."

"Goodbye, dear Anne."

"Oh, I cannot bear it. I bid you only farewell. Things will work out. We shall meet again."

"It is my fondest wish."

My friend leaves me with an aching heart. When Lord Dellingby comes to enquire how the visit went he discovers me lying prostrate, crying my eyes out.

"My dear, what ails you?" he asks, kneeling.

"It is only my distress."

"What on ever for? Surely nothing can be worthy of such sentiment."

"It is Lady Meltcham," I sob.

"Is she ill?"

"No. She is poor."

"What the deuce? I thought Meltcham a little low in spirits, but I had no idea he was destitute."

"See, Lord Dellingby, you see now? Promise me never to gamble again. You see what it does? And now my friend is ruined and is being forced to leave town, perhaps the country. And all because her husband plays cards and I know not what."

"Well, I daresay his illustrious parties did not help."

"Do not be glib, not now."

"I was merely…nevermind. It is all very unsettling."

He consoles and holds me until I can stop sobbing and draw breath.

"She means a great deal to you."

I nod. It was more a statement than a question.

"Is there nothing that can be done?"

"She refuses all assistance, not even the ten pounds I offered. She forbade me asking you for aid."

"Indeed, it would not be proper."

"What is propriety when one's friends are in distress?"

"Indeed. But what are they to do?"

"I implored her to seek out her papa. He had denied Lord Meltcham access and she declared she would not go without him. But I urged her to try again."

He kisses my forehead. "Let us hope he hears her pleas."

"Lord Dellingby, I am quite certain Queen Charlotte will understand my not being presented at court this visit. We have not sought a Drawing Room, and nor shall I. Standing around in a heavy dress in a hot room is not conducive to my current state."

"My dear, you quite mistake me. I merely mentioned it was a pity not to be done with the formality. I had no intention of seeing it through," he replies with a sigh and a glance to the heavens.

Bristling in my chair as best I'm able, I shoot him a glare. "I am glad to hear it."

He stands up to take his leave, but I reach out to take his hand. "No, please do not leave my side so soon. Forgive me my outburst. Indeed, I know not what has become of me of late. I seem to forever be at your throat. It cannot be helped. The more I try to control my temper, the worse it becomes."

He kisses my hand. "Do not think any more upon it. Did I not marry you for your vivacity?"

I smirk. "Perhaps, but surely there are limits to what even you can withstand?"

"And you are not near approaching them. Now, can anything be got to make you more comfortable?"

"Could you perhaps pass my fan? It is just beyond my reach, and it is such an effort to move, but I am grown quite warm. This August is mercifully not so hot as it could be, but I still feel it so."

He picks the item up, unfolds and wafts it before my face.

"Hmmm…" I moan, "You are most attentive."

"One does one's best."

"And succeeds. Thank you, my lord."

My eyes are closed, so the ensuing gentle kiss on my lips makes me jolt with surprise. However, a smile soon replaces the 'oh' on my mouth. I peck him back.

"You are too good to me, you know," I murmur.

"There is no such thing. But really there are pressing matters I must address, if you will forgive me," he says, passing me the fan.

I bow my head and lie back fully upon the chaise longue, a cushion beneath my back. Getting comfortable seems an impossible task now. Everything aches and my ankles are swelled beyond reason as well as my belly. Wafting my fan, I take deep breaths, trying to calm my nerves.

Mama enters the room with a knowing smile. She arrived two days ago and is doing her best to keep me in good humour. Even now she goes straight to the pianoforte and begins to play a sweet melody.

I have tried enquiring what to expect, but she will not be brought to speak upon the "vulgar subject of childbirth". Some form of hint would be helpful. Her silence only leads me to fear worse things than I had hitherto imagined. How ghastly is this to become?

On one hand, I wish this baby would arrive now, so my anxiety may be lessened. Yet, on the other hand, never before have I feared anything more.

My yelp of pain is somewhat unladylike. The pianoforte notes halt. My hand is rubbing my belly, my eyes scrunched in pain.

"Oh, my darling girl, are you alright?" Mama asks, rushing over.

"I do not know. Mama, it hurts."

"Your belly?"

I nod frantically, so she rings the bell.

"Help me get Lady Dellingby to her birthing room then send for the accoucheur," she commands.

"But it is too soon," I whine.

"Your baby appears to think otherwise. Now don't fret so. It is not so early as to be of concern. Come along," she cajoles, leading me away.

Hearing the commotion, Lord Dellingby runs up the stairs to join and assist us.

"Is it time, my darling dove?" he asks.

"It would appear so."

"Has the accoucheur been sent for?"

"It is all taken care of," Mama returns softly, a great deal calmer than him.

As we cross the threshold to the darkened room, I double over and cry out.

"Help me get her onto that contraption of a bed," Mama instructs.

She has made her feelings quite clear on birthing beds, asserting the chair is the only way to properly go about such things. However, Lord Dellingby has read up on the subject and has been advised this is now considered the best method and insists my safety is paramount. Of course, Mama and he had quite an argument over it, for she is equally concerned for my health. But I have promised to obey my husband and am inclined to think the thought of lying down preferable.

Clément arrives and helps me into my birthing dress, tucking up a layer under my arms. Fashion is hardly my key priority this instant, but it really is a ghastly garment.

The monthly nurse is by the bedside and ready with her own instruction. She chases Lord Dellingby through to the outer lying-in chamber, but not before he lays a familiar handkerchief beside my head on the pillow. It smells of him. I burst into tears at such sentiment, for surely it is his way of being by my side still, where I so long for him to be. Mistaking my tears, the nurse holds my hand and attempts to soothe my pain with words.

The nurse then sets about closing the curtains. No windows have been opened in this room since our arrival, the chimney has been stopped, and even the keyholes have been filled; there is no risk at all of drafts. But it is gloomy, even with candles lit. I reach for Mama's hand and squeeze it.

"Shh, it is alright, my darling," she soothes.

I want to tell her how scared I am. I want to cry more, and perhaps scream. Oh, Mama, how terribly frightened your little girl is, and how much pain she is enduring. Do you know? Help me, Mama.

But you raised a brave lady, and I am doing my utmost not to make a scene, to bear all with the greatest decorum possible. Trying so very hard. Yet a whimper escapes as my lower belly goes taught, ripping pain through me.

The accoucheur arrives and checks all the preparations have been made.

"Very good, she is progressing well," he declares, but I am unsure to whom he is addressing, for my back is to him.

The pain begins to subside, and I have the urge to get up and walk. Mama goes to stop me, but the accoucheur contradicts her, "Your Grace, her ladyship may walk if she is so inclined."

Mama glowers but helps me to my feet. I pace about the room in circles, stopping every now and then to gasp through the next bout of pain. The nurse encourages me to drink some barley water.

"Caudle was preferable for mothers in my day," Mama mutters, partaking in some herself.

The spicy, sweet, hot drink has been forbidden me, to my regret. I rather think Mama who has been through this might be able to form an opinion on such matters.

Bread is my only nourishment as the hours pass, and the pain increases. Lord Dellingby can hold back no more, and is now by my side, aiding me in my promenade.

"I could hear your discomfort, and thus it became my own," he whispers.

"I rather think not," I tell him, wincing with the next tightening.

"Be that as it may, I could not remain at bay and so am come to your side."

"Your ladyship, would you perhaps favour lying down now?" the accoucheur suggests.

I nod and find myself being assisted to the bed. A chorus of encouraging words floats about me as I lie down. The pain has worsened, and I cannot bear it. Something must be wrong. Squeezing Lord Dellingby's hand, I feel a bearing down inside me, which draws out a wail.

My world erupts into darkness and pain.

Never before have I seen anyone in so much pain. I saw ewes on my father's estate deliver their young, and it was nothing at all like this. My poor wife is bearing more than she is allowing, I know, but still she screams.

Fearing she no longer knows me, or perhaps herself, I squeeze her hand continually and whisper soft words to her. Her mama's concern is etched in her furrowed brow. And the accoucheur is making a great deal of fuss. I cannot think this is normal behaviour. My heart beats in my chest until I fully believe it shall burst its confines. My throat is dry but can take no refreshment. If men could but cry, I should disgrace myself alongside my wife whose tears can no longer be kept at bay.

"Good God, man, what-on-ever do you propose to do with those?" I all but yell as the accoucheur holds up a large metal implement akin to scissors.

"Your lordship, these are forceps. Quite common nowadays, I assure you. They will help the baby arrive more steadily."

"You are certain no harm shall befall either mother or baby?"

"I would hardly use them otherwise, your lordship."

"Of course. Forgive me."

I am left feeling rather stupid yet concerned. I cannot begin to count the many hours we have already spent in this chamber, but it borders on too many, of that I am certain. The nurse looks just as concerned as I but says nothing. Surely if there were any real danger she would interject.

The appearance of a man so near the area of my wife only I should have access to is most disconcerting. Rage bubbles within me, making my fists clench at my side. But my reason forces me not to strike the man who declares he is assisting. May God help him if he fails to keep both of them alive.

Lady Dellingby's hair clings to her head, and she is almost in a froth, making her appear more as if she's run the Epsom Derby; far from her normal perfect appearance. But this is not so alarming as her eyes which appear to roll when her eyelids allow sight of them.

Please, dear God above, do not claim Lady Dellingby. She is so very dear to me and is much needed here. Please show us grace and mercy. You cannot claim her.

Ear-splitting cries erupt. The accoucheur holds up a bloody, wriggly ball of flesh.

"Your lordship, your son is delivered," he declares.

"Do you hear that, Little Dove? Our son. You have brought us a son, you clever girl."

She smiles but makes no answer. I lean down and kiss her head. Her Mama is at her front, stroking her daughter's hair from her face.

"My wonderful daughter, you have made us all so very proud," she says, wiping moisture from her eyes.

"I'm so tired," Lady Dellingby whispers, barely audible.

The accoucheur fusses over the baby and hands it to the nurse.

"Just a little longer, your ladyship. Push when you feel you need to. Have no fear."

"Are you not going to pull?" the Duchess asks.

"No, Your Grace. It is not the done thing nowadays. Lady Dellingby is quite capable all on her own, are you not?"

She nods, but I am quite at a loss as to what they are referring. Is another child to be born? My wife does not seem entirely sure.

Bile rises to my throat and the rooms spins a little as a blood-soaked bundle of sheets is lifted away. So much blood.

The dry shift is pulled down to cover Lady Dellingby's modesty, and I am able to sit on the edge of her bed. Leaning down, I leave another kiss upon her head. She closes her eyes with a deep sigh, her grip on my hand is released.

Glancing up, I look at the nurse and accoucheur in turn, a silent question I dare not give utterance to held within my breath.

"Her ladyship is tired after her ordeal. Let us allow her to sleep," the male midwife says.

I sigh deeply. Sleep. Very well, that is acceptable. Of course she is tired. Now he comes to make mention of it, I'm rather sleepy myself. As others leave the room, I seek comfort in a chair near the bed and doze off alongside the mother of my son.

With no idea of whether it is day or night, I ring the bell as Lady Dellingby stirs. Her murmurs having woken me.

The accoucheur struts into the room, along with a servant carrying a bowl of steaming broth.

"How does her ladyship fare?" he asks, more in her direction than mine.

She groans a little.

"Hm, won't you try a little broth, your ladyship?"

I try to help her into a sitting position, but she cries out.

"Or perhaps a little laudanum first, hm?" the accoucheur quickly suggests.

He spoons some of the liquid into her mouth and declares more sleep will soon see her right. Until she full revives, I remain sceptical.

I do manage to partake of a little broth myself. Lady Dellingby is quite insensible as she sleeps soundly.

"Pardon me, my lord, but an express has come," my valet interrupts.

"Thank you, Oliver," I tell him, not entirely meaning it.

Whatever news is contained within can wait until my wife is recovered. Nothing can be as important as that. I place the letter onto the table without so much as glancing at it.

Oliver clears his throat. "There is also a change of clothes in your dressing room should you desire it."

Casting my gaze downwards, I acknowledge my dishevelled state. "Yes, perhaps that would be for the best."

Checking Lady Dellingby is still sleeping, I quietly make my way to change my attire and have a quick wash.

"Pardon my asking, but how does Lady Dellingby do, my lord? We are most anxious about her health below stairs. I hope you will forgive the impertinence of my asking."

Not having the strength to be angered, I inform him of her condition.

"I am most sorry to hear it, my lord. Please, let us know if there is anything at all she requires, and we will ensure her ladyship receives it."

"Thank you," I reply, and dismiss him from my presence.

He means well, I am sure of it, but he was correct; it was an impertinence. And my concern rises with every mention. I cannot bear to think of what may happen; the possibility is inconceivable.

Sitting back down by my love's side, I take up the communication which arrived so inopportunely. My heart stops upon seeing the black edging and sealing wax, as I consider perhaps my father has taken a turn for the worst. The notion halts my fingers in their progress of opening the letter.

Forcing myself to proceed, I tear it open.

Letter from Sir Reginald Rohampton, 7th July 1815

To the Marquess and Marchioness of Dellingby,

It is with deepest regret and sorrow that I write to inform you of the passing of Lady Rohampton. She passed away this evening during childbirth. The accoucheur successfully brought our daughter from her thereafter, who shall benefit from her mother's name only. I can write no more than this at present. It is more than I can bear to write these few words, but I am aware Lady Dellingby will be most affected by this news, and it should be brought to her attention without delay.

Yours faithfully,

Sir Reginald Rohampton

Good God! What is this? Surely such a calamity cannot befall so dedicated a pair. They were so happy. Panic constricts my throat and threatens to overwhelm me as I consider I may also soon become a widower. No, I will not join those ranks, damn it.

I rush nearer Lady Dellingby's side to check on her state of health, to reassure myself she still yet breathes. However, I am alarmed at the heat of her forehead and immediately call for the accoucheur.

"Dear me, this is an unfortunate turn of events. Her ladyship seems to have developed puerperal fever. I shall perform a bloodletting immediately," he announces, readying his instruments.

"You mean childbed fever?"

"I fear so. It should not be possible for any miasma to enter here, but it surely has."

I am asked to leave but flatly refuse. Lady Dellingby would not like me to abandon her when she is most in need of my presence. Whether she knows I am here or not, my place is by her side.

The procedure is rather grizzly, and I am forced to avert my eyes. To see such actions performed on one's wife is really quite horrendous. It seems to my uneducated mind that she has been through enough trials already but must bow down to superior medical knowledge.

Bloodletting has been performed on my father, but I was not present. A fact for which I am now grateful. The opening in the arm is larger than I had anticipated.

The doctor is still not satisfied as her temperature continues to run high, and she complains of severe pains in her abdomen and head. So, a dose of jalap is issued, and a purging ensues.

My wife falls into a feverish sleep. After a few hours, the accoucheur returns and takes more blood.

"I should like some pineapple," my dearest one mutters in a state of delirium.

I ring for a servant directly. "I say, is there some way of extracting the juice from a pineapple? Lady Dellingby has expressed a wish for some, and I hardly think her capable of eating such fibrous fayre."

"Juice from a pineapple, my lord? In all honesty, I cannot be sure, but I shall ask cook at once," he says, dashing away.

"Your lordship, do you think this course of action wise?" the accoucheur asks.

"What is there to doubt? Lady Dellingby wishes for pineapple, so she shall have it, by Jove."

"But is it too much? Surely barley water would be best? I fear Lady Dellingby knows not what she asks and perhaps should not be taken so literally."

For a moment I am stunned motionless, but then rise to my feet and look the devil straight in the eyes.

My voice is firm and admittedly a little raised. "Her ladyship has made a request, sir. As her very life hangs in the balance, no request is to be denied her. If she wishes for rabbit, a broth shall be brought, if she desires brandy it shall be provided. If she asks for the moon, by Jove, I would do my utmost to bring it to her. Do I make myself understood?"

"Quite so, your lordship," he replies quietly, slightly backing away as he bows before departing hastily.

As time goes by, I begin to worry such a task is beyond my kitchens, or that infernal accoucheur has intervened. However, as I am about to give up all hope, a glass filled with yellow liquid appears. Taking it from the servant, I hold the glass to Lady Dellingby's lips and encourage her to drink. She manages a few sips before falling back onto her pillow.

Another day passes with her writhing in pain, becoming incoherent at times, silent at others. Medical procedures are performed every few hours. More juice is brought; she has seemingly developed quite a taste for it.

Lady Dellingby's mama is a frequent visitor to the room but cannot bear to see her daughter so pained for long and so excuses herself at regular intervals. For now, I am alone, my wife is sleeping, but so terribly deeply as to appear quite lost.

"My dear, sweet Anne, come back to me. You cannot leave us. We have a son who sorely needs his mama. *I* need you," I whisper.

I take her pale hand in mine and caress it, sometimes kissing it, but never letting go. It is as if this is our only surviving link. She seems so very pale, more than is healthy. Her stillness is almost deathly. I am unmanned.

"Little Dove, do not leave us, I beg of you," I repeat, this time through tears, "I could not bear it, I tell you. You have promised to obey me. Well, I command you to live. Do you hear me? I order you to stay with me, with us. So, you see, there is no argument in the matter. Your duty is here, and mine will be done. Oh, merciful heavens, show me you hear me. I have never known you to shy away from me yet, and I insist upon being heard now. Please. Wake and tell me what a ninnyhammer your husband is become. That you see how wretched I am without you. Say…something, dash it all, Anne. Bally well answer me."

I am rambling, having become a blathering idiot in my desperation. Perhaps I shall take leave of my senses altogether and avoid this ache in my heart. My wrist paws at my eyes.

"You…are…quite…ludicrous," the most beautiful woman declares, barely above a whisper.

"Oh, my love, my love, you are returned to me," I tell her, covering her hand in kisses.

"You there, next door," I call for the accoucheur, who veritably flies into the room.

"Her ladyship is awake, I see. Jolly good. But still no movement of the bowels?" he asks, peering into her empty chamber pot.

He injects her with a clyster and dispenses calomel, apparently to help encourage such actions.

"And how is the pain?" he asks as he performs his task.

"All but gone," she replies, still too faintly.

I depart the room so she may evacuate in privacy and am only allowed entrance by the nurse who was ushered in to assist. To be thus ordered about by subordinates is humiliating, but I will forebear it for Lady Dellingby's sake.

The purging treatments continue. Clément is come in to check up on her mistress, having forced her way into the room, such is the strength of her concern.

"This doctor is so stupid," she declares, "he feeds her nothing but water and expects stools."

She flounces out of the room, and does not return for some time, but when she does it is with a large bowl of bone broth.

"My lady, will you allow me to assist you?" she asks, humble once more.

My wife nods and is helped to sit up. Her maid spoons broth to her mistress' lips as if she were a child, but she takes it with good grace.

"And here, I brought you your favourite. Do you think you could manage a little honey cake?" she asks holding up the treat.

Lady Dellingby's eyes widen at the sight and she nods eagerly. I cannot help but chuckle. Two pairs of eyes glare at me, but I shrug. In this moment I could laugh for the joy of having kept death from our door. My wife may eat and drink whatever she desires so long as she takes something.

"Eurgh, how can you bear such darkness? Do you not wish to see the sun?"

"Now, Clément, you go too far. I do not think—"

"Pardon, your lordship," she apologises, interrupting.

"We thank you for your care."

She curtseys and goes to retreat.

"Wait. Could you ask Nanny to bring Baby?"

"Of course, your lordship," she says, this time succeeding in her exit.

Lady Dellingby's grin is wide and her eyes are dewy as she at last meets our son.

"You have not named him yet?" she asks.

"I could not think of anything whilst you lie here so unwell."

"Well, we must remedy that," she says, looking deep into his brown eyes, "Mummy is so happy to meet you."

The little cherub giggles and gurgles at his mama.

"I was thinking perhaps George is a fine name?" I suggest.

"Oh, it's perfect."

"It curries favour with our prince regent, whilst we know its true worth."

"George Bamber."

"George Bamber Henry Edmund Gildcrest, Earl of Kemberley," I declare, knowing full well the reasoning behind the second name.

Had I not witnessed the pair of boys kissing at a party when they thought nobody could see them, perhaps jealousy would take hold. But gratitude is all I can feel, for he helped save my wife in the park that dreadful evening. Such a pity he had to flee the way he did. I owe him everything I hold dear.

Another two days pass with much purging. Slowly, Lady Dellingby seems to return to health.

"I should like to see the outside," she declares on the third day.

"If you think it wise," I reply, standing to open the curtains.

"No, I mean, I should like to go outside."

"Surely it is too soon for that? I will not risk your health."

"Do…do you think yourself able to perhaps carry me?"

I have her maid put a fresh morning dress on her, and then do as requested. Who could deny her anything?

Lady Dellingby Regains the Story

Lord Dellingby carries me as if I were light as a feather down into the garden. The light hurts my eyes at first, and I bury my head in his shoulder until I grow accustomed to it. He suffers the same, judging by his hissed breath.

He sits us down on the bench in the kitchen garden, which is nearest the house. The scent of herbs is almost medicinal in itself. My legs are across Lord Dellingby's lap and his arms are about my waist still.

"Thank you," I whisper.

"It is my pleasure," he whispers back.

It feels so good to have the breeze upon my face, its light fingers brushing through my hair. I must look terrible, but I care not. At least, not until Mama discovers us.

"Is it entirely wise to be out here?" she asks, fury shooting from her eyes.

"I felt it best."

"Need I remind you that you are only recently recovered?"

"Mama, do not scold so."

She opens her mouth to say more but is interrupted by Lord Dellingby. "I vow not to keep her out of doors long. Just enough to take some enjoyment."

"On your head be it if she catches chill," she huffs before storming away.

I hold on all the firmer to him

"She is only concerned for you," he says, hugging me closer.

"I know. But this is my house, and I have delivered a beautiful baby boy. I am a mama myself now."

He chuckles. "That, my love, you most certainly are."

He nuzzles my neck before kissing my cheek.

"However, your life was in peril, and she remains your mama. Let us not anger her. She was beside herself with worry."

"I hear you did not leave my side."

"Only for the barest of moments."

"Have I declared you the very best of husbands?"

"You know, I believe you have neglected to do so."

"Oh, what a pity," I shrug and giggle.

"Vixen," he cajoles, standing whilst still holding me, "Let us get you back inside."

We discover there are clean sheets on the bed, the curtains are slightly pulled back and the windows are cracked open as we reach the lying-in room. We both chuckle as Lord Dellingby lies me back down.

"Clément," I say with a shrug.

"She is a most determined young lady."

"And a truly marvellous girl. I feel better already."

For the next few days, I am slowly allowed more food of an increasingly strong nature. Lord Dellingby is persuaded to leave to attend household matters, and my son is brought in regularly. He begins to feed from me, and my heart overflows.

"My darling little boy, you are never allowed to leave your mama. No girl shall ever be good enough for you," I tell him as he takes his milk.

"My, what a milquetoast you will make him," Lord Dellingby declares, chortling as he enters.

"Hush, he shall be no such thing."

"Tied to your apron strings forever," he adds.

"Well, what of it? Is that so bad a thing?"

"And he shall be forbidden any education, so will be a ninnyhammer to boot."

"He can be home schooled."

"And afraid of his own shadow."

"Do not be so callous about your son."

"You know full well I jest. He shall go to school like any young lord."

"Oh, how can you speak of such things as he lies in my arms?"

He chuckles. "Quite cruel of me, I know."

He does not seem at all sorry, but he always has taken delight in vexing me. Perhaps I should be the one who is sorry if he did not.

❧ Chapter 43 ❧

I receive many visitors during the ensuing weeks of my confinement but am kept in my rooms, Mama having reprimanded me severely for my recklessness. Apparently carrying me was also an unreasonable expectation to lay upon my husband, who almost caused himself an injury under the effort. I am not entirely sure mothers should suffer such brow-beatings as the one she bestowed upon me on the subject.

Lord Alverbury is amongst the first of my male visitors. He seems cheered by baby Kemberley, which is pleasing. It is good to see them both smiling.

"I had not realised you were in London, my lord," I tell him.

"Ah, I have been here for the Season. One has to make a show as an eligible bachelor, does one not?"

I giggle. "Yes, I suppose you do. I had not thought of the men's duties being as arduous as those of the ladies."

"Ah, but now you see it is so."

"Poor Lord Alverbury. All those young ladies smiling and dancing with you."

"Admittedly, it is not all a chore."

"Well, I wish you every success in your endeavours."

"I have yet to accomplish my aim, and I fear time is growing short."

"Fie, you are yet young, my lord. Do not allow the end of one summer stop your quest."

"If my lady so commands," he says with a jovial smile and a bow.

Once our visitors of the day have all departed, and deciding it is time to discuss such things, I entreat Lord Dellingby, "My dear, I have not received word from Lady Rohampton. Is she not yet arrived in town? Surely she must, yet there has been no sign of her. And it is time we began discussions on godparents."

Lord Dellingby's face falls. It is as if I had hit him in the middle with my fist.

"My dearest love—" His eyes convey all with their worried frown.

"No."

"I am sincerely sorry, my lady."

"When?"

"The day before Georgie was delivered."

"And you tell me only now?" I ask, shrill to even my own ears.

He takes my hand. "My dear, consider how unwell you were. I could not inform you sooner for fear of worsening your own condition. I needed to be certain you yourself were out of danger."

"Oh, poor Sir Reginald. Is he in town, at least?"

"It seems they had taken the decision to stay at home."

"So we may not visit? How infuriating. I would issue my condolences in person."

He kisses my head. "I am sure you would. I have written to him, of course, and sent as much. He seems unable to meet with anyone as of now."

"But of course, he must be distraught."

"And has his hands full with his daughter."

"Good God, the baby lived and the mother did not?"

"Yes, apparently so."

"Dear me, what a to-do. This is not right. And a girl you say?"

"Julia, after her mother, of course."

"Lord Dellingby, I think my heart shall break," I say, my voice shaking.

He rubs my shoulder, but that merely encourages tears to fall.

"I think I must be alone for a moment."

"But of course."

As soon as the door closes, I give way to my grief. It cannot be. My dearest Julia, so happy, so in love, taken away from us? Impossible. But Lord Dellingby informs me himself; it must be so. But, oh, what calamity is this? My dear, dear friend whom I've known for most my life. How can this be?

My own mortality grasps me by the throat. How close was I myself to meeting my maker? Shock and fear tear at my throat and wrench more sobs from my breast. I really could have died. The possibility was all too real.

Whispered words, imploring me not to leave, but remain, echo through my mind. Did Lord Dellingby truly utter those desperate words, or was it a dream? It feels as if they were conjured up by my fevered mind. But no matter the mode of delivery, they helped me find him, brought me home when I seemed so far away.

If only Sir Reginald had been able to do likewise. He surely was equally eager to keep his angelic wife Earth bound. But she is gone even so. How cruel life can be. And what is to become of their daughter? The poor little dear has no mama. More tears and sobs wrack my body as that thought stabs at me. To have no mama; such horror.

In my grief, I send for my own mama, needing to feel her loving presence more than ever.

She sits by my side, and I throw my arms about her neck. "Oh, Mama, Mama."

"Hush, my dearest girl. You must not take on so."

"But Lady Rohampton…"

"I know, I know. It is too cruel. But stay your tears, they shall not bring her back."

"Oh, but if they could, Mama, I should never cease."

"Anne, do not give sway to your feelings. Come, gather yourself," she encourages, brushing my hair with her fingers.

"You are right, Mama, I know you are. But dear Julia —"

"Hush now, else I shall get cross. She has died. It is terrible but let that be an end to it. It cannot be helped. We must carry on as ever."

"Oh yes, yes, we must, I know it. But why was she taken and yet I live?"

"It is not our place to ask such questions. I am only glad God spared you, as selfish as that may seem."

"I am thankful for it too. Do not think me insensible of His mercy."

Mama rings for a servant and calls for some Madeira and for my son to be brought in. The wine arrives first, and I take a steadying sip.

When Nanny brings George to me, my heart swells.

"I am so exceedingly grateful to be here for you, young man," I tell him, droplets falling from my eyes anew.

He kicks his tiny feet and gurgles, which presumably means he is happy too.

⋘⋙

Clément is dressing me in something other than a morning gown for the first time in weeks. It is of modest taste, suiting the occasion, for I am finally deemed worthy of being churched. The *Thanksgiving of Women after Childbirth* is greatly appreciated now I am fully acquainted with the perils involved.

I journey out of the house, which seems daunting all of a sudden, especially as we travel through the busy streets of London. Everything is noise and chaos, whereas my rooms have been so quiet.

Arriving at the church, I make my way in, carrying a candle and kneel where indicated.

"Forasmuch as it hath pleased Almighty God of his goodness to give you safe deliverance, and hath preserved you in the great danger of Child-birth: you shall therefore give hearty thanks unto God, and say…" the priest declares.

I listen to psalms, join in prayers and give thanks.

"0 Lord, save this woman thy servant," the minister chants.

"Who putteth her trust in thee," I answer.

"Be thou to her a strong tower."

"From the face of her enemy."

"Lord, hear our prayer."

"And let our cry come unto thee."

Following another prayer, I make my offerings and take communion. My heart is brimming with gratitude, and it is as much as I can do to restrain my tears. To have lived to see this day, my joy is beyond measure.

I also offer silent prayers for the safekeeping of the soul of Julia. It is my first opportunity to do so, and take advantage, even if not out loud and not entirely appropriately.

Then it is home to celebrate with my family and friends. There is quite a spread laid out, which Mama helped me organise. She has been so good to me, guiding me to be as good a mother as she is, and assisting in the household duties.

࿇

Poor little baby Kemberley. Having been born on the 8th July, which his papa says was most patriotic of him.

"To arrive at the end of the war that way heralds a fine peace," he says.

Such a worrying start to the year; Napoleon escaped the island of Elba and somehow regained control of France. Quite how he managed such a feat is unimaginable.

Happily, the Duke of Wellington proved himself worthy of the honours bestowed upon him and chased Napoleon off at the Battle of Waterloo. The usurper is now confined to St Helena. I pray he may remain there and not cause any further trouble.

However, having been born on that auspicious day of victory, Kemberley has waited until now, the 6th August, an entire month before he can be baptized.

Lord Alverbury, of course, is nominated godparent. No-one could want for a finer protector. It is my sincerest hope he shall soon be married, but even if he is not, I should still choose him over any other.

However, my heart aches at not being able to select either dear Lady Rohampton nor Lord Beauvrais for the role. I would have invited Sir Reginald, but now is not the time, and is not entirely the correct choice. It was a passing folly, born of my concern over him. And Lord Longland simply will not do; I should not wish him within five miles of my son.

Lady Winterthorpe has kindly accepted the invitation of godmother and has remained longer in London for the occasion. Her husband is the other godfather, for there must be two, and he was a convenient choice. Lord Dellingby was in agreement once I had dissuaded him of his notion of Lord Grungate. They are marvellous parents, I'm sure, but a little too exuberant for my precious Kemberley.

We are quite a party as we arrive at church. Our baby, dressed in a very fine silk gown is introduced to the church, filling me with a pride which cannot be faulty upon such an occasion. He only wriggles and cries a little as holy water is poured upon his head. He has such a sweet nature.

Our voices ring out clear as bells as we call out our responses to the blessings. It is a solemn yet joyful ceremony.

Papa arrived the moment male visitors were permitted and shows encouraging signs of being a proud grandpapa. Many of his relatives are at the house for the celebrations. Dukes, marquesses and earls are amongst their number, along with their wives and children.

There is much gaiety as we dine. Oh, to be in Society once more…perhaps I shall never complain of it again. To be so kept away from one's friends is entirely miserable. To see them all so happy, and to celebrate our new arrival is surely one of the happiest moments of my life.

When Papa returned home, he took Mama with him, and I feel her loss keenly. However, the time has come for us to return to our own home up north. I can scarcely wait. It is diverting that the last time we made the journey up I was so filled with trepidation, and now elation. I miss our house. Sheringley Hall and its inhabitants have a place within my eternal heart.

Having reached our residence, we are soon pounced upon with outstanding questions and queries. Kemberley is verily ripped from my arms and taken to his nursery. I have not engaged a wet nurse here as of yet, having wanted to meet with her in person before offering employment. Looking through a list of names is one of my first duties, so Mrs Hinchley may extend invitations to a few girls to the house for me to speak with. I could not think of doing so before our departure, as it set my nerves on edge and felt too much of a temptation of fate.

We are still amidst discussions on other pressing matters some time later, when Lord Dellingby walks in.

"Might I borrow my wife, do you think?" he asks the housekeeper, grinning.

"But of course, my lord," she replies with a deep curtsey as if he had been in earnest.

Tightening my lips, I stop a smile, and glare at the jester.

"Why, thank you, Mrs Hinchley," he answers, bowing and then offering me his hand.

"What are you about, my lord? You have that look about you," I quiz.

"My dear, I about a mischief? Never."

Only once we are out of doors do I give way to the bubbles of laughter hitherto contained within. They are all the louder for having been repressed.

"Lord Dellingby, you are too cruel."

"It was not my intention to be so. Can I be held to account for Mrs Hinchley's lack of humour?"

"You know her manner full well, I tell you. You really are quite naughty for teasing so."

"Ah, but it has made you laugh, so worth any guilt I may otherwise feel for the poor woman."

"My good humour should not be at the expense of others," I say tugging his arm which I'm leaning on.

"Your good humour is worth a thousand discomforts."

"Why must you always descend into nonsense?"

"Would you have me otherwise?"

Pursing my lips, I give it a moment's contemplation. "Perhaps not."

A chuckle accompanies the kiss placed upon my cheek. Perhaps it is our homecoming which has encouraged such mirth. It is as if I am walking on little love clouds. A comfortable home, a fine husband, and a healthy happy baby; I have all anyone could ever want. My head inclines onto Lord Dellingby's upper arm as we slowly promenade.

Rounding the corner of a walled garden, a rich, sweet scent reaches me.

"What is that?" I ask, surprised by the unfamiliar scent in our garden.

His grin widens. "I do not know of what you speak."

"Lord Dellingby, you fib as dreadfully as I do."

"I am wounded, my lady."

"Pah. Hardly."

But any further teasing is halted. My breath stops. My heart stops. Water mists my eyes.

"Dellingby, what have you done?" I ask around gasps.

My hand flies to my breast in an attempt to contain it.

"My gift to you, Little Dove. For the safe arrival of our son."

"Oh, Dellingby! A rose garden. All for me?"

"All for you, my dearest delight."

I kiss him full on the lips, as tears fall from my eyes. My arms wrap about his neck.

"It is too much."

"No, it is not enough. Nothing could ever be enough to show my love and gratitude for having you in my life."

"Oh, what have you done to me?" I ask, wiping away the watery trails from my cheeks.

"I'm glad it meets with your approval."

"My approval? Oh, I love it. Almost as much as I love you."

He walks me around so I can lean over each rose and breathe deeply of its scent. The path encircles two rows of roses of all kinds. There are benches on opposing sides, and we make our way over to sit on one.

"It really is too much."

"I shan't tell you again, it is not," he whispers.

His mouth covers and sweeps over mine. Oh, how I have missed such kisses. He hisses out a breath at my neck, his grasp about my waist firmer. We both know we cannot go farther. Not yet. But I rather get the impression he would like to as much as me. I miss his attentions.

For now, I must content myself with the pleasure these beautiful roses bring. I am in great danger of becoming spoiled.

If I was surprised by the strength of my feelings for Lord Dellingby after marriage, I am utterly in awe of those for my son. Kemberley is the dearest little boy who ever did live. My life is his, there is nothing I would not do for his happiness. He already has a myriad of toys and shall never want for anything.

He seems to grow with each passing day, and I detest being parted from him. However, I am forced to pass him over to the wet nurse. I cannot be in all places at once. I have too many calls to make, too many visits, too many details to attend to.

How strange it is that he feeds from another woman. How empty my breast feels without him upon it. I am assured there is no failing on my part, and that I have spent a great deal more time mothering than most. Yet I wish to do more.

Lady snorts beneath me. I am out upon her, taking advantage of the dry weather. Horse riding is perhaps not a suitable pursuit for a mama, but it does clear my mind of the facts and figures whirling about when I have been at the books too long. It is an escape from all the demands on my time.

As if there were no cares in the world, Lady carries me across our land, leaping in a reckless gallop. But not for long. Images of my son impress upon my heart, and I slow us back down until we are at a walk. What would he do without me? And does Lord Dellingby not require at least one more heir? It would not do for me to take a fatal spill.

We complete our tour at no more than a canter, but it is still beneficial. I am alone out here, and not closed in. A rare freedom.

Returning to the house, it is to a grim-faced marquess pacing the halls. I had not thought him so disapproving of my activity.

"I have been waiting for you. A word, if you please."

My heart sinks as I follow him into his study. This cannot be good. But if he attempts to halt my one freedom, I will not remain silent, not on this.

He clears his throat. "I have received a letter from my sister. It would appear her hideous husband, the Lord Longland has met with an unfortunate end, having fallen drunk into a ditch."

I gasp.

"I shall not sport with your intelligence and pretend to be sorry for it. I am sure you cannot feel pity for such a man either."

"Indeed, I cannot own it myself. But it remains shocking nonetheless."

"Quite. Lady Longland has requested my attendance at the funeral as she fears there will not be many mourners and reminds me I was his brother-in-law and the expectation that places upon me."

"I see."

"It puts me in a bind. Naturally, I must attend. However, I would wish you to accompany me."

"Of course I shall. Any balm I can offer her wounds would be an honour."

He clears his throat again. "But what of our son?"

"What a question. There is no question that he will not accompany us. I cannot leave him so long a time. And Lady Longland has a babe herself. I am quite certain she will accommodate him and be in agreement of his coming. Should the new cousins not be introduced?"

He kisses my forehead. "I had thought you would say as much. Forgive me for questioning at all, but I had to be certain. I shall make the arrangements immediately."

I flee to my rooms to change and speak with Clément. Mourning clothes must be got without delay. A black crepe trimmed with gold is sufficiently dull.

On my own, I allow the information to sink in. Lady Longland is free from all danger, at least. Stifling a giggle, I think upon the manner of his demise. But then my mouth hangs agape. Had she not prophesied as much? My stomach lurches as the thought emerges that perhaps this was not entirely an accident.

But on this occasion, I will not march into Lord Dellingby's study and demand to know all. It can do no good. If this was part of his dastardly scheme, then my knowing may make me guilty by association.

However, if Lord Dellingby had not intended for this result, perhaps I should be disappointed in his lack of action. No, no good can come of me knowing definites. I shall hold the belief that perhaps he had a hand in it and be satisfied at the justice done.

One good thing from our journey is that it affords me the opportunity of showing my son off to his relatives, Lord and Lady Grungate, as we overnight with them again. They made such a fuss of him at his christening, and it is most pleasing to have him so admired.

I had almost forgotten quite how raucous they are within their own home but am soon reminded as we enter their doors. The twins are audibly mid-argument, but their bickering brings a smile to my face.

The babe who was in arms last we were here is toddling at his mama's feet as we enter the drawing room. A laugh is kept within when the realisation dawns that I am now the mama with a babe in arms.

"Welcome back, Henry. Good to see you both," Lord Grungate says.

"Indeed, it is so very good to receive you here, despite the circumstances," Lady Grungate greets.

"George, this is George," she informs her eldest, having beckoned him over.

"But I am George," the young boy whines.

"You both share that name. After all, does the Prince Regent not boast it himself."

The boy scrunches his face in thought, shrugs then runs off to play with the twins, who have stopped arguing momentarily.

My George, Kemberley, chooses this moment to start crying. Lady Grungate grabs him from me and starts bouncing him around in her arms.

"Oooh, now young man, what is wrong? Shh, sweet boy," she says.

Cooing noises ensue from her, as she bobs up and down. Perhaps from sheer alarm at such treatment, my son stops crying. She encourages me to feed him then and there.

Having so recently given up the practice, I am now brought back to it, happily without too much difficulty. I thought it cumbersome to bring a wet nurse with us, especially when I am capable and will have more time whilst away from home. Warmth floods through me as Kemberley and I are reunited thus.

"Such a happy picture. You make me quite envious, Anne. Perhaps I shall be rewarded with another before too long. Never have I been happier than when thus situated."

I give a non-committed smile. This first name familiarity still strikes me as peculiar. I truly wonder at their reasoning behind it. They mean no insult, it is clear. But it is remains an oddity.

There is, of course, a nanny in the house, not that she is much called upon. She happily takes my now sleeping babe so he can continue to do so in peace.

"Perhaps you would prefer to take some rest as well, Anne? You must be tired after travelling, and with an infant at that."

"That is most thoughtful of you. Perhaps I shall. I thank you."

Having received their full hospitality, we make our departure from Lord Dellingby's cousin and make the long journey to his sister. Kemberley sleeps a good deal of the way, the motion of the carriage seeming to soothe him. Goodness only knows how for it is not in any way soothing to myself.

Lord Dellingby takes a turn in holding his son so I may take some rest, which is most welcome. It is a long journey, and tremendously weary-making.

"Have I told you of the wonderful mother you make?" he asks me before I doze off.

"No, I don't believe you have," I reply, stifling a yawn.

Peeking through my closing eyes, I see his brown ones glimmering back. "Then please allow me to say it now. You are quite astonishing."

"I thank you, my lord."

Thankfully, he allows me to sleep. When I wake, he takes his turn to nap. We make a stop to feed ourselves and get refreshed. Kemberley is fed in the carriage at regular intervals. So, our journey passes quite peaceably, all things considered.

Lady Longland appears most sombre as she greets us into her home.

"Grief makes a hypocrite of me," she announces, holding out her black skirts, once we are safely alone.

"My dear sister, I am so sorry for your loss."

"I thank you, but please do not be. With you, I shall not pretend to feel anything but relief. You know how I suffered."

"Lady Dellingby, here you are arrived. Please forgive my delay. The opportunity of admiring your son was too great for me," Lady Mettingford says as she glides into the room.

Oh Lor', I had not thought about her still being here. She must have swooped upon him in the nursery, where he was taken the instant we arrived.

Placing a polite smile on my face as I curtsey, I greet her, "Lady Mettingford, how do you do?"

"Tolerably well. All the better for not having my every direction contradicted. I trust you had a good journey."

"Very good, I thank you."

"I must declare it a pleasure to meet with your good company again. Lady Longland is, of course, a fine companion, but she has been much repressed."

The lady in question moves to protest.

"Lady Longland, I will have it said. We are all very well aware of the nature of your former husband. None of us are sorry to see the back of him. That information is to be kept within these walls, naturally. But amongst family, I will declare he was most disagreeable."

Neither of us is quite sure what to say in response and so remain silent.

"Let us speak of pleasanter things. How do you find motherhood, Lady Dellingby?"

"It is a treasure, Lady Mettingford. I am truly thankful of being able to provide a son for Lord Dellingby."

"As well you should be. He rivals even the little Lord Longland in appearance."

I had not expected such adulation of children from her. Perhaps it is the comfort of the family name being continued which has her running so high?

"Speaking of the little lord, is he asleep at present?" I ask Lady Longland.

"Yes, he had gone up only moments before your arrival. How sweet it is that both are asleep at once."

"A welcome blessing."

"Come, shall we take a look together? I did not get full opportunity to gaze upon my nephew."

I agree most readily, but Lady Mettingford chooses to remain in the drawing room. So, not that enraptured by the babes after all.

"Oh, what a beautiful cot, such fine craftmanship" I whisper as we enter the nursery.

"I could not resist. And it seemed only fair to provide the same for our guest."

"You are too good. You needn't have gone to such expense though."

"No, but I wanted to. I owe you and my brother a larger debt than can ever be repaid."

"Lord Longland takes after his mama, most fortuitously," I tell her, peeking at her boy.

"It was certainly a great relief. How I feared he would take after his papa."

I cast her glance, one eyebrow raised higher, letting her know I know of the circumstances.

"Whereas your little earl does more closely resemble his papa," she observes.

"He is the pride of my life."

"Which, the father or the son?" she asks coyly, and we both stifle giggles so as not to disturb the slumbering boys.

We make our way out of the room, Nanny taking command again.

❧ Chapter 44 ❧

The day of the funeral is upon us. Black handkerchiefs and sprigs of rosemary were handed out to principal mourners. Nobody made mention of the lack of mourning rings.

Lady Longland and I return to the house in the carriage immediately after the procession, whilst Lord Dellingby pays our respects at the service. It would not do for us to display our grief in public, or perhaps even the lack thereof. Lady Mettingford, however, does attend, in no danger of having such speculation placed upon her.

Lady Longland and I have a rare moment alone together.

"Of course, my little earl now inherits all," she confides, "but he is gracious enough to allow his mama to remain in residence for now."

"Long may it be so," I reply, giggling.

"To be thus indebted to one's own infant, it really is quite a shocking turn of events."

We're both laughing, but there is a serious note behind the amusement.

"At least there is no need for you to worry, not until he marries."

"Ah, yes, all my love and attention may be poured into him, a far worthier recipient of the title."

"Not that that would be difficult. But, putting aside all show of decency, it must be a relief to be free of such neglect," I half-whisper.

"My dear, to you I must own it. It may make me a terrible person, but I can find no sorrow for the man, only relief. His departure was shocking, to be sure. And whilst sitting vigil, it was comforting to ascertain he was indeed departed of this world and not merely in a deep stupor. That being the case, the entire household seems lighter. I have even heard distant whistling when the servants do not realise I am near. It is as though the curtains have been drawn back and sunshine is pouring in. It is telling, is it not, by the necessity to hire so many for the procession?"

"It is terrible for one to be so despised. But he can only have himself to blame. If he had not been so loathsome, he would have more to mourn his passing. No, I can only be pleased for you. Oh Lor', that sounds dreadful. But truly, it is good to see you returning to yourself again," I tell her, rubbing her hand.

"Thank you. I am fully sensible of your meaning. I shall be myself again. I cannot begin to describe how intolerable it was to be so persecuted every hour…" her voice trembles upon the last utterance.

Taking firmer hold of her hand I urge, "Pray, think no more upon it. All is well now. And the little Earl of Longland is such a blessing."

She takes a deep breath and manages to smile. "Yes, indeed he is."

Lady Mettingford arrives home, accompanied by Lord Alverbury, presumably to ensure her safety.

"All passed without event," he confirms.

"That is of comfort. Thank you, Lord Alverbury," Lady Longland replies.

We all take our seats in the drawing room together.

"Lord Dellingby alone remained for the interment. Even Lord Longland's cousin took his early leave," Lord Alverbury informs us, subdued as ever, although it is befitting for this particular occasion.

Lord Longland had no brothers or sisters. His mama died during childbirth, as I've recently discovered, and his papa never remarried and followed his wife several years hence. It is almost enough for me to feel pity for the miserable man.

A deafening silence permeates the room whilst we wait.

"Ah, here you all are," Lord Dellingby calls, breaking the silence when he finally arrives.

We all stand to greet him.

"It is done," he says to his sister, taking her by the shoulders.

She nods most demurely.

"Well, shall we perchance take some refreshment then?" he asks not unkindly.

We are all eager for some distraction.

Lord Dellingby holds Lord Alverbury back.

"Do not forget yourself, I beg you. She is still in deep mourning, for pity's sake." It is said in a low, hissed whisper, but I cannot help but hear it.

Forcing my feet to continue walking despite the urge to halt, I take a sharp breath. It is such a curious warning, and so vehemently issued. My eyes close as a feeling of being doused in cold water assaults me. How could I be so ignorant? How stupid of me.

All this time, Lord Alverbury has been pining for Lady Longland. But of course he has. Did he not seem cheerier when she arrived in town? How keenly he greeted and attended upon her at every little opportunity. And his spirits were only so deflated once her marriage transpired. And now he is here, not as a friend of the deceased. Clearly not. And not even as a friend to my husband. Scandalous, to be so inserted into her company at such a time.

It is no wonder we were all at a loss what to say earlier. There was a great deal each would say to the other if left to their own company, I daresay. Does Lady Longland return his affections? Is there hope for such a dear sister and a friend?

A letter has been redirected to me here. I read it the moment it is put into my hands this morning, my heart thumping with trepidation, recognising the hand.

Letter from Lady Meltcham, 16th August 1815

To dear Lady Dellingby,

I trust this letter finds you in the best of health. Thank you for your letter informing me of the wondrous news of the arrival of your son, and my apologies for my slow reply. I can offer no excuse except fatigue. And at first, I had not wished to communicate any false hope which may arise from alerting you to our arrangements. All was so uncertain.

I offer you my felicitations. Your family must all be very proud.

You were correct in your assumption that your letter would reach me in the country house of my papa. I took your sound advice, my dear friend, and sought his protection. He begrudgingly accepted my husband under his roof also, but perhaps more owing to being unable to deny him access to his face.

Lord Meltcham is being kept under strict watch. He is unable to stir from the house unless it be in the presence of another. Betwixt you and I, it is rather amusing to see him treated in so ladylike a regard. He finds it insufferable, naturally. However, it does seem to be having some effect.

Being in the country, there is less temptation in his way, and he is slowly coming to realise his serious error. Indeed, he could hardly do otherwise, Papa is so severe upon him. But perhaps this is what was required. I consider myself most fortunate to have such a caring papa. He is so good to us.

I venture to say that Lord Meltcham's character does not bend easily, however. His varying moods are rapid and on a grand scale, taking a great deal of effort to appease. He is become quiet, angered, morose and melancholy all in turn. But Papa and I are both doing all we can to calm him.

So, we continue comparatively comfortable here. It is finer than we could otherwise have hoped for. Thank you for your sage advice and unfailing wisdom. I miss your company above all others.

We remain hopeful that we will regain our proper place and we will soon be able to mix in Society again, our heads held high. Then I may hope to visit your good self, honourable husband and darling boy as I long to.

Yours ever faithfully,

Diana Meltcham

Oh dear, what a to-do. Perhaps she should better have remained Miss Plimpton. My heart is lightened by her declaration of hope, but how chaotic she seems. But, as she correctly points out, it is more comfortable than was feared, and she is making the most of it. I add my prayers that Lord Meltcham truly is brought to sense.

Going down to breakfast, we all gather together; Lady Longland, Lord Dellingby and Lady Mettingford enter in turn.

"Your news was not serious, I hope?" Lord Dellingby quietly asks me as we meet, frowning.

"Not at all."

We are all seated, dishes are served.

"Please forgive the manner of my disclosure, but I thought it best to inform you all at once," he begins.

We ladies still our hands in whichever action they were performing, all heads turning in his direction.

"It is my inauspicious duty to inform you that I received word that the Duke of Wenston has breathed his last."

There is a clatter as Lady Longland drops her butter knife upon her plate, her mouth agape.

"Oh, my dear," I utter breathily, reaching out to squeeze his hand.

"Grievous news indeed, Dellingby. Do you not think it could have waited until after our breakfast?" Lady Mettingford queries.

"My apologies, Aunt, but I could not contain it within my breast, concealing it from you, making polite conversation when my heart was so heavy."

"Quite so," I console.

"I am to go to the Hall as soon as we are done here to make arrangements."

"But of course. Shall I accompany you?"

He looks to his sister to answer my query.

"Yes, I would very much appreciate your company, and I am sure there are things for me to do that will be easier if you are with me," she replies.

"I, of course, will offer my brother-in-law whatever assistance I may in his final preparations," Lady Mettingford adds.

"You are most kind, thank you," Lady Longland acknowledges.

Not a morsel touches our lips, and we all retire to make ready to travel, fortunately not very far, to Wenston Hall, each alone to deal with the news in our own fashion.

Sinking onto my bed, I take a juddering breath. Poor Duke Wenston. I hope he passed peaceably, but one does not like to inquire. Perhaps it is best not to know and keep to my belief that he died in his sleep, unaware of what was occurring.

Tears begin to full as my heart brims over with sadness for the passing of such a kind-hearted man. Oh, I shall have to inform Papa.

A knock sounds upon my door. Quickly wiping away the salty trails, I call out in a shaky voice, "Enter."

"Oh, my Little Dove, you shed tears for my father?" Lord Dellingby asks as he approaches.

"Is it so very surprising?"

He comes closer and holds me in his arms, rubbing my back. "Not entirely. But then I know not what to think. I cannot settle on any one thought for long."

I wrap my arms about him tightly, offering comfort in return. "It is no great wonder. Such shocking news."

We separate and sit side-by-side upon my bed, seemingly unable to venture so far as the chairs.

"Should it be so shocking? It cannot be said it was wholly unexpected. My father had been unwell for so long a time."

"But perhaps therein lies the surprise. For he had fought so hard for so long. One could almost believe he would live indefinitely as he was."

"Perhaps."

"And I suppose there was always the hope he would improve?"

"Precisely so. But now there is no hope left," he says, his voice cracking, his head hanging low.

"Oh, my love," is all I can utter as I place my hand in his.

Taking a deep breath, he says, "Forgive me. I came to see if there was anything you need."

"Do not make yourself uneasy about me, my lord." I have to swallow hard as bile rises; not lord any longer, but Grace.

The world spins and lurches as I recognise that sitting beside me now is the soon-to-be Duke of Wenston, and not Lord Dellingby. Oh Lor', what a heavy burden, weighing down what was already almost unbearable.

I catch his gaze. "What will we do?"

"I am sorry, but in what manner?"

"Are we ever to return to Sheringley Hall?"

"Oh. Err, I suppose not for a while at least. It seems — "

"It was a stupid question. Forget I asked it."

"Stupid? No, you take on too much. Is it not any wonder it arose?"

"Understandable perhaps, but hardly appropriate."

"Lady Dellingby, you may…oh."

I place my fingers upon his lips. "No, do not speak it. Not yet."

His smile is woeful and does not reach his eyes. "No, it is too soon, is it not? Due process will follow along with letters patent. Oh Lor', there is much to be arranged."

He kisses my forehead.

"Oh, my dear, what a terrible time," I utter with a sigh.

My head rests upon his shoulder as we fall into silent contemplation of all that has befallen us.

The duke lived within a convenient distance when not encumbered with infants, but their care means it is a difficult journey. Therefore, we are to remain at the hall once there instead of toing and froing. However, it is strange when a house is not yet truly our own, and yet not the property of any other living soul.

We all pull together to make the arrangements. There are a great many more involved this time, as the Duke of Wenston was much loved. Mourning rings most certainly are to be distributed in his name. Every care is being taken.

The household is thrown into chaos amidst its grief. It must be said the servants have seemingly welcomed Lord Dellingby back amongst them with great alacrity. Having been so long absent, I had feared there may be some resistance, but they seem most accepting and obliging.

Grief is wont to do odd things to a person, and the thoughts which occur can be of a random nature. Once arrived here, I found myself already regretting the loss of my rose garden. Assuming there are no challenges, we will settle here. I did not get to enjoy the pleasures of my gift above a day. It is curiously selfish and ridiculous to think upon such minor considerations, but there it is nonetheless.

It is not only the garden, of course. Having remained at Sheringley Hall for almost a year, we have made quite a home of it, and now we are forced to leave. I had not even the chance to say a proper farewell to Mrs Hinchley.

"We cannot avoid the call of duty, my dear," Lord Dellingby reminds me, "Wenston Hall is the family seat, and demands our presence."

I know he is right, but it rankles all the same. It seems I must start home making afresh and get used to new servants as well.

I do my best to be of use to my husband, but also his sister.

"Is this my punishment for being so wicked over my husband?" Lady Longland asks me once we're alone one afternoon.

"Of course not. Do not even entertain the thought for a moment."

"I should have been there for Papa. I was no longer kept prisoner."

"My dear, you could hardly neglect the duties which had sadly befallen you. You were not idle. You would have been with your papa if you could."

"You are kind to say so."

"It is not kindness, only truth. Perhaps your papa preferred it this way, thus avoiding distressing you with his ailing health? Have you considered that? Insomuch as one can choose these times, perhaps he decided upon this moment. Especially knowing you are now safe."

She pauses. "Yes, perhaps it is as you say. Do you really think he may have lingered long enough to ensure his error was remedied?"

"Would any good papa not do so?"

"He was always a good papa before. Yes, perhaps he did."

Smiling at her, I declare, "He did seem an affectionate, understanding man."

"I wish you had known him in full health. He was all you say and more."

I let her ramble about the good times, reminiscing about happy days gone by. It seems to bring her away from distress and into comfort.

Under guard, the funeral is performed without incident. Our goodbyes are bid, and well wishes flood in. It is a sign of a life well lived when so many arrive to pay their respects. Friends as well as family are in the number.

It is a trying time for all. Lord Dellingby has come to appreciate that it was a blessing, that his papa's pain is at an end; he is at peace, no longer in distress. A point he attempts to press upon his sister, with limited success.

Slowly, the dust begins to settle. Lady Mettingford accompanies Lady Longland back home. It must be assumed that the dowager countess will soon return to her cottage, having declared her anxiety to be by the sea again. And all begins to resemble life as it should be.

Lord Dellingby does indeed become the new Duke of Wenston, and we go about discharging our new and greater duties. Mrs Hinchley is happy to have her role back, I think, although I still feel guilty about making her take on so much. But perhaps without us there, it is not so very arduous. I miss her company and assistance.

Clément's familiar face is of great comfort. She remains a constant in my life, always ready with her skin treatments and fine eye for the latest fashions. Her art is well utilised, covering my tired appearance.

❧ Chapter 45 ❧

It is mid-September by the time I receive a return correspondence from Lord Beauvrais.

Letter from Lord Beauvrais, sent 15th August 1815

To the dear Marchioness of Dellingby,

You cannot imagine the joy I feel upon hearing both of the safe arrival of your son and also upon reading his name. How thoughtful you are to be so considerate in naming your first born after so worthy a man. I am not entirely sure I am worthy of being the second namesake but shall endeavour to be so.

How I wish I could be there in person to make a fuss over him. If but I could be an uncle to the handsome little chap, as handsome he must be, I have no doubt.

But it is with the heaviest heart I receive the news of Lady Rohampton. She was such a sweet young girl, so compliable with our games. So sweet a nature cannot ever be bettered. And to think her light shines no more is incomprehensible. I offer my sincerest condolences to you and all who must surely feel her loss to the keenest degree.

I have survived my first winter here and remain hopeful therefore that I shall see many more. It really is quite a pleasant land once accustomed to it. And I am kept occupied. Idleness is unbearable to me, as you well know, so am relieved to find good use of my time here.

The family business here has increased well under my scrutiny. Not, I daresay, you should care for such things, but my pen is wont to inform you even so.

There are parties and balls, and my attendance is increasingly requested. To be so accepted amongst one's peers in so foreign a land is humbling yet glorious. They are quite lively affairs, and most welcome. And at the cessation of war in February, we became quite raucous in celebration. Peace is a blessed relief.

The little masked creatures, the racoons I wrote of before, have outlived their novelty, and are become something of a nuisance. Their masks are more of a disguise for their identity whilst committing thievery, I suspect.

I am still as yet to eat any bear, mercifully. I do not fancy it much. However, I can reliably inform you that moose tastes like venison. Perhaps coarser and stronger, but similar. I suppose this should be no great surprise, but one had rather hoped for an entirely new flavour when braving new meat. It is somewhat disappointing to be thus rewarded. Perhaps I should try the bear. Curiously, I am told, they can taste fishy if they have dined on salmon.

You are forever in my thoughts and prayers, my dear, sweet sister, if I may call you such still. Knowing you are happy fills me with warmth. Had you informed me adversely, I should have had to make the return journey immediately to play protector. You know full well I would, my own safety notwithstanding.

Despite finding happiness here, I still pine for home. Even more so when I long to be there to wish you congratulations in person. I am immensely proud of you, please know that.

Perhaps one day, that return journey can and will be made. I live in hope. Until then, I shall continue to live as finely here as is possible. That is to say, very fine indeed.

Yours faithfully,

Beauvrais

He is doing well, at least, which is pleasing. He seems happy, I must content myself with that. One should rejoice in the happiness of their friends. But I miss him as much as he apparently misses me. Every correspondence seems to make the miles appear greater. Will I ever grow accustomed to this distance? Or dare I hope, like him, that one day he shall return? I cannot ask more of God than he has already kindly bestowed upon me, but I would beseech Him to grant me this if it be not so much to ask.

But for now, I must make ready for the day ahead. There are calls to make and a ball to arrange. Oh, and I must see to more servants. The good old duke did not need so many as our family, keeping so much to himself. And once engaged, they must be monitored to ensure they are a good fit for the household. We have got through two footmen already.

❧❧

My son is often in the care of Nanny, much to my chagrin, but she does so fine a job, and I find myself so much more in demand. As if I were not called upon enough at Sheringley, even more people now demand my time.

Being in mourning has some benefits; we are not expected out in Society quite so much as we could be. We attend the barest minimum of functions, and even then, one seems somewhat of an eccentricity. My black attire attracts many a pitying glance.

Lord and Lady Winterthorpe have already visited us here and are most welcome. I miss her vivacity and presence. However, I am grateful for Lady Longland's frequent presence, and new friendships are being formed here too. Indeed, I am in danger of having too many, for all seem to wish to curry favour with the new duchess.

It still feels strange to own such a title. It is what I was always intended for, what Papa had designed for me. But to have achieved such at still so young an age is overwhelming. However, I am equal to the task. Perhaps if I repeat this to myself often I shall begin to believe it.

My beloved days at Sheringley were indeed good training for this grand estate. Wenston, as he now is, although he will forever be Dellingby in my heart, has promised we shall summer there. But that means getting through this winter which is now descending upon us.

Lady and Rosalind are settled here too. Not that I am able to give them near as much attention as would be preferable, but they remain close companions and my means of escape when all threatens to become too much.

∾

It has been almost three months since baby Dellingby, as he is now named, came into the world, and I remain alone in my room. How I miss the attentions of the previous Dellingby, but it is entirely improper to suggest he does anything about it, especially as he is in mourning for his papa. Thus I remain silently lonesome.

Readying for bed, I gaze into the looking glass on my dressing table and spy a grey hair. A startling reflection of a young lady.

"Oh Lor', Clément, what is this?"

The girl inspects the outstretched strand, and plucks it from my head, making me wince.

"It was nothing, Your Grace."

I smile. "Am I grown old, Clément?"

"Old, Your Grace? Why ever would you say such a thing? You are not yet nineteen."

"I feel aged. And look at my appearance."

"Is there a wrong I have committed, Your Grace? Is there something amiss?"

"You? The very notion. The fault is mine. Look here, is this a wrinkle?"

She peers closer in the candlelight. "There is not so much as a frown line, Your Grace."

Leaning in closer, I judge my reflection further, pushing and pulling my face with my fingers. There must be something amiss for me to be left so untouched.

Standing, I pull my nightgown close about my body.

"Am I grown over plump?" I ask, running my hands over my belly.

"Your Grace is everything that she should be in every regard. Might I say, your figure is fully regained?"

"Are you certain? Perhaps it is too far reversed, and I should be fuller?"

"If you please, Your Grace, you are as beautiful as ever, which is to say a great beauty."

Sighing, I dismiss her. "Thank you, that will be all."

As I settle into my bed, it is with great discomfort. Perhaps my character is changed? Do I spend too much time with baby Dellingby, and not enough with Wenston? With these thoughts filling my head, I toss and turn, failing to find an easy slumber.

Feeling out of sorts due to lack of sleep and attention, the next morning I decide to take matters into my own hands. To continue in this vein would be severely reprehensible.

Once my most pressing duties are dispatched, I venture to the Duke's study and knock upon the door.

"Enter," comes the gruff response.

My footsteps are smaller than anticipated as I walk into the room.

"I find you all alone," I state.

"As you see."

"Is there anything so imperative it may not be put off?"

"Well, that depends greatly on what the alternative may be." There is a glimmer as he turns his eyes upon me, leaning back in his chair, which lends me some confidence.

"It occurred to me we are too shut in, and that perhaps a promenade may be beneficial?"

"This is what is upon your mind?" he asks, rubbing his chin.

"It is."

"And you propose I accompany you on such an outing?"

"If it pleases you." My heart is beating hard and fast, creeping into my throat.

He throws down his pen. "If Your Grace requests, who am I to refuse?"

Oh Lor', one feels wickedly wanton when he looks at me so. Am I being too forward? Frankly, I am almost beyond caring for propriety.

"In case it rains," I say, collecting an umbrella on our way out.

We stroll through the grounds arm-in-arm.

"Well, this is a most pleasant distraction," he notes.

"Indeed it is. Most welcomed," I reply, bringing the handle of the umbrella to my lips.

His breath hitches as he casts me a querying glance. I lower my eyes, dipping my head in what may be perceived as a slow nod. His hand clasps onto my arm a little tighter, sending hot tremors throughout my person. The flames of my nether regions are fully alight.

Carrying the umbrella closed in my right hand by my side, I gently persuade our direction towards the orangery. Tingles of excitement tantalise my every nerve.

With my most coquettish sidewards glance, I walk inside the brick building with its small windows, out of the chill October air. The Duke follows dutifully.

"Do you not love it in here?" I ask, looking about, the handle of the umbrella raised to my lips.

Looking directly at me, he replies, "I do, most fervently."

My bosom heaves under his intense gaze. His hand reaches agonisingly slowly towards my waist. I am but putty in his palm, fully pliable to his whim. The umbrella clatters to the floor.

His breath is warm upon my cheek as he embraces me.

"Oh, my beautiful wife, how I have longed for you," he whispers.

His lips are upon mine. Oh wondrous kiss, fill me with your pleasure. Remind me of how I am wanted and loved. Entice my lover to satisfy my hunger.

The wind is knocked out of me as my back is thrown against the wall. I had expected to sit on a bench first, perhaps kiss a little, let my openness to advances be known, but no. He has already taken my full meaning.

Frenzied, the duke pushes my skirts up where I stand. Lifting me a little, he rams himself into my depths. The force is sudden and brutal, but oh so desired. He is where I need, and it matters not the fashion in which he arrives there.

My head is thrown back as waves of ecstasy assault me. Wenston thrusts himself into me, grunting his passion. He is become more animal than human. All at once terrifying and tempting. My hands clench onto him, steadying my stance.

One of his hands pulls the top of my dress down. His mouth sucks upon my breast, and I am undone. Screams are ripped from me as I reel into oblivion. I am vaguely aware of his cries as I am lost in swirls of delight.

It takes several deep breaths before I am fully brought back to myself. The Duke buries his head in my neck, trailing kisses.

"Oh, Your Grace, I apologise. Tell me I did not hurt you? I quite lost myself. It has been so long, and the urge so sudden. Pray, tell me you are unhurt."

I giggle at his sudden earnestness. "No, I am not hurt. But the term Your Grace seems a trifle unfitting in this moment."

Surely the mode of this coupling was more fitting to the ladies of the streets, from what I have heard. Hardly befitting a duchess. How delightfully naughty.

"I have disgraced you enough in my fervour."

My fingers touch his cheek and travel to his jaw, urging his gaze up to mine.

"You do me nothing but honour with your every attention," I tell him.

His kiss upon my mouth is tender, loving and caring.

"Even so. Perhaps you will permit more tender ministrations? Might I come to you tomorrow night? I would give you time to recover from my rough, base behaviour."

"As you wish," I tell him with a smile.

He is mine again. I am whole.

Goodness heavens, we are just returned from a rout. What a lively evening we have spent, crowded into rooms to the extent that someone trod on my dress and tore it, and I could not positively identify who the culprit was. But much laughter was enjoyed throughout.

We are still laughing as we reach home. I am far too awake for sleep.

"Perhaps one more glass before we retire for the night?" His Grace asks as if reading my mind.

He has been most attentive since the occasion in the orangery, and I am as happy as may be.

Already merry from the free-flowing wine of the evening as well as the jovial ambience, this further glass of wine pushes me beyond all decency. We do not make it to my bedroom this evening.

As exciting as our unions in alternative locations are, one cannot beat the comfort of one's own soft bed. Besides, that location has induced the Duke to sleep an entire night by my side on a few occasions. Although, I am so fatigued it is entirely possible for me to fall asleep on this chaise tonight.

Our six months mourning period reaches its conclusion, and I cast off the black with delight. As if rejoicing with his mama and papa, baby Dellingby has begun to crawl and waves his arms up and down. I can't resist picking him up and giving him a cuddle in response. Of course, he wriggles and whines to be put down, so my moment does not last long, but it is much cherished.

"Now, you be a good boy for Nanny. Mama and Papa must go and greet our guests," I tell him, fooling myself into believing he can understand a word I say.

"Come then, Mama, let us make ready," the Duke cajoles, helping me back to my feet.

Casting one last glance to our son, I leave him most reluctantly. We have a house party descending upon us for four days, which will keep me away from his gloriously chubby-limbed presence. My heart is already aching from our separation. Chastising myself, I attempt to remember he is within the same house, not far away.

It is the last day of February, and a convenient moment before the Season of London begins in earnest. We are bound for the city almost immediately once our guests depart, many travelling in the same direction.

The Duke is a little late in arriving in town this year, but under the circumstances, it is excusable. The House of Lords is not so strict in its adherence to attendance as perhaps the House of Commons. And it is not yet Easter, so he is not so very tardy.

Wenston wishes to gain a better understanding of the current state of affairs from his cohorts before his arrival in town. He is particularly concerned over the rumblings of a repeal of income tax, and so landed gentry are to be amongst us, of all things. He has no pity.

Lord Alverbury rarely seems out of our company, so naturally, he is present. As is Lady Longland, who is now in half-mourning and appears in lavender accordingly. Not requiring much excuse to visit her godson, Lady Winterthorpe is arrived with her husband, as they are amongst those destined for London; he becomes our principal guest.

Even Sir Reginald has been coaxed into attendance and has brought his little daughter along with her entourage, seeing as I insisted upon it. Julia would not approve if I were to neglect her husband. So it is that we really are quite a mix of people; how modern.

Once we are all assembled, I take the ladies to the drawing room whilst the men immediately go out in search of deer to shoot. Needlework has been strategically placed should any lady require some, and music has been carefully strewn so anyone may select a piece to play.

We all start by opting for needlework, so we may converse socially. It is the first time some of the ladies have met, and there is much to speak of. With a little direction from myself, we rub along well enough.

The men return and we retire en masse to dress for dinner. A most sumptuous selection of dishes has been prepared. I had to hire additional kitchen staff in order to cope, but they have done exceedingly well. No taste is left uncatered for; quite a feat when there is so much variety amongst us.

The conversation flows as freely as the champagne. The duke catches my eye and gives a quick upward nod of the head which brings a smile to my face. He is in good humour and even seems to have brought about some cheer to Sir Reginald.

Lord Alverbury's demeanour is brighter, but that has less to do with Wenston and more to do with Lady Longland, I suspect. She blushes each time he catches her attention. Of course, she tries to disguise it, but there is no hiding from my keen perception now I have some insight.

Much singing and playing takes place following the meal, and all seem highly amused. It is exceedingly late when we find our beds. The first day can be considered a success.

The next morning, we all venture forth as it is a dry day and partake in some archery. The ladies target is set at fifty yards, of course.

If one was not informed previously, one would soon gain knowledge of whom amongst the party are single, for they stand tallest and proudest as they aim their arrows, their figures being shown to full advantage.

With a sneaky look towards the men, checking the Duke is paying attention, I take my aim. My first arrow finds its mark with full accuracy. My smile remains hidden, as one would not wish to appear to be gloating, but inside I am a peacock, especially when Wenston doffs his hat.

Eager to avoid full sun, we ladies retire back to the house, leaving the men to whatever pursuit next captures their attention. A light nuncheon is served as I foresaw refreshment may be welcomed following our exertions.

Later, after another elaborate dinner, the ladies play spillikins until the men join us. A fun round of charades is played, causing much merriment.

We are all happily exhausted as we retire.

"You could not possibly hope to keep me at bay after such a magnificent display," the Duke whispers as he comes into my room.

"I should be disappointed if I had not hit my mark."

"My not so innocent dove, what am I to do with you?"

I peel back the bedsheets in response. As quietly as we are able, we join our bodies together in blissful union. Wenston inconspicuously leaves my chamber, leaving nobody any the wiser of our activity, as is proper.

The next day is filled with a carriage ride, painting and dancing, and equally as much gaiety. One could become quite accustomed to such heady delights. It is most gratifying to bring so much joy to our friends.

The ladies partake in a game of pall mall on the last day, hitting balls with a satisfying thunk of a wooden mallet, sending them through iron arches.

It is almost a sadness to bid all a farewell. However, I am delighted at knowing I shall be in the company of some in London.

❧ Chapter 46 ❧

Lady Longland rides in our carriage to London as she is to reside with us in town, so we may show her the delights which have hitherto been denied her. It is almost as though she is making her come out, albeit in lavender.

The past few days have seen a return of the brightness to her eyes and pale pink in her cheeks. Indeed, her vivacious character seems to be rising back to the surface. I wish I could claim credit for such a transformation, but alas, it is more likely attributable to Lord Alverbury.

I have borne witness to their secret glances. How frustrating she must still be considered in mourning. However, she is clearly not enlarging. There is no danger of confusion now, if ever there was a concern, seeing as she had so recently brought her son into the world. There may be a reasonable argument for her period of mourning to end before the twelve month.

We all three are too quiet. Our babes are the only ones to disturb the silence. They seem to encourage one another in some form of competition for the loudest cry. Perhaps they should have travelled with the nannies, but I could not bear to spend these many hours worrying over whether their carriage had overturned, or some other disaster befallen them. They are far safer with us.

Each infant is slowly placated by means of feeding them a little arrowroot, shaking their silver rattles and handling of toy soldiers in turn. At long last, they fall asleep, and I am sorely tempted to join them. Travelling with offspring leaves much to be desired.

After stops and an interminable age, we arrive at our London residence and flee from the carriage the moment it comes to a halt. Our sons are immediately transported to the nursery. It is late, so we must change for a hasty dinner. We do not linger long after the meal, each of us eager for our bed.

I stay abed longer than intended in the morning, but it is surely excusable. My wash is an even more thorough one, ridding myself of the uncleanliness of travel which seems to cling to my every limb.

The Duke is immediately set to his duties and makes an early start. Lady Longland and I are alone as we meet at breakfast. A quiet day in seems advisable, not wishing to set foot out of doors without the company of Wenston, at least on our first outing. Tongues would be set wagging otherwise. As well they might in any case, upon seeing Lady Longland in town.

Wenston is most generous and takes us to the theatre the same evening, despite his early start. He is also sensible of the necessity of making a show of approval. Oh, but it is good to be back amidst such entertainments and lively people. Lord Alverbury is noticeably absent.

Our courage raised, Lady Longland and I take a carriage ride around the park the next day, in need of seeking a little freedom, and of further announcing our presence. A smile is quickly concealed as I think upon my daring horse rides across this ground. How little I knew then. I am but two years older, but it seems a lifetime ago. Fond memories leap through my mind.

We visit with Lady Winterthorpe afterwards. She is such a dear friend. How did I ever doubt her? We are heartily welcomed and enjoy a splendid time in her company.

A thought occurs to me; is it London which changes or myself? My first visit to the city was filled with nerves and excitement, new wonders were revealed. My second was for my confinement, so saw precious little, and it was a most trying time. But this third is the most strange yet. Where once I felt as if I were imposing myself into Society, now the Ton are showering me with invitations.

A duchess is always sought to improve one's appearance in Society, but I try to be careful which I accept. Influence is a terrible thing if misused.

There is a shocking fall of snow at Easter, and the weather continues changeable. However, our amusement is not in the least diminished for it.

Poor Lady Longland is denied access to some of the formal engagements my husband and I must attend, so remains alone at home on such occasions. But we have her with us as often as is possible, and I insist upon a visit to the circus which remains as fascinating as ever.

One evening, whilst in bed with my husband, gathering our breath after marital activity, I brave a suggestion.

"My dear, have you perchance considered Lady Longland's mourning may be reduced?"

"Do you believe me so much a ninnyhammer? My dear Duchess, why do you think she was brought with us to town?"

His gruff response holds me back in silence. But of course. How foolish of me. He is encouraging the match which will surely ensue.

The months fly by in dizzying activity. Balls, parties, operas, all manner of dinners and gatherings are savoured. It is as if the world has opened its doors to us. My only regret is not being allowed to dance with my own husband. However, sometimes there is an abundance of women, so I oblige them. And on occasion, Lord Alverbury and Lord Winterthorpe partner me, so I am not left out altogether.

We must leave town before I am aware of quite how much time has passed. We travel to Sheringley Hall to stay there until the onset of winter forces us home. Not wishing her to be alone, we invite Lady Longland to accompany us.

It is a far quieter time, although there is much to be seen to on the estate. And we still make merry with dinners. It is marvellous to spend time amongst my friends here again.

Enjoying a blessed moment alone in my precious rose garden, I inhale deeply and close my eyes. Ahh, what bliss is this, to enjoy such blessings.

Upon opening my eyes, I see a female form approach.

"Apologies. Am I disturbing your solitude?"

"Of course not, Lady Longland. You surely know your company is always welcome. Come, sit with me."

"It is such a sweet garden, is it not? How fine to have so many roses."

"Your brother is most generous."

"I sought you out. There is a matter which is troubling me."

"Then share it, my dear, if you think I may be of any assistance."

"I hardly know how to begin. Perhaps it is best simply to state the case. Lord Alverbury made me an offer when we were in town."

"Oh, how wonderful."

"You do not seem much surprised."

"My dear, I am not entirely blind. And when two people I love may be made happier, one takes a keen interest."

"You think it a good thing then?"

"How can it not be?"

"I am still in mourning."

"It has been almost a full year. Perhaps you may dispose of it altogether."

"You do not think people would mind it?"

"Lady Longland, I daresay people shall barely notice."

"If only that were true."

"Shed your dismal attire entirely immediately. Then, after a period of a month or two, formalise the agreement between you. Has your brother been informed?"

"I have been afraid to broach such a subject."

"And Lord Alverbury has not?"

"Well, the Duke has been so severe upon him about propriety, I believe he too feels trepidation."

"For mercy's sake. I do not think he is so menacing a person as to instil such fear. You are his sister. He wishes you to be happy. And this will make you happy, will it not?"

"Yes. But he is a second son."

"Of noble birth, and with his own income. He is not poor. And you have a home."

"Only until the little Lord Longland comes of age."

"And I suppose there is no house belonging to Lord Alverbury? Or that your son would throw his mama out of the house?"

"Truthfully, I do not know what property may befall him. And who knows what will happen?"

"Such considerations may be laid before your brother. Let him make the arrangements on your behalf, as is his duty."

"But…but…will Lord Alverbury…expect…will I…?"

"Oh, my poor sister. Have no concern. Lord Alverbury is one of the kindest men amongst my acquaintance. The thought of harming you would never so much as occur to him. Besides, such things may be…enjoyed."

Her mouth gapes wide.

"I say no more than that," I tell her.

"Duchess Wenston, you mean to say…?"

"Not all men are the same, I understand," I add with a wry smile.

We both giggle through our embarrassment.

"I will speak with Wenston, and pave the way, as you both will not," I confirm.

She takes my arm in hers and links our hands. "Can I ever thank you enough, Duchess? You are so very kind."

"Well, what else are sisters for?"

Of course, Wenston holds no opposition to their match, and arrangements are quietly made. This brings Lord Alverbury to Sheringley, of course.

What a splendid finale to the non-summer we have. It is not over warm, but our hearts make up for any lack of the sun. And we do manage a couple of picnics, despite being dubbed "the year without summer". There is no stopping us from taking pleasures.

Aware of an aching in my breasts, I have an earlier sign this time of my condition. The accoucheur is called as soon as he may be useful, and I take a pain. He confirms what I already know. Child number two is on its way. This may be the happiest summer of my life.

"Already?" is Wenston's response upon my informing him.

"It would appear so."

"Oh, what a wonder you are," he declares, sweeping me into his arms and showering me with kisses.

Years go by in the blink of an eye. We seem to be forever journeying to London so I may take confinement. We find a different accoucheur for the second birthing, and it is far easier. Air and light are allowed into the lying-in chamber, which feels far more comfortable. I am so well looked after that it is barely an ordeal.

All six of our children, four boys and two girls, all gather with the Duke and I to have our family portrait painted. Sir Thomas Lawrence obliges us.

"Hold still, if you please," he grumbles.

It as much as I can do to keep from laughing. After all these years he is the same as I remember. Nanny has her hands full trying to keep her charges from crawling or running off. I do what I can but am commanded to sit still as well. It is all a bit of a farce, but we muddle through. As much as can be said of life, I suppose.

Introducing Lady Julia Anne Margaret Gildcrest, third born child, and first daughter of the Duke and Duchess of Wenston.

Gazing upon my reflection in the looking glass, I am startled at the transformation.

Mama and Papa are holding my come out ball this evening as I have come of age.

My long dark hair, so like Mama's, has been pulled into an elaborate display with flowers intertwined. My brown eyes glitter back at me, full of promise and trepidation.

Mama walks in and smiles as she tells me, "You look beautiful, my darling. Every man shall bow at your feet."

Planting a kiss upon my forehead she gazes lovingly upon me a moment before sauntering out of the room, full of grace.

My parents are fortunate. They were seemingly matched in heaven. I have borne witness to their happy marriage. It is a great deal to live up to. I hope I shall not disgrace them.

With trembling fingers, I pick up my fan. My breathing is forced to deep, slow inhalations and exhalations.

Time stops for no one, and my clock is now striking. Now is the hour of my fate.

I pray God that my husband be half so good as Papa. Then I may be content. May he not be hideous in features nor disposition.

But I delay and must tarry no longer. The most important mystery of my life may soon be solved. Whether this is for the better shall be seen in due course.

***

Thank you for reading *Regency Love – Reflections of a Young Lady*.

Please do leave a review, they are more valuable to me than you can imagine and help other readers make an informed decision about whether to make their purchase.

About the Author

TL Clark is a British author who stumbles through life as if it were a gauntlet of catastrophes.

Rather than playing the victim she uses these unfortunate events to fuel her passion for writing, for reaching out to help others.

Her dream is to buy a farmhouse, so she can run a retreat for those who are feeling frazzled by the stresses of the modern world, and to rescue horses.

Her writing mission, which she has chosen to accept, is to explore love in its many different and intriguing forms.

Her loving husband and very spoiled cat have proven to her that true love really does exist.

Writing has shown her that coffee may well be the source of life.

If you would like to follow TL or just drop in for a chat online, you can do so on Facebook, Instagram, Twitter, Pinterest, YouTube or Goodreads.

@tlclarkauthor will find her on most social media

She also has a blog where she shares random thoughts and book reviews. She's very kind and supportive, so often reviews other indie authors as well as offering writing tips.

www./tlclarkauthor.blogspot.co.uk/

You can sign up for her newsletter on her blog, to ensure you don't miss any exciting news (about new releases or special offers).

Other books by TL Clark

<u>Young's Love</u> – Striving for independence and finding gelato in Tuscany.

A journey which explores Samantha's cry for freedom. She has an unhappy, controlled marriage that just keeps getting worse.

At breaking point, she goes on a couples' holiday to Tuscany. As she finds independence can she also find love? Can she become the woman she always wanted to be?

<u>Trues Love</u> – Suspense and suspended reality in Ibiza.

Amanda Trueman loves her single, wild and carefree lifestyle. Read about her erotic adventures in this rollercoaster of a book.

She heads off with her best friend to the sunny skies of Ibiza for a holiday which promises to supply even more fun memories.

A blonde bombshell certainly fits the bill, but he soon has her heart exposed as well as her flesh.

Feeling vulnerable, will Amanda sink or swim in the world of true love? Danger lurks. Is their relationship doomed to end in disaster?

<u>Dark Love</u> – A romance novel with BDSM in it too.

This book follows Jonathan, a male Submissive. His attention is grabbed by another woman, but can he bear to turn his back on the life he's always known and loved? Is it even possible?

This book investigates the love that exists in a BDSM relationship and beyond.

<u>Broken & Damaged Love</u> – a book with an important message.

This one comes with a trigger warning, as it features a sexually abused girl.

It was written to give hope to CSA survivors. They too can go on to have healthy, happy relationships.

It also aims to help others watch out for signs, so they can help stop abuse.

Profits are regularly donated to charity from the sale of this book.

<u>Rekindled Love</u> – Hatches, matches and dispatches.

We join Sophie just in time for her first 'experience', but she gets torn away from her first love.

We go on to follow her life, through marriage, birth and death. Hers is not an easy life but hold her hand through the bumpy bits to get to the good times.

There's a rollercoaster of emotions waiting for you.

<u>The Darkness & Light Duology</u> – formed by Love Bites & Love Bites Harder

The paranormal romance

Shakira didn't fit in. The reason why is tragic…the solution is unbelievable.

A rich tale of witchcraft, sorcery, elinefae and a dragon.

Shakira struggles to balance darkness and light.

<u>Self Love</u> – the importance of being kind to yourself

Molly is a self-deprecating florist, at least until The Incident forces her to look at herself differently. Internet dating features with varying results. As does a beautiful friendship.

Full of British humour as Molly discovers the path to personal growth is no bed of roses.

That's it for now. Don't forget to write that review. Happy reading.

Love and light,

TL Clark

Lightning Source UK Ltd.
Milton Keynes UK
UKHW012000101019
351361UK00003B/233/P